BURN

Also by Paula Weston

Shadows
Haze
Shimmer

BURN

THE REPHAIM BOOK 4

PAULA WESTON

Indigo

Originally published in Australia in 2015
by The Text Publishing Company
First published in Great Britain in 2015
by Indigo
an imprint of Hachette Children's Group
a division of Hodder and Stoughton Ltd
Carmelite House
50 Victoria Embankment
London EC4Y 0DZ

An Hachette UK company

1 3 5 7 9 10 8 6 4 2

The paper and board used in this paperback are natural
and recyclable products made from wood grown in
sustainable forests. The manufacturing processes conform to
the environmental regulations of the country of origin.

A catalogue record for this book is
available from the British Library.

ISBN 978 1 7806 2188 3

Typeset by Input Data Services Ltd, Bridgwater, Somerset

Printed and bound by CPI Group (UK) Ltd, Croydon, CR0 4YY

www.orionchildrensbooks.com

THE REPHAIM – WHO'S WHO

GABY/
GABE
Recently discovered she's not completely human – and that she knows how to kill creatures from hell with a sword.

JUDE
Gaby's twin brother. Also not who he thought he was. Not necessarily unhappy to discover he's more than a backpacker.

RAFA
Jude's best friend. Had a complicated history with Gabe. Now has a complicated relationship with Gaby.

JASON
Gaby and Jude's cousin. Keeper of secrets. Not keen on the rest of the Rephaim.

LOYAL TO THE SANCTUARY

DANIEL
One of the Council of Five. Gabe's ex. Nathaniel's right-hand man. Snappy dresser.

TAYA
Designated head-kicker. Punches first, asks questions later.

MALACHI	Taya's battle partner. Messy history with Mya.
DAISY	A close friend of Gabe's. Impulsive, loyal. Not a fan of Mya.
MICAH	Another old friend of Gabe's. Laid-back. Deceptively effective in battle.
CALISTA	One of the Council of Five (ex-soldier). Limited sense of humour.
URIEL	Another member of the Council of Five. Also an ex-soldier. Still jumps into the fray as opportunities arise.
ZEB	Reclusive member of the Council of Five; guides the Sanctuary's theological and philosophical thinking.
MAGDA	The academic on the Council of Five. Not a fighter.

OUTCASTS

MYA	Volatile, unpredictable anti-authoritarian with an excessive fondness for kohl eyeliner.
EZ	Calm and level-headed. Emotionally intelligent *and* deadly with sharp weapons. One half of the Rephaim's only functional couple.
ZAK	A man mountain of few words. Trusts Jude and Rafa implicitly. The other half of above-mentioned couple.
JONES	Easy-going, lethal. Doesn't hold grudges. Has more patience with Mya than most people.
SETH	Always up for a fight. Tall and strong – even for the Rephaim.

PROLOGUE

Up until a few minutes ago, here's what I thought I knew about my life.

Eleven days ago I was living in Pandanus Beach with my best friend, Maggie, holding down a job at the library, grieving for my twin brother Jude. I thought I was a backpacker; I thought I'd watched Jude die in a crumpled mess of metal and petrol and dust. I thought I was learning to get on with my life, despite weird and gruesome dreams that featured hell-beasts and mutilations.

Then Rafa came to town. Violence followed – and some mind-bending news. I wasn't nineteen: I was a hundred and thirty-nine. I wasn't a high school drop-out estranged from my parents: I was part of the Rephaim – a society of half-angel, half-humans. My father was one of the Fallen, a band of disgraced archangels banished from heaven and sent to hell thousands of years ago for seducing human women. A hundred and forty years ago, led by Semyaza, they broke out and did the same thing all over again. And then they disappeared without a trace. The only one of the Fallen who abstained was Nathaniel. He's the one who gathered together the Fallen's bastard babies and made us into a society. Raised us into an army and created a base for us at the Sanctuary. Called us the Rephaim. He murdered our mothers to do it – not that anyone but Jude and I knew about it until a few moments ago.

Nathaniel claims our destiny is to find our Fallen fathers and turn them in: hand them over to the Angelic Garrison. But we're not the only ones hunting them. Hell's Gatekeeper demons are also tracking them, and are itching to destroy the Rephaim along the way.

My role in all this is complicated.

About a decade ago, there was a major split among the Rephaim over what should happen if we actually found our fathers. Jude and twenty-three others including Rafa rebelled. They left the Sanctuary and became Outcasts. I should have walked out with them, but I didn't.

Then, a year ago, Jude and I made up. Jason – our cousin, who'd been hiding from Nathaniel all these years – reached out to us. He told us about a young girl in his family who had visions. She'd seen something important involving me and Jude, so we went to see her. At that point, as far as anyone knew, we disappeared. Both factions of the

Rephaim assumed we'd betrayed them; that we'd found the Fallen – and it got us killed.

But we were alive. With no memory of being Rephaim or what we'd done, each thinking the other was dead. Me living in Pandanus Beach with my grief. Until Rafa found me and told me who I was. Helped me find Jude. Reunited me with my brother, who seemed to take the truth better than I did. Who fitted back into his Rephaite skin so much quicker than me.

A few days ago, we discovered there's a family in Iowa that hates us; has done for generations. They claim to receive divine guidance about how to protect the world from us, including building an iron-lined room capable of trapping Rephaim despite our supernatural abilities. A family who lost a woman and teenager, horribly killed when demons overran that farm and took control of the iron room.

Then the demons took Rafa and Taya.

We rescued them. Got them back and destroyed the iron room. Along the way, we found out that Mya – de facto leader of the Outcasts – is actually a member of the family in Iowa. She gave herself away when she saved Rafa and me yesterday, then she went to ground.

And now the Gatekeepers are headed for Pan Beach to draw the Rephaim into a fight that could end us – or jumpstart a prophesied war between heaven and hell.

A few minutes ago, Rafa, Jude and I rallied a crew of

Outcasts and Sanctuary Rephaim to head to Pan Beach to try to stop the Gatekeepers tearing apart the town I love.

But on the way here, everything changed.

A few minutes ago, I didn't know my own story. Why I stayed at the Sanctuary when Jude and the others left to become Outcasts. What secrets Rafa was keeping from me. A few minutes ago, I didn't know what Jude and I were doing when we had our memories taken from us.

The difference between now and a few minutes ago?

Now I remember it all.

NOW

AWAKENINGS

Jude and I are looking at each other. Watching. Sunlight streams through the window, warms my back. I can hear the surf pounding the beach a block away. A magpie somewhere outside. My room smells of stale coffee and the half-melted vanilla-bean candle in a mason jar by my bed. My chest is a storm of emotion, thunderous and insistent.

'What do you remember?' Jude keeps his voice low, doesn't move closer.

I bite my lip. Memory after memory rises up like a wave, crashes down, replaced by another. They just keep coming.

'Gaby, we need to talk.'

'I know. Just . . .'

I close my eyes. I'm unhinged, spinning. There's a tornado under my ribs, surging and tearing at me. Voices in the kitchen, louder now. Mick Butler. Zak. Micah.

Daisy. Footsteps in the hallway. I force my eyes open, let the world back in.

'Gabe.' Ez steps into the doorway. 'What do you want us to do with the Butlers and their crew?' Daisy appears between Ez and Jude, still rattled about having chosen to defy the Sanctuary and come with us.

I cast around for some thought to anchor me to the moment. *Demons are coming to tear Pan Beach apart.*

That'll do.

I remember where I am. *Who* I am. 'They're human. They need to go home and sleep. We'll catch up later at the Imperial.' My voice is steadier than I expect. 'Tell Mick to stay off the mountain.'

Ez frowns. 'Are you okay?' She looks at Jude and then back at me. 'What's happened?'

I shake my head. Swallow. My heart is racing. Ez and Daisy are going to hear my pulse if I don't get out of here. 'Just relieved to be home.'

Home.

'When are you going to Rafa's?' Ez asks. 'We need to get everyone together to talk tactics.'

My stomach does a neat somersault. 'Soon,' I say. 'I need a run.' Because if I don't burn energy soon, the chaos in my gut is going to rip me open.

'A run?' Daisy says. 'Like, *now*?'

'Yep.' My mouth is dry.

'What about everyone else? Shouldn't we be—'

'You can all chill for half an hour. We'll work out a plan when I'm back.' I'm talking too fast. I look around for my running gear, spy three-quarter tights in the pile of clean washing on my desk. 'I need to change.' I force myself to make eye contact with Daisy. 'I won't be long.'

'I'll come with you.'

'*No.*' It comes out too loud. Daisy stares at me, her straight red hair tucked behind her ears. Freckled cheeks flushed. 'I need . . . space.'

Ez's forehead is still creased. 'But you'll call into Rafa's?'

I nod, non-committal, and kick off my boots.

The voices in the kitchen are louder. Micah's arguing with Rusty. Ez gives a meaningful glance in their direction. 'I need to sort out these clowns. Daisy – a hand?' Ez disappears back down the hallway. Daisy catches my eye for a second, shakes her head in frustration, and follows.

Jude stays. 'Can we talk?'

Anger stirs – or the memory of it. I can't tell what's real and what's an echo right now. 'Let me get my head straight.'

'Gaby—'

I grab a t-shirt and my running shoes and shift next door to Maggie's room without looking at him. I stand for a moment, my breathing quick and ragged, thoughts tumbling.

Maggie's bed is neatly made but her work table is a jumble of cloth bolts and patterns. Her sketchbook is closed, half-covered by a crimson shawl she started knitting last

9

week. Chanel No. 5 still lingers. It brings another flood of memories – more recent – of cooking with Maggie in our kitchen, walking down the hill to work together, sharing the bathroom mirror. Drinking beer in our regular seats at Rick's, overlooking the esplanade.

My throat tightens. I need to run. *Now*.

I shift with the shoes in my hand. It's easy now, like walking. I pinpoint my arrival to a spot behind a hulking fig tree on the rainforest track. The path is empty under the leafy canopy. I stomp my foot on the trunk to jam my heel into the trainer. I don't realise how much I'm shaking until the third time I fumble the laces.

Quick hamstring and calf stretches. I fix my eyes on the track, anticipating the cool air against my skin, the burn in my muscles. I need the release. I need the escape.

But I already know I can't outrun the thing I'm trying to avoid.

The truth.

11 YEARS AGO

ANOTHER DAY IN PARADISE

I don't want to be here.

I'm still wound tight from yesterday. It's hard not to be. I wish my katana was closer but it's hidden a few metres away, out of sight. I haven't even got a knife in my boot: we're not in a boot-wearing kind of place.

'Drink up.' Rafa gestures to the fishbowl glass in front of me. Frothy pink bubbles fizz at the edges. I pick out the umbrella and take a sip through a fat plastic straw. The assault is instant: strawberry, coconut, Grand Marnier. Sickly sweet with the consistency of wet cement. I unstick my tongue from the roof of my mouth.

'Yep. Disgusting.'

We're at yet another bar. We've been to hundreds over the years, maybe thousands – I've lost count. Usually it's all dull lighting, nicotine haze and stained carpet. Not tonight. Tonight we're outdoors under a thatched roof, breathing in sea air laced with exotic flowers and kerosene from torches lining the beach. Waves break beyond the guttering flames with gentle monotony. Couples with unnaturally vivid drinks stand chatting, skin scorched from the day's sun. Candles in jam jars are scattered around on crates. A guy with tribal tattoos and a wide, happy face strums an acoustic guitar in the corner.

Behind the bar, Jude tosses cocktail bottles like a seasoned pro and flirts with two blondes in sarongs. Daisy is next to him, slicing fruit, barely watching what she's doing with the knife. It's as if yesterday never happened. Not the undersea earthquake a few hundred metres offshore here; not the shit-storm back home.

Yesterday the island shuddered. A few kilometres inland, an old church cracked and slumped and the road split in two. The locals rode out the aftershocks and waited for the repercussions from the sea. Jittery tourists held their breath.

Not all that different from what was going on at the Sanctuary. Jude and Nathaniel arguing. Again. The rest of us keeping our heads down, waiting for the aftermath. The ground shifting under our feet.

But now, with the sea again calm and the sky a crisp blanket of stars, it's hard to believe the world was almost upside down yesterday – here or there. Ez and Zak are at a table behind me. Half-watching the shadows beyond the torches, mostly watching each other. Whispering, frowning. It's not the earthquake they're worried about, or even the promise of Gatekeepers sniffing around; it's what's going on between Jude and Nathaniel.

I straighten and stretch my neck side to side. 'I *really* need to hit something.'

Rafa's mouth quirks. 'I know what you need.'

'In your dreams.' I know where this is going: it's been the same banter for about five decades now. Usually he saves it for an audience.

'In *my* dreams, Gabe, you end up slick with sweat and moaning.'

'I have food poisoning?'

He laughs, a beer halfway to his lips. Condensation drips from the bottle. He's completely at ease here: three-quarter cargoes, frayed t-shirt, bare feet. 'I'm just saying that if you need distracting, I'm your man.'

'If I wanted to go places everyone else has been, Rafa, I'd take a trip to Disneyland.'

He leans in closer. 'Yeah, but don't you want to know why everyone loves Space Mountain?'

Jude walks down the bar and pushes a fresh beer in front of Rafa. 'Dude, what have I told you about talking that shit to my sister? At least where I can hear you.' He glances at my glass, still full. 'You're not even trying.'

'I'm not in the mood.'

'That's not the point. You're insulting my bar skills.'

This game of ours started forty years ago in Mongolia when he dared me to drink banana liqueur in yak's milk.

'So? You planning to make this a full-time career?'

Jude shrugs but it's too quick, too jerky. 'Depends on what happens when we get home.'

'It's not going to come to that.'

'It might.'

We share a long look. This secret we've been carrying for over a century has grown heavy on both of us. The weight of it makes every other frustration cut deeper, sting longer. It's the reason Jude keeps pushing Nathaniel. Well, that and calculated agitation from Mya.

She's around somewhere. She's the reason I'd rather be anywhere but on this island right now.

Rafa rests his forearms either side of his glass. 'You two are such drama queens. It'll sort itself out.'

I ignore him and nod down the bar at the cluster of bare chests, boardshorts and bikinis. 'What's the story here?'

Jude follows my gaze. 'None of them can surf for shit.'

'And . . . ?'

'The pit scum haven't made an appearance.'

'There's still a chance the fault line is a lead,' I say.

'Come on, sending us here was an excuse to keep us distracted. Nothing more.'

'Maybe. But Malachi and Taya saw Gatekeepers two islands over yesterday.'

Jude grabs a dishcloth and wipes up a beer spill with a

16

deft flick of his wrist. 'Zarael and his horde are as bored as us. If there was even half a chance the Fallen disappeared from here, the place would be crawling with demons and hellions. And Nathaniel would be looking over our shoulders by now.'

A brunette with bronzed skin in a soft cotton dress lifts an empty glass in Jude's direction. He smiles at her. It takes a second for it to reach his eyes. 'Well look, someone actually likes my cocktails.' He slides a glass from the rack above his head, tosses and catches it. He moves away from us. 'Same again?'

Rafa taps his thumb on the bar. 'When this is done, I'm taking him to San Fran.'

'Who's in San Fran?' Because with these two, it's always a 'who'.

'Two European history majors who go weak at the knees when we speak French to them. Your brother needs to blow off steam. Given how twitchy you are, you should come with us.'

'Yeah, 'cause there's nothing I enjoy more than watching you two hook up.'

'So find your own entertainment. Seriously, how long's it been?'

I fiddle with the straw in my drink. It's been almost a year, but I'm not telling Rafa that. I happen to be fussy about who I blow off steam with.

'Anyone else going?'

'Jones and Daisy.'

'And?'

'Me.'

I don't bother twisting round to see who it is.

'Got a problem with that?'

Mya leans on the bar, not too close. She's smart enough not to crowd me. She's wearing a turquoise bikini and a see-through white sarong tied low on her hips. Blonde hair frames her face. Her lips are glossy, her eyes shaded with kohl.

I ignore her and she drums short black fingernails on the bar. 'Jude,' she calls out. 'Make me something special.'

Daisy bangs her knife on the chopping board, halving a watermelon with enough force to split a skull.

'I thought we'd see action today,' Mya says. 'Maybe we should've made our presence more obvious.'

I pick at my straw, push it around in my drink. 'We're here to investigate the fault line, not provoke a brawl with demons.'

'Yeah, but who follows orders?'

'We do.'

Rafa scoffs. I ignore him.

'That's the problem with you lot,' Mya says. 'Not enough independent thought.'

I finally face her. 'No,' I say carefully, 'the problem is people who confuse arrogance with independent thought.'

She holds my gaze. 'Yeah, I can imagine that'd be a

bitch.' A taunting smile, and she saunters down the other end of the bar to watch Jude pour the electric blue cocktail he's made for her.

'When are you going to cut her some slack?' Rafa says, amused as always by how much Mya aggravates me. 'She's good value.'

'For what, trouble?'

'Says you, who can't go a day without goading her. Honestly, Gabe, I don't get it. It's been a year—'

'Exactly: one year. And she struts around the Sanctuary like she owns the place.' I push my drink away. 'She's next to useless in a fight, has already made an arse out of Malachi by screwing him and dumping him, and she's—'

My phone rings. I answer without seeing who it is.

'Hello.' It comes out clipped.

'Gabe?'

I look right at Rafa. 'Daniel.'

Rafa rolls his eyes and takes a long drink of beer.

'How's the weather there?' Daniel asks.

Small talk. Perfect. We never used to do this, but in the last few months we've been having a lot of awkward conversations. And I'm not having one in front of Rafa. I've already copped enough ribbing from him and Jude about Daniel's changing interest in me.

'Humid,' I say, 'and no sign of Gatekeepers.'

'What's the status?'

That's what I like about Daniel – he's easily distracted by duty.

'Jude felt nothing when he arrived this morning and he and Daisy aren't getting vibes from the locals about anything weird since the quake. If the Gatekeepers haven't been here by now, they're not coming.'

'Are Jude and Daisy working or drinking?'

'Working. They're doing a shift for free – their contribution to "quake relief".'

'And the rest of you?'

'Working *and* drinking.'

'Gabe . . .'

I turn my back on Rafa, focus on the flickering torches in the sand. 'It's been a shitty week, Daniel, give me a break.'

'It's not you I'm worried about. You know your limits. But your brother and Rafa—'

'Everyone's doing their job, Daniel.'

A pause. 'We need to talk when you get back about what's going on between Jude and Nathaniel.'

I close my eyes. 'It'll have to wait until tomorrow. We're taking a breather before we come home.'

'Who's we?'

'The usual crew.'

'For how long?'

'A few hours.'

Another pause, longer this time. 'Stay in contact.'

I disconnect and take my time turning back to Rafa. He's waiting, smug. 'So you're coming with us?'

I can see it now: Daisy watching Jude flirt, pretending it doesn't bother her; Jones trying to distract her and failing; Rafa throwing back shots, talking crap in French; Mya prowling the bar, finding her own brand of entertainment.

'No chance.'

'What then?'

'I'll hang here for a while. See if I like it more when Mya's not around.'

Jude is back down our end. He uncorks a white wine, pours two glasses. Pushes them across to Rafa and nods towards Ez and Zak.

'I look like a waiter to you?' Rafa says.

'As if I'd let you deliver drinks to real customers.'

Rafa grins. 'Fuck you.' He picks up the drinks and heads in Ez and Zak's direction.

I wait for Jude to have a go at me for dissing Mya, but he's distant, distracted.

'You okay?' I ask.

He stacks glasses in the dishwasher, not meeting my eyes. 'I think we have to go.'

He means leave the Sanctuary. Him and me. We've talked about it for years – done nothing about it for just as long – but things have never been this tense.

'I've found this great little beach town in Australia.'

My eyes track to Rafa, Ez and Zak – caught up in quiet

conversation – and then to Daisy. Her red hair is tied back, her eyes frequently sliding to Jude and me. Worried.

'You want to walk away from everyone?'

I try to imagine life without the rest of the Rephaim. Without the people I've known my entire life. People I've laughed with, argued with, fought beside. I can't.

'It wouldn't be forever,' Jude says, but I hear the doubt in his voice. Once we leave, how would we ever return?

Rafa is coming back our way, shoulders relaxed because he has no clue what Jude and I have got hidden behind our backs. Ticking away.

'He'll never forgive us if we go without him,' I say.

Jude's face folds a little. 'I know. But he'll be so pissed off at us for lying to him all these years it'll take a while for him to notice.'

UNDER THE STARS

Three hours later I'm sitting on the beach alone, toes buried in the sand. I stare out at the endless dark sea. Another wave breaks on the shore. The wash races towards me, reaching, straining. The pull of the tide drags it back.

Thoughts crowd in, about the past and its secrets. About the future. It's always stretched before me without shape or form, but never as uncertain as now. Nathaniel's lie about our mothers has been buried for too long, but what if we drag it into the light? It could shatter our world beyond repair. And it's the only world any of us knows. My chest constricts at the thought.

But if not now, when? And how many other lies has Nathaniel fed us? For a hundred and thirty-nine years he's claimed the Angelic Garrison lets us live for one reason only: to hunt the Fallen – our fathers – and deliver them to the archangels for punishment. And for a hundred and thirty-nine years we've had to take his word for it.

I sigh and lean back on my elbows, the sand cool and damp against my skin. A thousand stars fill the sky, ghosts of dead suns suspended in infinite blackness.

Infinite.

I've never been able to get my head around the concept. How can space be endless? How can time have no beginning and no end? How can I – made of flesh and blood and bone – live forever? How can other realities exist somewhere out there – or right here – side by side with ours? Hell dimensions and heavenly dimensions. Endless realms in between, one of which is probably hiding, or holding, the Fallen.

Where do we fit into the universe? We exist in this world but we're tied to other, unseen worlds. We are Rephaim, children of the forsaken. What future exists for us if we find the Fallen? What future exists for us if we don't?

God, my brain hurts.

Maybe I should've gone to San Francisco. Not with the others, but maybe to that funky wine bar a block from Union Square that Ez and I found last—

My stomach drops as if the ground's been ripped away beneath me. Demons. I spring to my feet, sword in hand. Here. Right now.

My insides twist again. They're near. I close my eyes, feel sand grit between my palm and the sword hilt. Adrenaline thuds through me. I strain to hear something – anything – but the night is silent. I scan the beach. The resort glows beyond the dunes, the only light for miles. That's where they'll be.

I sprint up the beach, too wired to shift. I hope it's Bel. I hate that smug prick.

I slow as I near the bar. It's dark when I creep past, chairs and crates stacked against the back wall. A few couples linger in the lagoon pool, faces lit blue from the lights under the surface. Splashing, laughing. Oblivious that creatures from hell are a stone's throw away.

I press my blade flat against my leg and skirt around the front of the resort. Stick to the shadows. Catch a flash of white through the palm trees further along the beach; a few more metres and I get a clear view. Bonus: Bel *and* Leon. I exhale and slip my katana from its saya.

Leon is on one knee, his palm pressed to the sand, doing whatever it is pit scum do to track the Fallen. Bel is beside him, hands on hips, staring out at the ocean. Long white hair trailing in the breeze. His trench coat flutters around his knees. I force myself to wait, make sure it's only the two of them. Ten seconds pass. Twenty. I don't want to miss this chance, but I make myself give it another five seconds. Then I shift while they still have their backs to me. I draw back my blade in the vortex and swing down where Leon's exposed neck should be—

And jolt to a stop, so shockingly that I bite the inside of

my cheek. Too late, I realise the demon straightened in the split second I was shifting and I've buried the steel in his shoulder. Leon shrieks. I duck, feel the fizz of Bel's blade nick the top of my scalp. I jerk my sword free, kick out at Leon – still hunched in agony – and spin in time to block Bel's next strike. I taste blood.

'Gabriella.' Bel's irises flare bright orange. His broadsword slides down until it locks with my katana hilt, his breath hot in my face. He looms over me, weight bearing down, all the advantage his. With my free hand, I crack the wooden saya against his knee. He buckles for just a second but it's enough for me to get out from under his blade.

Leon is standing now, sword drawn in his left hand. His right arm hangs at his side, as useless as his injured shoulder. 'Bitch,' he spits.

I spin the katana in one hand, the saya in the other. Hold them out at my sides, open, challenging. The sand under my feet is hard-packed. Firm enough ground.

Bel grins. 'Are you bored, Gabriella?'

'A little.' I focus somewhere between the two of them. Any second now . . .

Leon shifts first. On instinct I spring to the right, see Bel disappear from the corner of my eye the same time Leon's heavy blade comes at my face. He's slow. Sloppier than usual. I have time to knock it away and spin, ready for Bel. I bring the katana and saya up together, blocking the blow centimetres from my throat. I push back, find the rhythm: swing, duck, block, kick. Block, kick, spin, *strike*. There's nothing but this moment. Attack. Defend. Keep my feet. Blood roars in my ears. I'm all fire and spark. If I can just get the right opening, I can end Leon. All I need is—

The night explodes into shards of white. I stumble sideways. My head is all wrong, like it's bigger, heavier. The ground hurtles up at me and hits, hard. I groan, try to move. Can't. There's sand in my ear, in my mouth. I can't spit it out. I can't breathe. Darkness presses in, suffocating. Where did my legs go? Am I holding my sword? Boots stroll towards me. There's an extra pair. *Three* demons. Fuck.

I reach for the void, but I can't get to it. My heart thrashes.

The boots keep coming, blurry now. Is someone standing on my skull? Is it still attached to the rest of me? I can't feel anything except—

Sharp pain cuts through the throbbing. A blade against my throat, sinking slowly into my jugular.

A sick, strangled noise escapes me. A wave breaks on the beach, muted. A smoky laugh wraps around me. It could be above me, it could be in my head. The blade twists, deeper. Are they going to take my head slowly or just see how much I can bleed without dying?

Ohshitohshitohshit . . .

And then it's gone. The blade, the pain – nothing. There's a surprised shout, the sounds of steel on steel. Grunting.

'Stay conscious!'

It takes a moment for the voice to sink through the fog. *Rafa.*

I open my eyes, but everything is smeared. The night, the ocean, the demons. A second later I feel it, warm fingers clamped over my bleeding throat. 'Let go.'

I let Rafa drag me into the vortex – I doubt I could've resisted even if I'd wanted to. It's over in a split second. Too quick. I can still hear surf, smell the island flowers. Rafa catches me before I slump to the sand and hoists me into his arms.

'Whaaa . . .' I can't finish the question. My mouth isn't working right.

'Hang on.' Rafa holds me against his chest. He pushes hair back from my face, keeps his other hand pressed over the wound in my throat. I can feel the blood pumping out of me. 'Fuck, Gabe . . .'

I make another incoherent noise and his grip tightens. He lowers his head and whispers something into my hair. I almost catch it but then another wave of blackness washes over me. This time I let it take me.

THE HAPPIEST PLACE ON EARTH

The first thing I see when I open my eyes is the water-stained ceiling of the infirmary. The second is Daniel. He's sitting forward in the chair beside me, eyes like cobalt.

'What were you thinking?'

He's quiet, controlled.

'That I could take them.' It comes out croaky, but at least I can form words again.

'Three Gatekeepers and only two of you?'

I falter. He thinks Rafa was with me from the start. No wonder he's relatively calm. Daniel would be apoplectic if he thought I'd taken on Bel and Leon on my own. I lift my hand – it works! – and find my head wrapped in a bandage. I touch my neck. More dressings.

'Did they attack first?' he asks.

I fiddle with the bandage on my neck, avoid eye contact.

'Gabe . . .' A tiny sigh. 'I expect that sort of recklessness from Rafa, but not you and not now.'

'You've been out of the field for too long, Daniel. You forget how hard it is to cross paths with Gatekeepers and turn the other cheek.'

'It's our mandate—'

'To defend ourselves, not attack. Yeah, I know.' I lift my weight onto my elbows and wait for the brain-crushing pain.

It doesn't come. There's only a dull throb at the base of my skull. The sword hilt struck with enough force to crack bone. Rafa must have shifted with me more than once on the way back. I look around for Brother Ferro, find him restocking his supply cabinet. I breathe in familiar smells of antiseptic and disinfectant.

'How long was I out?' I ask him.

The monk pauses, a box of syringes in his hand. I notice how grey his cropped hair looks under the fluorescents and try to remember how old he is. I'm sure he's barely fifty.

'You had a bad concussion so I gave you a sedative,' he says. 'You've been sleeping for about an hour.'

'How's Rafa?'

'Exhausted from healing you; otherwise uninjured.'

I prod at the dressing, feel the lump beneath it. What made Rafa go back to the island? What would have happened if he hadn't? For a second I'm on the beach, sand in my mouth, bleeding, helpless as Bel pushes his sword into my neck. I shudder.

'Do you want to shift again?' Daniel asks.

'With you?' I don't hide my surprise. Daniel's one of the Five. He hasn't made that offer in years – that's what the rest of us are for.

He watches me closely. 'Yes.'

I'm well aware he's offering more than healing: this is the start of something else, officially. Something we've been dancing around for weeks now. Jude would be rolling his eyes behind Daniel's back if he was here right now. Actually, where *is* Jude? Maybe he doesn't know about Bel and Leon. But that would mean Rafa didn't go back to San Francisco—

'I take it that's a no.'

Oh. I give him a quick smile. 'I'm fine, really.' I haven't worked out how I feel about Daniel's interest in me, and I'm not quite ready to explore it.

He nods, moves back. 'Is your brother thinking more rationally?'

I push aside the sheet and sit up. I'm still in cargoes and a t-shirt, the front caked with my blood and Leon's. 'Mya's the one you should be worried about.'

'Jude is responsible for his own actions.'

'Can you honestly sit there and tell me he's being unreasonable?'

Something crosses Daniel's face: he's disappointed with me. 'I think it's unreasonable to question Nathaniel. I think it's unreasonable to accuse him of fabricating our destiny.'

I bristle. 'But that's not what Jude said.'

'Your brother wants proof of our commission to hunt and find the Fallen. That's no different than calling Nathaniel a liar.'

But Nathaniel is a liar.

I don't say it out loud. Instead I say: 'You need to let this play out.'

'To what end?'

'I don't know. But it needs to happen.'

He studies me for a moment. 'And where do you stand in all this?'

'You really need to ask?'

Daniel exhales. 'With your brother, of course.' He rises. He rests his fingertips on the bed, close to my thigh but not touching. 'I truly hope Jude is as smart as you think he is. Your loyalty is admirable, but it should never be blind.'

I watch him walk out of the infirmary, his designer shoes quiet on the cracked lino. Daniel's a strategic thinker. A *deep* thinker. He must have questions about our existence, but he's never said so. And he won't start now, not with Jude driving the push for answers.

I swing my legs over the side of the bed. Brother Ferro

shuts the supply cabinet and comes over. 'May I?' He gestures to my head. I nod and he unwraps the bandage. 'I would have preferred to stitch this, but the healing was too progressed by the time Rafa brought you here.'

I reach up and touch hair stiff with dried blood.

'Yes, Gabriella, it is all there.'

I let out a relieved laugh. Not that I haven't had patches of my head shaved for stitches before, but I'm happy to avoid it.

'Something else I need to thank Rafa for.' I drag my fingers through a tangled clump and retie my ponytail. 'Did he say which bar he was hitting for a drink?'

'I know you believe Rafa's stamina is limitless, but I don't think he was going anywhere but his room when he left here.'

I wait until Brother Ferro returns to sorting instruments before I reach for my phone. And even then I hesitate. Not sure why. Embarrassment? I should never have put myself in that situation on the beach. If anyone else had done what I did tonight, I'd kick their arse. But I'm going to hear about it from Rafa sooner or later, so I may as well get it over with. I tap out a text.

Where are you?

He responds a few seconds later. *My room.*

You decent?

Rarely.

Put some trousers on. I'm coming up.

I wait a couple of minutes and then shift to the hallway outside his room, knock twice.

'It's unlocked.'

I walk in, find him standing in the bathroom doorway, towel wrapped low around his hips. His hair is still wet and steam wafts around him.

'Trousers?' I shut the door behind me.

'Next on my list.'

'Brother Ferro said you were a wreck. You don't look so bad. Who'd you shift with?'

His eyes drift to my blood-caked hair. 'How about you tell me how you ended up face-down in the sand with three Gatekeepers arguing over who was going to decapitate you?'

An icy finger brushes the nape of my neck. I shrug it off. 'When I felt them arrive I thought I could take care of it myself.'

'Three of them? You might need to check that ego, Gabe.'

'There were only two when I attacked.'

'It didn't cross your mind they weren't alone? Seriously, what the fuck were you thinking?'

I don't know what to tell him. I let my eyes wander around the room to buy myself time. The walls are crowded with katanas, poleaxes, sais, broadswords, all neat and ordered in racks, but everything else is a mess. His bed is a tangle of sheets, motorcycle magazines and tattered manga paperbacks. Boots and running shoes scattered on the floor, the desk buried under a pile of dirty clothes and crumpled towels. There's a box of empty beer bottles by the door and I catch a faint whiff of bourbon.

'Why didn't you call?' He's not angry; he's genuinely curious.

I reach for his favourite katana, sheathed in an antique hand-carved saya, run my fingertip over the leather-bound hilt. I can't look at him. 'I needed a distraction.'

'From what? This crap between Jude and Nathaniel? Fuck, Gabe, it's not that big of a deal.'

'It is.' I take a deep breath. 'Jude's prepared to walk out the door over it.'

A beat. 'No he's not.'

'He is, Rafa. Doesn't it bother you that everything's on the brink of turning to shit here?'

'Apparently not as much as it does you.' He watches me for a second and then crosses the carpet, stepping over shoes without looking. He stops less than an arm's length away and a hint of sandalwood reaches me. I wait for him to tell me how it doesn't matter if the Sanctuary tears itself apart, wave it away like he does everything else. But he just stands there watching me, searching for . . . something.

Finally he rubs the back of his neck. 'A few seconds more and they had you.' His voice is rough. It brings a strange sensation to my chest. I'm aware of how close he is. Of the water dripping from his hair to his shoulder, running down his collarbone. The contours of his arms and his chest, the trail of hair low on his stomach. I've seen Rafa shirtless a thousand times, wrestled with him half-naked on the training mats just as often. I've always known how fit he is, but I've never been distracted by his bare flesh before. It must be the towel. We watch each other for a few more seconds.

'What made you come back?'

He shrugs with one shoulder. 'The European history majors weren't doing it for me tonight.'

'But why the island?'

Rafa doesn't take his eyes from me. 'You were twitchy. I wanted to check you weren't going to damage the first tourist who hit on you.'

'And then what, repeat your offer to distract me?'

'Would your answer have changed without an audience?'

'You wouldn't offer without an audience. That's the whole point, isn't it? To get a reaction?'

His eyes drop to my lips. 'There's no audience now.'

I try to read him. For once, I can't. I feel a flush creep up my neck. Get a grip. It's *Rafa*.

I push past him. 'I don't know what *this* is, but it's not helping.' I walk into the bathroom. I wet a face washer, dab at my crusty hair. The steam in here smells of apples. It throws me further off-kilter. I don't know if it's the tension between Jude and Nathaniel and knowing where it might lead, or the fact I was bleeding out on a beach two hours ago, but I'm off balance. Undone.

'You took on three Gatekeepers on your own.' Rafa is behind me now, watching in the mirror. 'That's a whole new level of aggression, even for you.'

'Fine. Get dressed and we'll go a few rounds.'

'I don't want to spar with you.' Rafa drags his fingers through his hair, looks away for a second. When his eyes meet mine again in the reflection, they're dark, serious. 'I thought you were going to die tonight. Do you know what went through my head?'

'Same as usual, right? Nothing.' I'm trying to keep the mood light, but I'm warm in places that haven't felt heat for a long time. I turn round and he's barely centimetres from me. I should move away. Palm him in the chest. Headbutt him. I don't do any of those things.

'That's right,' he says quietly. 'Nothing. I was about to lose you and I couldn't form a coherent thought.'

I lean back against the sink. 'That's a good line, Rafa.'

'It's not a line.'

'What do you call it, then?'

'An attempt to drop the bullshit between us.' I can see the pulse in his throat.

'And do what?'

He waits, and when I don't push him away, he moves even closer. Our hips touch. I feel the heat of him. He rests his hands either side of me on the sink. 'Don't' – his lips are almost on mine – 'hit me.'

The kiss is soft, tender in a way that surprises me so

37

completely I don't even think about it. I just respond. The kiss instantly deepens, but he doesn't take his hands from the sink. For the moment I'm distracted enough by his lips and tongue. I'm losing myself and he's barely touched me. Is this what I want? Is *Rafa* what I want?

His hand slips under my shirt. His fingers climb my back and then trace a light path down my spine. I shiver with pleasure. I'm still kissing him. He wraps his free arm around me and I let him lift me onto the vanity, position himself between my thighs. My body thrums with want and need. Heat everywhere.

He crushes me against him, fingers in my hair now, cradling my head against the force of his lips. I match him for intensity, getting a grip on his towel and pulling him closer. I'm struggling for breath, but I'm not breaking contact first. Rafa finally drags his lips from mine. He kisses my throat, his breath hot. Ragged. He unhooks my bra with one hand. I tug on his towel, let it drop to the floor. Run my hands over his bare hips and the muscle of his backside.

'Gabe . . .' His voice is raw. Our hearts thump together, racing each other.

'The door,' I manage.

His mouth covers mine again and I feel the vortex. I let him take me across the room. The sensation of kissing though the shift is obscenely intimate, deepening every sensation as the maelstrom tears and compresses us.

I materialise with my back against the door, legs tight around him. He flicks the lock with one hand and presses into me, kissing me harder.

I'm lost in a storm of pleasure and wanting. I pull at my t-shirt and we break apart so I can drag it over my head. He waits for a beat, breathing fast. And then his fingers find the button on my jeans. My zip slides down.

Our lips crush together, more urgent now. I loosen my legs from his hips and drop to the floor so I can step out of my boots. Rafa pulls my jeans over my hips along with my underwear, stopping to kiss my breasts and my hipbone on the way. I kick my clothes away and Rafa lifts me against the door again and in a single, assured movement he's part of me. We pause for a second, share a moment of astonishment. Chests rising and falling, checking ourselves.

Rafa doesn't hesitate when I pull us back into the vortex. The sensation is exquisite. I take us across the room, pinpoint our arrival so that his legs strike the bed and he has to topple backwards onto the mattress.

Rafa smiles against my lips as he steadies himself. 'What a surprise,' he whispers. 'You want to be on top.'

He flips me round so fast I'm almost not ready for it. But as soon as I hit the mattress I tighten my legs and use his momentum to roll him onto his back. It's almost like sparring. I straddle him, triumphant. His hands are on my hips. As he calculates his next move, I start to push against him. He closes his eyes, slowly, guides me with his hands. 'Unfair tactic.'

'Why?' I ask, trying not to lose myself too quickly. 'You think I might be better than you at this, too?'

Rafa smiles, dirty and sexy. 'We'll see who lasts longer.' He pushes himself up into a sitting position and wraps my legs around his hips. And then he runs his tongue up the side of my neck and grazes his teeth over my earlobe, arms tight around me.

'You can't tell anyone about this,' I whisper, pressing my cheek against his hair, want and need building, hips moving with purpose. 'And I'm not moaning.'

He laughs and it reverberates through every part of me. 'We'll see.'

AVOIDANCE

'Were you trying to get yourself killed?'

Jude's voice drags me out of the blackness. I keep my back to him while I surface. The morning light is subdued, not yet fully awake either. Pieces from last night fall back into place.

Oh. I bury my face in the pillow, try to focus. How much does Jude know?

'What happened to respecting my privacy?' I mutter.

'Fuck your privacy. You almost died last night.'

That answers two of three pressing questions: Jude has spoken to Rafa, and he knows what really happened on the beach. But what about afterwards? The memory washes over me again. The heat, the urgency. What was I thinking? My fingers tighten on the corner of the pillow. I close my eyes and try to settle my poker face. It takes a few seconds.

'Why would you go after them on your own? Is this about my fight with Nathaniel?'

I don't answer and I hear him take a slow breath, like he's struggling to keep his temper. And then: 'How could you drop your guard like that?'

I roll over and face him. He's next to the bed, hands resting on his hips. Bloodshot eyes and stubbled cheeks. Behind him, George Grie's *River Styx ferry* hangs on the wall, ominous in the dull light. Its black and grey sky seems almost cheery compared to my brother. I try to read his mood. A sense of distance. About me or Nathaniel? I rub my cheek on my shoulder and catch a hint of sandalwood. Heat flares in inappropriate places. I glance away, guilty. Jude can't know about Rafa and me: he'd be acting weirder than this if he did.

'I needed a fight,' I say. 'In hindsight, I picked the wrong one.' I sit up too fast and the room does a quick lap around me. Jude takes my elbow to steady me. He sits down and I can't help but lean into him as the mattress takes his weight. He smells of lime and tequila and the sea.

'I feel like an idiot.'

'It was an idiotic thing to do,' he says, but the anger's mostly gone now. 'You really scared the hell out of Rafa.'

Warmth creeps up my neck. 'What makes you say that?'

'I could hear it in his voice.' Jude sits back so he can see me properly. 'Why didn't you call me from the infirmary?

Why did I have to wait until this morning to hear about it from him?'

'I didn't want to disturb *your* choice of recreational release.' I gesture to his bloodshot eyes – and register that Rafa's only just phoned him. It's the reason Jude's back from whatever bar he was in.

'Gabe.'

'I was embarrassed, all right?' I'm not sure if I'm talking about the fight on the beach or what happened afterwards. Maybe both.

'No shit.'

I pluck at his shirt – the same one he had on last time I saw him. 'Not all of us have the foresight to stay out all night drinking ourselves into oblivion.'

'Beats lying in bed staring at the ceiling.'

I bring my knees to my chest, wrap my arms around them. 'Are you going to provoke Nathaniel again today?'

'Don't change the subject.'

'Same subject – forays into recklessness. Mine's done and dusted, let's talk about yours.'

His eyebrows twitch up. 'You think I'm being reckless?'

'In letting Mya drive the agenda? Absolutely.'

Jude lets out a loud sigh. 'This again? She mightn't have been here for as long as us but she's allowed an opinion, Gabe.'

'And what *is* her opinion?'

'The same as yours: that Nathaniel's kept things from us

43

and it's time to come clean. At the very least, tell us which archangel ordered him to track us all down as babies and train us up to be the Garrison's reserve force. Come on, we've been talking about this stuff for years, all of us.'

'Yeah, in hushed tones over bottles of wine, not getting in Nathaniel's face about it. And don't tell me her opinion is the same as mine. She wouldn't know mine – she's never asked for it.'

'I know how you think, and I'm telling you she's on the same page as us.'

I press my lips together. There's no point arguing with him about Mya. He can't see how destructive she is. She doesn't care about learning the truth: all she wants is chaos. Ever since she found out it would take decades before she earned the right to stand for the Council of the Five.

'Is this about Daniel? Are you worried he's going to think less of you?'

I stare at my brother. 'No, it's not about Daniel. Fuck, give me some credit.'

'Why? You're not giving me any.'

I feel the anger tightening my chest, shortening my breath. 'Jude, we could have confronted Nathaniel a thousand times over the last century and we didn't. Why? Because we didn't want to risk everything here unless we had to. I don't think Mya's need for rebellion is a good enough reason for a sudden change of heart.'

For all our baggage, for all our desire to tell the rest of

the Rephaim what happened to our mother – what most likely happened to theirs – we've never done it. Partly because it will rip the place apart. And partly because we've dug ourselves a hole. We know *keeping* a secret this big is almost as bad as the secret itself.

I pause. 'You haven't told her about Jason, have you?'

He looks at me as if I've slapped him and I immediately regret asking. Of course he hasn't. Even he knows there's no way Mya could keep that bit of information to herself.

'Sorry,' I say, and I mean it.

Jude breathes in deeply through his nose. We sit in silence for a good minute.

'I wish I knew what happened to him.' He says it quietly. It still grates on him that our cousin hid from us over a century ago and hasn't once reached out to see if we're okay.

'Maybe he's dead. That'd be easier to forgive than him disappearing because he panicked we might tell Nathaniel he exists.'

Jude strangles a laugh. 'Shit, Gabe, you can be cold sometimes.'

I shrug. He knows I'm a realist.

The light falling through my window is brighter now. Jude stands up, rubs his eyes. 'You want to grab breakfast?'

I think about running into Rafa in the commissary, feel a strange sensation in my stomach. 'I'll get something later.' I reach up above my bed to the sword rack, lift down the closest blade. I slide it out of the saya, check the line in a patch of sunlight on my bed, pretend that's all I'm thinking about. 'I lost a perfectly good sword last night. I need to get this one into shape before I do much else today.'

'Okay. I'll bring you something to eat.'

'Thanks.'

We share a weary smile. No matter how often we disagree – how much we piss each other off – we always find a way to be okay. The door clicks shut as he leaves and I flop back onto my pillow, throw my arm across my face.

I hooked up with Rafa.

What was I thinking? What if everyone finds out?

But even as I wrestle with the implications, I can't shut out the memory of him. The contours of his body. The assurance in his touch. How he buried his face in my neck and said my name as he shuddered. It completely destroyed my self-control. But I didn't make a sound. I wouldn't give him the satisfaction – not after all those years of being the punchline to his favourite joke.

But oh my god . . .

I touch my lips, remember his crushed against them. My skin is raw from his stubble, my hair mussed from his fingers. I catch another trace of sandalwood and the ache sets in without warning.

I pull a pillow over my face. God help me.

I'm crushing on Rafa.

STING IN THE TAIL

Usually when I need to clear my head, I run the mountain trail that snakes up from the southern wall of the Sanctuary. But I really do need to get my back-up katana into shape, so I'm set up under the canopy of Nathaniel's ancient apple tree, the one trying to punch its way through the Sanctuary walls. It's early autumn, and the tree is heavy with leaves and waxy fruit. Patches of sunlight filter through, casting abstract patterns on the grass. It's quiet, peaceful. Perfect.

To sharpen a katana properly takes weeks of concentrated effort – I'd never have the patience for it – but a few hours of working a blade over a whetstone is enough to freshen the steel and usually enough to clear out the cobwebs.

Not today.

I've been sitting here on my mat for half an hour and

I haven't progressed beyond preparing the whetstone. I keep getting lost in random fantasies involving Rafa on the training mats. We're sparring, alone, and when I pin him—

'What are you smirking about?'

Daisy's standing in the doorway to the scriptorium, dressed in black leggings and training singlet. I don't know how long she's been watching me but I hope she doesn't see the heat in my cheeks. I should slap myself. I'm blushing over *Rafa*.

'Nothing.' I reach for my sword, check the line even though I haven't started working the steel yet.

Daisy crosses the courtyard, picks a low-hanging apple on her way. She cradles it under her nose and takes a deep breath. 'New season apples. Finally.' She sits cross-legged on the ground opposite me, the bucket of water between us. 'I hear you had some excitement last night.'

I run the blade over the whetstone, focus on keeping the action smooth and steady. 'Uh huh.'

'As did Rafa.'

I wet the steel, keep up my rhythm.

'Caught on camera for all to see.'

The blade slips off the end of the whetstone. Daisy's still talking but all I hear is white noise. He filmed us? Blood thunders to my temples and I taste bile. I'm going to throw up. I'm—

'Are you listening to me?'

I force myself to swallow, breathe, finally look at Daisy. She must be mortified.

'They were going at it like crazy—'

Wait. *They*.

'Who?'

'Rafa and Mya,' she says, exasperated. 'The cameras are working again in the training room. They had no idea they were being filmed.'

Thoughts smash up against each other and it takes a second for her words to take shape. And even then I can't quite make them fit together properly.

Rafa didn't film us.

Rafa had sex with Mya in the training room.

Last night.

My stomach twists into a knot. 'When?'

Daisy shrugs. 'It can't have been too long after you two got back from your run-in with Bel and company.'

I need to swallow, but my mouth is too dry. I flash hot, then cold. Rafa had sex with Mya.

Then he had sex with me.

And I've been thinking about him all morning.

I scramble to my feet and make it to the edge of the courtyard before I dry retch.

'Gabe, are you okay?'

I retch again, everything in me straining. The wall is the only thing keeping me upright. I rest my head against the rough stones. Rafa was fresh out of the shower when I went to his room because he'd just been with Mya. I wipe my mouth with the back of my hand. My fingers are shaking.

'I must still be concussed.'

Idiot. *Idiot*. If anyone found out ... It's embarrassing enough that I went there with Rafa, but this ... this is humiliating beyond words. It was *Mya*. And the fact he was with me in the same night won't faze her. She'll gloat that she got there first.

'How badly did you get hurt?'

I push down the rage. It fights back, hard. 'Not badly,' I lie. 'Laceration to the neck and a knock to the head, that's all. I'm fine.' She looks me over, unconvinced. I haven't come this close to throwing up in fifty years. I go back to the tree and sit down, force an embarrassed smile. 'Did you go to San Fran last night?'

She rubs the apple against her t-shirt to polish the mottled skin. 'Only for an hour or so. Jude was really throwing back the tequila. I offered to shift and sober him up but he wasn't interested. He wanted to get hammered. I wasn't in the mood to listen to him rant about Nathaniel and the Five, so I came home.'

'You left him alone with Mya?'

'She left not long after Rafa. They were probably slamming hips at that point.'

The image is a sharp jab between my ribs. 'So she's lost interest in Jude, then.' I coax the words out, try to sound normal.

Daisy laughs, bitter. 'I doubt it. And honestly, if he's that stupid . . .' She takes a vicious bite of her apple. It crunches and snaps and she screws up her face, spits out the mouthful. 'Ugh.' She wipes juice from her freckled cheek and tosses the rest of the apple across the courtyard. 'Nowhere near ripe.'

Even Daisy's reached the end of her patience with Jude. She's wanted more than friendship from him for years, but he hasn't hooked up with another Rephaite for a century. He was the first of us to realise how much drama that could create in a society as small as ours.

Yes. Well.

'This arguing with Nathaniel,' Daisy says. 'It's got everyone on edge.'

I flick water on my blade. 'I know.'

She blames Mya for the tension – no faulting her there – but she doesn't know the decades of buried anger that have preceded Jude's rebellion. Mya just happens to be a very effective and aggravating catalyst.

'Nathaniel could answer his questions,' I say. 'They're reasonable enough.'

'You're defending Mya?'

'I'm defending Jude.'

Daisy tucks her hair behind her ears. It's longer than it's been for a while, almost to her shoulders, and vibrant red even in the shade. 'He's pushing too hard. He needs to pull in his head for a while.'

'I'm not his keeper.'

'He listens to you.'

'Yeah, but I'm not the only one in his ear these days.'

Daisy stands up, dusts off her leggings. 'I wonder how Jude's going to feel about Mya and Rafa?' She picks another apple as she leaves.

I know how *I* feel about it. I snatch up my sword and go back to work on the whetstone. Pain builds in my head. Blood pounds at my temples.

And I know what I'm going to do about it.

I'm going to fucking kill Rafa.

STICKS AND STONES AND A GLASS WINDOW

I find him in his room wearing a black vest and tracksuit bottoms, one foot on his desk, lacing up a running shoe. He doesn't flinch, even though I've shifted in without warning. The bed is still unmade, sheets strewn across the floor where we left them.

'Hey,' he says and gives me a lazy smile. 'You up for a run?'

I flex my fingers, control the rage churning in my chest. 'I've been thinking about last night.'

Another slow smile. 'Me too.'

'I'm curious.'

'About what?' He takes his foot off the desk and turns to face me, trying to work out my mood.

'Why it happened. Was it so you could brag you'd finally

screwed your way through this place?' It's an effort but I keep it light. I want to set him up. 'Why the fixation with adding me to that list?'

He measures me for a long moment and then he lets out his breath slowly. 'Gabe, you're the *only* one I've ever wanted. Everyone else was just killing time.'

'Is that what you were doing with Mya last night in the training room, *killing time*?'

He blinks.

'The cameras are working in there again, Rafa. It's on tape.'

A shrug, not as casual as he wants it to be. 'So? I ran into her and she offered to heal me, one thing led to another . . . It didn't mean anything.'

'Are you fucking kidding?'

Rafa waves away my anger. 'I had no idea what was going to happen with us.'

'It *wouldn't* have happened if you'd told me. Don't you get that?'

'Come on, you needed last night. Don't tell me you didn't enjoy it. And what went on in the training room was nothing compared to what happened in here.'

'Explain what was different.'

He moves closer, his eyes sharp. '*Everything* was different. For starters, I'm not in love with her.'

I stare at him. For a second I feel it – a faint prick of regret – and then the humiliation hits all over again. I lash out without thinking, connect with his jaw. He takes a step back to absorb the punch, and then he straightens, rubs his face. 'You done now?'

'Am I *done*? You think I'm going to hit you once and then we're all good?' My knuckles throb. The pain is familiar, welcome. It centres me.

'I just told you I love you. For fuck's sake, Gabe, I've never said that to anyone—'

'And yet I was the *second* woman you got naked with last night.'

A tight smile. 'Clearly you haven't seen the footage. I barely got undressed in the training room.'

I push away the image of Rafa and Mya having quick and nasty sex on the practice mats. It wrings me out, makes me feel like I need another shower. 'Wow, I feel so special.'

Rafa cracks a knuckle. The sound has never irritated me more. 'So you want to throw down? Will that make you feel better?'

'The only thing that would make me feel better is if I could erase last night from my memory. It was the biggest mistake of my life.'

Something shifts in his eyes. They're darker now, harder. 'I knew you'd do this. You were always going to find a way to regret last night because it was *me*. God forbid you admit to yourself I've been right all these years.'

'About what?'

'That I'm the only one here who can handle you. I'm the only one who's your equal.'

I scoff. 'My equal? Maybe in combat and drinking but have you ever had an independent thought, Rafa? One that Jude didn't give you?'

'Is that what you want, Gabe – an independent thinker? Then stop looking in Pretty Boy's direction. He doesn't know what he thinks until Nathaniel tells him.'

'At least he has the capacity to think with his brain instead of his dick.'

'He has to, his dick's not big enough to multi-task.'

I walk over to the bedside table, lift up a motor-cycle magazine draped over an empty glass. I fling it on the mattress. 'Yeah, because you're an intellectual genius.'

'When did your head get this far up your own arse? No wonder Daniel's got such a hard-on for you.'

'You're really threatened by him, aren't you? You know why? Because he's more man than you'll ever be.' It's a cheap shot but it has the desired effect. He wants to hurt me. And I want him to try. I don't want to think, don't want to *feel* any more. All there is now is this burning need to punish him.

Rafa moves forward and I snatch up the glass, hurl it at his head. And then I launch myself at him. He bats away the glass and blocks my punch, counters with a sharp jab to my ribs. I swing again, slam my fist into his kidneys. He kicks out my knee, elbows me between my shoulder blades. I stumble forward, catch myself on his desk chair. I use the momentum to swing round, bringing the chair with me. Rafa braces and turns his face away, blocks with both arms. The wooden legs crack against his forearms but the chair remains intact. It jars. I pull back to swing again, but Rafa kicks me in the ribs. I stagger back, almost trip on a shoe.

'Just fucking stop,' he says between breaths. He's seething. I've never seen him this angry.

Good.

I charge, drive him into the wall with my shoulder. Katanas rattle in the rack above us. I land another punch to his lower back before he shoves me away. We've sparred a thousand times, know each other's moves as well as our own. This isn't sparring, though. This time we want to hurt each other.

I land a solid punch on his jaw, harder than the first. His head snaps back and blood sprays from his mouth. It's not enough. I want him unconscious. I want to humiliate him like he's humiliated me. I swing again but he's already recovered, and now I'm fending off a barrage of punches and kicks. I duck, block, counter. Try to avoid the obstacle course of boots and sheets on the floor. He dodges a hook and I grab him in a headlock, trap him against my side, fire three hard jabs into his ribs. He gets his arms around my legs. Too late, I know what's coming. He lifts me off the floor and over his shoulder, and then slams my back on the floor. The carpet muffles the impact but all the air is driven out of me and in the vital seconds it takes me to recover, Rafa has the advantage. He straddles my chest, pinning my shoulders with his knees, and holds down my arms. His face is centimetres from mine, flushed and bleeding. Hair damp with sweat.

'Too slow, Gabe. You're well off your game.' His lips are flat, twisted in a tight smile. 'I rocked your world, didn't I?'

I go still beneath him, catching my breath. Gathering strength. 'Don't flatter yourself. I was concussed.' I swing my legs up and around him. I'm quick enough to hook my ankles together around his chest before he can block me. We're locked together now. I try to wrestle him to one side, get his weight off me so I can use my fists, but he's too strong. I tighten my legs, manage to push a boot up under his chin. He grunts, turns his face away. I grind the sole into his cheek.

'Fuck,' he spits. He leans back to get away from my boot. It's enough for me to tilt my hips and roll us both sideways. Rafa uses the momentum to change his grip and fumbles for a headlock. For a few seconds we scuffle around, both trying to get a grip.

I find an opening first, not for a submission hold but an elbow to Rafa's throat. He cough-chokes and I kick free. We roll away from each other and spring to our feet simultaneously. He rubs his neck, gives me a filthy look. I push hair out of my face and eyeball him.

'You know the worst thing about all this, Gabe? You're as uptight in the sack as I imagined you'd be.'

Another blast of rage hits me, a hot mess of fury and shame. For a second I can't breathe through it.

'At least Mya's not afraid to make a few noises—'

I shift and crash-tackle him. I hit so hard we both smash through the window. It's a two-storey fall to the piazza. My hand is clamped around his throat, his around mine. We wrestle all the way down. Neither of us shifts to avoid the impact.

We hit the grass. *Hard.*

Bones crunch. Something gives in my right shoulder. Pain splinters down my arm. We lie panting, side by side. The sun is too bright. I try to lift myself up – shit, everything hurts. I kick out at Rafa instead. He catches me by the calf and drags me closer. I taste grass, dirt.

'You done yet?' he rasps. He's in a world of pain. His cheek is split and swollen, his forehead grazed. A piece of glass is embedded in his lower lip.

'Not even close.'

Someone is running towards us, their footfalls soft on the lawn. I grab a fistful of Rafa's shirt, smell blood and sweat. 'You tell anyone what happened last night and I'll break every bone in your body. Do you understand?'

He watches me, unflinching.

'And, Rafa' – I swallow, taste blood – 'if you ever touch me again, I will end you.'

DISLOCATION

'What the hell was that?'

Micah leans over me and blocks the sun, blond hair like an aura spiking in all directions.

Rafa knocks my hands from his shirt and rolls over, lets out a small moan. 'Minor disagreement.'

Micah looks from me to Rafa and back again. 'How about I get you both to the infirmary before anyone else sees this mess.'

'Not the infirmary.' Rafa picks the shard of glass from his lip and winces. 'Get me to Zak.'

Micah hesitates for only a second. 'Fine.' He reaches for my wrist. We're in the vortex for barely a second, but it's enough to take the edge off the pain. Except for my shoulder – that's still screaming.

Zak is alone in his room, hanging from an inversion

table. Rafa leans against the wall. I slump to the bed, refuse to look at him. Zak stays upside down for a good five seconds after we arrive; doesn't say a word. Then he slowly hauls himself up the right way. He takes in the state of Rafa, checks me over, and runs a hand through his shaggy black hair.

'Demons?' He unhooks his feet and steps onto the carpet. The room is so much tidier than mine – Ez has always hated clutter – and smells of fresh cotton and orange blossom, a hint of liniment.

Micah gives a short laugh. 'They did this to each other. And Rafa needs a new window.'

Zak raises his eyebrows at me. 'That's extreme, even for you two.'

I ignore him. My shoulder is killing me.

'Right,' Micah says. 'If you finish taking care of Rafa, I'll get Gabe sorted.'

Zak nods and they wait for Rafa and me to speak to each other: an apology or at the very least a parting shot. It's how we'd usually walk away from a dust-up. But this isn't a bit of overenthusiastic sparring. This is so far beyond that. Out of the corner of my eye I see Rafa watching me, waiting to see what direction I take this. I ignore him, hold my hand out to Micah. 'Still in pain here.'

A small line creases his forehead. He flicks another quick glance at Rafa and then grips my wrist. We shift to his room and I immediately sit on his bed, wince at the pain radiating down my arm and across my collarbone.

'Are you going to tell me what that was about?' Micah asks.

'The usual stuff. Can you get this back in?'

He takes a good look at my shoulder. 'You know I've never done this before, right?'

'You've seen it done. You'll be fine.'

Rafa popped my shoulder back in two years ago after Zarael threw me against a brick wall. *Rafa*. Just thinking about him brings an instant spike in blood pressure. I hope Zak takes his time healing him.

Micah helps me lie down and then kicks off his boots. 'Sorry about the sock, but it's better than my bare foot.'

'I don't care about your stinky feet, Micah, just get my shoulder back in.' I turn my face into the pillow and breathe deeply. He takes my hand, gives it a reassuring squeeze.

'Do you want something to bite down on?'

I shake my head and the pillowcase rustles. I focus on the acoustic guitar propped against the wall, the scuff marks on the scratch plate under the strings. Micah positions his foot in my armpit, gets a better grip on my hand. 'Here goes.' He pulls on my arm, slowly increasing the stretch. I grit my teeth, squeeze my eyes shut. Oh god, I forgot how much this *hurts*. The seconds grind by, filled with knives and needles. It's an effort not to shift to escape the pain. And then finally my shoulder slips back into place. The relief is instant.

'Hey,' Micah says, his voice gentle. 'You're crying.'

I wipe my cheek with the back of my finger. 'No I'm not.'

'I haven't seen you cry since we were kids.'

'I'm *not* crying. Let's shift again.'

He gives me a level look. 'You might want to throw in a please and thank you there somewhere.'

I sigh. 'Please, Micah.' My phone rings. I ignore it. 'Another shift or two should do it. *Thank you.*'

My phone stops. Micah's starts. 'It's Daisy.' He answers it, glances at me. 'She's here, why?' A pause. 'Okay. I'll tell her.'

I rub my eye. 'What now?'

'Jude and Nathaniel are in the piazza. Daisy says it's bad.'

There are at least sixty Rephaim clustered under Rafa's window in the piazza. Word travels fast at the Sanctuary. But it's not the broken window or the glass scattered across the lawn they're interested in, it's Jude and Nathaniel, facing off under a pale blue sky.

'About time,' Taya says as I move between her and Malachi. Heads turn in my direction, expectant. Micah and I shifted via my room so I'm wearing a clean shirt and my shoulder has settled to a dull ache, enough that I can hide the injury. Daisy visibly relaxes, as if me just being here is going to fix everything. I stand between her and Jones – I need a feel for what's going on before I jump in.

They're both dressed in training gear, flushed, hair damp: they were sparring when the shit hit the fan.

'Who?' Jude demands. 'You keep going on about how the archangels give you orders but who are we talking about? Michael? The same Captain of the Garrison who ordered you all to be thrown to hell in the first place?'

Nathaniel is calm, his icy gaze flickering slowly, patiently. 'The secrets of the Garrison are not for you, Judah. Not yet.'

Daniel and Calista flank the fallen angel. Daniel meets my gaze and there's no doubt what he's thinking: *I told you this was coming.* Jude has his back to me, feet planted and shoulders tense. He's holding something in his left hand, it's . . . an apricot brioche in cling wrap.

And, like that, I can guess how this all unfolded. Jude was on his way back with my breakfast when he heard about Rafa and me crashing through a window. Nathaniel must have heard too, and the two of them crossed paths coming to check on us. It was too much to hope they could avoid each other for even a day.

Mya is at Jude's side, mussed blonde hair falling around her shoulders and jeans too tight for anything except drawing attention. Anger stirs under my ribs. She flicks a look over her shoulder in my direction, dismissive rather than triumphant. She doesn't know about Rafa and me, but it's a bittersweet consolation. She's standing beside my brother, energised by the conflict. Ez catches my eye.

64

Tense, anxious, silently urging me to do something. Damn it. If I hadn't been brawling with Rafa, this wouldn't be happening.

Rafa.

I rake the crowd and find him with Zak, pushing past Seth. They've just arrived. The sight of Rafa – healed, unbloodied – is like a hot knife between my ribs. He catches me looking, winks without smiling. The blade twists. I fight the urge to shift over there and break his nose.

Nathaniel sees me before he sees Rafa. 'Gabriella, good. Could you explain what happened here?' He gestures to the spray of glass around us. Jude glances my way and the tightness around his eyes eases a little. He might have Mya at his side but it's my support he wants right now.

'Rafa and I were sparring,' I say and shrug, as if he and I regularly smash through windows.

'In his room?'

'Close-quarters fighting,' Rafa says, drawing Nathaniel's attention. 'We needed the practice.'

'You need a bit more,' Jones says, pointing up at the shattered window. Nobody laughs.

'Nathaniel,' Jude says, his tone flinty. 'Don't dodge the question.'

The fallen angel is still focused on me. 'Gabriella, perhaps you can talk sense into your brother. He appears no longer to respect the sanctity of the Garrison.'

'My brother has always respected the Garrison,' I say, stepping up next to Jude and avoiding eye contact with Mya. 'And a full understanding of the archangels' role in our lives will deepen that respect, not diminish it.'

Daniel makes a small noise of disapproval and Daisy frowns at me: this isn't what she had in mind.

'Why don't we settle this once and for all?' Jude says. 'Call down your captain. Let Michael tell us himself what he wants from us. And while he's at it, he can explain why our fathers have to go straight back to hell if we ever find them.'

Behind me someone gasps; someone else swears – Malachi, I think. Nathaniel remains immobile. Rigid. Only his eyes betray him: the icy blue irises flare white.

'Trust me, Judah,' he says, his voice arctic, 'you do not treat the Captain of the Garrison as if he were a pet dog.'

Mya folds her arms, digs her fingers into her skin. 'What about Gabriel? He's supposed to be merciful. Summon him.'

'Do you forget, Mya, that the archangel of whom you speak executed two hundred and twelve nephilim? Gabriel may be merciful, but his mercy is tempered with justice. Do not give him an imperative to choose one over the other.'

We've heard this story a thousand times: a cautionary tale to remind us what happened the last time the Fallen fathered children. It's the first time Nathaniel has used it to directly threaten us.

'Maybe if you'd lost a child that day with the rest of the Fallen you'd share their opinion of the Garrison.'

I suck in my breath. Even for Mya, that's a low blow. We know Nathaniel fell, and we know his earthly romp didn't produce a child, but he was still thrown to hell with Semyaza and the others. It's not something we bring up. Ever.

'You think you understand what it is you are asking, but you do not,' Nathaniel says, not quite as calm now.

'Because you've never explained it.'

'Let me explain it now, Mya, so there can be no doubt. You do not summon the Host of Heaven. The Garrison is not ... acquiescent. The warriors you so desperately wish to face will kill you before you can draw breath to question them. They fight hell spawn that you have neither the experience nor the courage to imagine. Their war has been raging for thousands of years. You' – he sweeps his hand around the room – 'all of you, are but the blink of an eye to them.'

'Then why do they care what we do?' Her voice is louder now. 'They've never shown any interest in us, so why do we have to prove ourselves to them?'

'Your value to the Garrison will be determined by your actions. When we find your fathers, your value will be beyond doubt.'

Jude scoffs. 'You and the rest of the Fallen escaped on their watch. It's not our problem.' He searches the faces around us. There's uncertainty. Agitation. His eyes meet mine. Shit, he's really going to do this. I nod and he straightens his shoulders. 'If you can't produce a member of the Garrison, Gabe and I are leaving.'

I blink. Not the bombshell about Nathaniel murdering our mother. This is actually worse: he's really ready to walk away. Am I? I'd be happy never to see Rafa or Mya again, but everyone else . . . I haven't had time to think about that.

'You are behaving like a child,' Nathaniel says.

'We've done everything you've asked of us – we're your own personal army, for fuck's sake!' Jude says. 'We have a right to know who's pulling our strings, and we have a right to meet our fathers before they're dragged off in chains again.'

'Enough.' Nathaniel's voice echoes around the courtyard. 'Cease this disrespect right now.'

'You say you're in contact with the Garrison. Prove it. Summon them.'

'No.'

'I mean it. Summon one or all of them. Let's take our chances.'

'No, Judah. I will not do that, now or ever.'

Jude stares at him. The tendons on his arms stand out, my breakfast pastry a crushed mess in his palm. Nobody moves. Nobody speaks.

'Then we're going.' Jude says it quietly and turns to me.

My heart knocks against my ribs. We're really doing

this. Which means Jude is getting ready to lob our grenade as a parting gift. He looks to me again. I nod and—

'I'm going too.'

My heart freezes. Fuck.

Mya.

'And me.' Rafa steps forward. *No.*

'Jude, don't be an idiot,' Daisy says, panicked. 'Where are you going to live? What are you going to *do*?'

'Whatever we want, that's the point.' Jude points at Nathaniel. 'What has he told us over the years? Nothing! He says the Garrison showed him where to find each of us, but how does he know it was them? And how did the Fallen break out of hell in the first place? Come on, we've all talked about this . . . don't any of you want answers?'

Silence. And then: 'I do,' Jones says.

'Don't . . .' Daisy reaches for him as he steps away. Lets her hand fall. She looks at me, wounded.

'Does anyone else want to find out if there's another life for us?' Jude asks.

I see Ez slip her fingers between Zak's. They don't look at each other: they don't have to. They've made their decision. They walk forward together. More movement as others follow. Rephaim around them move aside, so there's no mistaking who's standing with Jude.

Taya walks right up to me. 'You're leaving? With *her*?' She stabs a finger in Mya's direction. Taya wasn't a fan of Mya before Malachi hooked up with her: even less so since

Mya made sure he caught her with a random guy in an alley behind a Paris bar a month ago. Public sex acts are apparently her thing.

'This isn't about me,' Mya says to Taya. She's standing between Rafa and Jude – so much shorter than both of them – chin up and eyes bright. She's loving every minute of the drama. 'This is about what it means to be a child of the Fallen. There's a life out there that's different to this one. I know: I lived it for more than a century.'

'And you've been here for all of eight seconds,' Taya says, lip curling. 'Don't act like you know what we're about.'

'I know that most of you wish you could take the fight to Zarael, not sit on your hands waiting to be attacked. Jude's not the only one who wants to know why our fathers abandoned us before we were born. Not all of us are sheep.' She levels a gaze at Daisy, sharp enough to draw blood. 'Why can't we meet the Fallen? We have as much right to them as the Garrison.'

Nathaniel takes a slow, deep breath. 'I know your fathers in ways you cannot. I have served with them, I was imprisoned with them for millennia. I know their rage. I know their obsession with the Garrison. Wherever the Fallen are – hiding or trapped – they are plotting. They are scheming. They will use your neediness to turn you against me, use you to bolster their ranks in their fight with the Garrison to stay out of hell.'

'You really think we're that naive?'

The fallen angel watches Mya for a long moment. 'Child, you have spent too long as an outsider. You do not know how to exist if you are not in opposition to someone or something. Semyaza will see that and mould it to his own advantage.'

His attention returns to Jude. 'Your only hope for redemption is to be accepted by the Garrison. Any attempt to interact with your fathers will destroy that possibility.'

Jude shakes his head. 'And yet again, we have to take your word for it.' He looks to me but Daniel steps between us and blocks him.

'Gabriella,' Daniel says. 'Look around. Your brother is about to take our best fighters out the door. It will leave the Sanctuary vulnerable. Can you live with that?'

I don't answer, but I don't move round him either. A breeze whispers through the pine trees beyond the Sanctuary.

'And if you go, how many others will follow you out the door? What does that mean for those left behind who aren't soldiers? What does it mean for the monks? Where is their protection?'

'For fuck's sake, Gabe,' Jude says, 'don't get sucked in by this bullshit. If we're that important, Nathaniel will do what it takes to keep us here.'

Everyone is looking at me, waiting to see what I'm going to do. The fact there's even a question has brought a new air of uncertainty into the piazza.

'Can we talk?' I say to Jude.

A flicker of surprise. 'Now?'

'My room.' I shift without waiting for an answer.

I arrive by my window in a patch of sunlight. My bloodied t-shirt is crumpled on the floor. I kick it towards my dirty clothes basket. Wait for Jude to arrive. The seconds stretch out, hollow.

Finally, my stomach dips.

'What's going on?' Jude is by the door. Unsettled.

'I thought it was only you and me leaving?'

'Isn't this better?'

'Better how?'

'We're not walking away from everyone.'

'No, only *most* of our friends.' Anger stirs. All he cares about is that Rafa and Mya are coming. 'And what happened to telling everyone about Nathaniel killing our mother?'

'We save it.'

It takes a second before I understand. He doesn't want the others to know about our secret, not now that so many of our friends are out on the limb with us. Ez and Zak. Jones. Rafa.

'Then why leave today? We can stay here, bide our time, drop the bombshell when the time is right.'

He crosses the room to me. His face is flushed, full of urgency. 'We can't stay here, not after everyone stood up with me. We have to go. Now.'

'Go where?'

'Anywhere, Gabe. It doesn't matter as long as we're together.'

Blood rushes in my ears. Can't he see the problem? It was supposed to be the two of us. I try to picture this new life, trying to coexist with Rafa, having to explain to everyone why we can't be in the same room without hurting each other. Watching Mya flirt with him and manipulate Jude. Jude treating her like she's his equal. And then I imagine everyone finding out Rafa slept with Mya and me within hours of each other. And I was *second*. Shame washes over me. I can't do it.

'I'm not leaving.'

It takes a few seconds for the impact of my words to hit. When it does it's like I've sucker-punched him. It almost finishes me.

'Why not?'

I look away. How can I tell him I've humiliated myself with his best friend?

'Because of what Daniel said?'

I swallow. My throat is packed with dirt. 'You know he's right about weakening our defences—'

'Bullshit. It's Mya, isn't it? If she was staying, you'd go.'

'And if I said yes, would you leave her behind?'

His expression shifts, guarded now. 'Is that what you're asking me to do?'

'God forbid.' I push past him. He reaches for my arm and I knock it away. Harder than I intend.

'You're serious. Gabe, what the fuck has got into you? This is what we've been talking about since the day we found Jason—'

'That's right, Jude, we've been talking about it for over a century, so why the urgency now?'

'Because I just had an almighty showdown with Nathaniel and I drew a line in the sand!'

'He'll get over it.'

'*I* won't. Fuck, I'm not backing down now. I can't.'

'I'm not leaving today.'

'Then when?'

'I don't know.'

'You'd stay here knowing what we know?' He sniffs, something he only does when he's really wound up. 'Does Daniel's opinion mean that much to you?'

'This isn't about Daniel and you know it.'

'Then tell me what it *is* about, Gabe, because this makes no sense.'

I pick up my bloodied t-shirt and hurl it into the wastepaper basket. It hits so hard the bin falls over. Balls of scrunched-up paper from my notebook spill onto the carpet. Torn pages of short stories that aren't working. 'I'm not running out the door because Mya thinks it's time to leave.'

'It's a little late for that now.'

We stare at each other and I watch it all play out across his face: the anger, the anxiety, the betrayal. 'I haven't got time to argue. There are people waiting down there who *do* want to leave.' The seconds draw out, each one clawing at me, ripping tendon, sinew, bone. I don't answer him. I can't say no again, not with him looking at me like that, so much hurt and anger.

'Well, thanks for not humiliating me in front of everyone.'

He hesitates for another second and then he's gone.

My eyes stay fixed on the indent in the carpet where he was just standing. The shaking starts in my legs. I walk to the bathroom, my steps wobbly. I stare at my reflection, sick and numb.

It's not too late. I can still shift down there, stand with Jude and fix this.

But all I see is Rafa, smug. Daisy fretting. Micah, uncertain. Mya, triumphant.

And I can't do it.

I have to let him go.

NOW

WIPE OUT

My feet pound the rainforest track. I focus on the ground, scanning for the roots that jut from the hard-packed soil round the next bend. Ferns reach out, brush my arms as I pass. Parrots flit through the trees ahead, flashes of yellow and blue, shattering the quiet with their squawking. I smell damp leaves, rain-sodden earth. A hint of salt from the sea beyond the fig trees and palms. The morning sunlight is muted in here, the forest full of shadows.

I'm running hard, arms pumping, legs aching. Twisting and turning along a track I know like the back of my hand. Sweat trickles down my face and neck, cool against hot skin. My t-shirt clings to my back, my heart thunders in my chest.

And still every jolt brings a new memory, each undercutting the other. Burrowing into me.

Jude walking away from the Sanctuary. From me.

Rafa goading, humiliating me. Both of us lying bleeding in broken glass in the Sanctuary piazza.

Memories from the Sanctuary. Memories from the past week. Real memories, fake memories. All pieces that belong to different puzzles. There's no way they can all fit together.

I reach a fork in the track and veer towards the beach out of habit. Patches of blue appear between the trees. The breeze picks up, carrying sounds of seagulls and pounding surf. I sprint right to the edge of the rainforest and then skid to a stop and collapse under a clump of pandanus palms, hands on knees, chest heaving. The sand blurs and I taste salt – sweat mixed with tears. It's a while before I can draw enough air to fill my lungs. Finally, I slump back in the sand. I draw my knees to my chest and stare out at the horizon, try to tell where the sea ends and the cloudless sky begins.

I feel exposed. Like I've been walking around naked and I've only just noticed.

Movement catches my attention closer to shore: three dolphins leaping out of a wave. Synchronised, playful. Water trailing from tailfins. I'd been in Pan Beach for two days the first time I saw a dolphin launch itself out of a breaking wave. It was one of the most amazing things I'd ever seen: still is.

And it hits me, hard and fierce: I love this place.

Further along, the water is crowded with surfers. A figure jogs down from the dunes, board tucked under his arm. Dark hair curling to his shoulders. Everything about him so familiar it makes my chest ache. He looks in my direction, shields his eyes. Sees me. I have no idea where he got the board, but it's no surprise that he did. When I need to think, I run towards water; when Jude needs to think, he needs to be in it or on it. Of course this is where we'd both come.

More memories crash in, these ones from the past two days: Jude on the dock in Hobart. Me, falling to my knees, clinging to him, sobbing. Jude defending me on the roadside near Pan Beach, putting Mya in her place. Standing beside me to stare down the Outcasts and the Five at the Sanctuary. Back to back with me last night, fighting Gatekeepers, the commissary on fire behind us.

I know I should talk to him. I *need* to talk to him. But first I have to work out where everything fits. What's real and what's not, what *feels* real – and if there's a difference.

Jude waits to see if I'm going to at least acknowledge him but I take too long. He bends down, secures his ankle strap. Then he turns to the sea, spends a good minute watching the sets roll in and break. He must feel my eyes on him, but he doesn't glance my way again as he jogs into the water. He jumps on his board, starts to paddle out.

Yesterday – or was it earlier today? I've lost track of time – he told me he hadn't surfed for a year. And as I watch him dive under a wave and come up the other side, I see how much he's missed it. He might have spent almost a year on a yacht battling the freezing ocean south of Tasmania, but he dreamed of a sun-kissed sea every day. I know this without him telling me. I knew it even when my memories of him were a lie. So much of him is the same as it's always been: attitude, sense of humour, obsessions. *Exactly* the same. The bits that aren't are the ones I'm wrestling with – and his role in shaping the lie I've been living for the past year.

Out on the water, Jude sits on his board and waits. The surf is decent, but it's breaking hard. The swell rises, lifts him. He lets the wave go. Two younger guys further along the alley chase it, miss it. Jude lets another wave pass. When the next swell rolls in, he waits until the last second and then flattens himself on his board and paddles hard. And then he's up, carving the face of the wave. Balanced, focused, as if doing this only yesterday. I don't have to see his face to know he's lost in the moment. He twists sharply to avoid a kid on a board too big for him. The wave peters out well before shore and Jude dives in. He surfaces near a girl in a black vest and hipster bikini – nobody I know. He says something, she laughs, and then they grab their boards and head back out.

Jude catches three more waves before I notice another figure on the beach, standing at the base of the boardwalk steps.

Rafa.

My heart gives a startled thump. His hood is up so I can't see his face, but even from here I recognise the tension in his shoulders. Images from the past week rise up, smudge all my edges.

Rafa turning up in Pan Beach. Telling me who I was. Lying to me about our history.

Rafa putting himself between me and the Outcasts in Dubai.

Kissing me on the beach. *This* beach.

Rafa caked in blood in the iron room, his life leaching out of him. Willing to die to keep me safe.

Me wrapped around him naked, wanting him more than air . . .

Jude rides a wave all the way to shore, milking it for all its worth until he has to jump off in the wash. He scoops up the board and walks to Rafa, hair dripping down his back.

Rafa starts talking before Jude reaches him. Jude's hand comes up, as if Rafa needs calming. There's gesturing. It's not angry – more . . . *emphatic*. Rafa flicks his hood down, pushes up his sleeves. He's frustrated. I could get up and go over there, find out what's going on between them. I don't. I'm not together enough for *one* of them, let alone both. They talk, heated, for a few more minutes. They're guarded. I've never seen them like this, not with each other.

And then Jude gestures in my direction.

My breath catches. Rafa turns, sees me sitting in the shade twenty metres away. He *knows*. Jude's just told him. I can tell from the way he's standing, shoulders slightly hunched, hands jammed deep in the pockets of his cargoes. Neither of us acknowledges the other. We stare, twenty metres of sand and a hundred and thirty-nine years between us. A line of sweat snakes down my spine. I can't push back the memories clawing at me, but I can't ignore everything I've felt for him this past week either. A rush of sensations: the feel of his body pressed against mine, the taste of his skin. Heat flares. Confusion. Shame. The pang that hits is painful, knots my insides.

Rafa watches me, motionless, and before I can untangle my thoughts he turns and walks back to the boardwalk. Away from Jude.

Away from me.

NO BEACH FOR YOU

I walk towards the esplanade, sweat cooling on my skin. I should go home and shower, but I'm just as likely to run into Rafa or Daisy or anyone else I'm not ready to face. I have to work out how to wear my old life. I've been someone else for a whole year; I'm a different shape now.

I take the stairs to the boardwalk opposite the Pan Beach library and gallery. The glass catches the morning light and turns the façade golden. A flock of lorikeets fuss and squawk on the rooftop. The parrots are obsessed with the gleaming arc of sea green that dominates the gallery roofline: a sculpted wave that's become Pan Beach's most controversial piece of public art. Half the locals don't think it's art; the other half do, and hate the fact it's always covered in bird shit.

Next door, the tables at the Green Bean are already filling up on the footpath. I head for the library.

I sense it as soon as I step through the automatic doors. The stacks crammed with books; the quiet hum of air conditioning; the smell of freshly ground coffee from the Green Bean. It feels like home – as much as the smell of leather and sweat in the gym at the Sanctuary ever did.

Jane, our head librarian, is at the service counter with her back to me, searching the reserved shelves. What day is it? If it's Monday, I'm supposed to be working. I look around for Gaz, spot his dyed black hair and army fatigue t-shirt through a gap in the shelves. He might be lazy but he's covered my shift without me asking. And it's not the first time he's done it in the past week.

I duck behind the *Firefly* display I set up a fortnight ago – comics, posters, small-scale replica of *Serenity*, a mannequin in a brown coat – and go upstairs to the gallery. Jacques' freaky installation pieces dominate the space. It feels like forever since I interviewed him downstairs, but it's only been nine days.

Nine days. My world has tilted dangerously on its axis since then. I don't even remember what it felt like before Rafa came to town.

I wander over to the wedding dress, meticulously created from blonde hair and nail clippings painted a pearlescent white. From memory, the piece has dead skin woven through it too. Lovely.

I've hacked limbs from hellions and beheaded Gatekeeper demons, and Jacques' collection still makes my skin crawl.

'This is some weird shit.'

Micah is standing at the top of the stairs studying a birdcage made from tiny braids of human hair. I'm so distracted I didn't hear him come up. He's changed into a white t-shirt and dark grey board shorts. With his broad shoulders, spiky blond hair and chilled vibe, he more than any of us could pass as a local surfer.

'What are you doing here?' he asks. 'Did you forget that your town's had a sudden influx of agitated Rephaim? You bring us all here and then you go AWOL—'

'I needed space.'

'Interesting timing.' He glances at a dove made from toenail slivers, shakes his head. 'Daisy's in your kitchen sharpening swords and getting twitchier by the minute. You've got the redneck brothers champing at the bit to barricade the town and stockpile weapons on the beach, the Outcasts wanting answers about Mya—'

'I *know*, Micah.'

I cross the room and open the French doors to the deck. The sea breeze ruffles flyers on the information table. The esplanade hums with cars and cyclists. Beyond the beach, another set of waves rolls in. There are twice as many surfers out there now jostling for position.

Micah's tennis shoes squeak on the polished wooden

floor. 'Why the urgent need to get away from us?'

'It's been a big few days.' I don't look at him when I answer. Instead, I watch a couple with ebony skin and fluorescent pink zinc cream weave a tandem bike along the boardwalk.

'I don't disagree, but—' He stops at the sound of boots on the stairs.

It's Gaz. He grins when he sees me. He's got at least three more rings in his top lip since last week.

'Gabzilla, I thought you must have died.'

I laugh. 'It's a common mistake.'

He blinks, his smile slightly confused. 'Yeah, well, you owe me.' He jerks his thumb in the general direction of the library. 'I've got better things to do than work on a Monday.'

'You'll still have plenty of time for wanking when you get home.'

His grin widens and a swathe of dark fringe falls over one eye. 'You've obviously spent a lot of time thinking about what I do when I'm alone. Who's your mate?'

I introduce Micah as a friend from school. It's close enough to the truth.

Gaz gives him a once-over. He has to tilt his head back to look Micah in the eye. 'Seriously, Gabster, do you know any short ugly people?'

'Just you,' I say, and he laughs.

'Burn.' He punches my arm – light, playful – and

moves past me to take up his usual spot on the deck.

Micah raises his eyebrows. 'Look at you, making new friends.'

Gaz lounges against the folded door, watching two girls in bikinis cross the road to the boardwalk.

'Don't you have work to do?' I prompt.

'We've been open five minutes. Plenty of time.' He frowns, his attention still outside. 'Bloody hell, check out that dude. And people call *me* a freak.'

Gaz points to a short guy with wraparound sunnies and platinum hair. He's wearing suit trousers and a white business shirt, undone at the neck and sleeves rolled up.

But it's not the out-of-place outfit that's caught Gaz's attention: it's the fact the guy's head looks too big for his body and when he lifts a hand to shield his eyes, his nails are long and sharp and black as midnight. My scalp tightens.

Immundi.

'Gabe . . .' Micah says.

'I know.'

Seeing the demon in broad daylight on the esplanade – my esplanade – stirs something dark and violent within me. Gives me a moment of piercing clarity. No matter what else has changed, I'm a warrior. And I'm not allowing filth from the pit to harm anyone in this town. Even Gaz.

I pat his shoulder as I turn away. 'You'll never be as freaky as that guy.'

He grins. 'I think that's the nicest thing you've ever said to me.'

Micah and I take the stairs two at a time. We watch the demon through the glass doors. He's still on the other side of the road, maybe thinking about crossing. The good news is that he doesn't have the trademark Immundi blades strapped to his forearms. The bad news is that he'll have weapons hidden on him somewhere.

'A reconnaissance trip for Zarael?' Micah asks.

I nod. 'Has to be. He won't risk his own horde, not so soon after last night.' Not while they're recovering from seeing Nathaniel's true form. I have a flash of the Sanctuary: the commissary a ball of fire, a hole ripped in its side from Leon's rocket launcher. It's still a few hours until the sun breaks over the mountains there. The damage will be so much worse in the daylight.

The Immundi turns in our direction but there's no way he can see us inside with the sun reflecting off the glass.

It's not the first time the Gatekeepers have used the lower demons to do their dirty work: they used Immundi in LA last week to draw the Outcasts to the club.

But this feels different. If Immundi are playing scout for Zarael, it means they're involved in more than their usual nastiness. It could mean Zarael is conscripting every kind of pit scum this side of the veil to bring with him to Pan Beach. An army of hell spawn. I steady myself against the glass.

The demon is scanning the beach now, his back to us.

'How do you want to do this?' Micah asks.

'Low key.'

We slip out between the electronic doors and jog across the road. The breeze is warmer now, salty. We're completely exposed on the street. The bobble-headed demon only has to turn his head and he'll see us. I check the gallery deck: Gaz is still there, watching. It doesn't change what we have to do.

The Immundi is six metres away. I glance over at the Green Bean and the row of surfboards lined up against the café wall. Is Rafa in there brooding over an espresso? Micah and I hug the boardwalk railing. A VW camper van drives past with its windows down, the John Butler Trio thumping from sub-woofers.

The demon is four metres away. He taps his deadly nails on his thigh, untucks the shirt from his waistband. I wish I had a sword. Two metres. Don't look this way. Don't—

The demon turns. Freezes.

I lunge but he skips out of reach, snarling. Slams into a woman in a tie-dyed dress, spins away and sprints onto the road. She drops the bags she's carrying; cans of baked beans and a loaf of rye bread spill out onto the footpath. I glance back to check she's okay and then dodge a cyclist and a taxi. Micah is right behind me.

The Immundi weaves around tables outside the Green

Bean, his white shirt flapping behind him. He flings an empty wicker chair in our path and I jump over it. I hope Maggie's mum is preoccupied inside. I hear gasps from a nearby table, a shout for us to stop. I catch a flash of steel before the Immundi ducks into the laneway beside the café.

I know exactly what I need to do.

And the certainty feels good. It feels *right*.

I sprint into the alley and check Micah is following, shielding me from the road. I slip into the void for a split second and materialise in front of the Immundi, plant my feet, and collect him with a straight-arm to the chest. He slams onto the concrete and his breath comes out in an ugly grunt. I'm on him, trying to pin him down, but he thrashes and gets a hand free. Something catches the sunlight – the glare blinds me for an instant – and I jerk back, feel a blade whisper across my t-shirt. The demon swings again, this time at my face. I catch his wrist and at the same time Micah slides to his knees beside me. He clamps a hand on my shoulder.

'Go,' he says. I drag him and the demon out of the alley, into the maelstrom.

I take them deep into the rainforest beyond the town. I'm still straddling the Immundi when we arrive and Micah immediately gives me room. I'm aware of the stillness – no cars, no seagulls, the surf too far away to hear – a second before the dagger comes at me again. I duck sideways and deflect the strike, use the momentum to flip the demon onto his stomach, wrench his arm behind his back. I push his face into the dark soil and dig my thumb into the pressure point on the back of his hand. He yelps and the dagger drops from his fingers. Micah scoops it up. The demon bucks and squirms underneath me but I've got him now.

'Keep that up and the next stop will be the Sanctuary,' I say, panting. Adrenaline surges through my limbs, singing to me. I feel strong. I *am* strong. The demon quietens, but tendons strain in his forearm.

Micah crouches near the Immundi, the demon's dagger swinging loosely between his thumb and forefinger. 'Why are you here?'

The Immundi bares pointed teeth. He struggles to look up at me, dirt smeared across the lens of his sunglasses. 'Hordes are coming for you, nephilim filth.'

'Yeah, yeah.' I press my fingers against the pulse in his wrist. It's fast, but not erratic. 'But why are *you* here?'

His lips stretch into something possibly intended as a smile. 'To peruse the menu.'

I flick his sunglasses from his face, stare into flat, black irises. 'Are you alone?'

'I am legion.'

'Spare me the fire and brimstone bullshit. Did you come here on your own?'

The demon swallows. 'There are others.' The steady beat

under his skin stutters, picks up speed. He's lying. I nod for Micah to hold him while I pat him down.

Micah obliges, all the while watching me, curious. 'Nice shifting in the alley.'

'Thanks,' I say, not meeting his gaze. I find a mobile phone in the demon's pocket and check recent calls. Nothing today. He hasn't made contact with anyone. I blow out my breath and sit back on my heels. We can't let Zarael find out we're here. It might bring forward his attack plans and we're nowhere near ready – me least of all.

Micah meets my gaze. 'What do you want to do with our friend here?'

I reach for the Immundi's sunglasses and brush off the dirt. Slide them back onto his face. 'Kill him, I guess.' But even as I say it, I know that's not happening. Beating a demon in a fight to the death is one thing. Executing one in my favourite rainforest is quite another. Micah knows it too.

'I'll take him to the Sanctuary,' he says and the Immundi snarls and squirms.

'You can't take him inside without Nathaniel's permission.'

'This piece of slime is proof Zarael's coming. Nathaniel can't turn me away without losing face with the Five. I'll let Daniel know—'

'Daniel's not going to help. You've turned your back on him.'

Micah shakes his head, frustrated. 'I'm going to hand him an Immundi who's confirmed that a horde of demons is about to attack a town full of humans. Trust me, there's no grudge in the world big enough to dull Daniel's interest in that.'

'And if Nathaniel still says no?'

Micah shrugs, musses the Immundi's platinum hair. 'Then I guess I'll have to stake this one out on the mountains for the wolves.'

A YEAR AGO

SO . . . WHAT'S NEW WITH YOU?

I'm buzzing with adrenaline.

I'm on a bench halfway along the pier, sitting on my hands. My right foot taps a staccato beat. Dampness seeps into my clothes. The sun will burn off the marine layer later in the day, but for now Santa Monica is cloaked in fog. The ferris wheel above me, the empty stretch of beach, the climbing ropes and fitness rings, all blanketed in grey. It's eerie and oppressive, and perfect for shifting in under the pier unnoticed – which I did five minutes ago.

I fidget and wait.

The fog is so low I can barely make out the date palms lining Ocean Avenue, ghostly sentinels of coastal Los Angeles. Even the traffic is muted: cabs, buses, cars, all monochrome in the early morning mist. I breathe in salted air, catch a hint of sugar, hot oil and cinnamon: donuts further down the pier.

This is one of the places Jude and I used to come when we needed a break from the Sanctuary. There's no surf, but it was always fun to jog from the pier down to Venice Beach around dusk. Join a drumming circle. Breathe in second-hand marijuana smoke. Watch muscle freaks pump weights and dogs ride skateboards in sunnies.

Maybe that's why Jude picked it: the memories here are all good.

I keep my eyes on the stairs where I climbed up from the beach. That's where Jude will appear too. And Jason.

My left foot picks up the beat. Jason, alive. Gone all those years, and now he reaches out. Why? Whatever the reason, it was enough for Jude to call me twenty minutes ago. The sound of his voice. Not shouting insults at Daniel in the heat of a brawl or ordering the Outcasts into formation – but quiet, cautious. It dislodged something in my chest. I've felt untethered ever since.

My hood is up but the mist frizzes my hair anyway. I snap the band on my wrist once, twice. It's not that I care what I look like ... I push back the hood, twist the band free and tie up my hair. I have a quick thought – this is the first time I've seen Jude since I've had my hair shorter – and push it away, annoyed. Who cares what he thinks about my hair?

Two heads appear on the stairs. One dark, the other

blond. My heart gives a sharp squeeze. It's them. I glance at Jason long enough to see he's exactly as I remember – curly blond hair to his shoulders, startling blue eyes – and then my attention locks on Jude.

We haven't been this near to each other for a decade. Usually the only time I see him is when our crews run into each other chasing the same lead on the Fallen. And then, when the inevitable fight breaks out, he and I keep as much distance between us as we can. It's not hard to avoid each other – I always go straight for Rafa.

I'm on my feet but I don't move to meet them. I see the tension around Jude's mouth and eyes. Is that from life with the Outcasts or from seeing me? He stops a few metres away and Jason does the same.

'Thanks for coming.' Jude says it in that same careful voice he used on the phone.

I can't stop staring. Whatever is loose in me is crashing around my chest now, wild, reckless. 'How could I not?'

Jude glances at Jason, rigid beside him. 'I know, right?'

And with those three words, the significance of the moment – the two of us standing here with Jason – passes between us. Unguarded.

For a second, the distance between us is as insubstantial as the mist. Jude's shoulders settle a little. I search his eyes and I see it: he's not looking to rip open old wounds. This is something different. Something new. I exhale.

I finally take a closer look at our cousin. Jason raises his hand. 'Hi.'

'Hi? That's all you've got to say after a fucking century?'

His hand drops. 'Well, no. But I thought it was a good place to start.'

'What happened in Monterosso?'

Jason runs his tongue over his teeth. He's nervous and not just because I swore at him. 'I'll explain everything if you'll give me a—'

'We didn't know what to think when you disappeared. We thought you were dead.' I'm aware of how freely I'm using the word 'we'.

'If you let me speak I'll tell you.'

I glance at Jude. He shrugs, walks over to me. 'Let's hear him out.' He waits for me to nod and then we sit down at the same time. He sits closer than I expect, but still leaves space between us. I steal a quick look at him, enough to see the start of stubble on his jaw, the hint of dark circles under his eyes. That his hair is forming ringlets rather than frizzing. Typical.

A seagull lands on the railing, turns its head to eyeball us. Jason scans the pier, scratches his neck. 'Okay.' We wait. He walks over to the chain wire fence around the amusement rides, stares up at the ferris wheel for a good five seconds. Comes back.

'Okay.' And he begins. He tells us why he and his mother left Monterosso last century. He tells us about his half-sister, who had premonitions as a child about angels and demons and knew Jason was half-angel without being told. About each first-born girl in the family line having similar gifts, until a girl named Dani came along with a very different set of skills. This girl didn't only see angels and demons. She saw us, the Rephaim. And not only in premonitions and visions, but any time she wanted. He tells us that for the past few weeks she's been having a vision involving Jude and me that's important enough to bring Jason out of hiding.

It takes him a good fifteen minutes to get the story out. It's a while longer before the reality of what he's saying sinks in. Jude fires a dozen questions at him, trying to understand how a child without Rephaite blood could be linked to us.

But there's really only one question.

'What did she see about me and Jude?'

'I don't know, she won't tell me. But she wants to tell you.' Jason drags his hand through his curls. 'I've kept away from you two to keep our family safe, and now along comes Dani with the most dangerous gift of all and she wants to meet you.'

Jude leans forward, rests his forearms on his knees. 'You think we're a danger to her?'

'What do you think Nathaniel or Zarael would do if they knew what she could do?'

'We're not going to tell anyone about her. Shit, Jason,

we've kept *you* secret all these years. You can trust us.'

'Even now?' Jason gestures to the space between Jude and me. The thing in my chest slams into my ribs.

'Yes, you can trust us,' Jude says, his voice tighter. 'Even now.'

We fall into a tense silence. On Ocean Avenue, a car blasts its horn. The seagull on the rail loses interest in us and starts to preen itself. What must Jason think of us—

'Hang on,' I say. 'How did you know Jude wasn't at the Sanctuary?'

'Dani knew where he was,' Jason says.

'But how did you know one of us didn't tell someone about you after you disappeared?'

His hesitation only lasts a second. 'She'd know if you did. Dani.'

'Okay,' Jude says, 'so you know all this stuff about us—'

'But I don't know what she's going to tell you or what that might mean for either of you.'

Jude sits back on the bench, stretches out his legs. His boots are scuffed, the laces loose. 'Sounds like she's telling us, whether you like it or not. So what's the plan? When do we meet her?'

Jason takes a deep breath. 'Dani wants you two to . . .' He exhales loudly.

'To what?'

A pause. 'Spend more time together first. She wants you to not be fighting when she meets you.'

I slide my eyes in Jude's direction. Catch him doing the same. 'We're not fighting right now,' Jude says carefully.

'I don't think that's what she means.'

'I thought this was urgent.'

'Apparently this bit's important enough to wait for.' Jason pushes up the sleeves on his body shirt. 'Right, then, I've played my part. Jude has my number.'

'Hang on,' I say. 'What is it you're asking us to do?'

Jason looks from me to Jude and back again. For the first time since he arrived, he's comfortable with the question. It strikes me then that he's come a long way from the teenager we found mending nets in Monterosso over a century ago. 'Having a conversation would be a good start.'

'That's a bit rich coming from you,' I say. 'You haven't told us what you've been doing all these years.' And that's a much easier conversation than the one he's suggesting.

'We'll get to that. It's more important that you two talk.' And then he turns and jogs down the stairs out of sight, leaving Jude and me.

Alone.

For the first time in ten years.

The seagull pokes up its head from under a wing, eyeballs us again. Neither of us speaks or moves. The gull blinks, digs its beak back into his feathers.

'So, Jason just stepped out of an alley somewhere?' The question comes out forced, awkward. God, it's ridiculous.

He's my twin brother. But I see him pick at his thumbnail and I know it's just as weird for him, us not knowing how to be around each other.

'Yeah, in Ho Chi Minh City. Not a job' – he says it quickly – 'I was in the mood for a bowl of pho. Jason waited until I was on my own before he showed himself.'

Jude doesn't mention who was in Vietnam with him and I don't ask. 'It was a bit of a shock to see him after all this time.'

'I bet.' I realise I'm tapping my foot again. I stop. 'And this girl, Dani . . .'

'I know. Crazy.'

'What do you think she's seen?'

'No idea, but I'd like to understand where her visions come from before we put too much stock in them.'

'There's obviously something to what she sees: she found you.'

Jude glances at his watch. 'I need to check my books, see if there's any precedent for it.'

'Yeah,' I say. 'I need to get back too.'

'I didn't mean right now.'

Oh. I run my palms over my jeans. 'How's Ez?'

A shadow passes over his face and he doesn't answer right away. I'm not surprised he doesn't want to talk about the nightclub ambush. It was a debacle.

'She's tough.'

'That's not what I asked.'

He closes his eyes for a second. 'The scarring is pretty bad. She says she can live with it . . .'

This is the moment I could go for the jugular, point out that Mya's recklessness is responsible for Ez being mauled by a hellion in LA. That sooner or later she's going to get one of them killed. But I can see from the fold of his shoulders that he doesn't need to hear it. And it's not the conversation Jason had in mind for us. What else have we got to talk about, though? Aside from our last conversation at the Sanctuary, and I need way more time to prepare for that.

It's my turn to check my watch. Crap. I've been here too long. 'I really do need to get back.'

He studies me, rubs a palm across his jaw. 'Can we meet again in a couple of days?'

A couple of days? 'What's wrong with tomorrow?'

'We've got a job.' He levels his gaze, waits for me to bite. It's an effort, but I resist the urge. It shouldn't surprise me that he puts the Outcasts first, even after what we've just heard. He shakes his head like he can read my thoughts. 'It would raise questions if I was a no-show, especially after disappearing today.'

'You didn't tell anyone you were coming to see me?'

'No. You?'

'No, though I ran into Daisy before I left. She knows something's up.'

'Which means Jones will by now.'

I can't hide my surprise.

'What, you think I didn't know they've been in contact with each other?' Jude asks.

'When did you find out?'

'Three years ago.' About the same time Daisy told me Jones had reached out to her.

'So who's playing who for information in that arrangement?'

Jude shrugs, unconcerned. 'I think they're working each other as an excuse to keep talking. They miss hanging out.'

'More like Daisy misses sparring with him. Nobody moves like Jones.'

His eyes flit to mine. 'Jones isn't the only one who misses people at the Sanctuary.'

I can't hold his gaze. Too much pain and regret there.

Down on the beach, a lone jogger appears out of the fog. If I had time I'd go for a run myself, but not on the path; I'd run barefoot down by the water where the sand is firm and cool, feel the pull of that great expanse of ocean.

'I like it.' Jude gestures to my hair. 'The new length, I like it.'

'Oh. Thanks.' God, this is like making small talk at a party. Sober. I clear my throat. 'So where do you want to meet?'

Jude's mouth twitches the tiniest bit, as if he's fighting a smile. 'Give me your phone. I'll put in the coordinates.'

I check the screen when he hands it back. 'Is that somewhere in the Aegean Sea?'

'Patmos.'

I almost laugh at the irony. He wants to meet on an island famous as a place of exile.

'The coordinates are for the church down the road. It's empty by five o'clock every day. Our place is four houses up on the bend: the one with the orange tree by the front door.'

'*Our* place?'

'Mine and Rafa's.'

A flare of anger. Faint, but still there. 'You two dating now?'

He measures me for a moment. 'I don't know about you, but I still need time out occasionally. So does Rafa.'

'Who else knows about that place?'

'Nobody.' He gives me a moment to let that sink in. That means no Mya.

'Will Rafa be there?'

A tight smile. 'I probably won't mention it to him.'

NOTHING IS SIMPLE

Daniel is in the library when I get back. It's humming with activity despite the chill in the air. He taps his watch as I walk in; I pretend not to notice.

'Are Taya and Malachi back from Oslo?' I ask.

Daniel's standing behind a bank of screens, looking over Magda's shoulder. She glances up at me, gives me a nervous smile. Everyone else in the room stays busy shuffling papers or tapping keyboards.

'You missed their call by a few minutes,' Daniel says. The tiny inflection in his voice is the only hint he's unimpressed that I'm late.

'And?'

'Zarael was in Norway this morning.'

I join him behind the desk, focus on the screen. Magda has highlighted half a dozen locations on a city map. I recognise one as the University of Oslo.

'Doing what?'

'Stealing research on the aurora borealis.'

'The northern lights, again? I thought he'd given up on that?'

'Apparently he's still interested, which means we need to find out why.' I can feel Daniel watching me, measuring me. 'We need further reconnaissance. Greenland, Iceland, Canada. Maybe even Alaska and Siberia.'

Awesome. I miss Santa Monica already – marine layer and all. Thinking of the pier reminds me of Jude, which brings a storm of emotion and a stab of guilt. Daniel, of course, sees it all play out across my face.

'Gabriella, may I have a moment?'

Magda gives me another nervous smile and her fingers stray to the prayer beads beside her mouse. I guess Daniel's been uptight over my absence – at least, enough for someone as observant as Magda to pick up on it.

I follow Daniel past the shelves and into the Council of Five's antechamber. Warmth instantly wraps around me: the fire in the corner is down to coals but the room is still toasty. I've always felt at home in here: the pressed metal ceiling, mismatched antique chairs and shelves crammed with hard covers frayed at the corners. The air is musty, but in the best kind of way. I head for the fireplace, stretch out my cold fingers.

Daniel kneels next to me. He removes the screen, takes

a poker and breaks up the coals. Then he adds another log, sending a shower of sparks up the chimney.

'What is it you're not telling me?' he says, stoking the fire.

I take a slow breath. I don't particularly want to lie to him. We might not be sleeping together any more, but I value his friendship.

'Jude called.'

He goes still. Doesn't look up. 'Why?'

'He wanted to see me.'

'And you went to him?'

I shift my weight. 'He's my brother, Daniel.'

Daniel rises to his feet, his expression neutral. 'What did he want?'

'It's been ten years. He wanted to talk.' I may not want to lie, but there's only so much Daniel needs to know. He studies me, standing close enough for me to catch a hint of spearmint on his breath.

'I know things have changed between us—'

'That's not why I went to see him. Fuck, not everything is about us.'

'Please don't swear at me.'

'I went to see him because he's my brother. I don't agree with his choices or the company he keeps, but that doesn't mean I've stopped caring about him.'

'He has an agenda.' It's not a question.

'He doesn't.'

Daniel watches me for a moment. Sighs. He knows there's more but he's not ready to push me. Yet.

'Was anyone else there?'

I raise my eyebrows at him. 'Did I come back with blood on my knuckles?'

A wry smile. And then he leans in and kisses me. It takes me by surprise – Daniel doesn't do impulsive – and I kiss him back without thinking. He steps closer, brushes his thumb across my collarbone. There's sadness in the kiss, longing. But no demand, no urgency. And that's always been part of our problem.

I break contact first. 'Daniel . . .'

'I miss you, Gabe.' He traces the line of my jaw. I miss him too, sometimes. The long conversations in the early hours of the morning; the way he would kiss the nape of my neck when I was getting dressed; his willingness to hike up steep mountains to prove he was prepared to break a sweat for me. After Jude left, I'd needed something to tether me to the Sanctuary: I thought Daniel was it. But everything about our relationship was a reminder of what I'd lost. A reminder that I'd turned my back on my brother. I thought I could live with that decision, but it's always eaten at me, knowing how much it would hurt Jude that I was with Daniel.

And then there's the other thing: Daniel was always so *controlled* in bed. He was considerate, he was skilled. It should have been enough. It would have been. Before Rafa.

I loathe Rafa for that.

'Please, don't let your brother get in your head,' Daniel says, misreading my distraction.

I step back from him. 'I can handle him.'

The warmth leaves his eyes. 'You're seeing him again?'

Crap. 'Yes.'

'When?'

'I don't know.'

The last thing I want is Daniel watching my every move. I need to meet this girl, Dani, find out what she wants to tell Jude and me and then work out what to do about it. And I need to deal with the confusion still churning inside me after seeing my brother.

None of that requires help from Daniel.

'So this is some sort of reconciliation?' he asks.

'I don't know what it is yet.'

Daniel picks a piece of lint from his shirtsleeve, so tiny I can't see it. 'When you didn't follow the Outcasts into exile, it carried enormous weight with everyone here. Taya particularly.'

'I know—'

'So while I understand a bond still exists with your brother, you need to bear in mind what message you send if you reconcile with him. How it may confuse the way the Outcasts are viewed.'

Ah, Daniel. Always the politician. 'That's not my problem.'

And there it is, that expression he saves just for me: a perfect mix of resignation and disappointment. 'Have you thought about how Nathaniel might feel about you reconnecting with Jude? Have you discussed it with him?'

'It's none of his business.'

'It is if you appear to be endorsing the choices of the Outcasts.'

Frustration stirs, grating and familiar. The kind of frustration that would've seen me walk out of the door a decade ago if things had unfolded differently. I push it down, like I've been doing for a decade.

'Nathaniel wants them back in the fold, you know that as well as I do. Did it occur to you that Jude reaching out might be the start of that? Or is your disdain for him and Rafa so strong you don't want them under this roof again?'

His eyes sharpen. 'It would take a significant show of contrition and humility for the Outcasts to return. I'm not convinced your brother is capable of either, let alone Rafa and Mya. But' – he holds up a hand – 'if they prove otherwise and Nathaniel accepts them, I'll welcome them back with open arms.'

Bullshit, it would be his worst nightmare. I don't bother arguing because it's not an issue: Jude's not coming back to the Sanctuary. He might have hinted at missing me, but the only reason he made contact today was because of Jason.

'You need to tell Nathaniel about this,' Daniel says.

'There's nothing to tell.' Plus, he might ask to read me – something he hasn't done in years. I move away from the fire. 'Daniel, do you trust me?'

'You know I do.'

I feel a twinge of conscience. Ignore it.

'Then trust me.'

THE SWEETEST THING

The cottage on Patmos is postcard-perfect. Whitewashed under a cloudless blue sky, built into a hill overlooking a harbour packed with fishing boats and luxury cruisers. I'm standing in the middle of the narrow road staring out at the Mediterranean Sea when I hear a door open behind me.

'Well?'

I answer honestly. 'I'm insanely jealous.' I turn to find Jude in the doorway wearing a white t-shirt and jeans. Barefoot. He's freshly shaven and his hair is damp as if he's just out of the shower. He's made an effort. I left the Sanctuary in old jeans, combat boots and a fleecy hoodie, my hair tied back. There's a sea breeze but it's still warmer here in October than in northern Italy. I unzip the hoodie and push up my sleeves. Wish I'd worn something a little nicer – and more climate appropriate.

Jude's smile is cautious. 'The first time I saw this place I thought of you.' I don't know how to respond so I just stand there looking out of place. He gestures behind him. 'Come in.'

I follow him down a bright hallway, through a sitting room – white stucco walls, copper artwork, rustic furniture (obviously Jude decorated the place, not Rafa, or there'd be motorcycle parts on a shelf somewhere) – and into a breezy kitchen. The window over the sink is open, framed by sky-blue shutters. It smells of oranges and freshly ground coffee. Jude grabs the container under the grinder, brings it to me. 'Smell this.'

I lean forward, breathe in. 'Oh my god, what is that?'

'Special Yemeni blend. I buy it under the counter from a café on the harbour. Wait till you taste it.'

He takes a copper coffee pot from a hook over the stove, measures two cups of water into it, adds coffee and sugar and lights the gas while I sit at the counter. I run my fingers over the terracotta tiles. The familiarity of the ritual is disarming. I've seen Jude make Greek coffee a thousand times. It's even the same pot he used to sneak into the kitchen at the Sanctuary to make coffee for Rafa, Micah and me. Brother Pietro was always so offended that our taste for coffee extended beyond his espresso.

Jude doesn't speak as he waits for the sugar to dissolve. He stirs the brew with his back to me, his hair falling forward.

The sight of him so focused on that tiny pot brings a sharp pang. I think of all the moments he's had without me and it's like the emptiness in my chest was just freshly gouged. He glances over his shoulder, sees me sitting at the bench – his bench. Or maybe he sees everything I'm feeling written on my face. Whatever it is, it makes his mouth tug down. He swallows but doesn't look away.

'It's boiling,' I say quietly and he turns in time to lift the pot from the flame before it bubbles over.

When it's ready, he pours it out into two small cups. Then he goes to the fridge and pulls out a plate. 'My friend at the harbour made it fresh this morning.'

I can't help it: I smile. Galaktoboureko.

My favourite dessert, or at least a close second to Turkish delight. He smiles back at me, less cautious now. I take the coffees and follow him to a patio off the kitchen. We're surrounded by colour: lemon trees in pots and bougainvillea along the low concrete wall, the ocean filling the horizon beyond the flat rooftops of the town. We sit on sun-blasted folding chairs at a small table decorated with a mosaic of a crescent moon, almost the exact shape of the Rephaite mark on our necks. We're side by side, facing the ocean. I sip my coffee. Thick and sweet.

'This is really good, Jude.'

His eyes flit to me as if he's pleased to hear me say his name. 'Thanks.' He hands me the plate of galaktoboureko and a fork, the silver warm from his touch. I dig into the puff pastry and custard, lift it to my lips and close my eyes. Feel sunshine on my face, savour the sweetness.

Jude waits until I open my eyes. 'So. How are you?'

I wipe syrup from the corner of my mouth. 'I'm okay. You?'

'Yeah, I'm okay too.'

A pause.

'Have you heard from Jason?' I ask.

'No. You?'

I shake my head and Jude loads up his fork. He chews and swallows, eyes straying out to sea. The silence starts to feel awkward again. He licks his fork clean. 'Okay, clearly neither of us has got any better at small talk.'

I laugh and immediately breathe easier.

'How about we say what we're thinking?' Jude says.

'Okay. You first.'

'Are you still with Daniel?'

Not what I was expecting. 'No.'

He nods, settles back in his chair.

'But you already knew that if Jones reports his conversations with Daisy to you.'

'I wanted to hear it from you.' He takes another forkful of custard pie. 'Your turn.'

'Why didn't you call after you left?' The question is out before I know that's what I wanted to ask. 'Was it that easy to walk away from me?'

He blinks, his fork dripping syrup onto the golden

moon. 'No, Gabe. It was not that easy. The *way* you stayed, it made it tough for me to . . .' He puts the fork down. 'And then we ran into your squad in India and you and Rafa attacked each other, which made it hard for me to convince the others you hadn't turned against us.'

I can't keep eye contact with him. That moment set the tone for the Sanctuary's relationship with the Outcasts. It's the reason Sanctuary squads and Outcast crews come to blows any time our paths cross. That's on me. And Rafa.

'I'm not throwing stones, I'm answering your question.' Jude's voice is gentler now. 'My turn?'

I blow out my breath and nod, eyes fixed on the ocean.

'Why didn't you come with me? I still don't understand.'

I rub my eyes. 'It's complicated.'

'No shit.'

'Can we work our way up to that one?' I hope he can't see how much my hand is shaking. 'How did your job go yesterday?'

Jude measures me. He knows me well enough to understand it's more than stalling. 'Nobody got hurt and there's half a dozen less Immundi infesting the world.'

'Is it just me or are there more of those ugly little turds setting up shop these days?'

'Definitely more, and Zarael and his horde usually aren't far away.'

It's a relief to talk to Jude about this stuff. 'Think Zarael's trying to organise the Immundi into a secondary force?'

'Maybe.' Jude takes another mouthful of dessert, keeps talking as he chews. 'But that would mean there's something coming that needs an army.'

'Like us finding the Fallen.'

'Or something bigger.'

A cold finger brushes the back of my neck. He means the prophesied war between heaven and hell. Nathaniel's always told us we need to find the Fallen before that happens. 'Do you think we've run out of time?'

'I don't know. And I still have no idea what it would mean for us if we have.'

'Maybe this Dani has some answers.'

'God, I hope so.'

We sit with the possibility of that thought for a long moment, the weight of it. Finally, Jude leans back in his chair, stretches out his legs on my side of the table.

'How's Micah?'

I relax a little; this I can answer. 'He still misses Adeline but he's stayed clean. And he's hooked up at least half a dozen times that I know of in the last two years, although I don't know if that's helping or—'

'Trust me, it's helping. He still playing guitar?'

'Yeah, and making playlists of musicians you should be listening to instead of banging your head.'

He smiles. 'Of course he is.'

I smile back – and that's when Rafa materialises behind Jude in the kitchen doorway. Maybe it's the sight of Jude and me sitting together, relaxed, that throws him, but Rafa breaks into a grin. For a split second it's like he's forgotten the past ten years.

And then he remembers.

The smile evaporates. 'You brought her *here*? What the fuck, Jude.'

Jude and I are on our feet, chairs scraping over concrete. I vaguely register that Rafa knows Jude and I are speaking again. Which means the rest of the Outcasts probably do too.

'Both of you stay calm,' Jude says. He doesn't get between us, which is optimistic – and uncharacteristically naive.

'She's the last person who should know about this place.'

'Shit, Rafa, and all these years I thought you trusted my judgement.' Jude says it like he's joking, but there's a hard edge to him. A warning.

'It's not your judgement I'm worried about.' Rafa's watching me now. His gaze flicks to my hands and I flex my fingers, shift my weight. Subtle, threatening. 'So what's the deal, Gabe? What's brought on this sudden need to talk to your brother?'

'That's between me and Jude.' My pulse kicks up a notch, adrenaline building. Rafa comes closer, stays on an angle to give me less of a target. I move forward to meet him away from the table – fewer objects to get in the way. Jude clicks his tongue in annoyance.

'For fuck's sake, you two, get over it. There's nothing to fight over any more.'

Rafa and I lock eyes, share a bitter, knowing look. *Yeah, there is.*

'Gabe.' Jude's voice cuts through my anger: the way he says my name, more entreaty than censure. 'Please.'

I take a slow breath. I can do this. I'm here for Jude, not Rafa, and things were going fine until he turned up. Better than fine. I don't take my eyes from Rafa, try to breathe through my need to hit him.

'Daniel sent you, didn't he?' Rafa pushes. 'Of course he did, you're his puppet. Does he pull your strings in bed too?'

I lash out, pure reflex. My fist connects with his nose and Rafa's head snaps back in a mist of blood. Pain explodes across my knuckles, forks up my wrist.

'Hey!' Jude is between us before I can follow up or Rafa can counter. My brother pushes me back, not rough, and holds a hand out in warning to Rafa. 'Don't.'

'Come on, man, she fucking broke my nose!' Rafa holds his palm against his nostrils to catch the blood, glares at me through his fingers.

'You got what you were asking for.' Jude eyeballs him, leaves no doubt he's not in the mood for an argument.

Rafa shifts his weight. 'So, what, you two have made up, just like that? The past decade doesn't count?'

'It's a conversation with my sister, Rafa. We're not

talking about the Sanctuary and we're not talking about our crew. It's twin stuff.'

Twin stuff.

Even before the split, neither of us had played that card for at least five years. It was the excuse we always gave when we wanted time on our own.

'Twin stuff, my arse,' Rafa says.

Jude doesn't react, he simply watches Rafa. Waits.

Rafa draws a slow, intentionally loud breath. Blows out a cynical laugh. 'Fine.' His eyes slice back to me. 'But next time I see you, it's on.'

I respond with a tight smile. 'Not a problem.'

A second later, Jude and I are alone again on the patio.

Slowly, I relax, rub the soreness out of my knuckles. I go back to the table and sit down. Jude does the same. He takes another mouthful of dessert, chews it thoughtfully. He swallows, wipes his mouth, and then lays his fork back on the plate. The sea breeze tousles his hair.

'Okay. It's time you told me what the hell happened between you and Rafa.'

AN AWKWARD CONVERSATION

I fold my arms and stare at the crescent moon on the table.

'Don't tell me it's nothing. I just had front-row seats to the drama between you two and I can see how personal it is.'

I wet my lips. 'A lot's happened since you and he left the Sanctuary, you don't think that's got something to do with it?'

'Oh, no doubt at all. But the day we left, you threw him through a second-storey window and forgot to let go. I know how much damage you did to each other: Zak saw you – and that was *after* the first shift with Micah.' Jude sits forward. 'Gabe, please. I need to know what it was about. I need to know why you didn't come with us.'

I hear the whisper of pain in his voice, an echo of the hurt and confusion from that day. It crushes the air out of me. I grapple for that old, familiar anger – the one thing that's protected me from the weight of the past – and come up empty. It's gone. All I feel now is sad. Fractured.

'Does it matter?' I ask quietly.

'Yes, Gabe, it matters.'

I pick up my coffee cup. I swirl the grounds, watch the sludge stick to the sides. 'But it's humiliating.'

He rests his fingers lightly on my wrist, so tentative and uncertain it breaks my heart a little more.

'I need to know.'

I close my eyes, breathe in and out. 'Okay.'

I tell him about me and Rafa, and Rafa and Mya. I can't sit still. I lean forward. Sit back. Retie my hair. Cross my legs and uncross them. Play with the fork. I avoid his eyes the whole time. By the time I finish, I've massacred the remaining galaktoboureko. It's now a forlorn mess and when I press the fork into the mush, I leave a deep imprint.

'So, if you'd come to San Fran with me that night after the island and you and Rafa had never hooked up, you would've left with me?' Jude's voice is quiet.

I nod, still flattening the dessert. 'I was always coming with you. The only reason I didn't was because Rafa and Mya said they were going. I couldn't face the humiliation if people found out what happened.'

'You stayed because of your pride.'

My head comes up so fast my neck cracks. 'What? No—'

'What else would you call it?'

'Self-respect?'

'Self-respect?' He stares at me. 'Do you want to know the reasons I thought you stayed?'

I don't, but he's going to tell me anyway.

'First, I thought it was about Mya. That you were so threatened by the fact I occasionally valued her opinion over yours—'

'Occasionally? Jude, she was in your ear constantly—'

'Let me finish.' He shifts his weight. 'I thought you were so threatened you were trying to make me choose between her and you.' He holds up a hand before I can argue. 'Then I thought maybe you liked life at the Sanctuary too much to leave. That even though you knew all of Nathaniel's bullshit, you'd rather put up with it and live a lie than take a risk and walk away. Which meant you'd either lied to me or yourself every time you told me you were willing to leave if we had to. I know you didn't want to leave Daisy and Micah – or even Taya and Malachi, for that matter – but they would've followed you if you'd left.'

'You don't know that.'

'Yeah, I do. And so do you. And then' – he runs a hand through his hair – 'when I heard you'd hooked up with Daniel . . . Shit, Gabe, I thought you'd stayed for *him*. That you'd been on with Daniel before we'd left and you'd kept it a secret.'

I gape at him. 'You honestly thought I'd lied to you – and I did it to be with *Daniel*?'

'What else was I supposed to think? You never told me the truth, and Rafa's never let on, so all I had to go on was assumptions. And you'd been changing that year—'

'Not to mention a certain someone putting that idea in your head, no doubt.' I mean Rafa. It must have been easy for him to convince himself I stayed for Daniel too.

He shrugs but doesn't argue.

'Jude, let's not forget that you had some pride issues too. Once you gave Nathaniel that ultimatum you were never backing down, even if it meant leaving without me.'

Again, there's no argument. He slumps back in his chair, drags his hand through his hair. 'I've gone over that day a thousand times, Gabe. Beaten myself up over it a lot more. And if I could do it again, I'd do everything differently. All of it.'

'Me too. But we can't.'

'No, we can't.'

For a while, we don't speak. I face the sea, watch a passenger ship cruise towards the harbour, a long trail of churning water in its wake. A weight has lifted from my chest but I honestly can't tell if it's made me lighter – or if it's made me vulnerable.

'Are you going to tell Rafa you know about what happened?' I ask.

Jude looks at me as if I've suggested he take an axe to Rafa's Kawasaki. 'Are you insane? That's not a conversation I *ever* want to have.'

'Good.'

'For what it's worth, he and Mya haven't been together for years. These days all they do is snipe at each other.'

'Has there been anyone for you?' I ask. I don't want to hear about Rafa and Mya.

Jude laughs without humour. 'It's been a decade: there's been plenty. But that's not what you're asking, is it? No, there hasn't been anyone like that.' He studies me for a moment. Shakes his head.

'What?'

'I always used to think you and Rafa were kind of inevitable. What do you think would've happened if he hadn't fucked it up? Would it have gone anywhere?'

I shrug, look away. 'I was embarrassed about anyone finding out – and that was before I knew about Mya.'

For a moment I allow myself to remember that night: the playfulness, the intensity. The sensation of being completely dismantled and put back together. And then falling asleep resting against a body as familiar as my own. Exhausted. Satisfied. I shove the memory away. It's meaningless now.

'It doesn't matter, because he *did* fuck it up.'

Jude sits forward, looks at me seriously. 'Yeah, but so did we, and we're talking.'

'Slightly different circumstances.'

'That's true, princess' – and I feel a comforting warmth at his use of my nickname – 'but forgiveness is forgiveness.'

I nod, but . . . I can forgive Jude for walking away from me – I know that now – but Rafa? What he did? What he said to me before I put him through that window? All the ways we've hurt each other since, with feet and fists and words?

I don't know if I can ever get past that.

I CAN SEE YOU

Nine days later, and Jude still hasn't heard from Jason. But we're talking on the phone every day now. The first few calls are a little stilted but once we get through the awkwardness, the conversation starts to flow. Some days we chat about the people we've missed. Other days we catch up on each other.

He asks about my writing and I confess I haven't done much since he left. I don't tell him the backpacking stories became meaningless without him to share them with.

I ask him about surfing and he tells me he doesn't get to the beach as often as he'd like. I get the impression Outcast life isn't all that different from the demands at the Sanctuary. Only once do we tiptoe through a conversation about respective recent missions, neither of us wanting to say anything that might undermine us with our own people.

I certainly didn't tell him about my trip to Iceland today.

It's nine o'clock now, and I'm alone in my room, getting ready to fall into bed. I stretch out my legs on the bedcover, flick through channels to find something to drop off to sleep to. My fingers brush over the new scar above my left knee: a ten-centimetre-long reminder of the demon blade that sliced through tendon and muscle a few hours ago. Taya, Malachi and I ran into the Gatekeepers outside Reykjavik. The surface wound has healed over thanks to Brother Ferro and multiple shifts with Taya, but muscles are always slower to repair: the dull throb radiating up my leg and into my hip isn't going anywhere in the short term.

There's a soft knock on my door.

'What?' I call out.

'It's Zebediah.'

'Hilarious, Micah.' I pull on pyjama bottoms and shuffle to the door. I wrench it open and falter. 'Zeb. Shit, sorry.'

Zeb stands there looking startled, but he can't blame me for my reaction. He's hardly left the scriptorium wing in five years: not since Nathaniel let him convert an office there into a bedroom and add a bathroom. All he does is study and attend Council meetings. I've probably seen him twice in the last month and both times were in the library.

'May I come in?'

He's wearing a light woollen jumper and jeans that look

almost new. His black hair is short and wiry, his beard neatly trimmed. I glance down at my threadbare t-shirt and baggy flannelette pyjama bottoms.

'Ah, sure.'

I clear newspapers and swords from my couch, gesture for him to take a seat. I sit on the bed. 'What's up?'

He clears his throat, looks uncomfortable.

'Spit it out, Zeb. I need sleep.'

'I'm curious about your reconciliation with Jude.'

Unbelievable.

'Daniel sent you.' It's not a question.

'No ... Well, yes, but that's not why I'm here. I would like to know if there is a reason behind it.'

'Other than the fact he's my brother and we're tired of not talking to each other?'

'Yes, other than that.'

'What makes you think there's more? You don't think we've missed each other this past decade?'

He rests his fingertips on the edge of the scarred timber coffee table. Even in the soft light of the bedside lamp I can see his fingernails are short and manicured, pink against his ebony skin. 'I've devoted the past century to transcribing the ancient texts from Nathaniel's library—'

'Yeah, I'm well aware of that.'

'So, I've had access to writings from every society and creed known to mankind. And yet there are truths that remain elusive to me and I can't help but think this is intentional, especially when it comes to the Fallen. If I'm right, then, by logic, it means there are other ways for us to glean answers beyond the written word – if we knew where to look for them.'

'And?' I prompt. My mouth is already dry.

'I wonder if the Outcasts have discovered one of those sources.'

'If they had, do you seriously think they'd tell me?'

He gives me a wry smile. 'No, but your brother might. Some things in this world are more important even than quarrelling with your sibling.'

Zeb's so close to the truth, and yet so far. And it burns at me that he's half right: Jude only reconnected with me because of Jason and Dani, and whatever it is she's seen.

'Do you think I'd run off with the Outcasts if they had information we didn't?'

'No, Gabe, of course not—'

'That's what you're suggesting, though, isn't it? Daniel's convinced there's another agenda running, and you think I'm signing on with the Outcasts because they've found something we haven't. Thanks for the vote of confidence, Zeb.'

'Gabe—'

'For the record, as far as I know the Outcasts have no more idea than we do about the Fallen.' It's the truth, but a thread of guilt still tugs at me. 'And if you think I'd sign up for anything that involved Mya—'

'I know that. Of course I know that.' He swallows, folds his hands in his lap. 'But you still haven't told me what prompted you and Jude to reconnect now.'

'Yeah, I have, you're just not listening.' I stand up. 'You need to leave.'

Zeb looks like he's going to argue, but then he glances at the rack of weapons over my bed and seems to remember whose room he's in.

'I'm sore, I'm tired and I'm not in the mood to be accused of betrayal.'

'Please, Gabe—'

'Tell Daniel the next time he wants to throw around accusations, he should come and do it himself, not drag you out of storage because he doesn't have the balls to face me.'

Zeb's still apologising when I shut the door on him. I crawl into bed, angry and resentful and unsettled. I haven't lied to anyone, not yet. Not really. And I don't care what this kid Dani has to say, there's no way in hell I will ever join the ranks of the Outcasts.

I lie there, stewing, and finally start to sink into sleep when my phone vibrates on the bedside table. I groan, grab it.

It's Jude.

'Jason just called. He's ready to take us to Dani.'

I'm instantly awake. 'When?'

'Now.'

'Like, right now?'

'Yep. He'll meet us under the pier. The marine layer is hanging in again so we should have enough cover. Then we'll go to the kid from there.'

I flick on my lamp and swing my aching leg out of bed. I reach for my jeans. 'Okay, give me five.'

The space beneath the Santa Monica pier is deserted. The forest of pylons is eerie in the murky light. I can't see the waterline through the fog, but I can hear it breaking calmly onto the sand not too far away, smell the damp sea air. I didn't ask what weather to dress for, so I layered: t-shirt, lightweight hoodie, leather jacket. My boots sink into the soft sand and I have an almost irresistible need to kick them off and run barefoot through the mist. Bad leg and all.

Jude and Jason arrive within seconds of each other, Jude so close to me that I flinch. We smile at each other, and for a second I think he might hug me – a crazy idea because we've never been huggers.

'So where are we going?' I ask Jason.

'Boise, Idaho.'

Jude laughs. 'Where else would an eleven-year-old prophet live?'

Jason shoves his hands in the pockets of his jeans, self-conscious. 'Please don't judge Maria if she comes off a little rude. This isn't easy for her. And be gentle with

Dani.' He glances at our swords. 'And try not to look too intimidating.'

Jude and I nod.

'Do you remember how to guide us in the shift?' Jude asks. He and I taught Jason to shift back when we were all teenagers but we only practised shifting together once.

'I think so.'

We move closer together.

'Are you limping?' Jude asks me.

I shrug. 'A little.'

'What happened?'

I think about lying, decide on an edited version instead. 'I had a job today. It ended with a run-in with Bel and Leon.'

He sucks in his breath. 'I really hate those two. How bad?'

'I took a blade. It's fine, no permanent damage. It's stiff and sore, that's all.'

'Who was supposed to be watching your back?' His eyes drop to my leg. 'Where was Daniel?'

I sigh. Of course his disdain of the Sanctuary – of Daniel – isn't going to evaporate simply because he and I are talking again. 'It was a surveillance job and we were ambushed. Taya and Malachi had my back and they had their hands full.'

Jude looks like he wants to say more, but Jason clears his throat before he can. 'Maria and Dani are waiting for us.'

I reach for Jason's wrist and after a brief pause Jude does the same. Jason pulls us into the vortex gently; it's like sliding into water. Two seconds later we slip out the other side into a warm kitchen that smells of fresh-baked cookies and gas heating.

A woman with short dark hair stands behind a kitchen bench, her eyes flicking between Jude and me. Her arms are wrapped tight around a child with long blonde curls. They're braced for us, barely breathing.

'You must be Maria,' Jude says and smiles in the way that makes his eyes crinkle.

Maria tightens her grip on Dani. 'Let's get one thing straight: I don't want you here.' She exhales and glances down at her daughter. 'But Dani believes she has to tell you whatever it is she's seen, and I have to trust that Jason knows what he's doing.'

Dani can't decide who to stare at, Jude or me. Her eyes, blue like a summer sky, are bright, curious. There's fear there too, but she's not as scared as she should be. 'Hi,' she says quietly.

'Hi,' Jude and I say together.

Jude unzips his leather jacket. 'Wow, it's toasty in here. Do you mind?' He takes off his jacket and I do the same. Jude's wearing an old Lynyrd Skynyrd t-shirt – one that I bought for him years ago. It's threadbare and faded, and he wore it for me. I feel inadequate standing here in a standard issue Sanctuary black tee. I wish I'd thought to wear something he'd given me, even the t-shirt that says *I run with scissors*. I haven't worn it since he left, but I know exactly where it is in my wardrobe.

'Nice place,' Jude says. It's old but well kept: a worn timber table with high-backed chairs, a spotless stove, a large fabric sofa with a vintage flower design. Thick carpet scuffed in places by someone else's furniture.

'Thank you,' Maria says, reluctantly accepting the compliment.

The cookies I smelled when we arrived are cooling on a rack near the sink. They smell delicious. Dani sees me eyeing them. 'Would you like one? Mom and I made them for you.' Her voice is soft and sweet, her east coast accent at odds with the northwest location.

'Sure.' I don't know how I'm supposed to behave around her – I haven't had a lot of experience with kids. It helps to remember that she's a distant relative (a fact that still spins my head). Dani pulls away from Maria and lifts the tray so I can take a cookie. Melting chocolate chips stick to my fingers. Dani watches as I eat it in three bites and lick my fingers clean. 'Not bad.'

Dani smiles. Seriously, this kid has no fear.

'Can we sit down?' Jason pulls out a chair at the table while I look around for somewhere to hang my jacket. Maria points to the pegs by the back door. 'Over there please. Along with your weapons.'

I hold out my hand for Jude's jacket and katana, and take

them across the room. I see the tiny backyard through the window: a swing, a bicycle propped against the fence and a planter box with bright purple flowers. What would it be like to have a mother who teaches you to bake cookies and makes you hang up your jacket? An old ache rises, taking me by surprise. I thought I'd buried that yearning a century ago. Maybe the family connection is stirring up those dry, dead things.

'How long have you lived here?' Jude asks, and we stumble through a few minutes of small talk, finding out that Maria and Dani moved to Boise two years ago so Maria could find work. She's a trauma nurse. The teenage girl next door babysits when Maria has nightshift, unless Jason is visiting. I get the impression he's here a lot. Dani goes to an elementary school up the road and pretends she doesn't know about angels and demons and the Rephaim.

'Where's Dani's father?' Jude asks.

Dani reaches for a cookie and proceeds to pick it apart but not eat it.

'Back east,' Maria says, her expression flat. 'He can't deal with Dani's nightmares. It's easier this way.'

I watch Dani's mouth turn down a little and wonder who it's easier for: Dani or Maria. 'He doesn't know the truth?' I ask.

'Of course not. Nobody does, except those of us in the family who have lived with the curse. Do you go around telling people what you are?'

'No, but I'm surrounded by people who know, so I don't have to pretend to be something I'm not. Must be exhausting.'

Jason doesn't say anything, but I see it in the way he reaches for Dani's fingers to stop her destroying a second cookie: he knows exactly what I'm talking about.

'What were your visions?' Jude asks Maria.

'I don't talk about them.'

'But—'

'Is there something wrong with your hearing?' She flicks a meaningful look in Dani's direction.

Jason clears his throat. 'Maria's visions weren't all that different from the other girls in her family, mostly battles between angels and demons.'

'But were they prophetic?' Jude interrupts.

'I don't know,' Maria says.

He leans in. 'Can you at least tell me if you ever saw Rephaim in those battles?'

I blink. What would it mean if she did? Confirmation that when the big war erupts between heaven and hell we'll be part of it – and on the right side?

She shakes her head. 'Dani is the first of us to see you. If the Rephaim were in the battles shown to me, I didn't know it.'

Jude sinks back in his chair.

'It doesn't mean anything,' I say. He nods, slowly, but I see the disappointment in the set of his jaw. 'And we're not here about that. We're here because of Dani.'

Dani sits up straighter, all business.

'So.' I'm not sure how to approach it. 'How does your . . . *thing* work?'

She shrugs. 'If I sit quietly and concentrate, I can see you. I also have visions every now and then, but mostly I use the gift to watch what you guys are doing—'

'Us, as in me and Jude?' I have a stab of anxiety. At least she's not old enough to have seen what happened between me and Rafa, not if her abilities only started a few years ago. Unless she can see into the past too . . .

'I can see all of you but I mostly watch you two, and Ez and Zak. You four have always been my favourites. I search for Micah sometimes too. And Daniel.'

I don't have to look at Jude to know his reaction to Daniel's name.

'You don't believe me, do you?'

I study her. She's so open, so trusting. 'Tell me something you've seen.'

She chews on her pinkie nail, thinks. 'I saw you hurt Rafa.'

'When?'

'Last week. You and Jude were sitting outdoors somewhere. It was really sunny. You were talking, and then Rafa was there and you got into a fight with him. I think you broke his nose.'

I glance at Jude, my skin prickling.

'I didn't tell anyone,' he says, looking as spooked as I feel.

'I went looking for you today, before I called Jason,' Dani says, ignoring our reactions. She points to my leg. 'You got hurt fighting a demon with long white hair and weird eyes. He cut you with a sword. And Jude had an argument with Rafa about you—'

'Okay,' Jude says, totally rattled. 'We believe you.'

She sits back in her chair, satisfied.

I reach for the tray of cookies, pick one up, put it down again. 'Okay, so what do you want to tell us?'

Dani glances at Jason and then turns to her mother. 'I need to talk to Gabe and Jude alone.'

'Oh no you don't,' Maria says. 'Under no circumstances—'

'Mom, I've told you: I can only tell Gabe and Jude.'

'And I still don't understand. Why can't you tell me?'

Dani spreads her fingers on the table. Her nails are short and neat, painted a delicate shade of shell pink. 'Because it's too dangerous.'

'That doesn't reassure me, Daniella.' Maria glowers at me. 'What's to stop one of you kidnapping her?'

'If we wanted to snatch her, she'd be gone already,' I say, matter-of-fact.

'Again: not very reassuring.'

'They're not going to kidnap me, Mom, I promise.'

Jason catches Dani's eye. 'Are you sure you're okay to do this?'

'You said I could trust them and I do.'

Jason squeezes her fingers, gives Jude and me a sharp look. 'Come on,' he says to Maria. 'We'll wait out back.'

Maria hesitates and then she kisses the top of Dani's head. 'We'll be right outside, baby. You remember what I told you: *you* are more important than what you see.'

Dani nods and then waits for them to grab their coats and leave through the back door. There's a strange flutter in my stomach. Dani wipes her hands on her jeans and pushes up the sleeves on her pink and grey jumper. Takes a deep breath.

'I had the vision for the first time a few weeks ago. Usually I only see them once, but this one kept coming back. Sometimes it happened when I was watching TV, other times I was outside playing. I had to stop riding my bike because I fell off and hurt my arm.' She holds up her wrist and shows us traces of a bad graze. 'I go into a kind of trance when it happens.'

'You're lucky you didn't hurt yourself worse,' Jude says. He sits forward. 'What did you see?'

Dani closes her eyes, and her face creases with concentration as she remembers. 'I see a man, taller than anyone I've ever seen, with huge wings. His eyes are like little fires, but the flames are blue. There are others with him, but I can't see their faces clearly.'

'Do you know who he is?' I ask.

Dani sucks in her bottom lip. Nods. 'Someone I can't see is called Orias. The one I can see is Semyaza.'

My heart stutters. Jude's eyes lock on mine for a good five seconds.

'How do you know their names?' Jude's voice is quiet.

'I hear them talking. Semyaza has his eyes closed and Orias is telling him to stop watching.'

'Watching what?'

'You and Gabe.'

'How can he do that?'

Dani shakes her head. 'I don't know, but he sees you.'

'Why us?' But I already know the answer. Why else would we be here?

Dani brings her knees up to her chest on the chair and wraps her thin arms around them.

'Because Semyaza is your father.'

WHO'S YOUR DADDY?

Semyaza is our father. The leader of the Fallen. The instigator of the fall and the angel most despised by heaven.

And wherever he is, he's watching us.

The walls and the windows and the kitchen become a smear of beige. The house is too hot. My t-shirt is too tight against my throat. I stand up. My chair thuds on the carpet behind me and the table sways under my fingertips.

'Gabe . . .' Dani's voice is far away. Blood rushes in my ears. I need to move. My legs are shaky but they're still solid, propelling me forward. I pass carpeted stairs, an alcove with a computer, a painting of the sky. I keep walking until I reach the front door. I wrench it open and step onto the porch. Cold air hits me, nips at my bare arms. I suck in a deep breath and the air stings my nose, my throat, my lungs. The world sharpens. I stare out at a street lined with two-storey houses, neat lawns, American flags and oversized letterboxes. Vivid trees hug the road – splashes of reds and yellows – and dried leaves lie in deep piles in the gutters. An ugly orange face carved with jagged teeth and crazy eyes stares at me from the neighbour's porch. I blink, try to fit it into the storm of thoughts and fears gathering in my head. And then I remember it's nearly Halloween. I almost laugh at the irony.

Goosebumps crawl over my skin, snap me back into the moment. It's cold on the porch and there are no answers out here. I go back inside. Jude is still at the table, staring through the window at the cloudless afternoon sky. Jason and Maria are hugged into jackets, standing near the swing, deep in conversation, oblivious to the fact our world just tilted sideways. I pick up my chair and sit back down.

Jude looks stunned, disconnected. 'What does it mean?'

I don't have the words to answer him.

'Who gives you these visions?' he asks Dani.

'I don't know.'

Jude rolls his shoulders and cracks a joint in his neck. Dani flinches at the sound. 'Sorry,' he says, and takes a steadying breath. 'Do you know what Semyaza sees when he's watching us?' Jude asks.

I suppress a shudder. That sentence totally creeps me out.

Dani scratches the back of her hand. Her nails leave angry marks on her pale skin. 'I'm not sure, but every time

I see Semyaza, the vision changes to show the three of us.'

'Doing what?' I ask.

'We're in a forest. You cut yourselves and I keep saying the same thing over and over again.'

'What do you say? Do you remember?'

She closes her eyes and wets her lips, and then speaks in a language I've never heard before. Guttural sounds, sounds that are barely human. But they reverberate in the marrow of my bones and my teeth itch. I clench my fingers into fists to still the trembling.

'Do you know what it means?' I ask and she shakes her head. I turn to Jude. 'Do you?'

He's staring at Dani, studying her as if she's the answer to a particularly challenging puzzle. 'No, but it has to be one of the tongues of angels. Why else would we not know it?'

Dani's fingers flutter to her lips.

'Does that mean an angel is sending her those visions?' I ask.

Dani isn't listening. She's still caught up in the idea she can speak an angelic language, her face filled with wonder. I don't feel wonder, I feel confused. And seriously freaked out. 'Why would they show you the Fallen?'

Dani finally registers I'm speaking to her. She stops touching her lips. 'There are things I don't see but that I sort of *know* when I come out of the trance. I think maybe Orias is my great-great-great-step grandpa, or whatever.'

She looks from Jude to me. 'He's Jason's father,' she says, as if we didn't understand.

'Does Jason know that?' Jude asks.

She shakes her head vigorously. 'No. I don't think I'm meant to tell him.'

'But you're meant to tell us? Why?'

She crosses her legs under her on the chair and lengthens her spine. She looks older all of a sudden. 'The Fallen are stuck in another dimension. The Archangel Gabriel did it. He found them and put them there after they escaped, rather than sending them back to hell.'

Dani talks about other dimensions, as if she's talking about countries she hasn't visited. I grew up knowing about other realms – shifting through at least one of them – and I still can't get my head around the idea.

'Why would Gabriel do that?' Jude asks.

'I don't know, but he used Semyaza's blood to bind the Fallen to wherever he trapped them. Now only Semyaza's blood – or Gabriel's – can break the seal and free them.'

'Why aren't they free already if Semyaza can do it?'

'The seal can only be broken from this side.'

Oh.

The full reality of that revelation dawns for Jude a second before I catch on. 'We're his blood,' Jude whispers. 'We can free them.'

Fuck.

I swallow. 'That's what you see us doing . . . freeing them?'

Dani shrugs. 'All I know is that I say the words and you bleed in the dirt. I don't know what happens next, I haven't seen that part.'

'Holy shit,' Jude whispers. He sits back in his chair, dazed. 'Ho-ly shit.'

We sit in silence. No wonder Dani didn't want to tell anyone else. This is bigger than Jason's existence and the secret about our mothers. This is even bigger than Dani and her abilities. If Nathaniel's right, finding the Fallen is the one thing that can give our existence meaning – give us a future. Even if he's wrong, finding and freeing them will change everything.

They've stayed hidden – no, trapped – for a hundred and forty years. And now, in the space of a short conversation with an eleven-year-old, we're the closest we've ever been to them.

'What are we supposed to do now?' I ask.

Jude drags both hands through his hair. 'Even if what Dani says is true, it means nothing if we don't know where the Fallen disappeared.'

He's right. It's the reason we've spent nearly a century and a half roaming the globe: trying to find the exact spot where the Fallen left the world. If we can do that, Nathaniel's always said he can track them.

Jude picks up a pencil from the table, absently taps it against his forehead.

'Maybe the exact spot isn't important,' Dani says.

Jude stops tapping.

'Maybe your blood is what's important, not the place.' She pushes a long blonde curl out of her eyes. 'You need to not be fighting, I know that much.'

'That's why you said we had to spend time together before we met you?' I ask.

She nods.

'But we're definitely in a forest?' Jude presses.

'Uh huh.'

'So maybe we could try it in any forest.'

Frustration flares, scorching and sudden. 'Can we have a word in private, Jude?'

He catches the edge in my voice. Nods.

I head for the front door and then remember how cold it is outside. I go into the study alcove instead. Jude follows and I close the sliding door behind him.

'What is it you think we're going to try?' I demand. 'Have you come to a decision you haven't shared with me?' There's not much room in here, especially with the space fizzing with my anger.

'I was thinking out loud,' Jude says carefully.

'That's what you want, though, isn't it: to see if we can release them.'

'I don't know yet. First I want to understand what Dani saw and then we can work out what to do about it. *Together.*'

'After you tell your crew.'

He stares at me, some of his calmness slipping. 'Are you planning on telling anyone at the Sanctuary?'

Am I? I find a spot on the wall behind him to study, a lighter patch where a picture once hung. I think about how that conversation would go – and its ramifications. Our century-old secret about Jason would be bad enough, but our link to the Fallen . . . it would complicate everything. Complicate life in ways that would never be unravelled.

'No,' I say. 'But if you tell the Outcasts, I'll have to tell the Five. If your crew knows, they should too.'

Jude nods. 'Fair enough. I have no intention of telling my crew at this point.'

'Me either.' I exhale. 'So what now?'

He's already thought it through. 'We lie low here until we know more. Stay away from everyone else so we don't have to lie to them.'

I imagine facing Daisy or Micah – or worse, Nathaniel or Daniel – knowing what I know now. 'Agreed.'

Jude and I borrow Jason's rental car and follow his directions to Whole Foods. We bicker about music all the way there and back, trying to agree on a radio station. Back at Maria's, we crack a bottle of pinot noir and take over the kitchen.

Maria wasn't overjoyed at the prospect of us staying – especially when she realised we meant overnight. With Jason already in the spare room, she suggested we try a hotel in town but we insisted we were happy to sleep in the living room. It was Dani who wore Maria down.

Once that was settled, Jude phoned Rafa to tell him he'd be away a bit longer – I didn't hear Rafa's half of the conversation but it obviously wasn't flattering to me. I sent Daisy a similar message, and ignored her follow-up texts fishing for more information.

Before everything turned to shit at the Sanctuary, Jude and I used to pester Brother Pietro to give us a corner of the kitchen to use. It wasn't that we didn't appreciate the meals he and his team served up – we did – it was that occasionally we wanted something less commissary, and less Italian, and we didn't always want to leave home for it.

We haven't cooked together for a decade, but Jude and I quickly find our rhythm. We're making rice-paper rolls, pad thai noodles and laksa. I chop herbs and Jude makes the pastes and dipping sauces. The kitchen soon smells of coriander, mint and fresh-roasted peanuts. I teach Dani how to soak the rice paper and roll up the mint, cucumber, carrot, and rice noodles. Her first two look like alien life forms – which she photographs on Maria's phone, giggling –but her third is near perfect. She lays them out in a neat circle around the sweet chilli sauce.

I bump elbows with Jude reaching for a fresh cutting board. He grins at me, eyes bright. I grin back.

Maria watches us closely, not drinking and not saying much. It must be strange for her to have us here, blood relatives and total strangers. Or, how she must see us after everything she's heard from Jason and Dani: half-angel bastards with a penchant for violence.

Jason finally starts to relax after half a glass of wine. He looks like I remember from Monterosso, but his fingers aren't calloused any more from handling salt-encrusted fishing nets. His skin is soft, devoid of the faint scars that crisscross my hands. It's fair to say he hasn't been battling demons since we last saw him. God, maybe he's never even seen a Gatekeeper or hellion. What would that life be like?

Dinner is delicious. Even Maria admits it. As we eat, Jude interrogates Jason about what he's been doing since Monterosso. Turns out he's been busy studying – history, psychology, law and theology. And for the last few years he's been able to keep track of us, thanks to Dani.

After Dani goes to bed and the dishes are done, the conversation drifts to the inevitable subject of the Fallen. It's enough to coax Maria out of her watchful silence.

'I've never understood why they were in such a hurry to seduce human women a second time around, knowing the consequences. What were they thinking?'

Jude's laugh is short, facetious. 'They'd had a dry spell that lasted thousands of years. They *weren't* thinking – at least not with their brains.'

'Thanks for the visual,' I say. Maria and I experience a brief moment of solidarity.

'They weren't stable when they came out of the pit,'

Jason says. 'How could they be? They'd spent millennia being tortured and then they escaped into a reality that held no good memories for them: the last time they were on earth, their offspring were murdered by the Garrison.'

Jude's amusement fades. 'Yeah, at the hands of Gabriel the *merciful*.'

'I guess Gabriel's mercy doesn't extend to abominations,' Jason says.

I frown. What has he seen – or learned – since I last saw him to put that idea in his head? I may not fully understand my purpose in this life, but I've never thought of myself as an abomination.

'The nephilim must have put up a fight, surely,' Maria says.

Jude uncorks another bottle. 'There's no evidence they were warriors.'

'Or that they were adults,' Jason says quietly.

Jude pours us each another wine. He swirls his, watches it cling to the side of the glass. Finally his attention returns to Jason. 'The Fallen could have gone anywhere in the world to find women. Any thoughts on how *two* of them ended up in Monterosso? Did your mother ever talk about it?'

'No.' Jason hesitates, glances at Maria. 'But my grandfather did.'

We wait while he takes a sip of wine and thinks about what he wants to tell us.

'Nonno blamed himself,' he says. 'Every year on my

birthday he'd drink too much grappa, then he'd pull me aside and tell me how Mamma ran wild with the gypsies the summer your mother, Ariela, came to visit.' Jason's fingers stray to the back of his neck, to the half-crescent moon marking his skin. 'To his dying breath, Nonno believed there was a connection between the rituals the girls were doing on the outskirts of our village and the arrival of the "shining ones".'

I rub my leg above my knee. The wound is aching again. 'That's not possible. The Fallen were in hell.'

'Yeah,' Jude says, 'but we know the veil between hell and earth isn't impenetrable. Demons can interfere here. Are you saying the Fallen found a way through?'

'Not physically,' Jason says. 'Metaphysically. Through dreams.'

'And then what?'

'The old texts talk about the Fallen teaching charms and enchantments to the women they slept with the first time around – the mothers of the murdered nephilim. Maybe it was the same with our mothers, except they taught them certain rituals *before* they got out of hell.'

I frown, not quite grasping what he's saying. 'Why?'

Jason dabs at a drop of spilled wine, shapes it into a crescent.

'I think it's possible they told our mothers how to bring them through the veil. They might have been the ones who broke them out of hell.'

THE PACT

Much later, after Jason and Maria have gone upstairs to their respective rooms, Jude and I sit on the carpet near a toasty gas heater. He shares the last of the wine between our glasses. We lean back against the sofa, shoulders touching. He takes a sip and then lets out a deep sigh.

'I've missed this,' he says quietly.

I draw my knees to my chest. 'Me too.'

'A decade. How did we let things get this far?'

'We're pig-headed.' I give him a gentle nudge, expecting at least a half-smile. Instead, he looks at me, deadly serious.

'I think we should do it.'

'Do what?' I raise my glass. I know exactly what he means, but I need a second to focus, prepare myself.

'Try Dani's ritual.'

I feel the buzz from the alcohol now, loosening my

muscles and my thoughts. 'Let's say we do, and it works. Then what? How do we deal with Semyaza and two hundred fallen angels, each with the strength to rip us apart with their bare hands?'

Jude shrugs with one shoulder. 'I guess we'll find out if Semyaza has paternal instincts.'

'Seriously, Jude, what if Nathaniel's right and all the Fallen want is payback against the Garrison for sending them to hell?'

'If they're going to war, they're going to war. The entire Rephaim army won't be able to stop that, so what does it matter who finds them?'

I concede a nod. All this time, Nathaniel's told us our duty is to find the Fallen and hand them over to the archangels. But the chances of us ever achieving that have seemed so remote over the years that he's never had to explain how we'd actually do it.

'Maybe Nathaniel's always intended to use us as leverage to get the Fallen to cooperate: take the gamble that we mean something to them.'

'Or at the very least that they don't want to kill us.' Jude takes off his boots, sets them over by the wall. 'There's an interesting conversation for Nathaniel: "Hey fellas, I raised your kids while you've been out of the picture and made sure they want to send you back to the pit. Oh, and those virgins you deflowered? Yep, I killed 'em all."'

I think of those young girls. Seeing Nathaniel in his true

form. Not understanding why he was there until it was too late.

'But why kill them? Especially Ariela. I mean, if Jason's right and she's the reason Nathaniel was free in the first place.' I can't bring myself to call Ariela our mother. She feels more real now, the reality of her more likely to wound.

'Think about it,' Jude says. 'If Semyaza is our father, then it must have been him and Orias who made contact from the pit with Ariela and Jason's mother. They taught them the ritual to tear the veil, and then seduced them. The rest of the Two Hundred then followed their lead, scattering across the globe to find their own action. How do you think Nathaniel would've felt about women who helped his brothers-in-arms disgrace themselves within hours of finally being free of the pit?'

My chest tightens. 'Manifesting in front of them was their punishment. Him in full glory. It would've blinded them. Burned their flesh to the bone . . .'

We sit with that horrible image for a long moment, and then the jarring reality hits again.

Semyaza is my father.

And now the ache returns, the one tied to my long-dead mother. The one that makes me feel empty and powerless. The one I've pressed down over these decades, tried to suffocate from the moment I was old enough to understand I would never know either of my parents. I want to ask Jude how he feels but it's too personal, even for us. So I ask something else.

'Is it worth dying to come face to face with Semyaza?'

He shakes his head, slowly. 'It's not just about meeting him' – although I can see in his eyes it's a big part of it – 'it's about changing the status quo. The Sanctuary and the Outcasts could keep searching for the Fallen for decades – centuries. We have a chance to end it all now, find out one way or the other why we exist and what we're supposed to do with our lives. Are we tied to heaven or earth or neither?' He sinks back against the couch. 'I'm over it all, Gabe. I'm no closer to the truth than I was at the Sanctuary, and it's worse now because you're not in my life. I can't go back – shit, I don't want to – and you're not about to join us' – he pauses in case I want to disagree, which I don't – 'so something has to change.'

I think about what I want to say before I say it, turning it over in my head to make sure it comes out right. 'What do you want out of all this?'

'I don't know. Meet our father. See the Garrison snap into action. At least if they show up, we might finally find out what the end game is.'

'Or they might kill us.'

Kill us, or worse. I don't let myself imagine the horrors of the pit if we get dragged down there with our father. 'And what if the ritual doesn't work, then what? Nothing changes.'

Jude takes a sip of wine, his eyes not leaving mine. 'We could drop off the radar. Just you and me, like we always planned.'

I blink. Does he mean that? Do I want that?

'Look, I love my crew. And we've done more damage to the Gatekeepers in the last decade than in all those years at the Sanctuary, but there aren't enough of us. There's always a risk one of us is going to get hurt again . . . or killed. If I left for a while, everyone might finally take time out. Mya mightn't be so gung ho without me around.' He says her name carefully, watching for my reaction.

I can see he means it – or at least he wants to – but I know it's not that easy. For a start, he'd struggle to walk away from Rafa. He always has. And I understand: I feel the same about Daisy and Micah.

'You're not going to leave your crew, Jude. Not after they've been loyal to you for a decade.'

He rubs a palm over his eyes, sighs, doesn't argue. I stand up, glass in hand. My brain always works better when I'm moving. Maria has left us a stack of blankets and pillows on the table. It tilts dangerously to one side, threatening to topple. I do a lap of the table and straighten it as I walk past.

'All right, let's break this down.' I count the options off as I go:

'One. We release the Fallen. They kill us.

'Two. We release the Fallen. The Garrison turns up, kills

us and/or sends us to hell with our father and the Two Hundred.

'Three. We release the Fallen. They make war on the Garrison and it triggers a greater war between heaven and hell and the Garrison is distracted dealing with the Fallen – Nathaniel's worst nightmare.

'Four. We fail. Go back to the mess of our lives.' I stop near the table. 'Or five, we desert the people we care about and spend years pretending it's not destroying us day by day.'

Jude smiles at me, sad. 'We've tried that last one already, remember. It didn't work.' He puts his glass aside and gets to his feet, comes over to me. Rests a hand on the pile of linen. 'What do you want to do?'

I tilt my head back and shut my eyes, let the evening settle into me. If I return to the Sanctuary, what am I going back to? The lies are still there, the undercurrent of tension. And how would Jude and I keep this connection if we return to our lives? How would we keep our people from each other's throats every time we tried to spend time together?

Jude lets me pick all these thoughts apart until it becomes clear to me there's only one possible option. I meet his gaze.

'Let's do it.'

THE BEST LAID PLANS . . .

The hardest part is Dani.

'You have to take me with you: I'm the one who recites the words,' she says.

We're sitting in the kitchen, soft morning light falling on the speckled bench. I'm washing our breakfast dishes, Jude's on tea towel duty and Dani is putting away the clean plates and glasses. The room still smells of rye toast and huckleberry jam. Maria left for work an hour ago – reluctantly – and Jason is upstairs taking a shower.

'What happens if it works and we end up face to face with the Fallen?' I ask Dani.

'They won't hurt me.'

'How do you know?'

She shrugs. 'I just do.'

I can see why Maria's so nervous about trusting Dani's conviction about things based solely on what she *feels*. She probably used the same argument to convince her mother to let us come to their home. And now we're about to take her out of the house without her mother's permission.

'Maybe Jason should come along—'

'No,' Dani says. 'He can't be there – it can only be the three of us. And you know he's going to freak out if you tell him. We'll leave him a note.'

I catch Jude's eye. I have no idea how to talk her out of this. Clearly neither does he.

'What are you worried about?' Dani asks. 'You can bring me back any time you want – just like that.' She snaps her fingers.

The water shuts off upstairs.

'We should go now,' Dani says.

'Go where?' Jude hands her another plate.

'This is Boise. We're surrounded by forests.'

I let the water out of the sink, watch the suds collect around the drain. Try not to think about how badly this could all go wrong.

'What about your mum?' Jude presses.

'She'll be at work for hours.'

I shake my head. 'She'll have a fit.'

'As long as we don't take too long and you get me back safe and sound, Mom will get over it.'

'I seriously doubt that.' Jude leans against the bench,

folds his arms and studies Dani. 'Are you sure? Really sure?'

'I'm sure.' She grabs a sticky note from the draw and carefully writes a message in neat lettering.

I'm with Gabe and Jude. Back soon. Don't worry. Dani xx

She opens the fridge and presses the note on the side of the low-fat milk carton. We use a maps app on Jude's phone to pick a remote spot in a forest to the north, and then slip into our jackets and grab our swords. A door opens on the floor above us.

'Last chance,' Jude says.

'Come *on*, already,' Dani says, exasperated. She holds a hand out to each of us, her fingers soft and warm. I hear footsteps on the stairs.

Jude and I exchange one last, tense look and then I guide us into the void.

It's brisk in the forest, the air clear and sharp. Almost cold enough for snow, even though it's only October. Dani clutches my hand as she steadies herself. She's pale from the shift and her fingers are like ice. I lead her into a patch of sunshine and rub her hands between mine to warm them. We've arrived in a small clearing ringed by pine trees and evergreens. Jude does a quick scout and comes back. 'Just us and the great outdoors.'

My pulse picks up, more insistent. I squeeze Dani's

fingers and she looks up at me, her blue eyes luminescent in the daylight. Determined. How does an eleven-year-old kid have this much courage?

'So, Jude and I cut ourselves, let our blood drop to the ground, and you say the magic words – that's it?'

Dani nods. 'Your blood needs to mix first.'

'Okay. You have your phone?'

'Uh huh.'

'And you'll ring Jason if anything happens to us?'

'Yes, *Mom*,' she says.

'Get his number up on your screen, now. Just in case.' If anything happens to Dani, I'll never forgive myself.

She pulls out her phone.

'And hide out of sight. What about behind that tree over there?' I point to an evergreen with a trunk as wide as Zak's shoulders.

She thinks about it for a moment. Nods. And then she throws her arms around my waist, taking me by surprise. 'Good luck.'

'You too,' I whisper, holding her tight.

She hugs Jude. He smoothes her hair, smiles down at her. 'Thank you,' he says.

We wait until she's out of sight and then Jude and I face each other, swords in hand. My heart knocks a steady beat against my ribs, my breathing quicker now. I spin my katana. Even in the cold, my palm is tacky against the leather hilt. This is it. If Dani's right, we're moments away from freeing the Fallen. Moments away from Semyaza. From our father.

Jude taps his blade against his calf. 'How do you want to do this?' His eyes are sharp, focused.

'Palms?' I hold mine out.

'Okay.' He blows out his breath. 'There's no undoing this once it's done.'

I nod, look away. Withstand a momentary blast of panic.

I don't want to do it.

I can't do it.

What if the Garrison turns up? What if they don't?

What if Nathaniel's right about everything and we're about to spark a war?

What if—

I meet Jude's eyes. He's scared too, but also . . . *resolved*. Whatever battle I'm having with myself, he's already had it and won. And suddenly I know. I'm with Jude. No matter what happens in this moment, we're in it together. It's enough.

I take another breath. 'Okay.'

He hesitates for a heartbeat and then scuffs a boot to clear the pine needles and dead leaves between us. 'I think we should stay on our feet.'

'Agreed.' Our blood will hit the dirt whether we're standing or kneeling. I don't want to be on my knees in front of the Fallen.

Jude lifts his sword and I do the same. We grip our blades near the hilt, carefully slice our left palms – not too deep. It stings. I grit my teeth. A muscle tics in Jude's jaw. He steps closer and we press our palms together. Jude's skin is already slick with blood. I feel my pulse beat against my brother's. Warmth spreads across my hand and blood trickles down my wrist and under my sleeve. I ignore it. The forest is silent except for the whisper of the breeze in the trees around us. No birds, no dogs, no distant hum of vehicles. We could be the only people on earth.

I concentrate on our hands. Blood gathers at the point where our wrists meet. *Our* blood. I glance towards the tree. Dani's well out of sight. Good. The first drop of blood falls. It spatters in the dirt without a sound. A second, right on top of it.

'Now,' I call out to Dani.

Immediately her voice rises up, strong and steady, reciting a language not of this world. I scan the forest behind Jude. He's focused on the space behind me. We're as ready as we can be.

My heart is punching my ribs now. I barely feel the cut in my hand.

Our blood drips in the dirt.

Dani keeps reciting the incantation from her vision.

Nothing happens.

She speaks the words again. And again. I recognise sounds and phrasing, even if I have no idea what they mean. Jude and I stay perfectly still, hands clasped, swords raised. It might be for a minute. It might be five.

'How long is this supposed to take?' Jude calls out.

She doesn't break her rhythm to reply.

My stomach lurches violently. I have a split second of surprise – the Fallen feel like demons when they arrive – before Jude sucks in his breath and jerks back his hand. And then everything happens at once.

A Gatekeeper demon – Leon – materialises behind Jude.

White-hot pain explodes across the back of my head.

Leon buries his broadsword between Jude's ribs.

My legs buckle.

Something solid slams into my side. A boot.

Jude shouts my name. It comes out choked. Yelling for me to shift.

I hit the dirt, hard. The forest is wrong. Sideways, blurred. I can't tell the trees from the legs surrounding us. So many legs, demon legs. *Not* the Fallen.

A mountain lumbers closer, blocking out the light. Snarls. I squint. A hellion. No – three hellions. Wait. The first is . . . *Iceland*. It can't be . . . I need to shift. I need—

Dani.

I panic, try to roll over to look for her. My head pounds. More blood. It's soaking into my shirt.

'No, no, no.' I hear Bel a moment before his boot smashes down on my thigh. The crack of shattering bone is impossibly loud. Shards of pain fork through my body.

I scream, taste dirt again. Darkness rushes in. I fight it, struggling against the pull of oblivion.

I hear scuffling, grunting. *Jude.* Oh god. Where are the Fallen? Where's the Garrison? Fuck, we're going to die.

Another kick, this time to my ribs. I grunt, try to curl into a ball. I reach for the void, can't get a grip. It's like the last time I was at Bel's mercy, but this time I'm not alone on an island beach. This time I brought my brother and an eleven-year-old girl.

Rough hands grab me by my hair, yank me up to my knees. My hands hang limp at my sides. Where's my sword?

My eyes flutter open. I try to bring the murky forest into focus, but it's too smudged. The throbbing behind my eyes is too much.

But then I see it. My brother, metres away, propped up on his knees too. Leon, fist clenched in Jude's hair. I try to focus on Jude's face, but it's beyond me. I can't feel my legs now. Or my broken ribs.

'You first.' The words seem to float down from the trees. Leon? 'Don't end it too quick.'

Fingers tighten in my hair, pulling at my scalp.

'Eyes open now, Judah. You don't want to miss it.'

For a long moment nothing happens. The seconds stretch out like soft toffee. And then Bel's fingers tighten in my hair and cold steel buries itself into the back of my neck.

Jude screams. Darkness swamps me.

I'm falling again. My head bounces when I hit the ground. It must still be attached.

I can't move. I taste mouldy leaves and blood. Feel the life draining out of me. Shadows flicker across a distant pinprick of light. I'm deep below the surface, slowly suffocating.

And then the light grows, brightens. Comfort washes over me. Am I dead? I must be. And yet . . .

I hear swords clash and raised voices around me. Muffled, frantic. The sounds fade, or I do. When awareness next finds me, there's a hand pressed against my neck. A warm hand. Strong.

Voices, garbled. My heart lurches: one of those voices belongs to Jude. I try to open my eyes. Can't.

Try to move. Can't.

Try to speak . . . Nothing.

I'm paralysed. Numb. I focus on Jude's voice, try to pick out his words but they fade in and out. Does he sound hurt? Dying? I finally catch a fragment, his words laboured.

'. . . whatever you have to do.'

A finger strokes my neck. And then everything goes dark.

NOW

WHO DO YOU SEE WHEN YOU LOOK AT ME?

That last memory clings to me like seaweed. Persistent, abrasive.

I'm back on the beach near the headland. I sit and lean against a dune. Close my eyes to ground myself. Feel the soft sand between my fingers, the sea breeze on my skin. Taste salt. Remember where I am. It doesn't budge the knot in my stomach.

I'm a mess. I might not be able to speak to Jude or Rafa yet, but I need to talk to *someone*.

I call Mags.

'Timing,' she says, slightly breathless. She's still in Rome with Jason, Dani and Maria. I wanted them away from the Sanctuary when we confronted Nathaniel. 'We're about to leave. Where are you?'

The sound of her voice tethers me more firmly to here and now.

'Back in Pan Beach.'

'Thank god. Who's with you?'

She sounds the same. I *feel* the same listening to her. Like I would if I'd made the call a few hours ago. 'The Outcast crew, plus Malachi, Taya, Micah and Daisy. We brought Simon and the Butlers with us.'

'Were you hoping for more Rephaim?'

Gatekeepers are coming to tear Pan Beach apart: yeah, I'd hoped for more. But I don't want to scare her. 'It's enough.' I stare out at the horizon, spot a freighter far out at sea. From here it looks like a toy. I blot it out with my thumb. 'What are Dani and Maria doing?'

'They're coming with us. Maria's not happy – no surprise there – but she caved in. Jason's offered them his room. We're picking up clothes for them on the way.'

'Tell Jason to go to the resort when you get here.'

'How come?'

'Our place is crawling with Rephaim.'

'Oh, okay.' A pause, and then: 'Is that surf I can hear? Are you at the beach?'

'Yeah. I needed some air.' I don't tell her about the Immundi. I don't want to freak her out any more than she already is. 'How long will you be?'

She holds the phone away and speaks to Jason for a second. 'Not long. A few minutes maybe.'

'Can we talk when you get here? Alone?'

'Of course.' A pause. 'Babe, are you okay?'

'Yeah, sort of. I'll meet you out front of the resort in five.'

I disconnect and get to my feet. I dust sand from my trousers, stretch my arms above my head. I feel stronger – physically stronger – than I have in a long time. I flex my fingers, shake out the tension.

There's no sign of Jude on the beach or in the water. Maybe he went after Rafa. They might be at Rafa's shack right now talking it out – or arguing. Could go either way.

I head towards town. The boardwalk is crammed with women power-walking their prams, so I jog along the hard-packed sand at the water's edge. The Lotus Resort is at the other end of the esplanade, right on the beach. It's all white shutters, climbing jasmine and manicured date palms. Jason's kept a room here all week, even though he's spent most nights on my couch or Rafa's or – more recently – in Maggie's bed.

The Lotus is where the local seachange millionaires bring their city buddies for foie gras and French champagne. I've only set foot inside once. Maggie, Simon and I had drinks there one Friday night before Christmas, and we each blew a day's wages to share a bottle of Billecart-Salmon Elisabeth Rosé. It was gone in half an hour and we couldn't afford anything else. We finished off the night on the beach with a six-pack of beer from Rick's Bar.

That's what I love about Pan Beach. The Lotus, Rick's

Bar, and the blood-stained Imperial Hotel are all within three blocks of each other, all existing in their own orbits, ignoring the other. Pretending their reality is the only one. Why can't my worlds function like that?

I lived at the Sanctuary for a hundred and thirty-eight years, in Pan Beach less than a year. And yet this place, with its lush mountain, turquoise ocean and chilled vibe feels more like home than the monastery ever did. Is that connection real or a lingering side effect of my fake memories? I fell in love with this place when I thought I was a teenage backpacker with shitty parents and a dead twin. When I was drowning in grief. Would I have reacted the same under different circumstances? Would I have become friends with Maggie? If I'd turned up as Gabe, would Maggie have wanted to share a house with me?

I'm fifty metres from the resort when I see Maggie half-jog onto the beach, peeling off the jumper she wore to Italy. She squints against the sun and holds up a hand to me. Her hair is tied back, two-tone blonde streaks shining in the sun. I veer towards her and slow to a walk. By the water, seagulls fight over an abandoned bucket of chips. Maggie scans my face when I get closer and stops a few paces away. She knows. She can see it.

'What's going on?'

I pause as if to catch my breath, but I can breathe fine. I'm checking if I really want to tell her. Because once this is out, I can't take it back. I tuck a stray hair behind my ear, shake out my legs to keep the blood circulating.

'Something happened in the shift, Mags. I remembered. I remember my old life.'

She frowns. Her lips part and then slowly form a single word: 'Oh.'

I give her a moment to absorb it.

'Oh,' she says again and lowers herself to the sand. I hesitate, then sit down as well, not too close. She's studying me more intently now, her jumper bunched in her hands. The seagulls keep arguing in the wash. 'Are you still . . . you?'

'Yes. I'm still me.'

'Not Gabe?' Not the hard-arsed, brother-shunning Rephaite?

Maggie swallows. She's holding her breath. God, she's unsure of me. It scrapes me raw to see that shift in her eyes, the tension around her mouth. I think about where all the pieces of me are settling. My past, my regrets. What shape they're taking.

'I'm still working that out.'

She nods, looks away. Why wouldn't she be freaked out at the prospect of me being Gabe? She hasn't heard too many pleasant stories about who I used to be. Maggie unzips her boots. Slips off one, then the other, and stands them in the sand. They slump a little, like soldiers at ease. Then she rolls up her jeans and presents her tanned shins to the sun. 'Okay.'

'That's it?'

A quick nod. Nervous, but resolved. 'I'm okay with whoever you are as long as you're still my friend.'

The idea that she thinks it could've been otherwise brings a sharp jab to my heart. 'Of course I'm still your friend. I wasn't *that* much of a bitch.'

'That's not what I meant.' She digs her French-polished toenails into the sand. 'I don't know how any of this works. Like, if you remember who you used to be, does that mean the last year doesn't matter? Then my Gaby would be gone.'

I feel a strange tug at the way she called me 'her' Gaby. 'I'm the same person I was an hour ago. And the last year means everything to me.'

She blinks rapidly, bites her lip.

'Something happened between the Sanctuary and the bungalow,' I say. 'And when we came out the other side, Jude and I, we had the pieces we've been missing.' A thought strikes. 'Did anything happen with you guys?'

She shakes her head.

'Nothing with Dani?'

A frown. 'No . . . although she was a little quiet when we arrived.' She squints against the sun. 'How's Jude coping?'

'We haven't talked about it yet.'

'Why not?'

'Long story.' I look away and we're silent for a moment.

'So, does this mean you remember *everything*?'

I turn back to her. 'Yeah. And I need to talk to someone about it before my head explodes.'

'You haven't spoken to Ez or Daisy? Or Micah?'

'They don't know yet. I wanted to talk to you first.'

'Oh.' Her face crumples a little, and then she smiles, wipes her eyes. 'Sorry, I didn't expect ... I thought maybe . . .'

I knock my trainer against her calf. 'Don't underestimate the impact you've had on me, Margaret Jane.'

Her smile widens and for the first time since arriving back in Pan Beach, I almost fit back in my skin. 'So. What happened with Rafa?'

And just like that, I'm smudged again. 'Bloody hell,' I say, trying for lightness I don't feel. 'Straight in for the kill.'

'You don't want to talk about him?'

'No ... Yes. Shit.' I stretch my neck to one side, try to ease the tension.

'Come on.' She picks up her boots and jumper and helps me to my feet. We climb the steps up to the resort, find a patch of shaded grass under a clump of palm trees. Maggie crosses her legs and waits, straightens the folded cuffs on her jeans. I take my time pulling my thoughts together. I lean back against a palm tree, find the freighter on the horizon.

I tell her all of it. What happened on the island, *that* moment in Rafa's room, finding out about Mya, and the fall-out with Rafa and then Jude. She asks questions as I go and when I finish – wrung out – she sits quietly, stares out over the sea while she assembles it all.

'Rafa told you he loved you?'

She thinks that's the most significant thing? 'Did you miss the part where he hooked up with Mya and then came on to me an hour later?'

'No, and I totally understand why you reacted the way you did, but didn't you go to his room?'

'That's not the point.' The memory feels new, raw. It still stings. 'The Sanctuary was falling apart and I almost died on that island. He took advantage of the fact I wasn't on my game.'

'It sounds to me like something he'd been wanting turned up at his door and he made the most of it.' She holds up her hands. 'Which was selfish and dumb and just plain *wrong*.'

I run my fingers through the grass, rip a few blades from the ground. 'Rafa never did anything that wasn't self-serving.' But even as I say it, I know it wasn't true, even back then. It was just easier to believe that after he was gone from the Sanctuary.

'Do you think he meant it . . . being in love with you?'

'I don't know if he was capable of loving someone.'

Maggie takes a slow breath. 'And what about now?'

I rest my forehead on my knee. Rafa spent a year thinking Jude and I were dead. And then he found me alive, oblivious to who I was and the danger headed my way. He could've walked away. He could've messed with me so much more than he did. But he didn't. He stayed and he kept helping me even when I made decisions that infuriated him. He tried to keep me at arm's length. He made me stronger, tougher. And yesterday, he was willing to die for me.

Maggie reaches out and squeezes my wrist. Behind us, on the other side of the jasmine hedge, someone splashes in the resort pool. Someone else laughs.

'Is it weird, these moments from your old life? Do they feel like your memories or someone else's?'

I take off my shoes and socks while I turn the question over. I press my toes into the cool lawn. 'They all feel like mine, but . . . I think the last year feels the most "real". Which I guess makes sense.'

'So, everything from when you woke up in the hospital in Melbourne?'

I remember lying helpless on starched sheets, sweating, sobbing, believing Jude was dead. Killed because we were arguing over music when he should have been watching the road.

That darkness ate away at me, hollowed me out even in the fug of pain from a broken leg, two broken ribs, twenty stitches in my neck, bruised spleen and the monstrous lump on my head.

'I've never hurt so bad for so *long*.' My bones ache again

just thinking about it. 'That's what it feels like to heal normally? God, it's so slow.'

She nods, a wry smile. 'Sucks being human.'

I'm ashamed at how relieved I am to be Rephaim. But at least now I know how I really got those injuries, even if I still don't remember how I got to the hospital. I push that troubling thought away.

'You really need to talk to Jude about all this,' Maggie says. 'It must be the same for him.'

'Maybe not.' I look away. Anger stirs, faint and indignant. 'He definitely had a hand in changing my memories.'

'What makes you think that?'

'I heard him talking to someone. And then I turned into the sister he always wanted.'

'You don't know for sure he did that.' She falters. 'Do you?'

I pull up another patch of grass, crush the blades between thumb and fingers. 'No,' I concede. 'Not for sure.'

Maggie taps her nail against a tooth, weighing up whether to push the issue. 'Okay, but you have to talk to him. Like, as soon as possible.' She holds out her palm. 'Give me your phone.'

I hesitate but I know she's right. And I really don't have the luxury of a few days to work through this in my own head. We're maybe a day away from a showdown with Gatekeepers. I stretch my neck one way and then the other. 'Fine.' I give her the phone.

'I need to see Mum, so let's make it at the Green Bean.' She taps out a message, glances at me, blows her fringe from her eyes and hits send. 'Good. Now, wait just a second—' My phone buzzes. She checks the screen, smiles. 'Excellent. He's on his way.'

MY BROTHER'S KEEPER

Jude beats us there. He's waiting for me at the back of the café. Maggie squeezes my hand and goes into the kitchen to find Bryce. The café wraps around me as I weave my way towards him: the hiss of the espresso machine, the clatter of plates and cutlery, laughter. Ten steps in and I already feel more backpacker, less warrior.

Jude stands up when I'm two tables away. He's changed into a black muscle shirt and mid-length chino shorts. His eyes drop to my right shoulder and I glance down, see a dark smudge on my t-shirt sleeve. Dirt from the rainforest.

'Trouble?' he asks as I slide into the chair opposite.

'Zarael sent a scout. Immundi.'

'Where is it now?'

'Micah's taken him to the Sanctuary. Exhibit A.'

Jude pauses. 'You went to Micah?'

'No, I ran into him.' The tendons in my neck tighten. He thinks I talked to Micah instead of him – so much for us not going back to who we used to be. 'We saw the Immundi on the street. Thought we should do something about it. I didn't tell him anything.'

Jude sits down, settles a little. 'I've ordered coffee,' he says. 'And friands.'

'You trying to soften me up?'

He checks my mood. 'Can't hurt.'

He still smells of the ocean. I smell like I've been running and wrestling a demon.

'You told Rafa,' I say.

Jude gives an unapologetic shrug. 'He went to your place after we'd both left and Ez told him something was up. You saw what he was like when he found me at the beach. I'm not ready to answer all his questions, so the conversation didn't go well.'

I think about their tense exchange, words whipped away in the wind. The set of Rafa's shoulders when he looked in my direction. At least it wasn't all about me.

'He wants to know what happened last year, why I didn't tell him what was going on. More than that, he wants to know where he stands – where your head's at.' Jude gives a short, sharp, laugh. 'I couldn't tell him that – *I* don't know.'

I rest my forearms on the table. 'My head's a fucking

mess, Jude, that's where it's at.' I don't say it with anger, just stating a fact.

'You think mine's not?'

'I have no idea.'

'I don't know what it's like for you, but I've got two versions of my life playing over each other. And I know which one I prefer.'

I raise my eyebrows.

'The fake one,' he says, exasperated.

'You didn't seem too disappointed a few days ago when you found out you were a badass half-angel.'

'Come on, I told you I'd always felt like there was *more* to my life.' When I don't respond, he lifts his hands in surrender. 'Okay, yeah, I liked that I could use a katana and handle myself in a brawl. But I never wanted to run off and join the Rephaim circus.'

'You've been slipping back into this life so easily—'

'Be fair, Gaby' – and I don't miss the name he keeps using – 'we've been under one threat or another since you found me. I've been doing what I have to do to keep us safe. So have you.'

We watch each other for a moment.

'How are you feeling about the Mya situation . . . now?' I'm not needling him: I'm curious. How does he feel now he understands the significance of her betrayal?

His eyes flit away and his jaw tightens for a second. He lets out his breath. 'I need to work things out with you before I worry about anyone else.' His attention drifts to my right. Maggie's on her way to us, carrying a tray above her shoulder to avoid being bumped.

'Right,' she says brightly when she reaches us. 'I've got an espresso, short macchiato and two raspberry friands.' She sets the macchiato in front of me without asking.

'Bryce put you straight to work?'

Maggie glances over at her mum taking orders at the counter. Bryce is in white linen, her blonde hair pinned back, smiling patiently while a woman with stooped shoulders and gnarled fingers counts out small change. 'I offered.' She measures us. 'How are you two doing?'

'We've been talking for two minutes, give us time,' I say, not looking at Jude.

She moves in closer and drops her voice. 'Dani says the Gatekeepers are coming in a thunderstorm. You know a storm can roll in out of nowhere, right?'

'Malachi's keeping an eye on the forecast,' Jude says, which is news to me. 'We'll have a few hours' notice.'

'Is there a plan yet?' Maggie asks, placing two glasses of water between us.

Jude glances at me. 'Next on the agenda.'

Maggie tilts her head a fraction, and I see her reframing how she sees him now too. It's no doubt an easier adjustment than the one she needs for me. 'Right then,' she says. 'I'll leave you to it.'

'Oh, hey,' I say. 'Can you put some feelers out for

accommodation around town? There's twenty-seven of us here now and they're not all staying at our place.'

I wait until she's a safe distance away before I ask the most demanding question rattling around in my brain.

'Did you do this to us?'

Jude picks up a sachet of sugar, shakes it by one corner. 'No. Sort of.' A frustrated sigh. 'Strange shit happened in that forest in Idaho.'

I swallow, taste the memory of dirt and blood. 'I felt that blade in my neck, Jude. How am I alive?' He watches me for a long moment and then tears the sugar open, empties it into his cup.

'Jude—'

'It was an archangel.' He locks eyes with me and for a second I can't breathe. A chair scrapes behind me. A bus sounds its horn on the esplanade. Far, far away.

'Which one?' I finally manage.

'I don't know, I couldn't open my eyes. You don't remember *any* of it?'

'I was drowning in my own blood with my spine almost severed. So, no.'

He crushes the empty sachet. 'Yeah, I saw. Bel had no intention of killing you quickly. He wanted me to watch you lying there, paralysed, knowing he could take your life whenever he wanted.'

I feel the fear again, marrow-deep. What power in the world was strong enough to make me forget that?

'And then what?'

'Leon was swinging at my neck when everything went white. He still got me, but it was sloppy. I remember hitting the ground, thinking the Fallen had turned up after all.' He smiles to himself, bitter.

'Where was Dani?'

'I don't know, but she was with us when we left the forest.'

'Left for where?'

'No idea. It was pitch black and cold and I could barely move, but there was no pain either.'

My skin chills. I remember the icy blackness less than two hours ago when our shift here was interrupted. When someone gave us back our memories.

'I knew you and Dani were there. I *felt* you, here.' He flattens his palm on his chest. 'Like I do when we shift together. Except no amount of shifting in the world could have healed your neck. I couldn't have saved you, no matter what.' Jude stares down at his cup and I wonder if he's seeing me broken in the dirt, bleeding out in that forest.

'I'm still here.' I say it quietly and he lifts his eyes.

'Only because an archangel saved you – healed you to a point where medicine could take over. And then he left us on the opposite side of the world. Separated.'

I sort through the mess of memories, find that moment I came to in the hospital in Melbourne. Pain radiating through my body with every breath. Grief suffocating me. What did the nurse, Hannah, say? *It was a miracle you survived.*

'What happened before the hospital?'

Jude reaches for a glass of water, takes a quick sip. 'Whoever it was, he wasn't happy. I couldn't see him, but his voice hit me like I was standing in front of a stack of speakers. He said he was *compelled* to separate you, me and Dani so we wouldn't try the ritual again.' Jude says 'compelled' the way Nathaniel would, archaic and authoritarian. Fleetingly, I wonder why an archangel let us live at all given we'd been trying to release the Fallen.

'He said we had to forget we were Rephaim.' Jude picks up his espresso. His gaze cuts away from me. 'That's around the time I started bargaining.'

'For what?'

A self-conscious shrug. 'You. I didn't want to forget your face. The fact that we loved each other.'

He holds my gaze and I don't look away.

'I told him I didn't care what we believed about ourselves as long as we remembered each other. The thought of us not knowing the other one existed, after everything we'd been through . . . it was too much.' Jude sits his cup back on the saucer. It's then I realise the scars on his knuckles are no longer strangers to me.

'He read me – like Nathaniel reads us – and I gave him everything I could scrape together. All I cared about was creating a history that bound us, that undid the damage we'd done to each other.'

I'm staring at him. I don't know what to say, what to feel. Jude manufactured my memories. My brother turned me into a backpacker. My mouth is dry again. I take a sip of coffee. It doesn't help.

'I used your stories, and anything I thought might help us find each other – and a few memories to keep us safe.'

'Like the Rhythm Palace massacre?'

Jude runs his fingers through his hair, still damp. 'I wanted us to be at least half-prepared if a hell-beast found us. I could only give you something I remembered, and it couldn't be a memory you were in or it wouldn't have made sense.'

Suspicion slides in. 'It's not because you wanted me to remember Rafa?' Jude knew the truth about what happened between us. Was he trying to undo that damage too?

'I didn't have a lot of time to think it through, Gaby. And I don't have too many memories of fighting hellions that don't involve Rafa. That mess at the Rhythm Palace was my single greatest regret – after walking away from you. I had nightmares about it long before we went to Idaho. Maybe that's why it settled in our psyche as a nightmare rather than a memory. Or maybe that was the compromise because I gave us something real.'

I shift my attention from Jude to a shelf above his head crowded with scented candles. Try to sort through a tangle of images and feelings. If it wasn't for that nightmare, I wouldn't have recognised Rafa in the bar last week. I wouldn't have let him get that close to me. (Or would I?) And I would have died in that cage match with the hellion.

Noise continues around us, laughter, a crying baby, cars passing by outside, the blender turning mangoes into a smoothie. I smell maple syrup – someone behind me is eating pancakes – and a hint of patchouli candle. Everything so normal. But there's nothing normal about this conversation. About the reality of what Jude is telling me. I'm grappling with each piece of my life, turning it over, trying to make sense of it before the next fragment flutters by.

'What are you thinking?' Jude asks.

I focus on him again. I see the brother I've known for thirteen decades; the brother who walked away from me – but who reached out to me when the chance came for reconciliation. I also see the backpacker who led me up mountains in Peru, who convinced me to bungee jump out of a cable car with him in Switzerland, and who held back my hair when I threw up after too many jelly shots in a London pub. Those last memories may not be real, but they're as much a part of me as the real ones are.

'That dream about the nightclub ... it's the thread that started all this unravelling,' I say. 'If I hadn't written that story and put it online, Rafa wouldn't have come to Pan

Beach and none of this would've happened. We'd still be apart.'

'And if Rafa didn't come here, Dani wouldn't have seen you in the rainforest. She would never have known you were alive. Never told Jason to come and find you.'

Dani. She was so determined to tell us the truth about our link to Semyaza and then insisted on being with us in the forest. We almost got her killed performing that ritual. And then I put her in danger again, yesterday, letting her project her mind into a room where Rafa and Taya were being tortured. No wonder her mother doesn't trust me.

'The archangel must have changed Dani's memories too,' Jude says. 'And then used her and Maria to cement the lie of our new identities.'

We know they visited Jude and me in our respective Melbourne hospitals – in an impossibly short window of time – to make sure we each believed the other was dead. And then had all of it wiped from their memories.

'Presumably, our archangel didn't give Dani the vision of Semyaza and the ritual,' I say. 'So who did?'

'No freaking idea.'

My head hurts.

'Why'd you make me think my name was Gaby?'

'I don't know.' A self-conscious shrug. 'It seemed ... softer.'

'What about all the other stuff: Foo Fighters lyrics, the

Dark Thoughts website ... both of us wanting to come here to Pan Beach?'

Jude straightens and I think I catch a tiny shadow of hope in his face. 'Mostly it was stuff floating around in my brain. Except for Pan Beach: that was intentional. I thought if we gravitated here, we might find each other. Maybe actually have that life you used to write about.'

'Except you ran off to Tasmania with a hot nurse.'

He dips his head. 'Yeah.'

This is the point I could let him know I understand why he did what he did in Idaho and that we're still all right. But I can't. Not yet. Because he blunted all my sharp edges and he—

The full reality of what he's said hits me like a gut punch. Stops me cold.

'What did you give the archangel in return?'

Jude picks up his empty cup, sets it down again. Doesn't answer.

'You said "bargaining". What did you bargain *with*? This archangel healed us, gave us the memories you asked for – and we both know he left you more prepared for the truth than he did me. He didn't have to do any of it, so what did you give him in return?'

My brother meets my eyes. 'Gaby ...' His voice is thicker now, rough.

'What did it cost you?' I push.

'I don't know yet.'

'What did he say he wanted?'

A pause. 'My *fealty*.'

'What the fuck does that mean?'

'I have no idea.' He gives me a tight smile. 'But whenever the times comes and he calls in that chip, I'm probably not going to like it.'

BACK INTO THE WOODS

I'm still absorbing the idea that Jude made a deal with an archangel – a faceless member of the Garrison with more power than I can comprehend – when I see Ez come in from the street. She moves with cat-like grace, tall and lithe. The claw marks that run from her cheek to her collarbone are stark against her caramel skin. More than a few people stare as she passes but she's too focused on us to notice. Her eyes skip from Jude to me and back again. We both sit up straight.

'What's up?' Jude asks.

'The Butlers have gone off the reservation.' Ez is still in combat clothes: black trousers and black t-shirt, her dark hair in a long plait. 'Simon gave me their address but the place was empty when Zak and I went to check on them.'

I glance at my watch. It's too early for the pub but that

doesn't mean they're not there. 'Did you try the Imperial?'

'Yes, delightful hovel that it is. They weren't there either, which probably means they're on their way up the mountain to get their weapons.' She gestures at our empty plates and drained cups. 'You done here?' She doesn't mention we shouldn't be here in the first place. We should be with everyone else, forming a plan to defend the town against Zarael.

Jude and I exchange a quick glance. I nod.

'Let's get everyone together,' Jude says. 'The Butlers' camp is as good a place as any. Two birds, one stone.'

'Is that smart?' Ez says. 'It's the first place Zarael will check when he starts reconnaissance.'

'He's already started,' I say, and tell her about the Immundi on the esplanade.

'We'll be fine on the mountain.' Jude brushes stray sugar crystals from the table. 'We'll keep our eyes open this time.'

'Your call.' Ez's gaze shifts from Jude to me again. She has questions we don't have time to answer. And part of me doesn't want her to know the truth: it will change how she sees me.

'Can you get the word out?' Jude asks Ez. 'We'll grab our weapons and meet you up there.'

A tiny crease appears on Ez's brow. 'Do you need a hand with the shift?'

Jude blinks, hesitates for just a fraction of a second.

'We're good.'

When Ez leaves – still unconvinced of Jude's plan, but not arguing – we go into the alley beside the Green Bean. There's more bite in the sun now, the bricks around us radiating warmth. Jude touches my elbow, tentative.

'We're not done with this conversation.'

'I know.'

'Are we okay for now?'

I'm so far off balance I'm surprised I'm not walking on a lean. But we have twenty-seven Rephaim and an unsuspecting town relying on us to get our shit together.

'We have to be,' I say. 'We haven't got time for anything else.'

The camp is deserted.

Mud-splattered utes and four-wheel drives still stand sentry around the site. Cold and silent. The tarp hangs limp from a palm tree like a deflated balloon. The trestle table is on its side, guns and ammunition scattered over the ground, swags kicked to one side. There's a blackened smudge around the fire pit where Joffa collapsed, his jeans in flames. Even the makeshift targets hammered into the banyan tree are askew. The place smells of coal and ash and diesel.

Something's missing . . .

The bodies.

Where are the guys from Mick's crew who didn't make it?

Jude prowls over to the table, scanning the forest. I follow, pretending not to see the grass and leaves stained dark at the edge of the camp. The smeared trail disappearing into the trees.

My skin chills. Some of that blood must be Rafa's. I see Bel's blade, shining wet. Rafa, caught totally unprepared. Afraid. For a second I feel the forest pressing in: palm trees blocking the sun; thick roots sprouting down from the banyan tree like bars of a living cage; the high walls of the rock gully hemming us in. There are no signs of life: no parrots, no cicadas. The demons are long gone, but some trace of them must still remain. Or maybe it's what they left behind that's keeping everything else away. I tighten the grip on my katana.

The faint sound of a diesel engine carries up from the valley, revving hard.

'Here they come.' Jude is by the keg. It's sitting in a tub of water now instead of ice. He taps the side with his knuckle. 'Maybe we should encourage them to have a drink first.'

'Yeah, because alcohol always makes those boys more rational.'

He gives me a wry smile. I sling my sword across my back – I remember how to do that now – and help him retie the tarp between the palm trees. Then we lift the table back on its legs, stack the rifles, handguns and ammunition into piles. All the while we watch the forest, waiting.

The engine revs louder, gears grind. We wait near the fire pit in clear sight, eyes on the wheel ruts that mark the only way in and out of the camp by vehicle. A faded yellow four-wheel drive bounces into view, fishtailing in the dirt and spraying leaves and black soil. Mick's mate with the blond mullet is driving, wrestling with the steering wheel as the mud-streaked car bucks and swerves. Mick's in the passenger seat, already eyeballing us, one hand on the dashboard, the other awkwardly gripping the seatbelt from his shoulder sling.

The car careens into the camp and for a heartbeat I think the mullet's aiming for us. But then he slams on the brakes and skids to a shuddering stop about three metres away. I turn my face to avoid a lungful of diesel.

Mick is first out of the car. His shoulder is still strapped, but the bandage is gone from his throat so I can see the ugly red hellion bite interrupting the ink on his neck. Maybe he's not planning on growing his beard back on that side at all. Maybe he thinks it's a badge of honour: he's survived two demon attacks and has the scars to show for it. I'm not so sure he should push his luck for a third.

'What happened to waiting for a plan?'

Mick kicks his door shut behind him. 'We got shit to do too, you know.'

Rusty climbs from the backseat, nods at me, and leans back in for a crushed packet of smokes. He lights two, hands one to Mick. He's lost the dressings from his buzz-cropped head and trimmed his beard back to his chin. It makes him look younger. Or maybe it's that he's spooked at being back at the camp.

'How long have we got?' Mick asks me. He takes a long drag, blows the smoke away from his brother.

'To do what?'

'Bury our dead.'

My gaze strays to the stained grass. 'I don't know if they're still here, Mick.' I say it quietly, hope he understands what I'm saying. I don't want to have to spell out that Zarael's hellions may have taken Mick's dead mates with them. For later.

A car door slams on the other side of the four-wheel drive and two more of Mick's crew shuffle around to us. Woosha, his hand bandaged (the one missing a thumb), his shoulder strapped. Lip stitched. And – unbelievably – Joffa. Before all hell broke loose up here on Sunday night, I smashed his nose and stabbed him in the leg. And then Gatekeepers showed up and the poor bastard ended up with both of his legs on fire. How he's even walking is beyond me. Either Brother Ferro sent these boys home from the Sanctuary with heavy-duty painkillers or they've been self-medicating.

'Where's the big one?' I mean the other surviving member of Mick's crew, the guy almost as big as Zak and fully inked with tribal tatts.

'Koro? We couldn't fit him in.' Mick pats the bonnet. The engine ticks as it cools. 'That's why we're here: pick up more wheels.'

Jude gestures to the table of semi-automatic weapons and ammunition. 'You didn't come for that?'

Mick flicks ash away from the car. 'It's no good to anyone up here.'

'We haven't agreed on a plan yet. You guys need to—'

My stomach dips the same instant Mick and Rusty flinch. Jude and I spin round and draw our weapons, and my stomach lurches again – nothing to do with shifting this time.

Rafa.

He's arrived with Zak. He watches Jude and me lower our blades, his katana still by his side. I meet his gaze without thinking. It hits me then, a flare of humiliation, hot and sickening. Followed by a wash of memories from the past week: of laughter, of heat and longing, of Rafa pushing me to fight, trying to protect me. Me watching him take a demon blade through the gut. The crushing fear of losing him; the desperate need to get him back. All of it a swirling mess of sensations that leave me unbalanced and totally ill-equipped for this moment.

Rafa's eyes are dark, wary. I can't pick his mood but he's on edge. Maybe it's seeing me. Or maybe it's just being back here. He's already scoured the trees around the campsite twice.

Now he takes in my track gear. 'Good run?' His tone is guarded, barely smart-arse.

'Cleared out a few cobwebs.'

Rafa and Jude share a nod. Neither speaks.

'Where's everyone else?' I direct the question to Zak but feel Rafa's eyes on me.

'Ez and Malachi are rounding them up,' Zak says. 'Taya's with the barman.'

'Daisy okay?'

'Touch and go. Jones is sticking close.'

'Oi, Zak,' Mick says, and I realise it's the first time he's called any of us by name. 'Did you touch anything else up here other than the launcher?'

Zak turns to him. He knows what Mick means. 'Yes.'

My first reaction is relief: the hellions didn't take Mick's buddies as snacks. My second is dismay, because their bodies are probably close by and we're going to have to deal with them. I do a quick calculation. They've been dead a little over twelve hours: rigor mortis will have set in but they're still a day or two away from being . . . worse.

I don't remember much of what happened during the attack after Rafa and Taya were taken – mostly shouting, gunfire, agonised screams – but I remember the names of the guys Mick lost from his crew: Tank. Gus. Maxie. Hawk.

'Where are they?' Rusty's voice breaks a little on the question.

'In there,' Zak tips his head towards a ute with a heavy-duty roo bar and a forest of aerials. The tarp over the back is strapped down. 'I came back a few hours ago.'

Mick limps over to it. He starts working his way around the tray, snapping the elastic straps from their hooks. Rusty takes the other side and the brothers meet at the tailgate. Mick grabs the tarp, hesitates. I can smell the blood already, dry and metallic.

'They're covered,' Zak says quietly.

Woosha steps in and he and Rusty fold back the tarp. Four man-sized shapes lie under swags. Arranged neatly, respectfully.

'Thanks, mate,' Mick says, not looking at Zak. He grinds his jaw, blinks rapidly.

My eyes stray to something not quite covered by the canvas. A hand. The skin is already greying, the fingertips slightly bluish. Rusty reaches for the swag.

'You might not want to do that,' Zak says.

Rusty's fingers stall. 'I need to see their faces.'

'Not that one, then.'

Mick's brother swallows hard and then reaches past the first body to the second, draws back the far corner of the swag. He does it slowly, as if something might leap out at him.

It's Tank. I recognise his shorn head and rough stubble, the Southern Cross tattoo on his throat. It looks tired against his waxy skin. His mouth is slightly open, frozen until rigor passes. Milky brown eyes stare out at nothing. Of the four who didn't make it, Tank is the only one I knew. He took on Rafa at the Imperial last week with a busted pool cue. He was wearing a sling from that encounter last night and the tattered fabric is still looped around his neck, frayed and bloodied.

'One of those pricks gutted him,' Mick says. His cigarette is still between his lips. It bounces up and down as he talks. 'Nothing I could do.' He leans down to uncover the next face. I feel a touch on my wrist.

'Come away.'

I turn at the sound of Rafa's voice. He's watching me, concerned, and then something shifts in his eyes – recognition, confusion – and his fingers drop. It takes another beat before I understand: for a second there he forgot. He thought I was still just Gaby, not the battle-hardened Rephaite. That's who he sees when he looks at me now. *Gaby*. I don't miss the irony.

He lifts a palm, apologetic. 'You can handle it, I know.'

'That doesn't mean I want to.'

His eyes search mine. I keep my back to the ute, hear a strangled sound from someone behind me when they check the next body.

'Are you all right?' Rafa asks the question carefully.

'Honestly, Rafa, I have no idea.'

Something changes when I say his name, a slight

softening around his mouth. It loosens something in me too.

The Butlers finish their inspection.

'What are you going to do with them?' Jude asks.

'Pay our respects and put the boys to rest.'

Rusty stares at his brother. 'Up here? What about their families? They need to know they're gone. They need closure, mate.'

'You want to explain how they died? Or drop 'em at the morgue and get the cops involved?'

'Mick, the cops are getting involved either way. Another day or so and someone's going to miss them.'

The brothers eyeball each other. Jude clears his throat. 'I assume you boys know how to burn a vehicle – properly?'

Mick gives him a flat look, but Rusty nods, catching on. 'Make it look like an accident? Yeah, mate, we could do that.' Rusty looks around at Mick and his mates. 'At least the boys'll be found.'

'You'd have to burn *everything*,' Jude says. 'It can't be obvious these guys were already dead.'

'I get it.' Rusty glances at his mates – covered again – and rubs a hand over his scalp. 'We can take the back roads to the other side of the mountain. Do it there. Maybe roll it into a gully first.'

Mick takes a last drag of his smoke, drops the butt and grinds it into the dirt. 'We'll need a coupla fuel drums in the back. Petrol. Diesel's not gonna explode just 'cause we push a ute off a cliff.'

'You'll have to position the bodies in the cab first.' Jude says. 'We can help if you—'

'Nah, we got it,' Mick says. He slaps the side of the tray and nods at Rusty. 'You drive this one. We'll follow.'

The blond mullet disappears behind the banyan tree. He comes back struggling with two ten-gallon petrol drums. Mick, Woosha and Joffa climb into the four-wheel drive. Rusty helps the mullet load the fuel and retie the tarp, and then slides into the driver's side, starts the car. The mullet takes the passenger seat.

'You lot need a plan by the time we get back.' Rusty leans out so we can hear him clearly over the idling motor. 'Because Mick's got one, and it makes blowing up a ute look like kiddies' play.'

TRUTH AND CONSEQUENCES

We watch the Butlers roll out of the camp. No revving engines this time, no fishtailing. It's a funeral procession.

'Right,' Jude says and looks around. 'Let's get organised before everyone else turns up.'

Rafa doesn't move right away. He's waiting for Jude to talk to him. Or for me to. And I know there's something I should say – give him some clue about where I'm at – but I don't know what it is. So I follow Jude across the camp and pick up two canvas chairs. I dust them off and set them near the fire pit. After a beat, Rafa grabs another two and does the same. Wordlessly, we set up the chairs and spread the swags over ash-smeared grass. Jude does a quick stocktake of Mick's weapons cache and Zak stands watch, focused on the forest. I'm on my way to help Jude when my insides plummet.

I draw my weapon again, just in case, but it's Ez who

emerges between a flatbed truck and a dented four-wheel drive. Everyone else is behind her.

'Take a seat,' Jude says. 'And keep your backs protected.' Ez heads for Zak and the other Rephaim file into the campsite, carrying or wearing their weapons. Taya's hand is still wrapped in bandages but there's colour in her cheeks again. Malachi's tidied up his goatee and finally dragged a comb through his hair. Taya sits in a canvas chair and he stands behind her. Seth rests a boot on the bumper of a pock-marked station wagon and the vehicle tips to take his weight. I search for red hair, find Daisy with Jones. She's carrying a katana, and the hilts of her twin-bladed sais poke up over each shoulder.

'So you didn't leave town?' she says when she reaches me. 'Good to know.'

'I'll explain. Just stick with me.' I hold her gaze until she nods.

'I've got her covered,' Jones says. He's wearing his black beanie low on his head, dark feathered hair framing his face. 'She's not going anywhere.'

Daisy clicks her tongue but doesn't contradict him.

'Anyone spoken to Micah?' I ask.

'He knows where we are.' Daisy scans the crowd, spins her sword hilt. She's wary around the Outcasts – old habits die hard – but she relaxes a little when she sees Jude. He's standing in front of a sedan with two flat tyres and grey undercoat flaking from the door panel.

Ez breaks from her conversation with Zak. Her knives are strapped to her arms, the leather biting into her skin. 'Where are the Butlers?'

'Looking after their dead,' Jude says.

Almost everyone's found a place now, in a chair, on a swag, or leaning against a car. I consider joining Daisy and Jones on the ground but one look at Jude and I know he wants me with him. I cross the clearing and sit on the edge of the sedan bonnet. Rafa follows and props next to me, avoiding eye contact. He's close enough that I catch a familiar hint of sandalwood. It stirs the storm under my ribcage. I try to ignore it, focus on the gathering. Our crew.

The Outcasts should seem different to me now that I remember my history with them. For a decade, they represented all the shadows in my life – the reason my brother left me. But now . . . Now I've fought beside them, seen what it is they fight for. Had them at my back. I punished them over the years, and yet when Rafa took me to them – when I needed them to not see Gabe when they looked at me – they found a way. I never thought I'd look at the Outcasts the way I do now. As allies.

And the loyalty they've shown Jude, the belief that he didn't betray them. Out of the entire Sanctuary, only Daisy and Micah extended me that faith. And even then it came with conditions.

Rafa slides himself further onto the car until he's right beside me. Then he leans back and takes his weight on his elbows, lets his knee rest against mine. I can't tell if he's keeping up appearances – hiding the fact there's weirdness between us – or if he's reverting to form and trying to get a reaction out of me. Before I can decide how I feel about it, my stomach drops again. Someone else is here.

We're on our feet in an instant, all of us twitchy. I scour the forest, catch movement in the flickering shadows a second before Micah steps into view. 'Don't shoot,' he says, and holds his hands up in mock surrender.

'How did it go?' I ask as he reaches the clearing.

'Daniel was more than happy to take a stray Immundi off my hands.' Micah lifts his eyebrows – *I told you so* – and joins Daisy and Jones on their swag. 'He'll let me know if our ugly little friend has anything useful to say.'

Rafa scoffs. 'Help us? That'd be a first for Pretty Boy.' He's pushing, testing – he can't help himself. He wants to know if I'll defend Daniel. I don't bite. I sit back on the car and, after a few seconds, Rafa does the same. Everyone settles again.

'Where's your mate Jason?' Seth asks.

'He's in town,' I say. 'And so are Maria and Dani.'

'That's a good thing, right?'

'Yeah, but Maria doesn't trust any of us, so we need to keep the two of them safe but also keep our distance.'

I feel a spark of resistance from Seth, reflected around the group. They want to meet the girl who can find them in her mind; who has visions of imminent demon attacks.

Jones clears his throat. 'What about Mya?'

All movement stops.

The last time we talked about Mya was at the Sanctuary. After Nathaniel dropped the news that she was related to the women who built the iron trap in Iowa. Jude looks to me. I press my fingertips against the chalky car. 'They want to hear it from you.'

His lips flatten. He's not ready to say it out loud.

'For fuck's sake,' Rafa says, leaning forward to glare at both of us. 'I'll do it.' He cracks three knuckles with his thumb in quick succession and faces Jones. 'Mya was born on that farm.'

Jones stares at him. Nobody else utters a sound. The silence stretches out, interrupted by creaking springs when Seth repositions his boot on the station-wagon bumper.

'Says who?' Jones demands. 'Nathaniel?'

'No, Mya. And her family.' Rafa shares what we learned at the Sanctuary from Virginia and Brother Stephen. How Mya's grandfather Heinrich was a Lutheran minister back in 1874. How he was so horrified his daughter had taken a roll in the corn with one of the Fallen that he murdered her after she gave birth and then burned her body. How good old Heinrich was all set to kill the baby – Mya – when his wife went into convulsions. And when it passed, she claimed she'd had a vision from the Archangel Michael telling her their family was the key to protecting the world from the Fallen – and from us.

While Rafa talks, Jude's attention is fixed on a clump of churned-up grass. I try to read the Outcasts. There's confusion, disbelief . . . and a slow stirring of resentment.

Taya lifts her bandaged hand to get my attention. 'In the commissary, you said those women in Iowa believe we're the key to finding and releasing the Fallen.'

'No,' I say carefully. 'Not finding, just releasing. The family agrees with Nathaniel – the *only* thing they agree with him on – is that the Fallen are trapped in another dimension. But they believe the only way the Fallen can be freed is if we all agree to it: each and every one of the offspring who are alive, if and when we find them. That's why the old man didn't kill Mya when she was baby. He needed her alive, but separated from us to guarantee we'd never be able to free the Fallen if we found them.'

'And they knew about Jason, too?'

'Not until 1940. Someone in the family had a vision and they found him in New York. They warned Jason he had to stay away from the rest of us. Until this past week, he didn't know about Mya and Mya didn't know about him.'

'There's been a lot of vision-having over the last century or so,' Taya says, 'between this family, Jason's family.'

'But what about Mya?' Jones presses. 'How are we supposed to feel about that? About her?'

Ez crosses the grass and positions herself between us and the rest of the gathering. 'Mya spent her life with people who treated her as an abomination. Try to imagine what that was like.'

'I thought she ran away from home when she was seventeen,' Malachi says, ignoring the black look Daisy gives him.

Ez shakes her head. 'Something bad happened then, but she didn't leave.'

I picture Mya in that barn as a seventeen-year-old. Defiant and angry. Scared. I imagine her older cousins circling her, predatory.

'She got her own back,' I say. 'Brother Stephen said she torched the family church in the forties – we saw the photos.' I feel Rafa and Jude watching me but I keep my eyes on Malachi. 'And meanwhile, Brother Roberto and then Brother Stephen were playing spy at the Sanctuary, keeping the family in the loop on what the rest of us were up to.'

The mention of the traitor monks brings more muttering.

Brother Stephen, so frail now. It must have been tough for him when Virginia finally sent Mya to the Sanctuary. Had he even met his infamous relative before that? Did he talk to her? Was Mya so aggressive towards Nathaniel and the Five because she knew he was watching and would report back to Virginia?

Malachi scratches his neck, frowning. 'If she was meant to stay away from us, why'd she end up at the Sanctuary?'

I think about what the old monk told us. 'The family

needed an insider to replace Brother Stephen, who would've retired by now if everything had gone to plan. Mya was meant to win our trust and then "sow seeds of discontent".'

'So she came to the Sanctuary to cause a rift?' Malachi's wrestling with it all, maybe trying to reframe his brief and disastrous hook-up with her.

'Pretty much.'

More silence, heavier now. Even Taya and Daisy – always so quick to sledge Mya (they learned that from me) – keep quiet. Jones slides off his beanie, runs his fingers through his hair. 'Then why did she stay with us after we left the Sanctuary?'

'That's something I hope we get a chance to ask her,' Ez says.

'Do you know where she is?'

'The last we heard she was with Virginia and Debra. And Jess.'

Jones frowns. 'LAPD Jess?'

'She's Virginia's other daughter.'

Ez lets the Outcasts absorb that piece of news: that Mya's contact in Los Angeles – one of only a handful of humans who know about demons – is connected with the farmhouse in Iowa. 'But . . .' Jones looks to me, confused. 'You've met her, Gabe. Jess isn't a psycho. If her family thinks Mya's an abomination, how can she and Mya be so tight?'

'Maybe the rest of the family isn't as hardcore as Virginia.' And then I remember Sophie, Virginia's teenage granddaughter. All lip gloss, jangling bracelets and righteousness. Butchered alongside her mother by Zarael and his horde. The old rage rises up. Blasting that farmhouse with a rocket launcher wasn't enough. We should've turned it to rubble.

Jones drags a knuckle down the middle of his forehead, presses it between his eyebrows. 'I don't get it. Mya must have known about the iron room . . .' He's looking to me for answers. *Me*. The person who blames Mya for everything that happened eleven years ago and everything that's happened since.

Last year, I would have used this information as a weapon. I could pretend otherwise, but I'd be lying to myself and I'm done with that. If I'd known the truth about Mya while I was still at the Sanctuary, I'd have phoned Jude, dropped the bomb, and sat back and watched the Outcasts implode. Waited for my brother to admit I'd been right all along about her.

It's not like she doesn't have it coming. She intentionally tore the Sanctuary apart. She took my brother from me, my friends. She screwed Rafa in the training room and spent a decade gloating because he and Jude chose her over me. Always so full of herself. And all the while, a traitor. Just thinking about it tightens my chest: another muscle memory.

But.

The same Mya saved my life this past week. Twice. Both times she could have walked away. And I've seen what being an Outcast means to her – watched her convince her crew to return to that godforsaken club in LA to save damaged kids from a fate worth than death. I've argued with her and fought beside her. Copped her criticism and her backhanded compliments.

'You should hear her out.' I say it quietly. 'If she wants to explain, you should let her.' I can feel Rafa staring at the back of my head.

'That's easy for you to say,' Daisy says. 'You don't remember what she did. What it felt like.'

I swallow. Feel clammy.

Shit. I have to tell them. Nothing I say now means a thing if I don't.

But I can't. They'll turn on me. All of them. They'll forget the past week and go right back to judging me on the Gabe scale.

I'm taking too long. I should say something – *anything* – but all I do is stare at the flaking rust on the car behind Daisy, aware of every muscle on my face, hoping I don't look as rigid as I feel.

Jude leans in, turns his face away from the others. 'Do it.' He says it so only I can hear. A parrot squawks down in the valley. Our eyes lock. I see understanding – and a glint of fear. He doesn't know what will happen either, where the conversation will lead. I chew on my lip. He leans even closer, his shoulder touching mine. 'Carefully.'

I wait three more seconds – everyone's watching, now, waiting – and then I blow out my breath. 'Actually, Daisy, I do remember.'

Her mouth drops open. 'What?' She looks around, sees that this is as much a surprise to everyone else as it is to her. 'Since when?'

'Since we shifted here this morning. Something happened to Jude and me on the way. When we came out this side . . . we remembered a lot of stuff.'

I feel the heaviness of those words in the silence that follows. The implication. And the reality that I can't unsay them.

Micah stands and walks towards me with startling purpose. I slip from the car, tensed. The only sounds around the camp are his footfalls. He reaches me in six steps, and I instinctively lift my hands, defensive – but then he grips my wrist and drags me into a hug. I resist for all of a second and then lean into him, my throat closing over.

'I've been wanting to do this since I saw you at the cabin but I didn't fancy a punch in the head.' He pulls back to look at me. 'God, I missed you.'

I blink once, twice. If I start crying now nobody's going to believe I remember being Gabe.

'Thanks,' I manage. 'For everything.'

He knows what I'm talking about: taking risks for me,

even though I wasn't the Gabe he remembered; reassuring me I wasn't a complete tool in that other life. Being willing to come to Pan Beach, to protect this town I care so much about.

'The least I could do.' Micah kisses the top of my head and steps back.

I feel a pang of regret. How would he feel if he knew Jude and I tried to free the Fallen on our own?

'So what happened last year?' Malachi asks.

I glance at Jude. Do we—

'Bel and Leon caught us off guard,' Jude says before I work out how to answer. 'Gaby took a blade to her spinal cord.' He pauses for a second, takes a breath. 'Next thing I know I'm in a world of pain in hospital, thinking I'm a backpacker and I've been in a car accident – and that my sister is dead.'

'That's all you remember?' Daisy directs the question at me and I nod. It's not a lie: that's all *I* remember.

'But we remember everything else before that.'

Rafa repositions himself on the car so he's facing Jude and me. His eyes are storm-dark. 'Where were you when you were attacked?'

'Idaho.' I try to say it casually. Fail.

'What the fuck were you doing in Idaho? Is that where Goldilocks took you to see Dani?'

The mood in the camp slides sideways again. This is news, even to Ez and Zak.

'Yes.' I hold Rafa's gaze, hope the tension between us doesn't cloud his judgement.

Somewhere to the west, an explosion shakes the mountain. Rafa turns towards it, briefly, and when he looks back he seems to register my expression. He lets his breath out loudly through his nose.

'It's been a year,' he says, his voice gruff. 'Why remember everything now? What happened to miraculously bring it all back?'

I feel the solid blackness again, that icy touch. If an archangel took our memories, it was most likely an archangel who gave them back.

'I have no idea,' I say, and I know Rafa doesn't believe me.

LIGHT THE FUSE

The questions keep coming, and Jude and I try hard not to lie.

I wait for someone to mention our mothers. It's ironic: the secret we were most afraid to share – the bitter slice of history we kept from everyone for more than a century – is the very thing we laid bare a few hours ago. Our parting shot to Nathaniel before we left: that he killed them and stole all of us.

But nobody brings it up. I don't know if it's because the news is still too raw, or too big to grasp. Either way, I'm relieved when I hear the Butlers' four-wheel drive in the gully.

Conversation stops as the battered car clears the trees. The boys park where the track ends, at the edge of the sagging tarp. They climb out and face us, shoulder to shoulder: Mick, Rusty, Joffa, Woosha and the blond mullet.

Mick glares at the Rephaim. Rusty folds his arms. All of them on edge. They smell of petrol and cigarettes. It's a wonder they didn't blow themselves up.

'Okay?' Jude asks Mick.

Mick sniffs, nods. 'The fireys and cops'll be up there in an hour. Then they'll come looking for us.' He digs a nail between his two front teeth and flicks away whatever he finds. 'Sarge won't believe us no matter what we tell him, but he'll have nothing so it won't matter.'

'Plus,' Rusty says, 'there'll be serious shit going down by the time they get around to harassing us. You come up with a plan yet?'

Mick hawks up something thick and wet from the back of his throat and spits it on the grass. 'I dunno about you lot, but we're clearing out the town.'

Jude raises his eyebrows 'And how are you going to do that?'

'Simple.' Mick taps the side of his head. 'We make a bomb threat and get the town evacuated – let a coupla charges go on the esplanade to get everyone moving. Then when the place is empty, we blow up the main road either end of town and block access. Nobody gets back in for at least a few days.'

'Yeah,' Rafa says. 'Genius.' He leans his leg against mine, almost absently. I don't move away.

Mick looks around the campsite. 'Okay, so what's your big plan then?'

'We're working on it.'

'What's so fucken hard?'

Jude sits forward, his boots resting on the car bumper and forearms on his knees. 'It's not hard. It's the first time we've had to plan a defence. Usually, the demons are already wreaking havoc wherever they've set up shop. We go in, check out the situation and make a plan to ambush them.'

I've only been on one Outcast 'job' – two if you count the farmhouse – and that's pretty much how it went down.

'This time we have to wait for Zarael and company to show,' Jude says. 'We know they're coming during a storm, but not exactly when. No idea of numbers, no idea where they'll strike.'

'They've never come after humans before,' Ez says. 'Not like this. So that's a whole other issue.'

Malachi catches my eye. 'It'd be better if we could draw Zarael away from the town.' He's still standing behind Taya's chair, katana loose in his hand.

'It won't work,' Rafa says.

'Why not? The Gatekeepers are only attacking Pandanus Beach to draw us into a fight. If Zarael knows we're already here, we could jump-start the whole thing on our terms.'

And, like that, everyone has an opinion.

'How? Send back Zarael's Immundi scout?'

'As if Daniel will hand him over.'

'Where do we take the fight – beach or forest?'

'When's that storm due?'

'Do we have the numbers if he's recruiting Immundi?'

And then: 'It doesn't matter what we do, Zarael's going on a rampage through the town anyway.'

The last comment – from Taya – cuts through the noise. The Rephaim fall quiet.

'He's coming to do damage,' she says. 'Trust me.'

I catch the look she and Rafa exchange. After their time with Zarael in that iron room yesterday, they know his appetite for fear better than the rest of us.

'It doesn't even have to be a rampage,' Zak says. 'Zarael might let Leon loose with his new toy. Hell, they might have a dozen rocket launchers by now.'

Rafa shifts his weight beside me. We flattened the farmhouse in Iowa with Mick's bazooka. Zarael retaliated by taking out a wall at the Sanctuary, blowing up the commissary. The Gatekeepers are definitely enamoured with the firepower now.

'What exactly did Dani see?' Malachi asks.

'Zarael and his horde advancing on the beach as a storm hits,' I say. 'Not hiding, wanting to be seen.'

'Has she ever been wrong?'

My skin prickles and I can't help but look at Mick and his banged-up crew. Dani saw that happen and nothing we did could stop it. For all I know, we *caused* it.

'Not in our experience.'

Mick nods. 'Then the place has to be empty when they get here.'

'I agree,' Ez says. She's back beside Zak. 'But we're not setting off explosions. Anywhere.'

'If we don't blow something up, the cops'll think it's a hoax. It's the only way you'll get those fat arses out of the station.'

Mick flips open a packet of smokes in his top pocket and pulls one out with his teeth, stows it in the corner of his mouth. He holds out a hand and Rusty passes his lighter. Mick fires up the end, takes a slow drag and then blows it out through his nose. 'I'm not hearing any other ideas.'

Mick's right. Nobody's got anything else. Maybe they all agree it's the best plan. Maybe they're waiting for Jude or me to come up with something better. I might have my memories back now, but it's not a magic bullet. Ez was right when she said none of us had faced anything like this before. Certainly not Sanctuary Rephaim: we were too busy ignoring demon activity unless it held up our search for the Fallen.

The Fallen.

Jude and I need to decide what to do about them. Or, more importantly, what to do now we remember who our father is.

'Does Pan Beach have an evacuation plan?' Ez asks.

Mick shrugs. 'Has to. We're on the coast, right – cyclones and all that shit?'

'What happens if it's activated?'

'No fucken clue.'

Ez takes a calming breath, right as her phone rings. She takes it from her back pocket, frowns at the screen before she answers. 'Hello?' Her free hand strays to Zak's shoulder. Mick carries on talking – something about remote detonation – but I'm watching the way Ez's grip tightens on Zak. Enough to make him look up. 'Slow down.' She turns away to concentrate on the voice on the other end. 'When?' She listens. 'Okay. Stay where you are. Leave it with me.' She disconnects and her eyes meet mine. 'That was Jess.'

Jones twists round so he can see her. 'Is it Mya?'

'She's gone back to the club looking for a fight.'

'In LA? Shouldn't that be out of action by now?'

'The basement and club are crime scenes, but the bar is still open.'

'Which means Zarael will still have someone in play. They'll tip him off.'

'I imagine that's the point.'

Nobody asks why Mya would put herself in Zarael's path: provoking conflict is her idea of stress relief. But this is offering herself up to Gatekeepers. It's suicidal.

'She took two handguns and a katana,' Ez says. 'She plans on going down fighting.'

Jones grunts. 'And we're going to let her?'

Daisy uncrosses her feet, crosses them again. Doesn't look at Jones, or Jude. I can read what she's thinking. *Not your problem.*

Jones stands up. 'Are we going to let Mya get herself killed?' His voice is harder now. The Rephaim look everywhere but at him. They don't know what they're supposed to do now Mya's a confessed traitor.

'We've got a situation to deal with here, too,' Daisy says quietly.

Jones levels his gaze at her. 'We're never going to get answers from Mya if a Gatekeeper takes her head as a trophy.'

Daisy lowers her eyes.

'Ez should go.' Zak gets up from his chair. 'And Jude.'

Jude stiffens.

'No,' Ez says. 'He's the last person she needs to see.' She walks around the fire pit to my brother. 'Your opinion means more to her than anyone else's and if she sees *that* look' – she gestures to his face – 'it will gut her quicker than any sword.'

'What makes you think my opinion means anything any more?'

'Yours is the only call she's taken in the last eight hours.'

Jude gives nothing away. I wonder if he's feeling the betrayal. Or is this more about the fact he spent a decade fighting beside her at my expense? How does that fit now?

Either way, Ez needs back-up.

'I'll go.'

All eyes shift to me.

'Yeah,' Rafa says, 'that's a brilliant idea.'

'No, it could work.' Ez measures me. 'Assuming you can keep your temper?'

'I'm not coming along so I can hug her.' I manage a tight smile. 'But there are a few things I'd like to sort out before she throws herself on a demon blade.'

YOUR SHOUT

We arrive in the alley behind the club. It's late afternoon in LA, the sky washed out and hazy. The air still. I breathe in exhaust fumes, stale bourbon and something funky from the bins; freeway traffic hums a block away.

I hate this place. The gate to the caged portico around the back door is shut and locked. The last time I was here, Bel had me pinned against those bars. I'd be dead if Mya hadn't put two bullets in his forehead and one in each bicep. Gave me a fighting chance before she ran off to help Jess get the kids to safety – the trembling, dull-eyed kids we found cowering in the basement.

Mya's responsible for a lot of shitty, underhand things, but what happened here on Friday wasn't one of them.

I still don't know what to do with all these shards, all

these pieces of Mya. I'm hoping for an epiphany when I see her.

Ez takes a moment to check her knives. 'Gabe, can I say something?'

I nod, unsure if I want to hear it.

She lifts her free hand to shield her eyes against the sun. 'You've always been fearless, that goes without saying. But what you've coped with this past week – how you've handled yourself, not knowing who you are or who to trust … It's the gutsiest thing I've ever seen.'

I swallow, try to hide how much that means to me. 'I didn't do it on my own.'

'That's part of my point. You let us help you.'

'Ez, I didn't remember who I was. Who you were.'

'You knew we hadn't been allies in a while. Zak and I made that pretty obvious.'

I give a short laugh, remember their reaction to me in my kitchen: bracing for an attack. 'You stuck around.'

She studies me. 'You remember who you are but you're not the same Gabe any more, are you?'

'What makes you think that?'

'The fact we're standing outside this club having this conversation. And because you haven't started throwing punches.'

She doesn't mention Rafa, but there's no missing her meaning.

I head for the end of the alley, look back over my shoulder. 'It's still early.'

A few traces of last week's riot remain in the street: a burnt-out van, blackened and gutted; graffiti-covered rollerdoors peppered with bullets; crime-scene tape over a broken window. The front door to the club is covered in spray-painted phallic symbols and scarred with cigarette burns. Bolted to the side of the building are vertical neon letters that spell out Angels Den, lit pink even under the insipid Californian sunshine. A twenty-four-hour taunt to the Outcasts.

I push open the door and we step into murkiness. There are no voices. No thumping music. More crime-scene tape hangs over the entry to the strip club, empty darkness beyond it. I draw my sword. Ez has hers pressed to the side of her leg.

We pass through a curtain of faded purple and green beads – they jingle behind us as they settle – and into a narrow, badly lit bar. It smells like every other shitty dive I've been in: stale beer and musty carpet. Cheap cigars and cheaper aftershave. The only sounds come from a television mounted on the wall. A baseball game. Even before my eyes adjust I know there are only three people in here: a skinny barman with bony shoulders; an old guy hunched over a beer glass; and Mya. She's at the far end of the bar. Her katana is laid out in front of her, a bottle of rum and a shot glass beside it. The resentment rises, old and familiar. But it slips away before I can work out if I need it. Or want it.

The barman notices our swords. He grunts and shuffles to a back room. Mya pours herself another drink, ignores us.

'Hey,' Ez says as we approach. She pulls up a stool, gives Mya plenty of space. I stay standing.

Mya throws back the drink, bangs down the glass and finally looks our way. Her face is ashen, kohl smudged around her eyes. She looks older than the last time I saw her, worn down and strung out. She scowls at me.

'Have you come to rub my nose in it?' She slurs enough to suggest the rum bottle was full not too long ago. Annoyance stirs. I can't help it.

'I've come to keep you alive long enough so I can.'

A bitter smile. She gestures to the katana in my hand. 'If you remembered how much you hated me, you would've used that thing already.'

'Mya, she does.' Ez says it sharply enough to drag Mya's attention to her. 'Gabe remembers.'

It takes a second for the words to penetrate the rum haze and then Mya stumbles back from the stool. She snatches up her sword, knocking over the empty shot glass. Points the blade at me as she backs away.

'We came to talk,' Ez says and lays her weapon on the bar.

Mya's not listening. The tip of the katana trembles,

pointed at my throat. 'You must be so happy with yourself right now.'

'Oh for fuck's sake, you really want to play the victim?' I don't have time to coddle Mya. We need to get back to Pan Beach. 'After everything that went down between us, you had a chance to do things differently and what did you do last week, Mya? You dragged me to this shit-hole to score points against the Sanctuary.'

'Does it kill you, knowing you did a job with the money-grubbing mercenaries?' she says. 'Or is it the fact you did something useful instead of cowering behind Nathaniel?'

'Save the martyr act. It might work on Jude. It doesn't work on me.'

A harsh laugh. 'I knew the second you remembered who you were you'd turn straight back into the same old uptight, heartless bitch.'

I lunge at her and pin her to the wall by the throat. A stool falls sideways and I kick it clear. I bang Mya's wrist against the wood panelling. Once, twice. She drops the sword and I lean in closer. 'Then what does that make *you*?'

Her face hardens. 'The piece of shit you always said I was.'

I tighten the grip on her neck, smell the drink on her breath. 'I didn't like you. I never said you were a piece of shit.'

'You thought it, though.' She tries to push me away but

I slam her back into the wall. She could shift. She doesn't. 'You never gave me a chance—'

'You didn't want one.' Anger thuds in my chest, at my temples. Our voices are loud now. 'You came to the Sanctuary with one goal: tear the place apart. And that's exactly what you did.'

'Maybe if you hadn't treated me like I was something you'd stepped in, things might have been different.'

'Bullshit. You were always going to create a rift. That mightn't have been the original plan when your psycho grandfather let you live, but it served his purposes just as well.'

Her eyes go wild. She thrashes against me, throwing punches and lashing out with her boots. I toss my sword aside and block her. She swings again; I catch her by the wrist, wrench her arm behind her back and shove her against the wall. I grab her neck and press her face against the timber. Ez stays out of the way, but I feel her anxiety.

'You had *everything*,' Mya spits at me. 'You had Jude. You had Rafa. Everyone thought you walked on water. How much would it have hurt you to cut me some slack?'

'So your scheming was *my* fault?'

'I wanted a home,' she says, teeth clenched. 'You have no idea what it's like to be despised by your family, to be the *abomination*, the thing that has to be tolerated because it's their holy duty.'

'And that gave you the right to take away people I cared about?'

She glares at me through one eye. 'I didn't take them away: you let us leave. And you were fine without us. You still had Malachi and Micah. And Daniel. And Daisy and Taya worshipped at your feet for staying loyal to the Sanctuary.'

I should tell her how wrong she is. How losing Jude almost crippled me; almost cost me every relationship I had left at the Sanctuary. She'd understand: she's feeling that debilitating remorse right now. We've both paid the price for our pride and our lies. The realisation steals the oxygen from my anger because there's a sting of truth in her accusations: I did think I was better than her.

'You're not helping yourself, Mya,' I say, lowering my voice. 'This is where you remind me how you saved my life twice in the last few days. How if it wasn't for you, Rafa and I would both be dead in that iron room.'

'Doesn't matter, does it? I'm a traitor.' All the fight goes out of her with that last word. All the rage. She sags against the wall. 'You win, Gabe.'

I have a brief moment of perverse satisfaction – closely followed by shame. I lean in. 'Of course it matters. That's the whole point of me being here.'

She stays slumped against the grimy wood panel, not moving. Her neck is blotchy, her blonde hair flat and lifeless. 'Do what you have to do.'

It takes a second for me to understand: she thinks I'm going to kill her – and that Ez is going to let me. And even thinking that, the most reckless of all of us isn't putting up a fight.

'You're a lot of things, Mya, but I didn't pick you for gutless.'

She stirs under my grip.

'Do you care at all about my brother? About your Outcasts?'

Mya closes her eyes and a tear slips out from her lashes, leaves a watery grey streak down her cheek. 'I would have died for them.'

'Then suck it up, take responsibility for your own mess. And get your head back in the game.'

I give her neck one last squeeze and walk back to the bar, pull up a stool. I can't look at her any more. It would be so much easier if I could keep blaming her for what happened a decade ago. So much easier if I still felt superior to her. But I don't. I'm in no position to judge. I never was.

'Mya,' Ez says, her voice thin. 'Come and sit down.'

We have to get back to Pan Beach, but I'm still rattled. I check the doorway where the barman disappeared. 'Any chance of some service out here?'

He creeps into view, grips the doorjamb like he's ready to run. 'What can I get you?'

'Whatever you've got on tap. Ez?'

She shakes her head.

I take the rum bottle and Mya's empty glass and slide them up the bar away from us. 'We're done with this. She'll have a club soda.'

Mya lowers herself onto the stool between Ez and me. 'And a beer.'

We sit in silence while the barman shuffles to the tap and pours two glasses with trembling fingers. He spills some of mine when he puts it in front of me. It barely has a head on it. Simon and Taya would be appalled. I pull out some crumpled bank notes and realise they're Australian. Mya snorts.

'I should've known it was too much to think you'd be paying.'

The beer is weak and watery, but by the third mouthful I feel the tension ebb from my shoulders. Mya wraps her fingers around the glass, her chipped black nails stark against the pallid ale. She hasn't touched the soda water. Ez picks up a coaster, folds a corner over and then presses it out flat on the bar. On the screen above us, someone scores a home run.

'Ez . . .' Mya falters, seems to change her mind about whatever she was going to say. 'Is Brother Stephen okay?'

Ez puts down the coaster and meets her eyes. 'I don't know. A lot has happened since you took Virginia.' She waits for the barman to go down the other end of the bar and then gives Mya the short version: about Zarael blowing up the commissary, Dani's vision of the Gatekeepers attacking Pan Beach and the latest walkout from the Sanctuary.

'The other guys left . . . knowing who I was?'

'It wasn't about you,' I say. 'It was about protecting a town.'

'Even Malachi?'

Ez glances at me. 'The farmhouse changed a few things.'

Mya sips her beer, watches me over the rim of the glass. 'This girl, Dani. If she can see the Rephaim, how come she didn't know the truth about me?'

'She can't see you,' I say. 'We think it's because of the ink over your Rephaim mark.'

Mya reaches for the crescent moon scar on the nape of her neck, hidden by a Celtic cross in faded ink.

'She hasn't been able to see Jude and me since last year either – not since our marks were scarred.'

'I suppose it's pointless asking if I can meet her.'

I tap the base of my glass on the bar, watch sluggish bubbles rise to the surface. I know how curious Dani is to talk to her. 'That depends.'

'On what?'

'If you come to Pan Beach and help us stop Zarael.'

Mya narrows her eyes. I see uncertainty – and guarded hope. Just like Jason, sitting in a rickety old farmhouse ripe with chicken shit and wet feathers. Beating himself up over his inability to protect Virginia and her family from demons and the Rephaim. Rafa – in a rare moment of charity – threw him a lifeline. Told him we needed his help to find Jude. Told him to get over himself.

We've all fucked up at one point or another. You can't live as long as we have and not make mistakes.

The memory pulls at me. I knew at the time Rafa was talking about himself, but now . . . Now, I think he was talking about me too. Was that his way of apologising for the past and letting me know I was off the hook for what happened between us? I tip my glass away from me. What's left of the foam clings to the sides. I need to talk to Rafa about the last two weeks. And the last eleven years. I feel myself dismantling just thinking about it. I take a steadying breath and focus back on the bar, on Mya. She's staring into her beer again, her grip tightening on the glass. 'Do the others want my help?'

'You'll have to ask them.' Ez leans forward and touches her wrist. 'Mya, this is the showdown with the Gatekeepers we've been talking about since we left the Sanctuary. We need every fighter we can get.'

'Do you have a strategy?'

'The Butlers want to use explosives. Needless to say, I'm not a fan.'

Mya's eyebrows go up. 'Use explosives how?'

I'm about to explain Mick's crazy-arse plan when my insides lurch like I've stepped out of a plane.

Demons.

HIT ME WITH YOUR BEST SHOT

Two Gatekeepers: bazooka-convert Leon is closest to me. Both are wearing trench coats and carrying broadswords.

I shift – snatch up my sword from the crusty carpet – and shift again, already swinging at Leon's neck as I materialise. His reaction is sluggish but he manages to block the blade centimetres from his throat. I kick him in the sternum, drive him backwards, swing again. My muscles hum with adrenaline. The other Gatekeeper – it's Agiel, I remember now – ducks past us and I hear steel clash behind me.

The bar is so narrow there's hardly room to swing a sword without burying it in furniture or the wall. My blade locks with Leon's above our heads, we strain against each other. Long white hair hangs over one eye.

'You will pay for Bel,' he snarls, and spittle lands on my cheek. Up close, I see his eyes are more yellow than orange today, barely flickering. In a flash, I understand: he and Agiel are only here because they thought Mya was alone and easy prey. Neither has fully recovered from being blinded by Nathaniel at the Sanctuary last night.

I shove the demon away, grab a glass with my free hand and fling it at him. He's still quick enough to block the missile with his sword – glass shatters, beer and shards spray everywhere – but he leaves himself exposed for a split second. I strike hard and fast at his ribs. My blade slices through Leon's coat, shirt and flesh. He grunts and twists away. I wrench the sword free, risk a quick look over my shoulder.

Ez has drawn both knives and is keeping Agiel busy as he fends off her precision attacks. Mya wouldn't have stood a chance against one Gatekeeper, let alone two. Not on her best day, and certainly not with the amount of rum she's got on board. Even now, tag-teaming with Ez, she's barely moving half speed.

We don't need to be here doing this right now. Even if we manage to kill Leon and Agiel, it won't stop what's coming. Won't change the fact we've got a bigger battle looming on the other side of the planet. But when I look at Leon, all I see is Rafa lying in a pool of his own blood, sliced up so badly that even shifting couldn't heal him. I imagine Leon watching Bel go to work on him, goading and laughing.

'Say when,' Ez says and kicks Agiel's thigh.

He staggers back into the bar, grabs a stool and flings it. She ducks and it crashes into the wall behind her. Leon backs away, pressing fingers against his wound. Bares his teeth at me.

'You will beg for death before we are done with you.'

I lunge at Leon – and meet nothing but air. I stumble against the bar and I spin around, expecting an attack from behind but the worthless piece of shit has shifted out of the room. Abandoned Agiel to fend for himself. Frustration grips me. I *want* to fight Leon. I know what I'm doing now – no more second-guessing, no more hoping my instincts kick in. I feel it in my bones, in every joint and muscle: I'm *good* at this. I toss my katana from hand to hand, wait for an opening to help Ez and Mya, but Agiel notices Leon's absence and shifts mid-swing.

Pathetic.

Ez, Mya and I instinctively draw together, backs to each other while we catch our breaths. Leon's blood drips from the tip of my sword onto the carpet. I doubt anyone will notice a new stain. The old guy and the barman have made themselves scarce.

'We need to go,' Ez says.

'I know.' I glance over my shoulder at Mya. 'You coming?'

She chews on her lip. 'Does Jude remember everything too?'

'Yep.'

She falls quiet and I break formation to look at her. 'Are you in love with him?'

'Not like that.'

'Like how?'

Ez has turned too. Mya checks her sword, even though it's clean. 'Jess was the first person ever to treat me like I mattered. Jude was the second, and not because he wanted to get in my pants. He was actually interested in what I thought.'

'What about Malachi? Maybe you weren't paying attention, but he had feelings for you before you humiliated him.'

She doesn't meet my eyes. 'I don't do relationships.'

I glance at the clock on the wall. We've been here too long. 'Are you coming with us or not?'

'I need to talk to Jess first.'

'You worried you'll upset Virginia if you come back to us now the truth's out?'

Her laugh is sharp, bitter. 'I've been disappointing Virginia for decades, one more black mark won't make a difference. No, I want to see Jess.'

'Are Virginia and Debra still here in LA?'

'That's not your problem.'

A prick of annoyance. 'You need to make sure they're safe. If Zarael thinks they can design another iron room—'

'I'm not an idiot, Gabe.' She takes a steadying breath. 'They're safe for now, from Zarael *and* Nathaniel. Don't be getting any ideas about taking Virginia back to the Sanctuary so they can keep questioning her.'

'Are you fucking kidding? You honestly think I want Nathaniel to know how Virginia built that iron trap? I never want to see a room like that again, I don't care who has control of it.'

Mya narrows her eyes. Clearly she can't reconcile the fact that I remember my old life *and* I'm willing to defy Nathaniel. Old habits die hard for her too.

Ez puts a hand on Mya's shoulder. 'Promise me you're right behind us.'

Mya uses the neckline of her t-shirt to wipe the kohl streaks from her cheeks. 'I can't promise much, Ez, but I'll show.'

Ez and I shift into the top of the gully and hike down to the campsite. The familiar tang of eucalypt is a subtle comfort, until I hear sounds of flesh smacking on flesh beyond the trees. It's not an attack – there's no ringing steel, no shouting. But there's no chatter either. No trash talking, no Zak barking orders at someone to watch their footwork. No, this is the sound of Rephaim working out their tension.

We clear a patch of ferns – and I almost walk into the business end of a double-barrel shotgun.

'What the—' I snatch the gun and duck sideways, stopping short of pistol-whipping the idiot pointing it.

'Fuck, sorry!' Woosha staggers back into a palm tree, one hand up and blood draining from his face. His left hand – the one missing a thumb – is strapped to his shoulder.

'What the hell are you doing?' I snap.

'Keeping watch.' His bottom lip has three stitches where a ring used to be. He still has the row of studs over his right eyebrow.

'On your own?'

'I was taking a slash.'

I hand Woosha the shotgun. 'You don't have enough injuries?'

He gives me a filthy look and falls into step with us. We clear the trees and I see Mick, Rusty, Joffa and the blond mullet perched on vehicles, supposedly keeping watch. Their rifles and shotguns are trained on the forest but their attention is mostly behind them, on the frenetic hand-to-hand combat in the centre of the camp.

Woosha struggles with his good hand to climb onto the ute with Mick. He takes a quick look over his shoulder and then makes a show of scanning the forest.

The campsite has been cleared of chairs and swags to make room for sparring. Even Taya is at it, figuring out how to block kicks and punches without using her bad hand, telling Daisy to go harder on her. Zak and Seth have teamed up. Jude is putting Micah under pressure. I can't tell who's more pumped: Micah, being able to spar with

Jude again, or my brother, finally back at full strength and speed.

I shake out my arms, the adrenaline still thrumming.

The only person not striking, dodging and blocking is Rafa. He's on the sedan, watching Micah and Jude in silence. I've never known him not to offer a running commentary on Jude's technique.

'Heads up,' Rafa says when he sees Ez and me.

Jude immediately steps back from Micah. Rafa gives me a quick once-over and his eyes drop to the stain on my sword.

'Leon made an appearance,' I say before he can ask. 'He left with his head, unfortunately.'

'And Mya?' Jude wipes sweat from his forehead on his t-shirt sleeve.

'She says she'll be here shortly.'

He pauses, mid-wipe. 'How badly did you hurt her?'

Ez and I exchange a quick glance. 'I didn't. Just her pride.' I move past him to put my sword on the car. 'Have we progressed beyond explosives yet?'

Jude shakes his head. He steps back into a fighter's stance, gestures for Micah to come at him again. I watch them trade blows. In the corner of my eye I see Rafa reach around through the sedan's open window and rummage in the glove box. He finds an old chamois and wipes down my sword. I roll my shoulders. Watch Taya and Daisy spar. Daisy's still holding back; maybe I should step in and—

'You want to go a few rounds?'

I look sideways at Rafa. My sword is beside him on the bonnet now, clean. 'With you?'

'Yeah.'

I feel a strange quiver of anticipation. 'Are you up for it?' I make a point of looking over his chest and ribs. I can tell there's no bandage under his t-shirt, but that doesn't mean he's not sore where Bel carved a crescent moon into his chest – or where he was repeatedly stabbed in the gut.

'I am if you are.'

The way he says it, I know he's talking about more than my fitness. I can't pick his mood, and this isn't the conversation I had in mind. But . . . 'Okay.'

He slides from the car and heads to an area of grass away from everyone else. He stretches out his arms and cracks a knuckle on each hand. I take up a position opposite and shift my weight so I'm balanced and ready. Rafa does the same and we watch each other, uncertain. It's like when we faced each other to spar on the mats in Dubai . . .

Ah.

I finally understand his reaction when he pinned me in that training room. It was a little too reminiscent of our last brawl at the Sanctuary, which ended when I put us both through a plate glass window.

If you ever touch me again, I will end you.

That's what he's waiting for now. The explosion of anger. Payback.

It's still there, the memory of that moment. My humiliation. The outrage. But it's like ink in water; it doesn't hold form long enough for me to remember its shape.

'Are we doing this?' His eyes search mine. He can't read me either.

'Any time you're ready.'

He cracks another knuckle. 'You first.'

Nervous energy crackles through me. I step off and we circle each other, more out of habit than intent. The campsite has gone quiet: everyone's stopped to watch. Nobody except Jude knows what really happened between Rafa and me, but they all know it was ugly – and they're all curious to see what it means now. Whether it still matters.

Nobody ribs us for hesitating. Nobody says a word, not even Jones or Daisy. Too late, I wish we'd had the sense to take this elsewhere. Rafa is urging me to action, dark eyes insistent. I circle closer, shape up with loose fists. He does the same. Adrenaline fires my pulse.

'Come on.' He mouths the words like a lover's whisper.

I rush him with a combination of rapid-fire punches, all aimed head-high. He moves back, blocks them with his palms and forearms, makes no attempt to counter. I aim a roundhouse kick at his shoulder. He ducks underneath, doesn't take the obvious opening for a leg sweep. I alternate with punches and kicks, and we settle into a frenetic exchange – except I realise pretty quickly that I'm the only one attacking.

It's an open invitation to go to town on him. The thing is, I still haven't sorted through the storm that stirs in my chest every time I look at him. I don't know how I feel. I don't even know how I *should* feel.

But I know I don't want to hurt him.

It's hard not to remember him in the infirmary, helpless, struggling in and out of consciousness. The life leaking out of him. And it's impossible not to remember him clean and bandaged, naked, in my bed. Sweet and tender and still a little broken.

I fall back to regroup and he stalks me, impatient. 'Stop playing safe.'

I flex my fingers, gather myself, attack again. Another combination of jabs, hooks and uppercuts; kicks to his legs. He counters now, but without aggression: elbows, knees, forearms. My strikes are precise, well away from his chest and his stomach. I drive him backwards with a combination of punches, forcing him onto the back foot so I can aim a roundhouse kick at his head. He knows it's coming: it's my trademark move. He blocks and ducks – and then he drops his guard. I see him do it, but it's too late to pull the kick. My trainer slams into his jaw. His head snaps back horribly and the impact reverberates through my foot and ankle.

I hop backwards and drop my hands. 'What the fuck was that?'

He steadies himself and rubs his jaw. 'A good shot.'

'Bullshit.'

Rafa settles back into the stance, hands up. 'Come on. Go again.'

'Forget it. I'm not using you as a punching bag.'

'Don't—'

He doesn't finish because his stomach must dip like mine. We turn to the western side of the camp along with everyone else. My t-shirt is damp around my neck and my pulse still thuds in my throat. Sweat trickles down my spine. It can't be Gatekeepers – not yet – but it could be Daniel or Uri or Callie or—

Rusty appears in the space between the vehicles. He looks spooked. There are two blonde heads with him. Mya and Jess. Was Mya scared to come alone? Jones and Ez are already moving towards them. I wipe my palms on my t-shirt. God, I need a shower.

I hear Rafa come up behind me. He stands so close I feel his breath on the back of my neck, not quite settled to normal. Heat radiates from him. 'We have to finish this.' Frustration in his voice, and need. I try to concentrate on Mya, try to read the mood of the camp, but my head swims with sandalwood and honey and sweat.

'Does it have to involve fists and elbows?'

'Isn't that what you want?'

I glance over my shoulder at him, at the red mark on his face from my trainer. 'No.'

He searches my eyes again and then his gaze flicks past me. 'Hold that thought.'

I look back across the camp to find Jess has grabbed Rusty and pressed a handgun to his temple.

FORGETTING WAS EASY.
FORGIVING . . . NOT SO MUCH

'Get your finger off that trigger. Now,' Ez says to Mick, firm. He and his boys have their rifles trained on Jess.

'That bitch has a gun to my brother's head.'

'And I'll handle it.' Ez stops a few metres from Jess, Rusty and Mya, her arms out to block anyone else from getting involved. 'We're all friends here, right Jess?'

Jess keeps the barrel tight against Rusty's temple. When I last saw the LA detective she was dressed as a nurse – a stripper nurse in red stilettos – leading a group of terrified kids away from the club in LA. Now she's wearing jeans, navy polo shirt and a police-issue holster across her shoulders.

'So we're clear,' Jess says, her voice loud and strong, eyes scanning for threats, 'we're not here for a lynching.'

Mya stands rigid at Jess's side, her sword against her leg, sheathed. Her skin is still pale, her blue eyes not quite as iridescent. But at least they're sharper than they were at the bar.

'You're gonna *wish* for a lynching if you don't drop that piece,' Mick growls. 'Why is she even still conscious?'

'Because she's our *ally*,' Ez says. 'She's not going to hurt Rusty – he's human, just like she is. And she's been through too much with us. She knows we're not her enemy, right, Jess?' she says again.

Jess's attention flicks from Mick to Ez, to the deep scars running from Ez's cheek to her throat. Jess was undercover in the Rhythm Palace when Gatekeepers let hell-beasts loose in the club, when Ez was savaged trying to get people out. If it wasn't for Ez and the Outcasts, Jess wouldn't be standing here right now staring them down. And she knows it – her family heritage notwithstanding.

I still can't see any resemblance between Jess and Virginia. She grew up surrounded by zealots, knowing how generations of her family felt about the rebellious half-angel they'd been charged with managing. The *abomination*. And yet Jess is here, knowing we can disarm her in a heartbeat, trying to protect Mya.

'Nobody's going to hurt either of you,' I say. 'Unless you keep that gun where it is.'

Jess raises her eyebrows at me, a challenge. 'You speak for the Outcasts now? For Rafa?'

'Yeah,' Rafa says behind me. 'She does.'

'Even though she remembers the bad blood between you?'

A pause. 'Yeah.'

I take a moment to let Rafa's response sink in – for me and everyone else. I snag Mya's gaze. 'Is this really how you want to handle this?'

Mya shifts her weight, clicks her fingernails against each other. She won't make eye contact with Jude and I recognise fear in that avoidance. Not of violence – *that* she could handle. She's afraid the Outcasts are going to reject her. That Jude is. She runs her tongue over her teeth. 'Let him go.'

Jess keeps the barrel in place for a few more seconds and then lowers her hand. As soon as the pressure is gone, Rusty jerks away from her. 'Who the—' He stops, gets a good look at Jess. 'Fucken cop.' It's not a question. 'You're lucky my brother didn't put a bullet in you. You'd better watch yourself, love.'

Jess gives him a flat look, holsters her pistol. 'Noted.' She's faced down demons and hellions. A crew of heavily armed roughnecks doesn't faze her. But seeing Mya floundering clearly does. She moves closer until their shoulders touch.

'Oi.' It's Mick, his rifle still trained on Jess. 'If you want us to cover your skinny arses, you might want to move 'em inside the perimeter.'

Mya hesitates and then she and Jess come further into the camp. Jude is on my left, Rafa still behind me. Silence settles over the gathering and a light breeze flows down the gully sharp with eucalypt, laced with accusation.

Mya squares her shoulders and lifts her chin, fixes her eyes on Ez. 'You asked for my help. I'm here.'

'Why?' Rafa demands.

'Because this is my family.'

He laughs, harsh. 'I've met your family, Mya. Not a fan.'

'Then you'll know why I found another one.'

'And you just *forgot* to mention those crazies in Iowa? Or the fact the lot of you are hell-bent on wiping out the rest of us?'

Her eyes flare. 'I never wanted to hurt any of you.'

'So you didn't come to the Sanctuary to rip the place apart?'

'I went to see who was ready to walk away from Nathaniel – and there were plenty of you. I didn't create that rift—'

'No,' Daisy weighs in, 'but you tore it wide open.'

Mya turns on her, explosive. 'You know what, Daisy? I lied to people I care about but you're just as bad with this lie you keep telling yourself that everyone followed me. They didn't follow me, they followed Jude. And you would've gone too if I hadn't been by his side.'

'Jude wasn't the one with the psychotic secret family driving the agenda,' Daisy snaps, her neck flushed.

'They weren't driving *that* agenda.' Jess steps between

them. 'My mother had a fit when the Outcasts broke away from the Sanctuary. That was never the plan.'

Daisy rests her hands on her hips. 'Yeah? Then what was?'

'Mya was supposed to undermine everyone's faith in your precious fallen angel so that when the time came you would all scatter to the ends of the earth – well and truly divided. Creating a renegade group to fight demons for cash was definitely not part of the agenda. Mya did it anyway because—' She pauses to give Mya a side-eye. 'Because she wanted to.'

'Why?' Jude asks.

Mya looks to him, guarded. 'To prove that I was more than a weapon for my family.'

'Is that why you stayed, even after the split?'

'Partly.'

'What was the other part?'

I can't read my brother. He's giving her nothing, no clue of his mood or how he feels about what she's saying. And it's killing her. But she doesn't look away.

'I was born to be an Outcast. It's the only time I've ever felt like I belonged.'

'Then maybe you should've come clean with us a long time ago. Not wait until you were caught out.'

She laughs, bitter. 'It's so easy for you, Jude. Never a foot wrong.'

Guilt slides over his face. 'I was on the wrong foot when I walked away from my sister for you.'

'You didn't do it for me. You did it for yourself.'

A movement to my left. Taya. 'What about that iron trap?'

Mya drags her attention from my brother. 'Jess's sister Louise saw the design in a vision. It took Debra a year to work out how to build a house to accommodate the cell. Two more to construct it and have the walls etched.' A bitter smile. 'I didn't know it worked on anyone but me.'

'They trapped you?'

'How do you think they tested it? Virginia kept me in there for six hours. She was trying to convince me to leave the Outcasts and move back to New York.'

Taya's fingers stray to her damaged hand. 'But your blood breaks the wards.'

'I didn't know that. Eventually Jess told me – shouted it through the door.' Mya glances at the detective. 'I cut myself, smeared the wings, and got the hell out. I hadn't set foot back in that place until last week when Rafa and Gabe got themselves stuck the first time.'

'How long ago did you leave?' Ez asks.

A shrug. 'Two years. I didn't speak to anyone except Jess after that. And then the farmhouse was attacked and I wasn't there . . .' She falters, looks away. Mya wasn't there when Louise and Sophie were butchered in the cornfield after Zarael showed up. She saw Virginia and Debra for the first time in two years in that shitty old farmhouse.

Jones is studying Mya, a slight crease in his brow. 'If

your family is so horrendous, why did you rescue Virginia from the Sanctuary?'

'She's still my flesh and blood.' Mya taps the flat of her katana blade against her calf. 'And Nathaniel doesn't get to terrorise her.'

A light breeze shakes the leaves in the banyan tree. For a long moment, nobody speaks.

'So this is it then? Nothing I've done in the last decade counts?' Finally, the anger I've been expecting from her.

'You lied to us,' Jude says, his voice flat.

'Yeah, I did. So did you.' She's harder now, surer of herself. 'What happened last year? Have you and Gabe come clean about that now you've got your memories back?'

My mouth dries a little. We can't dodge this a second time without straight-out lying. 'This isn't about us right now, Mya.'

'Why not?' She's still glaring at Jude. 'You can't sit there judging me if you're keeping secrets.'

Ez faces us. 'You said you didn't remember.' Jude's jaw tightens and she lifts her eyebrows. '*Do* you remember?'

Jude and I exchange a long look of frustration and uncertainty and fear of what will happen when it's not our secret any more.

'Fuck it,' he says. 'Let's put it all out there.'

ALL OF IT

My pulse spikes. 'All of it?'

Jude nods and points at Mya. 'You're still not off the hook.'

She doesn't react. I catch Rafa watching me. He raises his eyebrows in a silent question.

'Wait for it,' I tell him.

Jude drags fingers through his hair again. 'Last year—' He pauses, scratches the corner of his eye, swallows. Starts again. 'Last year when Bel and Leon attacked us, we were trying to free the Fallen.'

Someone hisses; someone else swears. Everyone stares. Of course they do: we just admitted we did exactly what they've all been accusing us of for the past year.

'You were *what*?' Daisy demands. 'How? *Why*?'

I force myself to look around the gathering. At Daisy,

Micah, Malachi and Taya. Jones, Seth, Zak and Ez. Mya. I feel their disbelief. Shock. I clear my throat. 'We found out Semyaza's our father.'

A long pause. 'Fuck,' Rafa says. And then he frowns. 'Who told you?'

'Dani.'

'Ah.'

'She had a vision about Jude and me and wanted to tell us. Only us. Jason was against it, but she convinced him to reach out.' I shift position so I'm talking to Ez. Her face is the least accusing. 'That's what brought Jude and me together last year. And then we met Dani and found out what she'd seen. Not just about Semyaza, but about a ritual using our blood that could open the portal. So we tried – but we failed because we didn't know the rest of the prophecy, about all of us having to agree to it.'

'Why didn't you tell anyone at the Sanctuary what you were doing?' Rafa asks me, and then to Jude: 'Why didn't *you* tell us? Why'd you go it alone?' He's frustrated. Stung. 'What the hell were you going to do if you released them?'

Jude doesn't flinch. 'We were both done with the bullshit. All of it: the lies at the Sanctuary, our crews despising each other, not knowing why we exist. Being apart. We figured that even if we died releasing the Fallen, the Garrison would at least show up. That there might be some resolution for the rest of you.' A grim smile. 'Of course that plan backfired big-time.'

Rafa's eyes flick from Jude to me and back again. 'So who stopped Bel? Who changed your memories?'

'Seriously, man, we don't know. But it has to have been an archangel, right? I have no idea who but I know why – he didn't want us trying to get to the Fallen again. I still don't get the point, given we only had half the prophecy. We were never going to be able to release them on our own.'

Rafa shifts his attention back to me, as if everything will make sense if he stares at me long enough. I feel exposed, scraped raw.

In the distance, a siren starts up. Sounds like Mick's burning ute's been found.

I take a moment to check the mood of the camp. Rephaim stare at me. Stare past me. Stare at their boots. Expressions caught somewhere between shock and bewilderment. Except Daisy. She's pissed off and makes no attempt to hide it when our eyes lock.

'So Daniel was right?'

I bristle. 'No, he wasn't.'

'You just admitted you tried to free the Fallen.'

'But we didn't betray everyone.'

'Then what do you call it, Gabriella?' A new voice, behind me.

Rifles are cocked as I turn to see Daniel step out of the forest.

'Why the fuck do we even bother with a sentry?' Rafa snaps at Mick.

Mick glares over his barrel. 'There's a lot of shit going down here at the moment. It's distracting.'

Daniel is wearing jeans, hiking boots and a t-shirt and his hair is damp around his forehead. He shifted in far enough away that we wouldn't feel him and hiked in. It's not like he doesn't know the way now.

'You and Jude were going to loose Semyaza and the Two Hundred. You were prepared to die and leave them for us to deal with, without warning. What do you call that if not betrayal?'

Memories of Daniel rush over me. Our friendship, our brief intimacy; his varying degrees of disappointment in me. And then I remember my visit to the Sanctuary in search of Maggie.

He's standing there calmly pointing out *my* mistakes, after everything he's done this past week?

I don't think. I shift. When I materialise, I give him a half-second's warning before I lash out. It should've been enough time for him to defend himself, but he wasn't expecting an attack. Not from me – the old me *or* the new one.

I kick him hard in the solar plexus before he starts to counter, and then collect him with an uppercut to his chin. The punch reverberates up my arm and into my shoulder. He staggers sideways, grunts.

'That's for the cage,' I say between gritted teeth as Daisy skids to a stop next to me.

'What are you doing?' she says, but doesn't attempt to interfere.

I ignore her, watch Daniel steady himself and turn delicately to spit blood behind him.

'I didn't remember how to fight and you fed me to a fucking hell-beast. Did you really believe I'd understand *that* act of betrayal once I remembered who I was?'

He straightens and rubs his chin. 'Do you want to take another swing, then, for the other hellion?'

'What other hellion?' Daisy asks. Behind me, I hear everyone else moving closer.

'How do you think Bel found Jude and me in Idaho? Remember the hell-beast we brought back from Iceland? Daniel fed it my blood when he knew I'd gone to meet Jude and then Nathaniel used it to try to track me. Daniel didn't only lose his hellion in that little experiment, he delivered it straight to Bel. A hellion with my scent fresh in its filthy nostrils.'

'Oh shit,' Micah mutters.

'*Do* you want to take another swing at him?' Jude asks.

Do I? It would be so gratifying to make him bleed a little more. But it's not going to change what either of us have done, so what's the point? I shake my head.

'Pity,' Jude says. 'Okay, Daniel, what are you doing here?'

Daniel finally acknowledges Jude. 'I took an educated guess you would be reckless enough to come back to this camp.'

'That wasn't the question.'

A pause. 'I wanted to see if you had a plan for Zarael.' Daniel's gaze slips back to me. 'When did your memories return?'

'A few hours ago.'

'Are you here officially?' Daisy asks.

'No.' Daniel dabs at the corner of his mouth, checks his fingertip for blood.

'Are you joining us?'

Daniel gives her a flat look. 'No, Daisy. But I am curious about the timing of Gabriella and Jude's memory recall.'

'Get over it,' Jude says, losing patience.

'As usual, you miss the forest for the trees.'

'As usual you're a patronising dickhead.'

'Did it occur to you there's a reason your memories have been returned to you right now?'

'And what would that be?' Jude asks.

'If you're right, and an archangel took your memories only to give them back a year later, it might be because Zarael's retaliation for the farmhouse attack is more significant than you believe. If he leads his horde here, it might be the trigger for the final war between heaven and hell.'

'Wow,' Jude says, bitter. 'You're laying *that* on us? Bloody hell, Daniel, you're on fire.'

I stare at Daniel. Is it possible he's right? My stomach twists at the thought.

Then I realise what he's *not* saying.

'You didn't know I had my memories back before you decided to come here,' I say. 'You came to see if we had a plan. Why?'

He studies me for a moment, seems to be about to respond. And then his gaze flicks to Rafa. To the mark on his jaw.

'Gabriella has her memories back and that's the extent of your injuries?' He doesn't hide his disappointment.

Rafa eyeballs him, dark and dangerous. 'You worry about your fuck-ups, Pretty Boy, and I'll worry about mine.'

Daniel's lips twitch in a bitter smile. 'So you, Jude and Rafa . . . you've sorted your differences?'

'It's a work in progress,' I say.

'And this is where you want to be right now, with this group?'

'Yes.'

He studies me for a long moment, and I can see him readjusting his thinking. 'Then this group is in good hands.' He disappears.

Leaves swirl where he was standing. I watch them settle back to the ground and try to get a grip on my frustration. But my insides churn with anger and guilt.

And a creeping certainty that everything's about to turn to shit.

TIPPING POINT

'You know why he came here,' Daisy says, clipping her words. A strand of red hair falls over her freckled cheek. 'He came to make sure we've got the situation handled.'

Rafa scoffs. 'And if we don't? Is he sending us back-up?'

'I don't know what he was planning, Rafa, but everything's changed, now, hasn't it?'

'Why, because the truth's a lot more complicated than any of us would like?'

'It's changed because now we all know how much we've been lied to.' Daisy's voice is getting louder. She doesn't look at me, but she doesn't have to. I've already seen how deeply it cuts her that I didn't tell her what was going on last year.

'Then why don't you run back to the Sanctuary?' Rafa says.

'What's the point? Nathaniel's a liar too.' Her eyes graze over the rest of the Rephaim. They're restless now. Agitated and unsure. Tightening weapon straps. Flexing fingers. 'Nobody else here got anything to say about all this?' Daisy demands.

Taya glances at Malachi and then away, cradles her bandaged hand. Jones fiddles with the leather on his sword hilt. Micah watches me and I can almost see him putting the pieces together, assembling the bigger picture. Mya is tensed, ready to fight or shift, and Jess's hand rests on the butt of the pistol holstered against her ribs.

'What do you want to hear, Daisy?' Zak's deep voice fills the clearing. He's on the far side of the camp, gripping his sword so tight I can see the tendons on his forearm. 'You want us to turn our backs on Gabe and Jude now? Is that it?'

'That's not what I'm saying. I want to know how you lot feel. What are *you* thinking, Zak?'

'I don't know.'

'Me neither and that's my point. We're about to go into a battle – maybe the biggest and shittiest of all time – and the trust is gone. How are we supposed to do that?'

'What's the matter, Daisy? Scared to go into a real fight without Nathaniel to hide behind?' Mya snaps. She's hanging here by a thread and still she can't help but pick a fight with Daisy.

Daisy turns on her, eyes blazing. Rising to the bait. *This* is a feeling she understands. 'No, Mya, I'm scared to go into a fight if you're the one covering my back because you're a traitor.'

Mya takes the insult. Feeds on it. 'Yeah, well at least I don't just play at being rebellious when there's nothing at stake.'

'What am I doing right now?'

'Whining like a bitch.'

Daisy draws her twin-bladed sais a good second before Mya unsheathes her katana. They lunge towards each other – and then Ez is between them. Shifted from beside Zak. Her knives are out and she points one at each of them, brings them up short. She's breathing hard, eyes wild.

'Don't move, either of you. I fucking mean it!'

They both falter and I sense the shock around the camp. Ez never loses her temper. *Never*. Even Mick looks startled, and he barely knows her. He lays his shotgun on the roof of the ute, slowly, nods at his boys to do the same.

'I am sick of all this fighting.' Ez stands firm, arms outstretched and blades steady. Daisy and Mya lower their weapons. 'No wonder Jude and Gabe tried to force an outcome last year. Yes, they kept secrets they shouldn't have. They weren't alone.' She glances at Mya. 'But ripping each other apart doesn't change any of that, any more than it brings us closer to the truth.'

Relief ripples through me. Ez hasn't wiped us yet.

'The last twenty-four hours have been tough on all of us, and the last twenty minutes have not helped.' Ez finally relaxes her arms, although she doesn't sheathe her knives. She scans the group: Outcasts and Jess, Sanctuary exiles, the Butler crew. Rafa, Jude and me. 'Everyone needs time out. So go do whatever you need to for a few hours. Get some sleep, train, eat, hook up, I don't care. Just get your heads straight.'

I have no right to ask anything of anyone right now, but I have to. 'Listen, no matter how you feel about Jude and me – or Mya – Zarael's still coming and we need your help.'

Ez is the only Rephaite who meets my eye. Nods. She checks her watch and holds up a hand to the others. 'Zak and I will be in town at five, at a bar called Rick's. If you're still in, you can join us there.'

There's shuffling and muttering, and then half the group is gone without saying goodbye. Mya glances at Jude – he doesn't meet her gaze – and reaches for Jess. They disappear.

'Thank you,' I say to Ez.

'Don't thank me yet.' She says it over her shoulder on her way to Zak. 'I need time too.' Zak nods at Rafa and then he and Ez shift. My stomach dips as more Rephaim leave. Malachi, Micah, Taya. Daisy and Jude have a tense, silent exchange and then she's gone too.

Now it's only Rafa, Jude and me, and the Butlers.

'Think they'll show at Rick's?' Rusty asks, climbing down from the flatbed truck.

'I don't know.' Jude leans back on the car, glances at Rafa. 'I have no clue how this is going to play out.'

Weariness washes over me. I need a shower and another hour or so of sleep. But there's something else I need to do first.

'I'm going to see Dani.' I check Jude was listening and then lock eyes with Rafa. 'I'll be back at my place later if you want to talk.'

'What do you—'

I shift without waiting for him to finish.

I arrive halfway down the mountain, next to a large Moreton Bay fig tree.

It's quiet here too, but without the tension and recrimination of the campsite. I reach out, press my palm against the cool trunk. Run my fingertips across a patch of dried moss.

Thick, twisting branches stretch out overhead. Here, the forest shelters. Embraces. Morning light flickers down through the canopy, dappling the ferns. It seems impossible that a hellion could lumber out of these shadows. But it's going to happen – here, or on the beach, or right in the centre of town.

I see the faces of the Rephaim again. Watch them absorb the truth about Jude and me. If Zarael's pending attack really is the start of something much bigger, we need to find a way to fight together, but I have no idea how that's going to happen.

I reach for my phone, text Jason to tell him I'm coming. I wait for his response and then shift to his first-floor suite at the resort. The French doors onto his balcony are open and the room smells of the sea and guava juice.

Dani already knows what I've come to tell her. She was watching.

'I couldn't help it,' she says, sitting cross-legged on Jason's couch. 'I needed to know what was happening.'

She's wearing a sleeveless chambray shirt-dress and white knee-length leggings with tiny blue starfish on them. From the freshly cut labels on the coffee table, it looks like she's been shopping downstairs. From the prices, I'm guessing Jason paid.

'Do you know what's going to happen?' I ask her.

'No, but I remember everything from before, like you do.'

'Did something happen in the shift?'

She shakes her head. 'I don't think so, but I remembered it all when we got here.' She glances at Jason. 'I wasn't going to say anything, but I didn't want to lie to Mom and Jason. They know everything now.'

Jason is in the open doorway, blond curls framed by a cloudless sky. Anger radiates from him. At least Maria's in the bathroom, so I don't have to withstand accusing stares from both of them.

'They're not very happy.'

'I don't blame them. We should never have involved you.'

'I explained that I made you take me—'

'You were eleven, Dani,' Jason snaps. 'And they are Rephaim. How could you make them do anything they didn't want to?'

She twists round on the couch to face him. 'The same way I get you to. I'm a pest.'

He shakes his head and goes out on the balcony.

'Are you still taking me to see a koala later?' she calls out.

'Yes,' he says, not turning our way. Even mad at her, he can't say no.

I sit on the arm of the couch, nudge an oversized cushion out of the way with my shoe. Check her eyes. Try to see if the memory of the forest has stolen anything from her. 'What do you remember?' I ask gently.

'I didn't see what happened but . . . I heard it.' For a second she's back there. I hear it in her voice, see the colour leach from her cheeks. The terror. 'I hid, just like you said. A hellion found me' – she swallows, glances at the bathroom door – 'but then everything turned bright . . . I don't remember what happened after that.'

I reach for her and clammy fingers find mine. She still

trusts me, even now. What sort of monster am I, putting her in the path of demons again?

'I see the Gatekeepers on the beach every time I close my eyes. It's going to happen soon.' Dani traces a starfish on her leggings. 'Do you think everyone will stop fighting before they come?'

'You don't know?'

She shakes her head. I sigh, sink back into the leather couch.

'Me neither.'

And I can't bring myself to think about what's going to happen to Pan Beach if nobody shows up at Rick's this afternoon.

BARE NAKED

I don't want to get out of the shower.

The water is tepid – too many Rephaim beat me in here this morning – and there's barely enough pressure to rinse my hair, but there's something calming about our cramped bathroom. The powder blue tiles and the shower screen with the hairline crack in the middle panel. The smell of Maggie's cherry blossom shampoo and my pink grapefruit shower gel. The ceramic soap dish shaped like a giant shell.

It's home. It's safe.

If I try hard enough, I can pretend I'm still a backpacker sharing a cheap bungalow with my best friend, working a few shifts at the library to pay my bills. Not have to think about my mistakes. Or how many people I've let down in this long life of mine. Or the fact an army of demons is coming to terrorise my town.

I finally turn off the tap but I don't get out. Water drips from the showerhead and hits the floor in fat splashes. I feel myself start to air dry. Absently, I trace the collections of scars puckering my skin. Wounds on my legs from knives and swords and claws. Old and new. Gouges across my side from my cage match at the Sanctuary last week. Claw marks on my chest from last night. I feel for the hellion bite on my collarbone and then my fingers search under my hair to the thick scar on my neck.

Who am I kidding? I wear the body of a one-hundred-and-thirty-nine-year-old warrior, not a teenage library assistant. The time for that fantasy has passed.

I towel-dry my hair and put on undies and a t-shirt – the only clean clothes I brought in with me. I listen at the door. The house is silent, but just in case I'm not alone, I shift into my room – and freeze.

Rafa is sitting on the edge of my desk.

His eyes drop to my bare legs and then lift to meet mine. 'Hey.'

I'm acutely aware that I'm not wearing a bra. So is Rafa, even if he's trying to keep his attention on my face. It wasn't so many hours ago we were naked, entangled, breathing each other's air. Now our history has loomed up between us.

'Where's Jude?' I ask.

'He was still up the mountain talking to the Butlers

when I left.' Another quick glance at my legs. I should get dressed. But there's a part of me that likes Rafa off balance. It reminds me I'm not the only one whose edges are a little softer now.

I walk over to the pile of clothes on my desk. 'Let's hear it then.'

'Hear what?'

'What you've got to say about last year. What Jude and I did.'

'That can wait. I want to sort this out first.' He gestures to himself and me. 'I gave you a chance to punish me—'

'Punish you for what?'

'You know what.'

'What's the point? We both know what happened between us at the Sanctuary was a total fucking disaster.'

His gaze slides away but not before I see the injury there. The capitulation.

'Not last night,' I say, frustrated he could even think that's what I meant. 'The first time. We stuffed that up from start to finish. That fight . . . You tried to tell me how bad it was, but bloody hell, the things I said—'

'You weren't alone.'

I don't want to pick apart that decade-old slanging match. I find a mark on my t-shirt near the hem, probably chocolate. Spend a few seconds rubbing at it but all it does is smear.

'What about the past week?' Rafa pushes. 'How I've handled things.'

He's talking about stalking me in the rainforest. His impatience. His avoidance of questions about our past. And the lies: that he and I never slept together. That I stayed at the Sanctuary to be with Daniel.

I sigh, give up on the stain. 'I get why you didn't want to tell me the truth. If our situations were reversed – if it was you who didn't remember – I wouldn't have told you either.' I glance at him sideways. 'But I probably would've got more mileage out of it.'

'More mileage than licking your neck in public?'

I feel the slow spread of heat, surprised that after everything that's happened between us, that memory still affects me. I pick up a pair of jeans. 'I can't believe you had the balls to come to Rick's.'

A guarded smile. 'Now you understand why I was surprised you let me close enough to touch you. Then you kissed me and I kind of forgot myself for a second, especially when you seemed so into it.'

And I was. It was so unlike me – either version. But my body remembered Rafa, just like it remembered how to fight. Muscle memory of a different kind.

'What's it all mean, then? Are you back to being who you were a year ago?'

I drop the jeans back on the washing pile. 'Are you?'

'No.'

Of course he's not. He and I never would've had a conversation like this a year ago. Or a decade ago. We didn't do deep and meaningful.

'Me neither,' I say. I've been someone else for a whole year and I can't undo that – I don't want to. It's who I am now. I just happen to remember another life as well. I'm still figuring out how it all fits.'

Green eyes search mine. 'Gaby, I know I've fucked up—'

'We both made this mess and we've both suffered for it.' I glance at his chest. 'Things are different now.'

His mood shifts. 'Don't go easy on me because you feel pity.'

'It's not pity—'

'Then don't tell me this past week undoes the last ten years. I knew what I was doing back then – that you wouldn't have touched me if you'd known about Mya. But I wanted you so badly I didn't care. *I'm* the reason you and Jude were apart—'

'I made my own choices—'

'I'm the reason you hooked up with Daniel – don't think the irony of that was lost on me all those years – and I lied to my best friend, never told him why you stayed behind.'

Frustration radiates from Rafa. I give him space. 'Jude knows.'

He falters. 'Since when?'

'Since Patmos, last year. After our little run-in, he pushed me for the truth, so I told him.'

Rafa laces his fingers behind his head. 'Ah, shit.'

What I didn't tell Jude was what I couldn't even admit to myself back then: that it took a near-death experience for me to drop my guard with Rafa because I'd always needed to be better than the girls he hooked up with. And then I'd needed to despise him, so I could live with the choices that followed.

'Rafa . . .' The truth gnaws at me. I have to say it out loud to him before I bury it again. 'You and I fucked up monumentally, but I could've left with the rest of you, even after our brawl. I chose my reputation – my fear of humiliation – over my brother. Over the truth.'

He drops his arms but doesn't respond. He's too busy feeding his own guilt.

'Do you want me to hurt you, Rafa? Is that what it's going to take for us to move on – me taking you through another window?'

He meets my eyes. 'What else is there?'

'How about forgiveness?'

His chest rises and falls. 'Too easy.'

'Too easy? More like we haven't had enough practice.' I splay my bare toes against the hardwood floor, try to control my breathing. 'Does that mean you can't forgive me?'

'I didn't say that.'

'Oh, so *you're* capable of forgiveness, but I'm not?'

'Gaby—'

'I'm not going to hit you or kick you or run your head

through a wall, Rafa, so either you can accept I'm dealing with our past or you can't. And believe me, forgiveness isn't the easy option. It takes a hell of a lot more effort than breaking bones.'

He's still propped against the desk, arms folded, grinding his jaw. 'How can you forgive what I did?'

'Because I *know* you. Because I've seen the best and the worst of you. Because of everything we've been through in the last hundred and thirty-nine years and what we've been through since you found me in the bar. God, because I want to move forward.'

'Yeah, but—'

'Because I love you, you idiot!'

The sentence hangs in the air. It's taken us both by surprise. We blink at each other, take a breath. I feel the flush climb my neck, check that I mean it.

I do.

Not just for who he's been for the past two weeks, but for our friendship before that. Before we screwed everything up.

'No you don't,' Rafa says. But the guilt and frustration are gone, replaced by something more fragile.

'Don't tell me what I do and don't feel, Rafa.'

He watches me, unreadable. The seconds stretch out.

'Then say it again.'

I look him the eye. They're difficult words because they strip me bare. 'I love you. You idiot.'

Rafa doesn't speak and I can't tell what he's thinking. This quiet intensity is something new. I close the distance until I'm standing between his legs. I don't touch him.

'That's not easy for me to say.'

'Because it's me?'

'Because I've never said it before, and because I mean it. Rafa, the way I felt about you a few hours ago . . . that hasn't changed. If I'd told you then, would you have believed it?'

His eyes soften at the memory.

'Then believe it now.' I press my hand to his chest, feel his heart thump against my palm through his t-shirt. 'Do you want to add anything, or am I out on this limb alone?'

He guides me closer, his fingers light on my hips. 'How I feel about you scares the hell out of me. I've got no counter-moves. No defence. And now you remember everything, I've lost the upper hand.'

'You had the upper hand?'

A short laugh. 'Apparently not.'

We watch each other. *See* each other. I feel him inhale and exhale under my hand. He touches my jaw, feather-light, and then slides his fingers into my wet hair.

'I'm sorry.' He says it simply, quietly.

'Me too.' I swallow. 'I'm sorry too.'

He brings his face closer. When he hesitates, I meet him halfway. The kiss is slow, tender. I slide my hands under his t-shirt, needing to touch him. He makes that low sound in the back of his throat and heat spikes through me. I love the way our lips fit together, the taste of him. The way he uses his tongue . . .

I break contact first, but only to drag his t-shirt over his head and toss it on the floor. I step back so I can see him, and I can't help but falter. His torso really is a disaster. The crescent moon Bel carved into his flesh and the violent slash through the middle of it. I brush my fingers over the puckered scar tissue, over other fresh scars, all the work of demon blades. Rage, deep and dark, stirs in the pit of my stomach but I push it aside, focus on the heat of Rafa's skin instead. I kiss the point of the crescent near his collarbone.

Rafa's fingers tighten on my hips. 'What did I say about pity?' His voice is rough.

I straighten and meet his gaze, trail my fingers down his chest and over his abdomen.

'Trust me, Rafa, this isn't pity.' I hook my fingers into the top of his jeans and walk backwards to the bed, tugging at him to follow. His eyes don't leave mine.

I find the button on his waistband, slide down his zip.

He lifts my t-shirt over my head. I finish helping him out of his jeans and low-rise boxers. He peels down my underwear slowly, still not shifting his gaze from my face. And then we stand before each other, naked. It's not like we weren't together a few hours ago, but this feels different. More exposed.

My mouth finds his again, and now there's no hesitation. His response is all heat and wanting, arms circling my waist, lifting me onto the bed. My skin is alight, my breathing already ragged. The fire between us, this urgency . . . it's not about teasing, or pleasure, or even desire. It's about need. For connection. For forgiveness. I wrap my legs around him, pull him down until he's a part of me. His breath catches and his eyes find mine.

'God, Gaby . . .' he rasps, and I love that he still uses that name. That he can see me for who I am now: more Gaby than Gabe.

We move together, watching each other with an intensity that unravels me so totally I can't tell where I end and he begins.

We lose ourselves too quickly.

Afterwards we lie tangled together, pillows scattered around us, catching our breath. I'm warm all over, waiting for the feeling to come back into my legs.

'Unfair,' Rafa says into my hair. 'You're turning me into a seventeen-year-old with no self-control.' His stubble scratches my shoulder. I kiss his ear. He takes his weight on his elbow so he can look at me. 'Give me time to recover and we can go again. Maybe a little slower this time . . .'

I laugh – he's got more stamina than me – and then my stomach rumbles. Way too loud.

'Gaby, when did you last eat?'

I absently trace a circle on his thigh with my thumb while I try to remember. 'I don't know, a few hours before I went to Iowa? Unless beer counts.'

He sits up, draws me with him. 'I can't compete with an empty stomach. Let's get some food into you.'

I laugh and push him away, reach for my clothes with jelly arms. There's a demon army marching on Pan Beach and the Rephaim are more fragmented than ever. But right now, in this moment, Rafa and I are okay.

Maybe there's hope for all of us yet.

IS IT HAPPY HOUR YET?

It's like a plague of locusts have been through the kitchen. My pantry and fridge have been emptied. Locusts wouldn't have cleaned up after themselves, though. At least the Rephaim wiped the sink and packed the dishwasher.

'You hungry?' I call out to Rafa as I dig through the freezer.

'I am now.'

I look around to find him pulling up a stool by the kitchen bench, shirtless. Daylight streams through the window onto the worktop, highlighting every scratch and wine stain. He grins at me and that irrational sense of hope rises again.

I find a couple of blueberry bagels buried behind a frozen chicken and pop them under the grill. The coffee machine is already on, so I make us cappuccinos while we wait. Rafa gets out plates and knives, finds a scrap of cream cheese in the fridge. It's the most helpful he's ever been in my kitchen. *My* kitchen.

I watch the milk froth in the jug, hissing and spitting, think about how many times Maggie and I have prepared meals together in here, and I know it's true: the bungalow is my home. Even now.

'Okay,' Rafa says when I take the stool next to him. 'Now you can give me the full story about last year.'

I push the sugar in his direction and, over bagels and coffee, I tell him everything, from Jude's first phone call to what happened in the forest in Idaho. Rafa listens, making the occasional disparaging remark about Jason – more out of habit than genuine derision – but grows restless when I mention Jude's deal with whoever saved us.

'I wish he'd told me what was going on,' Rafa says, swirling the dregs of his coffee.

I use the tip of my finger and gather up crumbs on my plate. 'What would you have done if he had?'

'Whatever he asked me to.'

'No you wouldn't.'

'Why not?'

'Because it involved me. Anyway, it would've meant telling you we'd met Jason over a century ago, and that wouldn't have gone down well either.'

He drains his cup, doesn't argue.

I make us another coffee and conversation drifts to the

things we've missed over the past decade. I tell him about Brother Ferro wrapping his beloved 1949 Fiat Berlinetta around a tree halfway down the mountain after one glass too many of grappa. Rafa tells me about Jones taking up skydiving and Seth having a brief fling with a footballer in Manchester. About the Outcasts going to Bolivia to investigate demon activity near a mudslide and spending a week digging out victims instead.

'Mya said Immundi have been turning up in bigger numbers,' I say.

We're outside now, sitting on the front steps of the deck. I've got one leg draped over Rafa's thigh. The sun is on the other side of the house, starting its descent.

'If they're all in league with Zarael and he brings them along . . .' A chill creeps up my spine. I check the horizon. At least the sky is still cloudless. Someone starts up a lawnmower a few doors down, oblivious to the coming threat.

'We'll be ready.'

'You think everyone will show?'

Rafa leans in and kisses the top of my shoulder. 'What else are they going to do?'

I guess he's feeling hopeful too.

We head to Rick's a little before five. Rafa suggests shifting – no surprise – but I talk him into walking down to the esplanade. I love this time of the day. The sun is starting to dip below the headland and the sky is streaked orange, turning the sea purple and gold. Lorikeets gather in the park, shrieking and squawking in their usual pre-dusk chatter. The smell of burnt sausages carries through the trees; sounds of children playing, dogs barking. It's Monday, but there's always somebody on holidays in Pan Beach.

We're both wearing jeans and boots, our heavy-duty soles loud on the steep road. Occasionally my knuckles brush against Rafa's, and a few times I catch him glancing at me.

'What?'

He gives me a lopsided grin. 'Nothing.'

We're passing the shopping centre car park. I nod in the direction of his shack. 'Do you want to round up the stragglers at your place?'

'Nah. Let's just see who turns up at the bar.'

The esplanade is buzzing. Black-clad waiting staff are preparing tables for the early sitting, setting cutlery, lighting tea candles in glasses, straightening chairs. A handful of surfers are out on the water and two stand-up paddle boarders beyond the break are starting to make their way in. We round the bend to Rick's just as the fairy lights come on in the poincianas. It's beautiful and familiar and it makes my heart ache.

Jude, Ez and Zak are at a stainless steel bench under the verandah. They're in front of the window where Maggie and I usually sit to scope the street. The three of them pause mid-conversation to watch Rafa and me approach. Based on the empties between them, they're onto at least their second round. At least they're speaking.

'Neither of you is limping,' Jude says when we reach them. 'I'll take that as a good sign.'

I pull up a stool. 'Yep, all windows are intact.'

'Does this mean you two are . . . together?' Ez asks and Rafa and I glance at each other.

'Yeah,' I say, sitting next to him. Not wanting to care what they think, but caring just the same. 'We are.'

'About freaking time.' Zak holds out his fist and Rafa bumps it. I raise my eyebrows and Zak offers his fist to me, grinning. I half-laugh, slap it away. Rafa still hasn't made eye contact with Jude.

'Drinks, then?' Zak stands. 'It's fine, Gabe, I've already been in once. Nobody ran out screaming.'

Ez rises too. 'I'll go with him. Really give them something to talk about.'

I know she means her scars, but that's not why people stare. They stare because she's beautiful – even with the claw marks – and Zak is impossible to miss with his flawless ebony skin and massive shoulders. He ducks to clear the doorway as they go inside. Heads immediately turn. Murmuring follows. They make their way to the bar, and I'm surprised to see Simon behind it. His movements are tentative but he can reach the glasses and work the tap, so he's managing. He carefully pours a beer and hands it to Taya. She's sitting with Malachi, half-turned to the street, ready for action. But she makes a show of inspecting the beer and nods her approval.

'She can do better,' Rafa says, following my gaze.

'The beer or Simon?'

'Both.'

I roll my eyes. 'Get over it.'

I turn back to the table to find Jude bending back the edges of a coaster, lost in thought. Rafa glances at him and reaches for an empty beer bottle, peels a strip off the label. Neither of them speaks for a good half a minute. I should say something, get them started—

'Fuck, Jude,' Rafa says in a burst of impatience. 'If you didn't want me to know what you were doing last year, why'd you leave all that cryptic shit on your laptop?'

Jude tears a corner from the coaster. 'I set all that up before I had any idea what was going to happen.'

'What for?'

Another piece of coaster drops to the bench. 'Back in the day, Gabe and I used to joke about seeing the world without demon blood on our hands. After we left the Sanctuary, I hung on to the idea of us still disappearing one day to sort ourselves out – without everyone else weighing in with an opinion.'

'Everyone, as in me.'

Jude lets that slide. 'A few times, after too much tequila,

I'd trawl the web for places we could go, bookmarked sites – stupid stuff like that. And then last year, Jason called. Next thing, I'm sitting on the pier at Santa Monica with my sister, and the idea didn't seem so crazy. I didn't know what was going to happen when we met Dani, but either way, I was going to float the plan to Gabe of us taking time out. Before I left that last time, I cleaned out the laptop except for those few bits and pieces—'

'Yeah, but *why*?'

'Because I didn't want to disappear without leaving you some hint of where I'd gone.'

'You could've just told me.'

'And when would I have done that – on the patio at Patmos? Before or after Gabe broke your nose?'

'If I'd known what the fuck was going on, that exchange might have gone down differently.'

'No it wouldn't have, and you know it. Not how things were back then. And by that point, it wasn't only about us. Gabe and I knew enough about Dani to put her at risk if we talked to anyone else.'

'Leaving random clues was an idiotic plan – even before Mya stole your laptop.'

'Yeah, well,' Jude says. 'Nothing quite worked out the way I intended. And I wasn't the only one being selective with information.'

Rafa peels another strip from the bottle, pastes it next to the first one. Between the label and Jude's half-destroyed coaster they're making a mess of the bench. 'How the hell was I supposed to talk to you about *that*?' Rafa says.

'You're certainly not discussing it now.' I'm all for them talking through their issues, but not if it involves my sex life. 'And enough with the craft projects.' I snatch the coaster from my brother and the bottle from Rafa. They both look at me, startled.

'Do you want to keep picking apart your mistakes, or can you move on?'

Jude gestures to Rafa. 'I can if he can.'

'Of course I can,' Rafa says. 'It's not like I've got the high ground here.'

They watch each other for a full five seconds. And then they slap their palms together, lean over the bench and thump each other on the back.

And like that, they're good.

Guys. Unbelievable.

Rafa straightens. 'Right. Where's our beer?'

He heads inside and Jude and I sit without speaking while half a dozen motorbikes rumble past. Exhaust fumes waft over us.

'Princess . . .' He says it tentatively, as if he's not sure how I'll react to the nickname now.

'It's okay,' I say. 'We're okay.'

Jude meets my eyes. 'I need to say it.' He reaches for the scraps of coaster, stops himself. 'When you found me on the dock in Tasmania – when I realised you were alive

– that was the biggest moment of my life. It still is, even remembering everything else.'

I nod. The world dropped away for me too when I saw him on that boat. I remember how it felt to cling to him, feel his heart beating, his tears hot on my neck. *Alive.*

'That life we remembered might have been a lie,' he says, 'but I miss it more than the real one.'

The lie: travelling the world together. Laughing. Looking out for each other. Promising we'd always have each other's backs. And the more recent promise made in ignorance: that no matter what we found out about ourselves, we wouldn't let it tear us apart.

'Me too,' I say.

'Really?'

'They were good memories.' I brush my cheek, smile at him through wet eyes. He takes my fingers, holds them tight. For the first time since arriving in my kitchen this morning, I finally fit this skin.

Rafa is on his way back out with Ez and Zak. At the bar, Taya says something to Simon – he looks unnerved now – and then she and Malachi follow. I check my watch. It's well past five. Is this it then? The seven of us against Zarael and his horde?

The sky is darker now, bruised in the dying light. I see it in the gathering dusk, far out on the horizon, and my heart gives a painful thump.

A bank of thunderclouds.

THE LAST SUPPER

'We ordered pizza.'

Ez hands me a drink and the others bring over two more tables – Taya helping one-handed – and claim the spare stools. There's nothing like optimism. A couple of surfers lean on the railing at the other end of the verandah, hair damp and board shorts low on their hips. Actively ignoring us. Maybe they were here for the brawl last week and remember seeing Rafa, Jones and Taya in action.

Ez glances at the clouds over the sea. 'I thought we had until Wednesday?'

'Maybe that storm won't make landfall,' I say. Or maybe Zarael's summoned something so nasty from the pit it's messing with the weather. 'Hey Malachi, I thought you were keeping an eye on the radar?'

Malachi looks to the east and grabs his phone. 'There was nothing half an hour ago.' He taps the screen, frowns. 'Huh. Now there's a storm warning. It's supposed to hit sometime in the next few hours.'

I feel a chill, even though the breeze coming off the water is warm. We're not even close to being ready for Zarael. I try to ignore the image of Gatekeepers overrunning the esplanade. The first priority is having a force to greet them, and right now we're seriously low on numbers.

'We can still eat,' Taya says. She sits next to me, clinks her glass against my bottle. 'Here's to you forgiving me for that little incident in the park.' She means the night she kicked the shit out of me: my introduction to the Sanctuary Rephaim post-memory loss. 'I thought you'd run off with Rafa and joined the circus' – she tips her glass in his direction – 'no offence.'

'And at the Sanctuary?' I say, willing myself into the conversation. 'When you suggested I deserved to die?' I'm not pissed off at her, just remembering.

Alarm flickers across her face. It's the same look I got at the Sanctuary when I tried to bluff her and Malachi into thinking I remembered how to fight. 'We thought you'd screwed up our chances with the Garrison.'

I laugh without humour. 'It wasn't for lack of trying.'

She takes a swig of beer. 'So, now you remember who you are – that doesn't change anything here, does it?'

'Did you think it would?'

Taya studies me for a second. 'I've given up trying to second-guess you.' She scans the street, absently fiddles with the edge of the bandage on her hand. 'About time.' She's spotted Daisy, Jones and Micah crossing the road. There's no mistaking Daisy and Jones for tourists. They walk with too much purpose, too much tension. They head straight for the bar but Daisy glances our way before she goes inside. Seth and a handful of Outcasts cross from the opposite direction and follow them into Rick's.

'Never let it be said those boys back down from a fight,' Ez says. The Butlers are stalking our way a few doors down from the bar. Mick has lost the sling, though his arm doesn't quite hang naturally. He's surrounded by denim and ink: Rusty, Joffa, Woosha, the blond mullet, and the giant with the tribal tatts. Their numbers are bolstered by the hoodie brigade – the barely pubescent chain-smoking, footpath-spitting crew led by Mick and Rusty's younger brothers.

Mick and Rusty come straight to us. Mick signals for the hoodie brigade to keep going. The tallest of the five boys scowls at him, facial piercings catching the light from the bar. Definitely a Butler. He's the smart-arse who sassed me on the street last week. He checks me out – more respect now – and shoves his hands in his pockets. Then he jerks his head at his mates and they amble along to their usual loitering spot under a blue neon sign promising Pan Beach's best steak sandwiches.

'You recruiting them out of high school?' Rafa says to Mick.

Mick ignores him and glances through the open window to the bar. 'The world must be ending for me to be drinking at Wankers Central.'

It's then I notice Mick and Rusty are the cleanest I've ever seen them. Beards trimmed, faces scrubbed. Rusty's scraped the crud from under his nails. Even Mick's oil-stained fingers are more pinkish than black. They're in jeans – threadbare at the knees but clean – and fresh flannelette shirts with the sleeves rolled up past their elbows. This is their idea of sprucing up – court appearances notwithstanding.

'Had a visit from the cops this arvo,' Mick says, watching the drinkers inside part to let his mates through. 'They found the ute. Sarge didn't push it today, but he'll be back.'

Around us, more Rephaim arrive. The weight finally lifts: we're not in this alone. Rusty raises his eyebrows at Ez. 'Where's the crazy blonde and her pet cop?'

'Not here yet,' Ez says. 'And don't ever call Jess that again.'

Daisy, Micah and Jones sit at the next bench, not quite ready to talk to us. By the time our food comes out, the verandah is crowded. I do a quick head count and feel a ripple of relief. We're all here, the same disobedient crew that left the Sanctuary less than twelve hours ago. Back then, of course, we were united. Now, not so much. The

Rephaim cluster around tables and wine barrels, talk to each other in low voices. Eyes flick in our direction, wary, as if Jude and I are dangerous. Whether we like it or not, our link to Semyaza sets us apart now.

I take a bite of wood-fired pizza: roasted pumpkin, sage, goat's feta, caramelised onion. It's never tasted better.

'By the way,' I say in Daisy's direction, still chewing. 'Who cleaned out my fridge this morning?'

She shrugs. 'You should've stocked up before you invited half the Sanctuary back to your place.'

'Nice to see you're still good on the tooth.'

She half-smiles, her mouth full of souvlaki. 'Look who's talking.'

I half-smile in response, feel the distance between us shrink a little.

'So, you're here to fight with us?' Jude directs the question to the entire table, but looks only at Daisy.

'No, just the food.' She wipes her mouth on a paper napkin and meets his gaze. 'Like Ez said, there's still a town to protect.'

Jude nods, satisfied.

'What is this shit?' Mick picks at the crust of his pizza like it's something he found on the bottom of his boot. 'Where's the pineapple?'

'Bro, it's *gourmet*,' Rusty says. 'Ton of fucken rabbit food where the pineapple's supposed to be.'

I look around at the unlikely gathering: Outcasts and

Sanctuary Rephaim. Mick and his crew. And me – *me* – here with Rafa and Jude. Things aren't perfect, but they're the best they've been for more than a decade.

Rafa leans in. 'You getting misty-eyed over the Butlers?'

'Yeah, right.' I laugh, embarrassed, and reach for my glass. But then I see the softness in the set of his lips, a knowing. He gets it. I touch the bruise on his jaw, the one I gave him when we were sparring. 'You need to let me heal this.'

'May as well wait until I have a few more.'

'I'd rather you ease up on the bruise count.'

His lips curve a little. 'Does this mean you worry about me now?'

'You've always been a worry.' He's close enough to kiss and for a second I seriously think about it. And then I remember where we are. By the time I draw back at least half of the Rephaim are watching us, fascinated.

'Look who else has decided to show,' Jones says.

Mya and Jess are standing on the footpath beyond the verandah. Mya is wearing jeans and a loose-fitting t-shirt. Her hair is tied back and she's been unusually sparing with the kohl. Battle-ready.

Jess has come without the shoulder holster – good call – but she's wearing boot-cut jeans, which probably means there's a small handgun strapped to one or both of those ankles. Waves break on the beach across the road, louder now under the streaky orange sky. Am I paranoid or have storm clouds swept closer in the last ten minutes?

Mya is defiant, chin set, her back to the sea. 'I'm here to help. Take it or leave it.'

'That's it?' Rafa says. 'That's all you've got to say?'

She gives herself away with a sideward glance at Jude. 'Here.' She tosses something on the table between Jude and me. The journal from the farmhouse. Red leather flaking at the spine, held together with fat rubber bands. 'Everything you want to know about my life is in there.'

The sepia edges of old photographs stick out one end. I know what they are: men in top hats and waistcoats burning Mya's mother's body in a cornfield in 1874. I don't need to see them again.

'They call me *Verdammt*, the damned, never my name. That book lists every ritual, every test.'

'Rituals for what?' I ask.

A bitter smile. 'The family thought more visions from Michael would come if I was bleeding, like the first time.'

The thought sickens me. 'Even Virginia?'

'No, the cutting ceremonies stopped after I torched the church. By the time Virginia was running things, she was more interested in learning the extent of my skills.'

Like whether or not Mya could shift out of that iron room.

'Why didn't you leave decades ago?' Jones asks.

'I tried. I always ended up back there. I didn't know how to live anywhere else.'

Jude has been watching Mya, listening, his thumb tapping the side of his glass. When she falls silent, he exhales and the beat stops. 'You hungry?'

Mya blinks. 'Why?'

Jude gestures to the plates of pizza. 'There's plenty.'

She chews on her lip, still unsure of his mood.

'Over here.' Jones gestures for Mya and Jess to sit with him. Daisy moves her stool to make room, keeps on eating. Doesn't acknowledge either of them.

'They do vegan here?' Jess asks.

Mick scoffs. 'Course they fucken do.'

Jess lifts her eyebrows at the oldest Butler. 'I hear you've got a half-baked plan to clear the town.' There's enough chatter floating out from the bar that her voice doesn't carry beyond our group.

'Maybe.' Mick wipes his mouth on his shoulder. He's managed to force down an entire pizza, despite the lack of pineapple.

'Do you have a map on you?'

'Why?'

Jess breathes out, impatient. 'Because I'm confident I know more than you about emergency planning.'

Rusty produces a crumpled piece of paper from his pocket and Jess joins their table, clearing plates and empties so he can flatten the page.

I move closer. The map is smudged and stinks of motor oil and cigarettes, but it's legible. It shows the cluster of streets hugging the coastline, the two main roads in and out of town, and the estate on the headland.

'Right then,' Jess says, mostly to herself. Her fingers hover over the page, not quite willing to touch it. 'Evacuation protocols are driven by the nature of any disaster and the degree of warning. You want to give emergency crews time to get everyone out without panic, long before there's any real trouble. Is this area prone to hurricanes or earthquakes?'

Rusty nods. 'Cyclones.'

'That means there will be an early warning system. Mobile phone alerts, radio announcements, door-to-door warnings—'

'Yeah,' Rusty says. 'Before Fletcher hit the year before last, the cops went through town with a megaphone mounted on the paddy-wagon.'

'Good. The sooner we can get that system activated the better. Evacs rarely go smoothly. There are always a few idiots who refuse to leave, no matter how big the threat.' Jess gives Rusty and Mick a sharp look. 'I'm guessing that would usually be you guys.'

'Bang-on, sweetheart,' Mick says, not without a hint of pride.

'Don't call me sweetheart. Where are you planting the devices?'

'Here for the first one.' He stabs his finger on the map to a spot that looks suspiciously like where we're sitting.

'Think again,' I say. 'I mean it. And not the library.'

He glowers at me and then returns his attention to Jess. 'Once the town's empty, we'll blow here and here' – more finger stabbing, this time on the main roads in and out of town – 'to keep everyone out.'

God, we're really doing this. A dull sense of dread creeps over me. 'Those clouds are definitely moving closer. We need to get ready.'

'Where are the best lines of sight?' Mya's beside Jess now, eyes fixed on the map.

Rusty indicates the resort at the top end of the esplanade – where Jason is staying with Dani and Maria – and the lifeguard tower.

Jude turns the map so it's the right way up for him. The rest of the Rephaim are around us now, jostling to see. 'Let's get sentries in place. Once the preliminary charges are set and blown, the rest of us will hang back out of sight while the town clears.'

Daisy glances in the direction of the sea. 'What if that's not *the* storm?'

'We can't take the risk,' Jess says.

I catch a flash out of the corner of my eye over the water. There. Another one. Sheet lightning. The sky is heavy now. A low rumble follows, louder and so much closer than I'd like. 'Whatever we're going to do, we need to do it now.'

'No argument here,' Rusty says. 'We've got—'

He turns at the sound of boots slapping on concrete. His

younger brother is sprinting towards us, phone in hand. He skids to a stop next to Mick.

'Heads up. Some weirdo's sniffing around the resort.'

'Define weirdo,' Jude says, craning his neck to see up the street.

'A tall dude with long white hair and a trench coat.'

DEMONS, DEMONS EVERYWHERE

The resort. Dani.

My heart slams into my ribs.

'Go,' Jude says. 'Check Dani. I'll take a team and sweep the resort grounds, get our sentries sorted.'

I make fleeting eye contact with Rafa and then duck under the table out of sight to slip into the void ... and come out the other side in Jason's suite. Maria gasps and drops the plate she's drying. It smashes on the marble tiles. Jason and Dani turn together on the balcony. Maggie's with them now too, her hand is pressed to her chest.

'Oh my god, you scared the—'

'Come inside,' I say, pushing past them to haul shut the French doors. 'Gatekeepers.'

Maria leaps over the broken plate and grabs Dani, pulls

her further into the room. 'Close the shutters,' she hisses.

Maggie lunges for the main window and yanks the cord, blanketing the room in shadow. It's already darker outside than it should be and I smell rain in the air. She ducks down behind the couch with Maria and Dani and I hear their panicked breathing. Feel their fear.

Jason and I flank the French doors. Gatekeepers can't fly, but they can shift from balcony to balcony. There's nothing we can do to cover the glass: no blinds and no curtains. It could be a coincidence a Gatekeeper's here at the resort. Or not.

The sky brightens again and then a gust of wind shakes the latch on the doors. Shit, it's totally overcast now.

'The storm's almost here,' Dani whispers. She's scared. My sudden arrival hasn't helped. I join them behind the couch.

'You have to leave.'

'No, Gabe,' Dani says, gripping my wrist. Her slender fingers are warm. 'I need to be here. So does Jason.'

'Not right now you don't. Jason can get you and your mum to safety. You can watch us from wherever you are and—'

'Please don't make me go.'

'Dani,' I say, impatient. 'There's a Gatekeeper right *here*, lurking around downstairs. I guarantee he's not alone. You're not staying. None of you are.'

'We're safer where you are.'

'Baby,' Maria whispers, 'for once listen to sense. Even Gabe can't protect us now.'

Maggie's fingers are splayed on her throat. 'What about the town?'

I tell them the plan.

'I need to be with Mum,' she says.

'Of course.' Jason crowds in. 'We'll take her with us.'

'Jason, Mum and I can't leave Pan Beach. People will notice if we don't make it to the evacuation centre. They'll put themselves in danger trying to find us.'

'I'm not leaving without you.'

'I need to be here. For Simon too.'

I touch Maggie's wrist.

'We could go with Maggie and her mum,' Dani says. 'Jason will be with us, so we'll be safe.'

I try to mount an argument against it. Fail. 'Fine.' I catch Jason's eye. 'But the first sign of trouble, you get them to the other side of the planet. I don't care who you have to shift in front of.'

The first charge detonates about three seconds after I arrive in the car park behind Rick's. Car alarms start up half a second later. Followed by shouting. I weave between parked cars and sprint to the street. People are streaming in all directions from cafés and bars, trying to get away from the blast. I cross the street to the beach side to get a better view out of the way. It looks like Mick's boys paid a visit to the surf shop on the next block down. Smoke billows through shattered windows, stinking of burning fibreglass. It's murky enough now the streetlights have come on.

Another blast – at the opposite end of the esplanade. Screaming. Panic.

'Gabe!'

I scan the footpath in front of Rick's, see Micah break free from the crowd and jog across the road.

'Sentries are in place,' he says as he reaches me. 'We're running sweeps of the town and then regrouping at the end of the boardwalk near the rainforest.'

'What about the evacuation?'

'Mick's made the call.'

I nod. A bomb threat plus two explosions: surely that's enough. I glance back at the resort. I should have made sure they got out safely. But maybe the demons don't know about Dani; if they see her with me, they'll know she's important. What the hell's the best way to protect her?

Sirens now. Cop cars. Two fire trucks.

'Come on.' I spring over the railing to the beach, ready to shift again. Before my boots hit the sand, the air shudders from another blast. Something else has gone up in the surf shop. A mob surges across the road. Frightened drinkers and diners jostle us before I get a chance to slip into the void, gaping at the fires bookending the esplanade. A gust of wind whips past, bringing with it the promise of rain. The temperature drops a few degrees.

Another flash of lightning. A heavy crash of waves.

The storm is here and the beach is crowded with humans.

Oh shit.

'Get the others.'

Micah nods and sprints into the gloom. I follow, shifting as soon as I can duck behind a dune.

I arrive in my silent, shadowy bedroom, grab my sword and shift to Rafa's kitchen. The shack is empty and smells of coffee, the floor littered with discarded weapon bags. I rifle through them, find a saya and two knives. I sheathe my katana and sling the strap over my head, tuck one knife into my boot, the other against my hip.

And then I'm back on the sand, not far from where I left. The wind is stronger now. More shouting further along the beach. I jog closer, see Jess pointing and shouting at Pan Beach's bulky police sergeant, Des McIvor. He lifts the speaker, forcing her to step aside.

'People, calm down.' His voice crackles. 'I need all of you to make your way to the golf course. Remember the speed limits. I repeat: we are evacuating to the golf course. If you are a visitor, just follow the signs once you reach the highway.'

The crowd keeps milling, unsure. Surfers, stoners. Couples dressed for dinner. Kids holding ice-cream cones, clinging to their parents. Dozens of people. Exposed and vulnerable.

'We are investigating what caused the—' McIvor breaks off for a heated discussion with a silver-haired man in a crisp shirt who's not convinced the sergeant knows what he's doing.

Forked lightning – the beach is lit up in serial staccato flashes. I try to get an idea of how many people are here, but for a few seconds all I see is retina burn. Thunder cracks so close it reverberates in my breastbone. Another speaker further along the esplanade is repeating the instructions to evacuate. I reach for the hilt between my shoulder blades, touch the woven leather strap. An old habit.

A fat raindrop hits my nose. Another gust of wind, laced with salt and ozone and fear. It's about to bucket down, and these people would rather get caught in a storm than risk going back onto the street.

No sign of Rafa or Jude or anyone else. Are the sentries still in place?

I climb the sandbank to get a better view. I'm almost at the top when my insides plummet. A split second later another flash bathes the scene in vivid light and my stomach lurches again. And again.

The beach beyond the agitated crowd isn't empty any more.

The long stretch of sand is filled with more demons than I've ever seen in my life.

TOSSED AND TURNED

Dozens of Gatekeepers, broadswords drawn.

Hellions in chainmail, carrying clubs.

And Immundi. So many Immundi. There must be at least two hundred. The beach is black with them. Where the fuck did they come from?

My gut roils. Time slows and grinds out.

I can't think.

We're not prepared for this.

We'd never be prepared for this, not in another hundred years. What can we possibly do in the face of that advancing horde? How did Zarael get them all here?

A wave smashes in the shallows. Cars rev in the street, tyres squeal. Shouting. Burning plastic and acrid smoke.

The crowd on the beach hasn't scattered. Haven't they seen the nightmare? The demons keep coming, no more than fifty metres away, waiting to be seen. Itching for the terror.

Lightning slashes the sky. The hellions snarl and roar as one, a horrifying noise that carries over the wind and the traffic and the surf. Promising violence and pain. The response is a collective scream – a sound borne of bone-deep terror – and the lights go out in town.

I need to put myself between the horde and—

'Get down!'

Two gunshots crack through the air, sharper, more demanding than thunder. The crowd drops to the sand. I crouch and turn towards the voice, see Rusty a split second before the flash on his shoulder. Feel the blast of heat as the missile scorches past and then—

Boom.

The world fractures. The ground shudders through the soles of my boots. My head buzzes. There's a stunned pause in the wake of the blast – even the wind seems to catch its breath – and then a war cry erupts from the demon army.

It's greeted with a burst of rapid gunfire behind me.

Men, women and children scramble up the sandbank on hands and knees to the boardwalk. Screaming, crying – backlit by the fire taking hold in the surf shop. The thunder clouds are low, the sky heavy, as if night has already closed in over us.

'Gabe!'

It's Jess, trying to scuttle free of the crowd on her hands and knees, a gun in one hand.

'Get them out of here,' I shout, and then shift to where the Butlers are advancing on the darkening beach with their arsenal. I arrive a few metres behind them to the deafening sounds of semi-automatic gunfire. My nose instantly burns with the stink of cordite. In a heartbeat, I understand the tactic. Mick and his boys – all of them, even the hoodie brigade – are advancing shoulder to shoulder, firing steady rounds into the front ranks of Immundi. The Rephaim stalk behind them, weapons ready, coiled to shift into the fray as soon as the firestorm stops.

Jude and Rafa turn when they feel me arrive. I push past them and grab Mick's shoulder, absorb the shuddering recoil as he empties another clip. His mouth is a grim statement, his eyes locked on the hell-spawn army invading his town.

More sheet lightning. The rain heavier now, streaming down my nose and into my mouth. The Gatekeepers and the hellions have abandoned the frontline, leaving Immundi to stumble and fall as bullets rip through them. But the Butlers' weapons are only slowing the demons, not killing them. Zarael's army keeps pressing forward. Sharp teeth, sharp claws, sharp swords.

'Get to high ground,' I hiss in Mick's ear.

Mick pauses to change the clip on his rifle. 'Hang on.' He empties it. The blasts thud in my ears.

More screaming from the street. At least three hellions are chasing the crowd along the esplanade. Gunshots in the midst of it all: Jess, trying to stop them.

'Now!' I yell. 'Go help Jess. Let us get in there.'

But even as I say it I know we can't stop this many demons. Not with only twenty-seven Rephaim – even with Mick and his militia thinning the enemy ranks. But what else are we going to do, sit back and watch Immundi overrun Pan Beach? Let hell-beasts devour anyone not quick enough to outrun them? I draw my katana, squint against the wind and rain.

'Ready?' Jude shouts, loud enough for his voice to carry up and down the line. He turns to me. 'Stay alive.'

'You too.' My heart is thrashing now.

I scan up and down the line. I'm looking at everyone I care about: Ez and Zak, Taya, Micah, Malachi, Daisy and Jones. Mya – yeah, I care what happens to her too. She's beside Malachi, fidgeting but resolved.

And Rafa.

'I've got your back,' he says and leans in, kisses me once, hard, on the mouth.

I feel strangely bereft when his lips leave mine. 'Likewise.'

Any of us could die here. We all could. I can't breathe, can't feel my legs.

'Now!' Jude yells.

My pulse leaps. Adrenaline surges. No time to think. I suck in a deep breath and shift with the others – and come face to face with a wall of enraged Immundi.

The bobble-headed demons let out another battle cry and stomp their own injured to breach the distance.

They surround us in seconds.

Rafa and I stand back to back, fending off the onslaught. Jude and Daisy are a few metres away, already surrounded by snarling pit scum. The wind carries the angry clash of steel on steel. The ocean pounds the beach. I block and strike, using wide sweeps to keep the demons at bay. There's four – no, five – trying to break through my defence. In the open, I could take out five Immundi easily enough. I'm too quick, too skilled for these vermin. But pressed in close like this, working in soft sand in driving rain? Much harder.

The wind whips up, bringing with it a new stench: sulphur. *Fuck*. Zarael's summoned this army straight from hell. No wonder the sky's at war with itself. That's no simple thing. He didn't pull this attack together in the last few hours: the leader of the Gatekeepers has been planning a full-scale assault for years. We simply gave him the excuse to launch it now. Here.

I swing hard at the nearest demon, take his arm clean off at the elbow. He howls and collapses, tripping the Immundi behind him. I take advantage, bring my blade down on the second demon's neck.

Blood. Everywhere. And the awful reality: this is what I do. This is what I've done for more than a century. I take no pride in it, but at least I know what I'm doing now. Timing is everything.

Sideways rain, so heavy the world is turning white. Plastering my shirt to my skin, my hair to my face and neck. My calves ache, my arms already heavy. The lightning is constant now, illuminating the beach as if we're at the world's most terrifying dance party. Flashes of teeth and blades. Black irises turning silver. Behind me, Rafa swears, grunts. At least he's still on his feet. I can't tell where anyone else is – Zak, Ez, the others – all I can do is keep swinging and blocking. Not think about Dani and Maggie. Not worry about where they are right now, if they're safe.

I slice my way through flesh and bone, use my knees and elbows when the demons get too close. My hands are slick – with blood or rain, I can't tell. I use my saya to block, my katana to strike. Over and over again. The Immundi keep coming. I still haven't crossed swords with a Gatekeeper. Where are they? What are they waiting for?

I push back three Immundi. Countless more flow around us like a river, streaming towards the esplanade. Thunder splits the sky. And then another two Immundi barrel into the demons closest to me, bleeding. I glimpse red hair, see who drove them there. Hope explodes under my ribs.

Uri.

'You bring friends?' I manage between ducking and

blocking. I can't take my eyes from the demons lunging at me, but I hear Uri's words loud and clear.

'Yep – the entire Sanctuary.'

I don't know how, or why, but we just gained an army.

And with that, I find my second wind. I cut down four more Immundi before Rafa moves up to my shoulder. We press forward, side by side. Uri is with us now, and when I can risk a look, I spot Callie. *Daniel.* Our numbers mean we can form something resembling a line as we press forward. We step over (mostly on) Immundi as we drive them back. The rain comes at us in gusts now and my wet clothes drag at me. Still no sign of Zarael and his Gatekeepers or their hell-beasts. More gunfire, targeting the rearguard of the Immundi. Mick's boys have taken up positions on the boardwalk.

We push the hell spawn back up the beach a good twenty metres before a siren wails from the esplanade. It sounds old-fashioned, like the one at local footy matches. For a second, I think it must be part of the evacuation, but then the Immundi on the beach turn and run as if on cue. Why are they retreating?

Actually, I don't care.

'Fall back!' Daniel's voice carries on the rain-sodden wind. The order's not for our crew, so I ignore it and instead sprint for the esplanade. There's screaming up there, more gunshots.

I take a quick look over my shoulder, see Rafa, Jude

and Daisy following, more Rephaim behind them. Mick's militia keeps firing at the Immundi: flashes from rifle muzzles light up the other end of the boardwalk.

I vault over the rail in time to see a ute with oversized wheels and a dozen aerials bounce over the kerb and careen into the esplanade. Rusty and Woosha hang off the side, firing into a pack of Immundi running towards the resort. Are those demons retreating like the others, or hunting human stragglers? My legs burn from the sprint through the sand but I push harder to keep pace with the Butler crew.

'We got these cocksuckers!' Rusty yells as the ute swerves to avoid slamming into the fire truck outside the surf shop. The blond mullet guns the engine and the ute skids, then straightens.

I slow to a jog and Rafa draws level with me, breathing hard. 'It's a fucking war zone.'

He's not wrong. A sports car is wrapped around a power pole outside the juice shop. An SUV lies on its side against the bike-hire rack. The fires at either end of the esplanade are still raging, spreading to neighbouring shops. God, I hope everyone got out – or they're at least well hidden. We've missed our window to guarantee an empty town. Thank god Jason got the girls away.

Daisy stalks the street, twin-bladed sai in each hand. Jude is with her, wiping his sword on his jeans. Behind them, the Rephaim fan out to cover the street. Taya races out of the cut-through from the beach ahead of us. She's got a sword in her left hand and clutches a serrated hunting knife with the four good fingers of her right. One of Mick's crew must have given her the blade – definitely not Rephaite issue.

'I'll check the bar,' she calls out and sprints across the road, face turned against the squalling rain.

Police sirens a few blocks away. Up ahead, the Immundi swarm over the boardwalk and onto the beach, away from Rusty and his mates. The ute brakes hard and the boys pile out, join Mick and the rest of the crew lined up along the handrail. By the time we reach them, they're all firing indiscriminately into the mass of demons.

Jess is wedged between Mick and Joffa. Mya is further along the line, hair plastered against her scalp, aiming a pistol at the retreating hell spawn. At least the girls are picking out targets before they shoot.

The beach is littered with dead and wounded Immundi. When the fleeing demons are out of range, Mick and his boys turn their attention to anything still moving on the sand. Each gunshot is a punch in the side of my head. The scale of the carnage turns my stomach, demon or not.

'That'll do,' I shout. 'Enough.'

Mick lets off a few more rounds and then the blasting stops. A crack of thunder follows, muted in comparison. The rain stops abruptly, like someone's turned off the tap. The Sanctuary Rephaim have fallen back to the other end of the beach near the headland at the edge of the rainforest. Uri wasn't exaggerating: he and Daniel brought the entire might of the Sanctuary.

Jones touches my shoulder. 'We'll do a sweep of the town.' He jogs off with Daisy, Micah and Malachi. Jude leans against the handrail to catch his breath. The rest of our crew does the same. It's a relief to not have rain pelting in my face. I take a moment to enjoy the sensation.

'What now?' Mick asks, reloading.

I'm still buzzing, finding it hard to stand still. 'I don't know. Give me a second.' Water drips from the palms and the fence railing. Do we have the numbers to take them now? Should we attack? Do I have time to call Maggie, check she's safe?

'Think quick,' Rafa says, standing close. I follow his gaze.

The Immundi are gathering on the beach in front of the resort, resettling into formation to charge again.

Looks like they've made the decision for us.

THE GANG'S ALL HERE

Uri materialises. Too close. I'm so wired, I almost take his head off. He ducks sideways and blocks my blade with his own.

'Fuck!' My heart gives an almighty thump and I lower my sword.

'I thought you saw me.' He straightens, still twitchy.

'No, Uri, all I can see right now is that horde regrouping.'

'Then tell us your next move. This is your show, remember?'

Shit. This is what happens when you act like you're in charge. The Immundi are definitely back in formation but they haven't moved. Are there more of them now? Bloody hell, I think there are – how is that possible?

'Is Nathaniel coming?' I ask.

Uri scans the beach, doesn't answer. I try to ignore the stab of panic.

'Go.' Mya pushes rain-slicked hair from her forehead. Kohl has smeared down her cheeks like charcoal tears. 'I'll send Jones and the others when they get back.'

'You come with them too.'

Mya's gaze flicks to Jude, avoiding Uri. 'That means Jess will have to manage this lot on her own.'

Right now, Jess is giving Rusty a lecture about the state of his rifle.

'She's got this,' I say. I step from the kerb, make sure I have everyone's attention. Ez is wiping down her knives. Zak dabs his temple where he took a heavy knock last night outside the Sanctuary. 'Let's get down there.' I point to the crowd of Rephaim in the distance.

'Shift,' Rafa adds. 'No need to set *that* lot off before we have to.' He gestures to the demons at the other end of the beach. Our eyes meet, and I slip my fingers between his so we can exchange a quick burst of energy on the way.

We materialise behind the Sanctuary army, and I feel and hear the rest of our crew arriving around us. Cobalt clouds hang low, flashing and rumbling, but the rain is holding off and the wind has settled to a sigh. The air remains electric, fizzing with menace.

'Daniel,' Jude calls out, loud enough to carry over the crowd of soldiers.

'Here.'

We make our way through the throng. I acknowledge every Rephaite I pass with a touch on the arm or shoulder, take quick stock of their injuries. Mostly cuts and welts, a few deeper wounds, already healing. I hear hushed greetings and back-thumping as our crew joins theirs. Everyone as bedraggled as each other.

Daniel is with Uri and Callie. Like them, he's wearing combat gear – black shirt, black trousers, boots – his forearms spattered with Immundi blood. Three members of the Five well and truly getting their hands dirty. He gives Jude, Rafa and me a quick once-over, seems happy enough to find us intact.

'Micah rang and told me what you were facing.' He glances up the beach. The Immundi are still holding formation. 'What do you want to do?'

'Wait for Zarael's next move,' I say. 'That first attack was about testing our strength.'

Daniel nods. 'He wanted to see who else is going to show before he commits his full force.'

The rest of the Rephaim – all one hundred and fifty-eight soldiers – stay close, tensed for the next threat. 'What changed your mind?' I ask.

Daniel gives me a small, ironic smile. 'Zebediah.'

'Seriously?' Zeb's the least influential member of the Five. He and Magda provide religious and philosophical expertise, they don't mount arguments for demon attacks.

'He was adamant we all needed to be here. Himself included.'

'He's here?' Jude stands on his toes to check the faces around us. It makes no sense. Zeb barely leaves his private library to eat, let alone shift to the other side of the world to spectate at a battle.

'He's with Magda and the others in a room at the resort,' Callie says. 'Your little seer reached out to him and—'

I don't hear the rest because I'm back in the void – and then in Jason's shadowy resort room. Two dozen Rephaim turn in my direction – Magda and Zeb, some other academics and IT techs from the Sanctuary. Not the faces I want. The power is out here too, but tea lights are lit in frosted glasses on the kitchen bench. The glow faint enough not to be visible from outside. Hopefully. At least it's not totally dark out there yet.

'Where's Dani?'

'Here, Gaby. I'm here.' Her tiny voice carries from the main bedroom and then she appears in the doorway, holding Jason's hand.

Relief surges through me. I sheathe my katana, ignore everyone else.

'Why are you still here?' I cross the floor, my boot heels loud on the timber. 'Where's Mags?'

I look past them. A tea light flickers in the ensuite, casting soft light into the bedroom. Maggie and Maria turn from the window.

'Is it over?' Maggie asks.

'I thought you were leaving?'

'Mum rang before the phones went down—'

'The phones are down?' I pull out my mobile. It's dead.

'The signal dropped out a few minutes ago. Mum's with Simon and Rick at the golf course. She's freaked, but she's safe. I told her I was with you and that we're okay.'

'But why are you still *here*?'

'Nobody listens to me,' Dani says, dropping Jason's hand and sliding her fingers into mine. Her skin is warm. 'I need to be where you and Jude are. Everyone does.'

'You called Zeb?'

'*Everyone* has to be here,' she says, exasperated.

Jason catches my eye. 'I didn't know what to do, and then that lot turned up and—'

'Hang on.' I let go of Dani and move around the bed, peer out the window. The Immundi and Rephaim armies are still at opposite ends of the beach. What is Zarael waiting for?

'Gabriella.'

Zeb crowds the doorway. His beard is trimmed neat, as always, but his jet-black curls are longer than I remember. I can hear prayer beads clacking. Magda must be nearby.

'I've met with Brother Stephen,' Zeb says. 'I believe there is more at stake here than a simple battle.'

Spoken like a true civilian: there's nothing simple about what's happening below us outside. Which is where I need to be. 'You've got five seconds to tell me why you're here.'

A flash outside momentarily lights up his face and I'm surprised by what I see in his eyes: nervous excitement. 'Brother Stephen says the Fallen can only be released if we are all in agreement, but I don't believe that means what he thinks it does.'

I gesture for him to get to the point.

'I think we only have to be in agreement generally. In other words, *not* be at odds with each other. That has never happened – there's never been the possibility of it happening – until now. Here, today, you have Mya, this boy Jason and the Outcasts. As I understand it, you also remember that your blood is the key to connecting with the Fallen, and that this miraculous child here knows the incantation.' He glances over at Dani, hovering in the bedroom doorway watching us. 'The rest are here too, every single one of us, united in our desire to drive Zarael back to hell.'

'And?' I flex my fingers, needing to be back down on the beach.

Zeb swallows, loud enough for me to hear it.

'We may very well have the first opportunity in our sorry history to fulfil our destiny.'

LIGHTS OUT

I materialise on the beach, feel the agitation.

Rafa meets me. 'Everyone okay?' He looks wild, rattled. Something quivers in my chest.

'I'll explain in a second. What's happened?'

'Take a look.' Rafa moves aside so I can step up between Jude and Daniel. Neither acknowledges me. I peer into the gloom and it takes a second for me to understand what I'm seeing.

The number of Immundi has doubled while I've been at the resort. No, tripled. No ... more. There must be over a thousand bobble-headed demons. Nausea bubbles up. My palms are instantly slick again. The Immundi lift their short blades and rattle them together. They're like an ancient barbaric force screaming at the sky, and it's deafening, even at this distance.

'What the . . .' My mouth is so dry I can hardly speak.

Boom.

The ground beneath me shudders. Another explosion in town, this one further away. The highway. I drag my eyes from the horde and check the boardwalk. Was that one of the Butlers, or something else? No sign of Jess or the Pan Beach crew. Please let them be far away from this nightmare. I hope the rest of the town made it out.

'The odds aren't in our favour,' Daniel says. I barely hear him over the waves. Sea spray kisses my cheeks, settles on the back of my throat. The wind has picked up again.

'You leaving then?' I ask, anger stirring beneath the fear.

'No, Gabe. We're here until the end.'

I look from him to Jude. Clearly I've missed something.

'Daniel's with us,' Jude says. 'Either we'll get support or we won't, but we can't just hand this town over to Zarael.'

I don't know if he means support from Nathaniel or the Garrison or both, and I don't get the chance to ask because the Immundi army surges forward.

'Now,' Jude yells and I have a heartbeat to prepare myself for the violence.

The shift gives us the element of surprise – for a split second – and then we're swamped by the monstrous pack of snarling Immundi. I attack with katana, block with saya. Kick, elbow, headbutt. Smell blood and sulphur. Demon sweat. Something foul from spilled intestines. I keep moving, don't think about what I'm stepping in, and on and over.

I feel it quicker this time: the burn in my calves, the ache in my shoulders. The way my bones rattle with every block and thwarted strike. The pull and tear of muscles as my blade finds its mark. The fierce concentration, how hard it is to spot the nearest threat with so much shadow and movement. Whenever lightning cuts over the beach, I see the endless sea of demons pressing to reach us.

It's like fighting against the tide.

Jude is ahead of me, so I see when he stumbles. He keeps swinging and blocking, but he can't buy himself enough time to get up from his knees. I fight my way towards him, decapitating an Immundi, running through two more. Jude's holding his own, he's—

A demon blade slashes across his back, slicing through fabric and flesh and muscle. Jude arches away from it, tries to turn. Exposes his neck to the snarling Immundi now behind him. The scream is there, right in my throat. And then Daisy materialises between Jude and the blade flashing down. She blocks it – at the same time I have to duck to avoid a sword aimed at my temple. I hamstring the two demons hindering my view and spring up to see Daisy in a stabbing frenzy, her sais plunging in and out of Jude's attackers with blinding speed and precision. And then she and Jude are gone. I have a heartbeat of relief, and then the next wave of Immundi sweeps towards me.

Before they can strike, the beach is bathed in blinding blue-white light. The horde snarls and shrinks back. I turn, squint against the glare. Nathaniel is on the beach behind us.

Thank god.

But the Immundi don't retreat. They lower their heads and rush past me, as if Nathaniel's arrival is a signal. They smash against me. Shoulders knock mine, spin me one way, then the other. My sword is almost wrenched out of my grip. I grapple for the knife at my hip but I can't get to it because I have to use my hands to push away the crush of demon bodies.

It's only going to take one of these pricks to stab me on the way past—

'Boardwalk!' Rafa shouts from somewhere to my left. I don't need to be told twice. I slip into the void – it's almost a reprieve after the chaos of the beach – and re-emerge a few metres from Rafa. I look around, frantic, for Jude and Daisy.

There. Jude is leaning over the boardwalk railing, shirtless, shielding his eyes to watch the beach while Daisy cleans his back. She's using his torn t-shirt. The boardwalk is crammed with Rephaim. I scan faces as I push my way to my brother, find Micah, Malachi and Taya. Mya – blood soaking the right side of her head, matting her hair – Uri, Callie, Seth and Jones. Zak and Ez.

'It needs *stitches*, Jude,' Daisy says as I reach them and I can see the gouge running from his shoulder blade across to his spine. The shift has stopped the bleeding, but she's right.

'I don't care about it scarring.'

'*I* do,' she says. 'It won't take Brother Ferro long to—'

'We're not going anywhere, Daisy. *Look*.'

I force my eyes from the two of them to see what Jude and everyone else are watching on the beach. Nathaniel is still in full glory so my eyes sting with the effort. The fallen angel is clearing a path through the Immundi like he's wielding a scythe instead of a broadsword, light radiating from him.

The Immundi scream – the blue-white brilliance actually *burns* their flesh – but it's not slowing them. They keep swarming, rushing him. The fallen angel stands head and shoulders above them, his entire being blazing, watching the demons stumble before they reach him, shielding their eyes. They keep falling, piling up around him. But they're not falling haphazardly. They're dropping to their knees and *positioning* themselves. And then the next wave does the same, on top of the first. Holy shit . . .

They're sacrificing themselves to build a wall around him.

Nathaniel realises what's happening. With a strong beat of his wings, he's airborne. But before he can clear the mass of demon bodies, half a dozen Immundi scale the backs of their brothers and launch themselves at him, faces turned away. Nathaniel beats his wings, harder now, slashes at them with his broadsword. More jump and grab the legs of the dangling Immundi, weighing the angel down.

What is he doing? Shift, for fuck's sake.

Nathaniel tries harder but there are too many. They're howling, skin burning where they touch him, though they don't let go.

Shift!

He looks in our direction, his chiselled face bleak, and my breath catches in my throat.

Nathaniel doesn't shift.

He falls.

And then his light goes out.

HELL BREAKS LOOSE

Gatekeepers and hellions materialise on the sand right below us, between the boardwalk and Nathaniel and the sea of Immundi. Zarael lifts his eyes to the raging sky, long black hair whipping around his scarred face. Laughing. At his back, the writhing mass of demons swarm over Nathaniel.

Panic claws at me. My mind spins.

'Mobilise!' Daniel shouts. 'Get Nathaniel out of there!'

I think about Zeb and Dani. In a flash I find traction. We have to do the ritual. *Now.* I grab for Jude and Rafa before they can shift with everyone else. Even Daisy is gone.

'The Fallen,' I say.

'What about them?' Jude's injured and bare chested, and straining to be down in the sand fighting with the others. For once, Rafa gets what I'm saying before he does.

'Will it work?'

'I don't know, but Dani's watching, ready when we are.' When I left the resort, she was sitting in the middle of the bed, preparing to sink into that meditative state where she can see us.

'Where would we do it?' Jude asks, and takes one last look over the boardwalk: Rephaim pushing Gatekeepers and hellions back, trying to get close to the spot Nathaniel went down. Rephaim stabbing at Immundi, dragging them away from the fallen angel. Shifting every few seconds to confuse the demons. 'Resort rooftop?'

Smart. It's close to Dani and we can keep an eye on the chaos. I nod, and am about to step into the void when my stomach dips and fingers grab my wrist.

'Wait—'

I duck and spin and then register it's Mya. But there's not enough time to stop the sweep that takes out her legs. She lands hard on the boardwalk, her katana catching the fence on the way down. The right side of her face is smeared with blood now – is she missing half an ear? I grab her wrist and shift without explanation, taking her with me.

My shin hits something solid and unforgiving on the other side and Mya bumps into me. Jude springs forward, steadies us before we both topple over.

'Mya—'

'You're breaking them out, right?' she asks, breathless. It's a demand, not a question.

'We're going to try,' Jude says. 'We have to.'

I move back from the thing that almost tripped me: a low-set timber table, the first in a long row, bolted to the rooftop pavers. Lounge chairs and umbrellas are strewn across the resort roof, upturned and battered by the wind. The noise of the battle carries up to us: shouting, snarling, steel on steel.

Rafa wipes his blade clean on a tattered umbrella. 'You want to help me cover these two while they do their thing?' he asks Mya.

She nods and I catch her eye. 'Are you sure this is what you want? It won't work if even one of us is against the idea of freeing them.'

'Anything's better than what's going on down there.'

I can't bring myself to follow her gaze. I take a steadying breath, fight off an assault of memories from the last time we tried this. The taste of dirt and pine needles. The feel of sharp steel breaking the skin on my neck. Blind terror that I was about to lose my brother, or die, or both.

And here we are about to do it all again, with the entire Gatekeeper horde and a monstrous Immundi army within shouting distance. This is what Zarael wanted all along, to draw all of us into a fight. Isolate Nathaniel. Come after Jude and me. Ironically, we're trying to give him exactly what he wants: the Fallen.

My heart is a jackhammer. What if we free the Fallen and they don't help? What if they despise the Rephaim as much as the Garrison does and attack *us*? What if—

'We need to do this now.'

I lock eyes with Jude. Swallow. He's as freaked out as I am, but there's determination in the set of his lips. Grim resolution. I sheathe my katana with trembling fingers, fumble with the knife tucked in the front of my jeans. Blood rushes in my ears, thunders through me. I feel it at my temples, my throat, my fingertips.

Mya sheathes her sword and draws two handguns. Rafa has a katana in each hand, spins both. They take up posts either side of us, ready. A bloodcurdling cry carries up from the beach. I can't tell if it's triumph or rage. I shove the thought aside and slice open my palm. It stings like a bastard. Jude takes the knife and does the same and then we slap our palms together. His skin is hot and sticky. He thrums as if there's an electrical current running through him.

This is it.

I hope Dani's ready. I hope she's right about remembering the incantation.

I hope we all survive this.

Jude and I keep our swords in our free hands. Tighten our grip on each other. Rafa and Mya prowl around us, impatient, agitated. Rafa leans over the timber handrail to see the beach. 'Anything yet?' he asks over his shoulder, and his urgency tells me how badly things are going down there.

A slash of lightning splits the sky, so close my hair

crackles and lifts from my scalp. Thunder booms. Somehow, the storm is right over us again. But where's the wind? The rain? Even through my haze of adrenaline and impatience, I notice the stillness. Not quietness – the battle still rages between the resort and the ocean. But the clouds are lower, heavier. It's as if the world is shrinking, closing in around us. I feel a strange surge of energy catch at the tip of my hair and rip through me, blasting out through the soles of my boots. But that's not the weirdest thing.

The weirdest thing is that Jude's face is lit up, flickering, like there's a bonfire between us.

'Gabe . . .' He looks up and I follow his gaze.

The sky is on fire.

No. Wait. That's not right. The night is shot through with flecks of oranges and reds, but not like flames: like embers. As if the clouds themselves are glowing.

'Are we doing that?' I whisper.

'I don't—'

He doesn't finish because Zarael materialises on the roof.

Of course he does.

The night grinds down. Suspends. And in that moment – the blink of an eye – I see hell's prime Gatekeeper with strange clarity. The cruel criss-cross of scars on his cheeks and throat. The easy way he grips his broadsword. Orange eyes reflecting the flickering sky. The sheer *delight* in the curve of his mouth.

Rafa launches himself at Zarael, his katana smashing against the demon's broadsword. Time snaps back.

Jude and I rush forward, hands still linked – we can't lose contact, not now, not if we're the ones changing the sky – but Mya shifts and beats us. She raises her guns and Rafa dives out of the way as she unloads both into the demon's chest and head. Zarael's body twitches as each bullet rips into him, driving him backwards. His head snaps back, taking one in the forehead.

It might be enough to slow him – or not. He's the hardest of all of them to keep down. Mya presses the triggers until the firing pins click. Once, twice, three times. She's empty. She tosses the guns aside, draws her katana.

Zarael stumbles against the timber rail and recovers immediately, his face streaming with blood. He's not smiling anymore. The four of us attack simultaneously. Jude and I are useless swinging one-handed and Zarael knows it. He skips sideways, blocks a strike from Rafa and collects Mya with a backhand blow. It lifts her off her feet. She lands on the pavers, bones crunching, barely missing an overturned deck chair. She doesn't move and I feel Jude waver.

My insides plummet. I glance over my shoulder; Leon and two hellions have arrived. Leon's sword is streaked dark. One of the hellions carries a club, the other flexes razor-like claws, bares its long teeth.

I half-turn, prepare for a second attack. Should we shift?

Will it nullify the ritual – if it's even working at all? Can we afford to be further away from Dani? Fuck. She's right *here*, a few storeys below us. In the middle of this nightmare. So's Maggie – unless Jason's finally taken all of them to safety. If he has, is there any point in us being here?

God, I don't know what to do. I don't—

The night shatters with another sky-splitting bolt of lightning and cracking thunder. And it's in the flare of orange light that I see them arrive. Leon staggers back and the hellions snarl. My heart stumbles.

The rooftop is seething with angels.

CAREFUL WHAT YOU WISH FOR

Angels. Everywhere.

Zarael shifts. I don't know where he goes because I can't take my eyes from the beings in front of me. Their shoulders rise and fall, chests heave. They're wild, untamed. Hair long and matted. Beards unkempt. Tunics and trousers faded and threadbare. Boots scuffed and wings ruffled. Even their broadswords are dull. But their eyes . . .

Their eyes flare icy blue.

My fingers slip from Jude's. My pulse thunders as violently as the sky. I skim their faces: every shade like their children. I can barely form a single coherent thought.

There's movement in the host. The angels are stepping aside to let someone through, someone with unruly dark hair hanging in curls to his broad shoulders. Whose face in this weird orange light looks a bit like . . . mine.

Blazing eyes find Jude and me, and then drop to our bloodied hands. He falters.

Semyaza.

Our *father*.

For a long moment, I forget to breathe.

How can he be our father when he looks no more than a decade older than us?

Beside the overturned deck chair, Mya moans and sits up – and then scrambles backwards on her hands when she sees the army of Fallen. A fallen angel with dreadlocked blond hair breaks ranks and strides towards her. She tries to get to her feet, stumbles. Jude shifts and puts himself between the angel and Mya, now pressed against the door to the stairwell.

'Don't touch her,' Jude growls.

The angel raises his sword to bat aside Jude's blade, but then abruptly stops. The rest of the host looks on, restless. Their eyes flicker, completely unreadable. At least they're keeping their light to themselves. The thought of them all revealing glory at once is terrifying.

'I am Hadrial,' the angel says, looking down at Mya. His voice is rough, like he hasn't used it in a while. 'She is mine.'

Jude holds his ground. 'Back off.'

Hadrial pauses and then takes a single backward step. Mya stares at Hadrial, eyes wide, her bloodied arms wrapped around her knees. I tear my gaze back to Semyaza. He's fixated on me, unblinking. He radiates strength, volatility. I haven't raised my sword – I don't want to invite violence – but I will if he comes any closer. I'm meant to say something here, but my mind is a flat ocean.

A hellion snarls and Semyaza's head snaps in its direction. I risk a look and see Zarael, Leon and the hell-beasts on the far side of the roof watching our stand-off. Zarael is drunk with glee.

'*This* is my reward for all the decades in this putrid realm.' He makes a sweeping gesture to take in the roof and the beach. 'I shall slaughter your bastards in front of you and then drag you back to the pit.' He grins, and then he and Leon disappear, taking their hellions with them.

Nobody moves.

Do the Fallen even know what's happening here? The urgency of the moment crashes over me.

'That battle down there,' I say, trying to smother the swelling panic. 'That's the rest of us fighting off Gatekeepers and a thousand Immundi. We need—'

And then they're gone. Semyaza and every single member of the Fallen: simultaneously shifted without a word. Rafa, Jude and I sprint to the edge of the building. This is it. There's no way any demon army can withstand two hundred angels manifesting in glory. I scan the teeming mass, see clusters of Rephaim, flashes of long white hair. The churning mound of Immundi still covering Nathaniel.

No.

I look harder. Straining to see wings, even the faintest tinge of blue-white light.

But the Fallen aren't there. They aren't anywhere.

We've freed them, and they've left us to face this nightmare.

Alone.

DADDY ISSUES

'Mother*fuckers*,' Rafa spits.

Dread claws at me, scrapes at my bones. Nobody's coming to help us. I fight a wave of desolation. A hundred and thirty-nine years of searching for the Fallen. A body covered in scars. All the questioning, the unknowing. The lies and blame and doubt. All the bullshit.

It was all for nothing.

Rafa scours the sky, still shot through with a hundred shades of amber. 'The Fallen are free so where the fuck's the Garrison?'

My palm throbs. It's still bleeding. I wipe it on my jeans, try to sweep my thoughts into order. 'I think it's safe to say we're on our own.'

Jude lets out a harsh laugh. 'We've always been on our own.'

'Yeah, and we're still alive,' Rafa says. 'Our old men are spineless – nothing new there – but this fight's not over, so how about we get back down there and do some damage?'

Jude stretches his neck from side to side. 'It's what we do, right?'

I look from Rafa to Jude and my heart hurts, too full of everything I feel for them. 'Let's just stay alive so we can keep doing it.'

Rafa brushes his knuckles along my arm. 'Let's stay alive so we can keep doing a *lot* of things.' And even in the midst of the dread and the uncertainty, I find a small smile for him.

Jude moves past us to where Mya is picking up her handguns and tucking them back in her jeans. 'You all right?' he asks.

She rubs her hip where she landed. 'I don't . . . I thought . . .' She shakes her head, frustrated that she doesn't have the words.

'Jude,' I say, 'Your shoulder.' The wound has torn open and fresh blood dribbles down his bare skin.

'You can sort it again in a second. I'll survive.'

I scour the beach, spot Zarael on a sand dune. Spindly hand on the hilt of his broadsword, surveying his handiwork. Secure in the fact the Rephaim are too busy fending off his army to even know he's there, gloating. Waiting.

The leader of the Gatekeepers thinks the Fallen are

coming for him. He thinks he can overwhelm them like he did Nathaniel – oh, god, *Nathaniel* . . . I quash the anxiety, jam it down with all the other fears: for Ez and Zak, Daisy and Jones. Micah, Malachi, Taya. Daniel. We haven't lost anyone yet. We can't have: the pit filth would let us know. The thought flips my stomach.

'Triple-threat attack?' Rafa shakes out his shoulders. 'I'll take the neck.'

'Torso,' Jude says, which means I've got Zarael's legs. If we time it right, one of us should strike home. We take a second to fix his position and then shift, each of us pushing as much energy as we can at Jude.

I arrive in a crouch and swing where Zarael's legs should be—

And meet air. I drop my shoulder and let momentum carry me into a roll, and then spring to my feet, blade up protectively. But Zarael's not here.

Rafa spins around, fizzing with anger. 'Where is he?'

Jude scans the battle. 'Gone. Let's get Nathaniel.'

Mya is already in the fray, trying to reach Malachi. He's battling a Gatekeeper, Daisy at his back.

I take a breath. Plunge back into the roiling chaos, katana in one hand, saya in the other. Jude and Rafa fall into position either side of me and we carve a path through the Immundi. I smell sweat and blood and sulphur. Traces of ozone on the sea air. The eerie light is constant now, even with the Fallen gone.

The battle is deafening. Shouting, grunting, the clash of steel meeting steel. Fists and boots pounding flesh. We push our way through, slicing and stabbing and stomping. Brutal and uncompromising. I block out all thought except finding a way forward. Focus on my breath, my technique almost instinctive. A century's worth of training coded into every muscle, every ligament, every movement. Rephaim strength flowing through me, a part of me as much as my hands and feet.

Leon and the rest of the Gatekeepers have formed a guard around the wall of dead Immundi. I catch a glimpse of red hair – Uri – and Ez, each fighting a Gatekeeper one-on-one. Zak is on my left. He hamstrings a hellion so Taya can take its head. She's fighting left-handed.

So much violence. I shove down the horror and press on.

Leon materialises in front of me. He knocks an Immundi aside to make room, giving me time to block his broadsword – about five centimetres from my jugular. He's playing for keeps.

I strike his ribs with my saya and kick out his knee. He stumbles, lifts his blade with two hands to block the blow aimed at his head. Rafa and Jude are preoccupied behind me with Immundi, Gatekeepers or hellions – or all three. The battle rages around us. God knows how many Immundi are pressing in, stepping over their dead and injured brothers to take their turn at us.

Leon and I are trading blows, striking, blocking and side-stepping each other. I attack with blade and saya – one deadly, the other a distraction – until Leon drops his double-handed grip and catches my saya. He rips it from my fingers and hurls it towards the sea without interrupting his attack. There are too many threats: I'm exposed now. I can shift, but then I'll have to fight my way back in again to get to Nathaniel.

Is Nathaniel even alive? Should I care? But I do. Whether I want to or not.

I swing again. Kick, block. God, I'm tired. My arms are heavy. My breath comes in sharp gasps. Leon's tiring now too, I can hear it in the way he grunts with each thrust and block. So when his eyes flick to the sky, I don't hesitate. I aim for his neck.

I'm sluggish and my blade buries itself in his shoulder, right above his collarbone. He snarls with pain and collapses to his knees. I kick his wrist and he drops his sword. I try to rip out my blade so I can finish the job, but as soon as the katana comes free, Leon is gone and the next line of Immundi rushes me.

That's when I know it for sure. We're never going to get to Nathaniel. We're never going to beat this army.

'Jude,' I call out, even though it costs me air I can't afford.

For a few terrifying seconds, there's no response and it takes all the discipline I possess not to turn around and check he's still alive.

'I'm here.' He's closer than I expect, his voice strained. He's hurting badly.

I lock swords with an Immundi with a platinum buzz cut, knee him hard between the legs. 'Rafa?'

'I'm good,' he calls out, further away. He doesn't sound good. He sounds tired and frustrated.

The Immundi in front of me is on the ground, clutching himself. Another two leap over him to rush me. And then . . .

They look at the sky and recoil.

I slice open the nearest demon while he's distracted and the second one scrambles backwards. But it's not from me. And he's not the only one. All the Immundi are floundering, eyes skyward.

I risk a quick look.

Movement over the rainforest catches my eye. Dark clouds gathering high above the canopy, strange shadows flickering across them . . .

Holy. Shit.

Rafa props beside me, blocks a blade centimetres from my shoulders, finishes the Immundi wielding it.

'What are you doing?' he hisses.

Jude bumps my shoulder as he joins us. I barely register the Immundi streaming around us. I can't stop staring at the mass below the clouds. 'Look.'

It's the Fallen.

The entire host, wings beating steadily, propelling them

forward. They're in a series of V formations, like a fighter squadron. A lone angel flies ahead of the rest. Semyaza. A chorus of panicked shouts rises up from the demon army. The Fallen, as one, pin back their wings and dive.

Relief washes over me, and then a thought strikes like a sliver of ice.

What if they're not just coming after the demons?

What if they're coming after us too?

EVERYTHING BREAKS . . . EVENTUALLY

'Rephaim,' I shout. 'Fall back. NOW!'

I hear the call repeated further up the beach before I slip into the void, feel Jude and Rafa shift with me. We materialise at the rainforest end of the esplanade, halfway up the sandbank.

For a heart-stopping moment it's just us, and then the rest of the Rephaim materialise in groups of three and four, panting. Ez arrives close to me. She puts a hand on my shoulder to steady herself. 'What's going—'

She doesn't finish because she sees it for herself. Her fingers dig into me. I wait for the Fallen to wheel around, change direction to come at us, but the host stays straight and true. Plummeting towards the fleeing demons. A murmur of astonishment ripples through the Rephaim.

The orange sky flares brighter. The ocean churns and roils, flashes gold.

'Hold!' Zarael shouts at the Immundi. 'They are but two hundred. We are legion!'

The Fallen are almost on them. My breath catches. And then the angels plough into the swarm like hawks on a plague of mice. I stand with the Rephaim, watching our fathers hack and slash at our enemies with dull blades. It's utter chaos.

'They're free, then.'

Daniel stands near Jude. I can't tell if it's observation or accusation. Either way, he's as culpable as the rest of us – the Fallen wouldn't be here if we didn't all want it at some level.

'Where's the glory? Why aren't they manifesting?' It's Daisy who asks. She's slipped beside Jude to get a better view. Her right eyebrow is split, her blades dark.

The Immundi have stopped trying to get away from the Fallen. They've noticed the absence of blinding light now too. They're turning . . . and charging. And still no glory from our fathers. I don't get it. They're fighting Gatekeepers, hellions and a seething horde of Immundi without glory. Unless . . .

'What if they can't light up?'

There's a tense pause on the boardwalk.

'Then they've got no chance of finishing this on their own,' Rafa says.

The Fallen are taller than us, stronger and faster, but without their trademark weapon they'll have to fight Zarael's army of Immundi the hard way.

I look to Daniel. 'We have to get to Nathaniel.'

'I know.'

'Then we have to help them.'

Daniel's hair is slicked back with sweat, his chest still heaving from exertion. 'You want us to fight beside the Fallen?'

'You got a better idea?'

His eyes skim over the Rephaim: Jude, Rafa and Ez. Daisy and Uri. Beyond to the others. I know how difficult it is for him, how the idea goes against everything he's ever believed about our purpose and our destiny.

'No,' he says, bitterly. 'I don't have a better idea.'

'Okay then. Let's focus on reaching Nathaniel – and take out as many demons as we can along the way.'

We've reached critical mass now, enough to push back the Immundi, buy us time to get Nathaniel out from under his macabre burial mound. Most of the demons smothering him are already dead or badly burnt, having taken the brunt of his scorching light before it winked out. We finally reach the wall of dead demons and Daniel takes the lead in digging through the bodies. Others join him and the rest of us form a circle, keep fighting off Immundi.

I don't know which job is more sickening.

I've never killed and maimed this many demons before – not even close. The sand is littered with their hands and arms and guts. Blood spattered everywhere. There's nothing glorious or badass about it. It's death, pure and simple. Mayhem. Not war. Slaughter. But then, that's all war is: killing and dying.

In fleeting moments between opponents, I try to glimpse the battle raging between the Fallen and the Gatekeepers: between former members of the Garrison and the demons who were their masters and torturers for millennia. The battle that was always theirs to fight. Never ours – or never meant to be.

I catch Rafa straining to see, and I know it's not that simple. He wants to be in the main event, not because he's desperate to bolster the Fallen's ranks but because we have history with the Gatekeepers too. The animosity between our fathers and their jailers became ours the moment the Fallen disappeared and we were allowed to live. Or, more to the point, the moment Nathaniel decided to make us into an army.

The movements behind me turn frantic.

'Move that one – no, that one.'

'Oh, *no* . . .'

I smash my sword hilt into the side of an Immundi's skull and look over my shoulder. Zak and Seth have dragged away the last Immundi corpse, stinking of burnt flesh to reveal—

Dear god.

I can't quite comprehend what I'm seeing.

Nathaniel is facedown, crumpled, his face pressed into the sand. Completely still. Every bit of exposed skin is covered in bite marks – his hands, forearms, neck. His clothes are in tatters. Clumps of blond hair ripped from his head. But worse are his wings . . .

One is bent beneath him at an angle that's all wrong. The other is splayed, spattered with blood and gaping where feathers have been ripped out. The exposed flesh is pink, torn and clotted. The sand is littered with his feathers. He must have lost consciousness before he could hide his wings. Why else would he let them do this to him? Daniel is on his knees, lifting the angel's head, brushing sand from his mouth and nose.

'Get him to the infirmary.' Jude joins Daniel on the sand and feels for a pulse at Nathaniel's wrist.

Nathaniel's eyes flutter open. 'No.'

He's alive. The force of my relief takes me by surprise. Rafa – or Ez, I can't tell – pushes me out of the way, rough. Protects me while I'm standing, stunned, with my back to the fighting.

'The Garrison will come now.' Nathaniel's voice is stretched thin, every word an effort. 'I need to' – he swallows, grimaces – 'be here.'

I stare at his mutilated face, taste bile. Did he sacrifice himself in the hope it would bring the archangels? Daniel helps him sit up. Nathaniel moans, grips Daniel's wrist hard enough to turn his knuckles pale.

'Nathaniel.' Jude waits until the angel's eyes are open again. 'The Fallen are free.'

He stares at my brother. His irises are faded, barely flickering. 'How?'

'We released them.'

He closes his eyes and lets out an exhausted, defeated sigh. 'Where are they?'

'Here. Fighting Zarael.'

Nathaniel lifts his head. 'Let me see.'

'Can you shift?' Daniel asks. He's still supporting the angel, a hand pressed between Nathaniel's broken wings to stop him slumping back to the sand. Nathaniel shakes his head.

'I'll help,' I say, and I don't only mean getting Nathaniel to higher ground. I crouch next to Jude and hook my fingers around Nathaniel's elbow. I almost draw back: his skin is burning. I have no idea if we can even heal an angel – we've never had to try before. We let Daniel guide the shift to the top of the dunes. It only takes a millisecond, but it's long enough to feel my energy slam against a solid wall. I glance at Jude and then Daniel as soon as we materialise. They both shake their heads.

I guess not.

We position Nathaniel against the boardwalk fence, his back to the road. Giving him an uninterrupted view of the churning violence. Daniel is crouched beside him, silent and pensive. Nathaniel makes no attempt to move or hide his wings. They stay spread out either side of him, tinged pink. But Nathaniel's not worried about his wings: he's focused solely on his fallen brothers-in-arms.

The Rephaim have pushed up to join the Fallen now. Two hundred warrior angels, wings folded at their backs. A hundred and fifty Rephaim, give or take. Rafa's down there, shouting orders, and everyone is following his lead, filling the spaces between the Fallen, creating an impenetrable phalanx. They drive the demon army onto the back foot. Stepping over the dead as they go, Immundi and Gatekeeper alike.

A pack of Gatekeepers materialise behind the Fallen/ Rephaim force, but Rafa's been waiting for that last, desperate move. He turns and Rephaim turn with him: Micah, Malachi and Taya. And then four of the Fallen join them. One with dirty blond hair hanging in dreadlocks down his broad back shoulders his way to Rafa's side. Glances at him before swinging his ancient sword at the nearest Gatekeeper.

I reach for Jude. 'We should—'

I don't finish because Zarael materialises. Right next to us.

He doesn't gloat or goad, he swings for Nathaniel's neck without a word, straight and true.

Jude reacts quickest, blocks the first strike. The second is already arcing down – Zarael is wielding two swords now – and I lunge to stop it. The impact jars, hard. It rattles my bones.

I kick to take out his legs, but he's already shifted and he's on my left, swinging at Nathaniel again. Jude and I move on instinct, block him. I feel the heat of Zarael's breath, feel a blast of his rage, and then he's gone again. Daniel is up now, covering Nathaniel. The angel is slumped against the fence, unable to stay upright under his own strength. We have to spread out to protect him, to avoid stomping on his broken wings.

'The Garrison will come.'

I can barely hear Nathaniel over the blood pounding in my ears. I try to steady my breathing. My eyes flick between skirmishes on the beach, searching for Rafa, for the others, and I have to force my attention back to the immediate space around me. Zarael's not done up here. He might have the Fallen and their bastards to subdue, but his hatred for Nathaniel is too strong. He's coming back for him.

My stomach wrenches, though it's not Zarael who materialises and blocks my view of the battle. It's Semyaza. His eyes fall on Nathaniel. Harden. He disappears, and all three of us are too slow, caught off guard because this wasn't the opponent we were expecting.

I spin around and find the leader of the Fallen – a

former member of the Garrison, *my father* – standing over the angel who raised me, his wings hidden and his blade pressed against Nathaniel's jugular. There's so much blood caked on Nathaniel's throat I can't tell if Semyaza has broken the skin or not. Nathaniel lifts a hand to stop us interfering and we all falter, even Daniel.

'Brother,' Semyaza says. His voice is raw as if he's been shouting. The unexpected familiarity of it tugs at me. 'You have been busy.'

Nathaniel looks at him out of the corner of his eye. 'I saved them from annihilation,' he says, trying to move his jaw as little as possible. 'I protected your twins.'

I blink. He *knew*. All this time, Nathaniel knew we belonged to Semyaza.

'You turned them against me. You slew their mother. You created a generation of orphans.'

The injured angel bears the accusation. 'If your women had survived the testing, I would have taken them with me to raise their children.'

'It was not your place to judge them.'

A shaky breath. 'It was my commission. My glory was returned to me so I could accomplish it.'

Semyaza lets out a gravelly laugh. 'There was no commission.'

Nathaniel turns his face so he can see Semyaza with both eyes, ignoring the insistent blade at his neck. 'The Garrison led me to each of them. They—'

'It was not the Garrison. It had nothing to do with them, you fool.'

Nathaniel glares at him, bruised and bloody but defiant in the presence of the warrior he's hunted for a hundred and forty years. 'How could you know, Semyaza, you were not even in this realm when I received the calling.'

The leader of the Fallen leans in, but I still hear his words.

'I know it was not the Garrison, brother, because it was *we* who led you to each of those women.'

NO TIME TO LOSE YOUR HEAD

Everything else drops away. The ringing steel, the shouting, the breaking ocean. Even the imminent threat of Zarael. Semyaza's words are the only reality.

And they can't possibly be true.

Nathaniel presses his hand into the sand and tries to sit up higher, winces. 'It is not possible.'

'It is and it was.'

'The stars and moon aligned.'

'It took the remnant gifts of each of us to guide you from beyond the veil.'

'But how—'

'We were bonded to those women, Nathaniel. Have you truly forgotten what that means?'

Nathaniel swallows. And then all that's left of his strength drains away. All the certainty. Whatever lies beneath that question, it's taken something from Nathaniel, diminished him in ways I barely understand.

He's not defiant any more.

I look to Jude. Is it possible it was the Fallen and not the Garrison who led Nathaniel to us? What would that mean? But the truth of that question already creeps over me like a chill on the wrong side of midnight.

It changes everything.

There would be no greater purpose for us after all.

A dozen questions – more – skitter through my head and career away before I can grasp them. I feel as if I've been sucker-punched, except I'm still standing. My gaze drifts over the battle. The carnage. Immundi bodies piled up on the beach, scattered between skirmishes. The blood on my sword. For a slow, sickening moment I feel the weight of all the death. All the violence. All of it my heritage . . .

I feel someone else arrive. I'm sluggish to turn, still lost in questions and confusion.

'GABE!'

At Jude's shout, I duck and bring up my katana, but it's too little too late. Another, heavier sword smashes into it, slams the flat of my blade into my forehead. The impact reverberates through my skull. It's like being kicked by a horse. I stagger back, but not quick enough to avoid the steel-capped boot that crunches my ribs. Pain forks through my ribcage and steals my breath.

And then something cold and hard slams into my

temple and the whole world tilts. I land with a muffled thud. Blackness stains my vision and the evening drifts out of focus. I don't have to look up to know I'm in serious trouble.

A fierce shout breaks through the fug. Swords clash so close I feel the air vibrate.

There's fighting now, all around me. I have to get up. I have to help. I roll over on my side, think about taking my weight on my knees and elbows. I gag, let a wave of nausea pass. I try to focus on the world, but everything is sideways. Boots and legs flash around me. Shifting or just moving lightning fast? I can't tell. My vision clears and I can make out Jude and Daniel tag-teaming against Leon a few metres away. Rafa trading blows with another Gatekeeper. Micah and Ez fending off three hellions. When did everyone else get here?

My view is interrupted by two more sets of boots, moving forward and back in an erratic dance, kicking up sand. I lift my head slowly, see Semyaza driving Zarael away from Nathaniel. Away from me. Ferocious, reckless with a millennium's worth of hatred and rage. Striking with such force I can feel the impact through the dune beneath me. Semyaza's power, his speed, his fury . . . beside the Fallen, we truly are children.

My head throbs. My ribs scream. I claw at the wet sand for purchase.

And all I see is Zarael's pinched face above me again.

Too close. The scars punctuating his cheeks and forehead are angry against his moon-white skin. He's sweating and panting and spraying spittle.

'You are rusty and dull, like your steel, Semyaza, and still without glory.' He brings both blades down at once, but the angel times the block, traps the swords against his own and kicks Zarael away. I'm struggling to draw breath but I can't look away.

'I need not glory to destroy you.'

Strike, block. Spin. Slice.

'You will need it to save your half-breed spawn.'

Semyaza launches himself forward – achieves impressive height even with his wings tucked out of sight – and brings down his heavy blade. Zarael blocks, barely centimetres to spare.

'They are more than a match for you,' Semyaza says. 'And they are no longer alone.'

The words wind around me, take vague shape, but the leader of the Fallen and his jailer are already done with sledging. Semyaza drives Zarael backwards, but he's not quick enough to finish him off. They're too evenly matched.

I need to move. If I could shift, could I help Semyaza?

The answer takes a few seconds to form, but when it does I know what to do. And it's going to hurt like hell.

I calculate the distance to Semyaza and Zarael, and push myself into the void. I materialise on my hands and knees, take a breath filled with knives and stifle a groan –

if I give away my position I'm dead. I open my eyes as the hem of Zarael's trench coat brushes my scalp.

This is it.

Semyaza doesn't look down, doesn't let on that he's seen me, but he must have because he lunges at Zarael, forcing the demon to scuttle back—

And stumble into me.

My ribs splinter. A thousand razor blades. I slump to the sand, wrap my arms around myself protectively, only half-aware of Zarael falling and Semyaza leaping over me to get to him. I gasp, squeeze my eyes shut and hope I've done enough.

Something hits the sand close to me. I open one eye and see Zarael's face. But it's all wrong.

He's not blinking, or moving, or breathing.

And his body is missing.

HELL FREEZES OVER

I recoil on instinct, sending a jolt of fire to every nerve ending.

Zarael's mouth is frozen in a snarl, his orange eyes static and opaque. The seconds stretch out – I can't look away from the horror of it – and then Semyaza snatches up the head by a handful of long black hair. The angel's wings snap out from nowhere. He launches himself from the sand with a single beat, pushing a gust of cool air over me. I grit my teeth, ride another wave of pain and push back at the shadows crowding in. I move my head a few centimetres, find Zarael's body lying truncated where it fell. Gag.

Above me, Semyaza is airborne. In his left hand, he carries Zarael's severed head; in his right, a dark-stained sword. I try to watch him, but I can't sit up. I hear his wings beat as he flies over the beach. The sky glows orange, brightens momentarily with a flash of sheet lightning followed by a low rumble of thunder. The evening is breathless. Even the ocean is finally subdued.

'Zarael is no more,' Semyaza shouts. His voice, rough at the edges, resonates with authority and carries over the ringing steel. 'Return to the abyss or be annihilated.'

The demons, those I can see, falter. Turn their faces skyward.

'Cohort, fall back,' Semyaza orders.

The skirmishes near me end abruptly: Leon and his buddies are nowhere to be seen. What's going on?

There's not enough air in my lungs to feed that thought and the night – is it night now? – blurs. A gust of air washes over me. I'm vaguely aware of someone striding towards me . . . Semyaza, back on the ground. His wings disappear as he walks, or at least I think they do. He's all smudged at the edges.

'That's close enough,' Rafa says. He's next to me on the sand. He wasn't there a second ago. His fingers shake as he brushes hair from my forehead. I close my eyes, exhausted from the knives and lack of oxygen.

Semyaza looms over us. 'I will heal her.'

My heart does a weird flip.

'Like hell you will.' Rafa's voice is tight.

'Boy, you are injured and useless to her until you are whole.'

'Fuck you, *old man*.'

I try to roll over. 'Are . . . you . . . hurt?'

'A few nicks, that's all.'

'You are bleeding all over her.'

'Rafa—'

Semyaza is suddenly beside me. His fingers clamp around my wrist, and then I'm in the void with him.

I don't fight it, and I don't know why.

I don't even know if I could've stopped him, given he's my—

The thought is obliterated by a blast of energy. I'm standing behind a fighter jet on full throttle. Scorching. Skin-flaying. I can't speak, can't open my eyes against the furnace. Panic builds: this fire is going to consume me. It's—

It's gone.

Feeling slowly returns and I register each sensation: cool, damp air rushing over me, dousing my skin. Orange light, flooding under my eyelids. A slow, rhythmic beat, buffeting me. The smell of the ocean.

I'm flying.

I look down, see ocean flashing past, my legs dangling below me. Feel Semyaza's tight grip around my waist, holding my weight away from him with massive strength, so there's space between our bodies. His wings beat powerfully, propelling us forward as I hang in his arms. I take a quick inventory of my injuries. My head is tender, but I can think clearly again. My ribs, only a dull ache.

Semyaza's healed me all right, but bloody hell . . . it was far from gentle.

The sky and ocean ripple with shades of amber, so we're still in Pan Beach. Thank god we didn't come out in a different dimension. I lift my head and see the town in the distance, dark under the glowing sky except for the fires burning on the esplanade.

'Align your body.' Semyaza says it loud enough so I can catch his words before they're whipped away. 'You are causing drag.'

Okay, so my father's first words to me aren't going to be sentimental. I draw back my legs so my body is in a straight line . . . it's a tough ask of my abs and I know within seconds I'm not in good enough shape for a long flight. I inhale deeply, relishing the fact that I can breathe again.

We draw closer to the beach. I could shift ahead, make the point that I don't appreciate being snatched away and don't need Semyaza to carry me home. But we're almost there. And flying's not so bad . . .

A hundred metres out and the shapes on the beach take form. The Immundi are fleeing – they're well beyond the resort now – even though nobody's chasing them. I strain to see long white hair in the retreating horde, but if the Gatekeepers are still here they've gone to ground. So have the hellions. The Fallen and Rephaim are facing off in front of the esplanade, neatly divided into two camps.

The Rephaim are in a loose formation on the banks of the dunes, the Fallen spread out on the sand below. I can tell which is which even from here because the Fallen have their wings out.

I see the front of the Immundi pack. That can't be right. I blink, try harder to focus, but I'm still seeing the same thing: the Immundi funnelling into a panicked line, four or five abreast – and then disappearing into thin air.

I turn my head, find Semyaza's bearded face startlingly close. 'I thought they couldn't shift?'

His eyes meet mine, icy and unapologetic. Matted hair trails back over his shoulders, barely bothered by the wind. 'It is a portal.'

Ah.

I knew portals existed – they have to if the Fallen were trapped in another dimension, otherwise how did they get there? – but I've never seen one until now. 'To where?'

'An outer circle of the hell where the veil is in tatters.'

The veil. Semyaza's words to Nathaniel catch up with me. Semyaza pierced the fabric that separated his dimension from ours to manipulate Nathaniel all those decades ago. I remember what that means and the coldness leaches back in. The Garrison was never interested in us. We have no higher purpose.

I don't know what's more unsettling: having a destiny I didn't ask for or having none at all. Thoughts snake around me, squeeze tight. And then Semyaza pins back his wings and takes us into a steep dive. The night rushes past, bleeds together. Adrenaline surges – I can't help it. Even as we plummet towards the beach, towards uncertainty, I can't help but think how much Jude and Rafa would love this sensation.

Semyaza buzzes the Immundi, scattering their formation and sending them into a heightened state of frenzy, trampling each other. If I didn't know better I'd say he was doing it to amuse himself.

All I want is every last hell spawn gone from my town. I want this carnage to be over, even though it brings on the moment when we face the consequences: the Fallen are free, and we don't know what that means. For the Garrison, for Nathaniel . . . or for us.

It's only when Semyaza swoops up and banks right that I catch flashes of movement between the Rephaim and the Fallen. Weapons drawn on both sides. Semyaza mutters something in a language I don't understand and changes course. Faces lift in our direction.

'Cohort, hold!' Semyaza shouts.

Daniel, Callie and Uri have placed themselves between Nathaniel and the Fallen, their swords lifted. Callie's favouring her bad leg, but she's not giving ground. I scour the faces of the Rephaim, find Rafa and Jude together, shoulder to shoulder. Their swords are drawn, but not to defend Nathaniel: they're already moving forward to meet Semyaza.

I don't know how to land, but I manage to get myself into position so my feet don't tangle with the angel's as we touch down. Semyaza steadies me for two steps and then lets go. My legs are shaky but they take my weight.

Rafa blocks Semyaza. 'What gives you the right—'

'She is healed.' Semyaza barely glances at Rafa as he steps around him and heads for Nathaniel. I grab Rafa by the t-shirt before he can go after him and pick a fight. 'Hey. *Hey.*'

Rafa stops, faces me.

'I'm okay,' I say firmly. I check him over. His arm is streaked with blood. 'Are you still bleeding?'

'No.' He's still thinking about challenging Semyaza. I slide my hand down to his elbow, keep a grip on him while I check on Jude.

'You?'

My brother offers his back to me so I can see the wound is scarring. It must have taken at least half a dozen shifts to get the healing to this point. But I know from experience that he'll be feeling the deep muscle ache about now. And Daisy was so right: it's ugly.

'Did Semyaza say anything to you?' Jude asks.

'Yeah,' I say, letting go of Rafa and moving closer to the stand-off between Daniel and the Fallen. 'Told me I was weighing him down.'

Two of the Fallen have moved up onto the dunes, both taller and more muscled than Daniel. The other angels stand in restless formation on the beach, faces flushed from battle. A hundred metres away, the Immundi are still crushing through the portal. Where are the Gatekeepers?

'You're not touching Nathaniel.'

Daniel's sword is remarkably steady in the face of two hundred warriors. The angel on the right is the same one who fought beside Rafa against the Gatekeepers. Dirty blond hair hangs in a messy plait down his back. An old scar marks the bridge of his nose.

'We led this traitor to your mothers and he executed them,' the blond angel says. 'He has earned his fate.'

There's a beat – and then the Rephaim stir. Understanding dawns. For most of them, this is the first time they've heard the truth about what happened to the women who gave birth to them. Eyes turn, accusing, to Nathaniel, still slumped against the boardwalk railing, bleeding out. The blond angel levels his blade in Nathaniel's direction.

'If he lives, he will not cease until he has seen us delivered back to hell.'

'He has the right to defend himself,' Daniel says. 'But he needs to be whole to do that, and we can't heal him.'

The blond warrior barks a laugh. 'You think we should *help* him?'

'Yes.'

'Truly, Daniel, you would let him live after all he has done?'

Daniel's attention snaps to the second angel. He has thick, dark dreadlocks and a beard down to his chest, but there's something familiar about the shape of his nose, the set of his mouth under those whiskers. The disappointment in the question.

He's Daniel's father.

Daniel sees it too because he's run out of words.

Semyaza draws his broadsword from the sheath between his shoulders and steps into Nathaniel's line of sight. 'You would allow these children to defend you, even now?'

Nathaniel fumbles behind him for the post, watches Semyaza through swollen eyelids. He grips the wire and hauls himself to his feet. Stands there, swaying, his torn wing hanging at an awkward angle. Chiselled face distorted with bruises, bites and anguish.

'I have failed them in every way possible.' A ragged breath. 'I have no more to ask of your offspring.'

Semyaza nods. 'Barakiel, Jael.'

Jael – Daniel's father – holds Daniel's gaze for a second longer and then he and the blond Barakiel step around Daniel. Nathaniel watches the two angels approach. They grab him by his arms and haul him forward. He grimaces but offers no resistance, no sounds of protest. Nathaniel's legs don't work, so the angels drag him through the sand and drop him at Semyaza's feet. Nathaniel takes his weight on his hands and knees, broken wings draped either side of him. With considerable effort, he lifts his ravaged face.

'Is it your plan to gather the Rephaim and make war on the Garrison?'

Semyaza's irises flicker in a steady rhythm. 'That is not your concern, brother.'

Nathaniel watches him for a long moment and then sits back on his heels. His eyes find Daniel's. Then Jude's and then mine. A tear slips down his mangled cheek. The revelation that it was the Fallen and not the Angelic Garrison who reached out to him all those years ago is unmaking him piece by piece.

He has no destiny either.

He drops his head to expose his neck. He's ready for Semyaza to kill him. For a second I forget how to breathe. Nathaniel murdered our mother – the mothers of all of the Rephaim – and he's lied to us for a hundred and thirty-nine years about a greater purpose that never existed. And yet . . . My blood cries out for him. That this is wrong. He fooled himself as much as he fooled us. However heartless Nathaniel was, however twisted his motives, he believed he was following orders given by the Host of Heaven.

And how can I ask for forgiveness for my mistakes if I can't offer it in return?

Semyaza draws his blade.

'Wait.'

I put myself between Nathaniel and Semyaza. My father blinks at me, slowly.

'Move aside, child.'

'No.'

Rafa and Jude step up next to me. Daisy too. Then

Daniel, Uri and Callie. The others. Semyaza's gaze rakes over us.

'You choose this traitor before your own fathers?'

'Oh, for fuck's sake,' I snap, and Semyaza's eyes flare. 'Why is it always about a choice with you lot? I'm not taking his side, I'm asking you not to kill him.'

'Because you care for him more than our need for justice?'

I hold his gaze. 'Because it's not your place to judge him, any more that it was his to judge our mothers.'

'I think you will find that in present company, we are the *only* ones qualified.'

'I disagree.'

I flinch at the sound of a new voice behind me, every nerve ending shot. I look over my shoulder, find a guy I've never seen before standing calmly between Daisy and Jones like it's the most normal thing in the world to be on a beach surrounded by sword-wielding soldiers, winged creatures and butchered demons. He has rain-slicked hair, sharp jawline, sinewy build. Wearing board shorts and a loose-fitting white t-shirt. Hands in his pockets. Barefoot. And taller even than Zak.

'And who the fuck are you?' Rafa asks.

The newcomer blinks and his dark eyes suddenly flash icy blue. 'I am Gabriel, Second Lieutenant of the Angelic Garrison.'

TRUTH, LIES AND
EVERYTHING IN BETWEEN

I feel my mouth fall open. The Rephaim skitter away from
him, leaving the angel alone on the sand.

Gabriel.

An archangel.

Not just any archangel: the warrior who murdered the
original offspring of the Fallen all those thousands of years
ago.

Jude and I did this. We set the Fallen free. We brought
him here.

We wanted to face down the Garrison, to know what
they want from us. And now we do: nothing. They don't
want anything from us, they never have. If we'd known
that half an hour ago, would it have changed our decision
to free our fathers? I stare at Gabriel, try to find my

way through an onslaught of panic. The sky shifts from oranges to pinks, bringing the cobalt clouds over the sea into sharp relief. Thunder rolls across the headland. The night is breathless, electric. Rafa moves closer until our elbows touch.

'Are you going to kill us?' Jude asks, somehow keeping his voice steady.

'Why would I do that?'

'Because we freed the Fallen. And because that's what you did the last time Semyaza and his cohort fathered children.'

'If that was my commission today, would you war against the Angelic Garrison?'

'Would we fight you for our lives?' Jude doesn't need to look to Rafa or me. He knows the answer. 'Absolutely.'

Gabriel watches Jude for a moment before his attention shifts to Semyaza. The leader of the Fallen holds his ground. 'You did not adhere to our covenant, Semyaza.'

'You offered no covenant, brother, only a new prison.'

'Did you prefer the company of Gatekeepers? Should I send you back with them?'

Semyaza flicks the tip of his broadsword in Nathaniel's direction. 'Do you think *that* punishment did not cut as deep into our flesh as Zarael's blade?'

'It was not I who led Nathaniel to your women.'

'He was meant to gather and protect our brides, but you rewarded him with a glimmer of glory and he used it to punish them.'

'I returned to him what he would need to protect himself in this realm. It was never intended as an instrument for judgement.'

Wait. What? My mind scrambles.

'*You're* the reason Nathaniel can show glory and the Fallen can't?' Jude asks before I can form the question.

Gabriel turns from Semyaza, gives my brother his full attention. Intent. Panic slices through my confusion. Rafa tenses. This angel destroyed an entire generation of our half-siblings, has the power to command the attention of two hundred and one fallen angels. He so terrifies Nathaniel, he still won't look up.

Gabriel weighs the question. He tilts his head, birdlike, and his focus drifts elsewhere for a long moment. Nobody speaks. Nobody moves. In the stillness, a wave breaks on the shore. Our world is being up-ended and shaken out but the tide keeps rolling in, oblivious.

'Let us wait for the others.'

I follow Gabriel's gaze to the resort. Does he mean the Rephaim up there? When does he think they're coming?

My stomach dips.

The rest of the Rephaim materialise. Magda, Zeb and the other non-combatants. And – *oh no*.

Dani.

She's with Jason. But they're not touching. He snatches her to his hip, his face pinched with fear. Maria and Maggie aren't with them; they must have left the women behind.

'Jason, what the fuck?' I demand.

He looks stricken. 'I didn't—'

'I bade them come,' Gabriel says. It's only now I see how bewildered and shaken the newly arrived Rephaim are. *Holy shit.* Gabriel plucked them out of that room. Can he do that to the Fallen too? Is that why they haven't fled from him already?

I shift and put myself between Dani and the Fallen. Between Dani and Gabriel. I force myself to look Gabriel in the eye. 'You'll get a war if you touch this girl.' I'm like a flea threatening a lion, but I eyeball the archangel anyway. Because I mean it.

'The same thing goes if you touch Gaby,' Rafa says.

Gabriel blinks, slowly. 'You, children, have spent too much time in the company of pit excrement. I am Second Lieutenant of the Host of Heaven. I would no sooner harm humans than I would offer my throat to a hellion.'

'But half-humans are fair game?' It's out before I can consider the wisdom of the accusation.

The archangel's lips tighten. His irises flare. I wait, my heart working double time.

'All actions have consequences,' he says, carefully. '*Your* existence is a consequence of the decision made the day the nephilim were extinguished.'

'They weren't *extinguished.*' Semyaza spits out the word. 'You slaughtered them in cold blood while we stood in chains and watched. They were defenceless, utterly ignorant of their crimes. They were not warriors, they were *children*.'

Gabriel doesn't acknowledge Semyaza. He keeps his attention squarely on me. 'The Fallen paid for their transgressions in ways that were justified, but perhaps not just.'

Warm fingers touch my elbow. Dani is reaching for me. I nod for Jason to let go and her bony arm snakes around my waist, slender fingers gripping the top of my jeans. She's studying Semyaza, no more frightened of him than she was of Nathaniel at the Sanctuary yesterday.

'Is that why you all made more children?' she asks Semyaza. 'Because you lost the others?'

A storm of rage and grief darkens his eyes and tightens his shoulders. Two hundred warriors fall dangerously still. Nathaniel stays on his knees, ready to be executed. Dani lets go of me so she can crouch down. She brushes her fingers over his feathers, so gentle and sad.

'Is that why you didn't want another child?'

Nathaniel's hands ball into fists, grazed knuckles pressing into the sand. I look to Jude. Nathaniel always told us he didn't father a child the first time around. Was that another lie?

'Nathaniel,' I say. 'Was one of the nephilim yours?'

His broken wings shudder.

Bloody hell. Nathaniel was a father once . . . and he watched that child die. The significance sinks in. No wonder he wanted to believe so badly that we had a destiny. He wanted to convince himself as much as the Garrison that we were different from the half-angel bastards who came before us. Even if none of us were his.

'Semyaza and his cohort did not learn the lessons of their recklessness,' Gabriel says. 'They repeated their transgression at the first possible opportunity. They lusted for the pleasures of the flesh, and they yearned to create life once more.'

'Why didn't you go with them?' I ask Nathaniel.

He lifts his face. His wounds are weeping. 'I could not bear the desolation a second time.' He finally looks at Gabriel. The sight of the angel seems to sharpen his pain. 'And then I was spared when my brothers disappeared. When I saw the signs, I knew it was a chance for redemption, to save this new generation from the fate of the last—'

'Nathaniel.'

The fallen angel pauses, swallows. Waits for Gabriel to continue.

'You were spared from exile with your brothers-in-arms because of your discipline. *That* was your redemption. You had freedom, Nathaniel, yet you could not see it. You could not accept a gift so simple.'

Nathaniel stares at Gabriel, understanding dawning. Everything he's done over the last one hundred and forty years was for nothing. His slate was already clean.

I watch as the archangel's words further crush him. He

starts to shake. His feathers rustle as his wings spasm and shudder. He slumps forward to the sand and clasps his hands over his head as if to ward off an attack, mutters words I don't understand. Completely unravelled.

I have to look away. But there's no relief here. The beach – my beautiful, sun-drenched beach – is a battlefield. The surviving Immundi are still pushing through the portal like frantic commuters at peak hour. The esplanade is a war zone, fire and smoke and overturned vehicles. The stench of ash and burning plastic carries across the road to us and the sky is still all wrong.

The rest of the Rephaim are as lost as I am. Ez and Zak are together, hands clasped. Jones prods a cut on his neck. Taya, Malachi and Micah stand close, swords hanging loose in their hands. Shirts bloodied and torn. Daisy has moved next to Jude, freckled cheeks flushed, eyes sharp.

I need space. I squeeze Dani's shoulder and guide her back to Jason.

'Why didn't you just send the Fallen back to hell when they broke out?' Jude asks. 'Where have they been?'

Gabriel nods: this is what he wants to tell us.

'Semyaza and his second-in-charge – Orias – pierced the veil and touched the minds of your mother and her cousin. I saw this, and I watched and I waited. I proposed that the Garrison let our brothers escape and give them the freedom to choose their own destiny. My captain, Michael, agreed, but only on the terms that I must take responsibility for whatever transpired. I accepted, with terms of my own: that Michael not interfere unless commanded to do so.'

I wish I could read Gabriel and understand what's going on here. Is he explaining because he's going to spare us, or does he want us to understand before he kills us? Or sends us to hell with our fathers.

Gabriel checks Semyaza. The leader of the Fallen scowls at him.

'As soon as they were loosed from the pit, Semyaza and Orias entered this realm in the place you call Monterosso, Italy. The others scattered to the corners of the earth, to willing women. Fertile women.'

'And you let it happen.'

The accusation comes from Ez.

'Your fathers chose their own fate.'

Ez clicks her tongue. 'You allowed the Fallen to create life – create us – and then you took them away. You left us alone.'

'What would they have learned if they had remained here?'

'What did they learn being away from us?' Her voice breaks a little on that last word.

'They learned to *watch*.'

'Watch what?'

Gabriel's lips twitch in what could be a hint of a smile.

'You.'

CHIP OFF THE OLD BLOCK

'Me?' Ez asks.

'All of you,' Gabriel says. 'These warriors are first and foremost watchers.'

Semyaza grunts. I can't tell if it's derision or annoyance, but he doesn't interrupt the archangel.

'All the suffering they endured in the abyss taught them nothing, so a different approach was required. I let each of *you* live so that they could watch, see the consequences of their actions. To witness the shame of their abandoned women, to see their offspring grow and struggle as they understood they were different from their mothers and from everyone around them. I wanted the Fallen to see the legacy of their selfish desires. I trapped them in a dimension where they could live freely but with the burden of knowledge and understanding. A place where they could witness but not intervene.' A quick glance at Semyaza. 'I underestimated how profoundly your fathers would yearn for you.'

I scoff. 'For freedom, you mean.'

'No, child. For each of you.'

Semyaza locks eyes with me, challenging. Daring me to contradict Gabriel. A long-buried yearning of my own stirs, but I refuse to expect anything from this scruffy warrior.

'Semyaza sent signs to Nathaniel and when that did not unfold as he anticipated, he reached out through Orias' bond to his human bloodline.'

An angel with fair hair and a long curly beard steps out of line and positions himself in front of Jason. His eyes are unexpectedly kind, his lips soft. 'I am Orias.' The family resemblance is striking.

Jason draws Dani closer. Blows out his breath, shaky. 'Are you saying the gifts given to the girls in my family came from you?'

'Yes.'

'But the girls are from a human bloodline.'

'Your mother bonded to me.' Orias says it quietly, respectfully. 'A connection such as that cannot be easily sloughed off. It permeated every fibre of her being and was passed to the daughter she carried after you, and beyond.'

Jason swallows. Blinks rapidly. Orias lowers himself to one knee so he's at eye level with Dani. His irises settle to a slow dance. 'Our connection has carried through your bloodline for six generations, and yet it is stronger in you than any other in your line. Because of you, I am finally free. Thank you.'

She lifts her hand to touch the bristles on his cheek. 'It's nice to meet you.'

He closes his eyes. Smiles. 'You too, sweet child.'

'What about *my* family?'

It's Mya who asks the question – not of Gabriel, but of her own father.

Hadrial stands to attention with the rest of the Fallen, as near to Mya as he can be without breaking ranks.

'Did you give my grandmother *her* vision?' she asks.

'If it had been me, Myanna, it would not have driven a wedge between you and my brothers' offspring. If it had been me, you would not have spent your life feeling so broken and damaged.'

Her eyes harden. 'You think I'm worthless too.'

'No,' Hadrial says quietly. 'I do not.'

Mya's lips tremble, but whatever she's feeling, she fights it. Her right ear is torn and bloodied, her hair loose and wild. She's all fury and grief. 'So which of you screwed up my family then?'

A revving engine cuts through the tension, gears crunching. Mick's dented four-door ute barrels along the esplanade and skids to a stop near the boardwalk, loud in the stillness. Mick, Rusty and Jess pile out, falter when they see the second army below us on the beach. A cigarette dangles from Mick's lips.

'What the—'

Jude holds up a hand to warn the three of them to stay on the road. Not that it will keep them safe if trouble breaks out, but they might have half a chance to get clear. The beach beyond the resort is deserted now. Wherever the demons have gone, they've closed the gate behind them.

'Who messed with *my* life?' Mya hasn't noticed Jess. She's too caught in the moment.

'I did,' Gabriel says.

Mya's head snaps in his direction, and then she looks to me – *me*, not Jude – confused. Opens her mouth, closes it again.

'Why?' I ask for her.

Semyaza shakes out his feathers. 'A failsafe.'

I raise my eyebrows at my father – feel that weird sense of being unstitched when he meets my gaze.

'When Gabriel ripped us from this world, he sealed the portal with my blood. He set a ward upon it that only the blood of my offspring could reopen it, and – as you now understand – that would remain sealed until all of our children were of one mind to release us.'

The archangel stands between Fallen and Rephaim, perfectly still except for his eyes, which move from Semyaza to me. 'I had thought it would take centuries – longer – for the progeny of the Fallen to find each other. But when

Semyaza led Nathaniel to each of you and he brought you under one roof, my hand was forced. Nathaniel had not yet found Mya. By keeping her alive and instructing the family to hide her from him, I ensured there would always be a child alive and separate from the rest of you. You would never be of one mind.'

'But Jason was already separate,' I say.

Gabriel nods, once. 'He was insurance. And then you compromised him.'

When Jude and I found him by accident not long after our eighteenth birthday.

'That's why you led Mya's family to him.' It's not a question: I understand now. Mya's family told Jason the Rephaim were an abomination, but if he kept away from us he'd be spared the punishment coming our way.

'Yes.' Gabriel is unapologetic.

Mya wavers, unsteady on her feet. Hadrial is beside her in a heartbeat – shifted – his wings tucked away out of sight. She's so off balance she lets him help her to the sand, where they sit cross-legged facing each other.

'But the feather . . . the trumpets?' For the first time since I met her, Mya sounds as young as she looks. She stares at Gabriel. 'I heard that story a thousand times. That it was Michael, the mighty Captain of the Garrison, who chose our family to protect the world from the abominations fathered by the Fallen.'

Gabriel's shoulders move a fraction, the hint of a shrug.

'I cannot help what mortals choose to see and believe.'

I think about the story Brother Stephen told us last night, about Heinrich cutting Mya, his grandchild, to see if she would bleed, and then preparing to execute her as he'd killed her mother. The only thing that stopped him was his wife's vision.

'You saved Mya's life when you gave her grandmother that vision,' I say, holding eye contact with the archangel, even though it makes my head swim. 'But you did it in a way that encouraged her family to revile her.'

'That was not my intention.'

I pick through all the pieces we've been given. 'What possessed you to give them the knowledge to build the iron room? You couldn't see how it might backfire, giving them the keys to a prison for us?'

A muscle jumps in Gabriel's jaw and I know I've hit a nerve. He hasn't shown any urge to repeat his genocidal tendencies – yet. Maybe I shouldn't be giving him an excuse.

'The connection Orias formed with Daniella changed everything,' he says, glancing at her. 'She was able to see what he and the rest of the Fallen could see. She could see you. Sharing the knowledge that enabled the holding cell to be constructed was a moment of frustration intended to balance the scales. It was an error.'

I look from Gabriel to Semyaza to Nathaniel, still shuddering on the sand. The three angels who have shaped our lives. Manipulated us. Who have failed us each in his own unique way.

'Okay, enough with the drama,' Rafa says and cracks a knuckle. 'We get it: Nathaniel fucked up. The Fallen fucked up. You fucked up. We all did.' He spins his sword hilt, points the blade at Gabriel. 'So the question is, have you finally shown your face to give us a history lesson, or correct your mistake? What happens now?'

Awesome. So much for not giving Gabriel an excuse to end us. Only Rafa would provoke an archangel. I try to catch his eye, but he's not looking my way and not likely to any time soon. He has no intention of backing down.

'Do not tempt fate, Rafael.' It's Barakiel, the blond angel with the dreadlocks and scar across the bridge of his nose.

Rafa turns on him. 'This is all one big game to you lot, isn't it?'

'Enough, son—'

'Don't fucking *son* me. You're my father? Big deal. You want me to fall at your feet and weep? I've survived a hundred and thirty-nine years without you, so whatever's coming next, I can face it without you too.'

'You have some skill as a fighter, however you are but a mote of dust to Gabriel—'

'*Some* skill? You want to throw down, old man?'

Barakiel bristles. 'You are well overdue for a lesson in respect.' He snaps out his wings to their full span.

Oh yeah, they're related all right.

'Respect for who, you?' Rafa starts down the dune. 'Why? Because you got a hard-on and knocked up a virgin a century and a half ago? Hardly makes you father material.'

The Fallen move aside, give Barakiel space.

'That is ironic coming from you' – Rafa's father waits for him – 'given your history with women.'

Rafa spins his sword, taunting. 'You're a gutless old prick.'

'And you, *son*, are a hypocrite.'

Laughter carries across the beach. It's enough to break through Rafa's anger. He rounds on Gabriel.

'What's so funny?'

Gabriel's expression eases to a smile that reaches his eyes and completely transforms his face into something luminous. 'You wished to know what happens next, Rafael? This is it.'

'What is?'

'The Fallen and their children finding a way to live with each other.'

FREE WILL IS OVERRATED

'Not a chance,' Rafa says. 'We won't be living together.'

Gabriel raises his eyebrows. 'The Fallen are free, Rafael. That leaves only two choices: I return them to hell or I consign them to live in this world. If they remain here, you will need to find a way to coexist.'

Rafa looks to me. 'What sort of choice is that?'

'I don't know,' I say. 'But why don't you come back up here and stop tormenting your father. You can antagonise each other later.' I hold Rafa's gaze, testing whether my advice counts when he's this riled up. He cracks another knuckle, holds his ground a few seconds longer, and then climbs back up the dune.

God, this is exhausting. I sit on the sand, pull Rafa down beside me.

A few other Rephaim join us – Ez, Zak, Jones, Taya

and Micah. The Fallen stay on the beach. Dani squeezes between Rafa and me. She tightens her grip on my knee until I look down at her.

'We're going to be okay,' she whispers.

'Have you seen something?'

She shakes her head. 'I just know.'

I nod and try to smile, but something a little more concrete would be comforting about now.

Jude stays on his feet. His jeans are low on his hips, his chest grazed and caked with sweat and sand. Next to him, Daisy uses the hem of her t-shirt to wipe her blades clean.

'So how do you see this working?' my brother asks, gesturing to the Fallen and then to us.

Gabriel turns and takes in the carnage on the beach. 'Today's battle was a skirmish compared to what is coming when the gates of hell break open and the final war begins. We do not know the hour or the day, but it will come.' He nods to Semyaza. 'You and your brothers will remain here and prepare for that war.'

Semyaza gives no reaction to the news.

'And us?' Jude asks. 'Are we expected to fight too?'

I think of the horror of the past few hours. How much worse an actual war would be. And not against pit-scum, but higher-order demons. Quicker, more brutal demons. Being conscripted into the Garrison army would hardly be a reward.

'Patience, Judah.' Gabriel says. He crosses the dune to

Nathaniel and Semyaza. Nathaniel keeps his face pressed to the sand; Semyaza watches him approach, impassive. The two angels face off, silently. The sky grumbles, the storm well away from the town now. Gabriel folds his wings and kneels beside Nathaniel, places a hand on the fallen angel's blood-matted hair.

'Look at me, brother.'

Nathaniel doesn't raise his head. His ribs expand and contract with an anxious breath.

'Nathaniel. I have a commission for you.'

A beat. Then slowly, painfully, Nathaniel struggles to a sitting position. Nobody moves to help him. God, his face is a mess.

'You will help your brothers assimilate to this world. You will give them a place to live and to train. When our war finally comes, and only then, you will know if you have earned your place on the battlefield with your brothers.'

Nathaniel closes his eyes, nods. I don't know if Gabriel's given him a lifeline or a sentence. I don't think Nathaniel's sure either.

Now Gabriel stands, faces Semyaza. 'It is time to heal your brother.'

Semyaza laughs, ignores him.

'You will do this thing, and then you shall swear allegiance to each other. All of you.'

Allegiance.

Fealty.

The reminder of Jude's bargain drags all the air from me. I glance at my brother, see the pulse jump in his throat.

'And if I do not?' Semyaza says.

There's a flash of searing light. Beside me, Dani gasps and I panic, throw myself over her. But she's already trying to wriggle out from under me, keen to see Gabriel's wings. His glory is gone as quickly as it came – with no more effect on Dani than Nathaniel's – but the archangel keeps his wings extended. His first show of authority.

'Semyaza, if you are to remain here you must reconcile with your brother. If you do not, I will return you and your cohort forthwith to the abyss, where I have no doubt Leon is already grovelling for the right to succeed Zarael. There are no more second chances for you and the Two Hundred.'

Semyaza's eyes cut to Jude and me. He grunts and sheathes his sword, and then reaches down and grabs Nathaniel without care or concern. They disappear. I blow out my breath and pull Dani onto my lap. She still smells of pears, even here. She links her arms around me, rests her head against my shoulder. She's as exhausted as the rest of us.

'So the Gatekeepers are back in hell?' It's not the question I need answered the most, but it's easier than asking what happened in the forest in Idaho last year.

'They are in chaos without Zarael,' Gabriel says. 'It will be some time before they venture back through the veil.'

'What about us?'

He looks at me – into me. 'That discussion we shall have soon enough.' Gabriel glances at the sky. 'Right now, you need to clear this beach of death.'

THE MORNING AFTER

I wake with Rafa's arm draped along my hip, his fingertips resting on my bare thigh.

I'm lying in a patch of sunlight, eyes half-closed against the glare. Rafa's chest rises and falls against my back in a slow, steady rhythm. His breath tickles my shoulder. I can hear the surf down the hill, muffled, and magpies fuss on the fence outside. The power's back on: my alarm clock blinks at me. Dust motes float in the light, settle on the windowsill.

It took us three hours to clear the beach yesterday, even with two hundred extra pairs of hands. We shifted every dead Immundi – every dismembered limb – far out to sea and dumped the remains as shark bait. It was beyond revolting. I don't intend doing that again. *Ever*.

By the time we'd finished, the sky had darkened from

oranges and pinks to a thousand shades of blue, and then the rain came. No thunder, no lightning and no wind, just torrential rain that drove us under cover. I don't know where the Fallen took shelter, but we – the Rephaim – gathered under the awnings along the esplanade to watch the downpour. It was deafening on the corrugated iron. The tide rushed in, faster than it should have, and when it was sucked back out, the beach was washed clean. Like that, all traces of our battle gone – from the sand, at least. We'll wear our scars a little longer.

I breathe out, lace my fingers through Rafa's and draw his arm around me. He mumbles something into my hair, doesn't wake. I should get up but I'm not ready to face the mess yet in the kitchen. Last night, when the rain eased to a drizzle, Jude and I took two cartons of beer from Rick's, left a scribbled note under the till, and came back to the bungalow. About a dozen of us crammed into our kitchen: around the table, on the bench, stretched out on the floor.

Jason went straight to the resort to get Maria – Gabriel had left her unconscious when he ripped Dani and the Rephaim from the room, and she was beyond frantic when she woke. Then Jason took Maggie to check on Bryce and Simon at the evac centre.

The power was out, so we lit candles, drank half-chilled beer and took turns under a cold shower. Maggie and Jason joined us just as the beer ran out. Maggie found pillows and sheets, and opened the cheap bottles of red we keep in the top of the pantry for emergencies. We were all exhausted, but we managed to keep talking, trying to fit together the pieces of the past twelve hours. Comparing stories about the moments when, amid the carnage and the clean-up, awkward introductions were made.

Nobody has a clue how to feel about the Fallen.

Not even Mya. Hadrial worked by her side during the clean-up, making an effort even though she ignored him. However she feels about him, she didn't share it with us last night. By the time she was slumped at my table, bottle in hand, she was too worn out even to insult the state of my house.

Sometime around ten, Jones and Daisy shifted to pick up noodle boxes and laksas from their favourite hole-in-the-wall in Chiang Mai. By midnight, Dani was asleep in Zak's lap. He and Ez took her and Maria back to the resort so Jason could stay a while longer with Maggie. Daisy claimed the couch and nobody had the energy to argue. When Rafa and I finally fell into bed, Jude was crashed on a mattress under the lounge-room window and Jones and Micah were sprawled on blankets on the floor either side of him. Everyone else found a room at the resort; it might have been deserted and without power, but there were plenty of empty beds.

I trace a crease in the sun-warmed sheet near my pillow, hear movement at the other end of the house. The coffee machine grumbles to life. Jude must be up. Way too early for Mags.

'Morning.' Rafa's voice is thick with sleep. He brushes his lips across my shoulder and I nestle against him.

'Get any rest?' I ask.

'Yeah, until the trucks rolled in.'

The first vehicles made it into town around dawn, gears crunching as they rounded the bend a few blocks over. It must have taken all night to clear the road from the highway. The Butlers weren't exaggerating about their prowess with explosives. It's going to take a bit longer to get the esplanade back in shape.

I yawn and Rafa makes room so I can roll over and face him. There are shadows under his eyes and his jaw is still discoloured, but he looks better than he did last night.

'What's the time?' I ask.

'No idea. My phone's still fried.'

'You think we're late?'

Rafa squints at the sun through the window. 'We've got at least an hour or so.'

Gabriel ordered the Fallen to the Sanctuary as soon as the beach was cleared. He gave the rest of us twelve hours. I don't want to be half-dressed if he gets impatient and summons us. My pulse kickstarts at the thought of the Fallen being at the Sanctuary. I sit up and stretch out my arms. I'm stiff and sore, my skin marked with fresh cuts and fading bruises, but I'm in one piece. We all are.

Rafa's fingers slide under my vest and climb my back.

'You that keen to see Semyaza again?' He runs his thumb down my spine.

I look over my shoulder at him. 'Not particularly.' That's not entirely the truth, though. I'm curious, fascinated. Nervous.

'I don't think he likes me,' Rafa says, deadpan.

I laugh. 'I'm not convinced he likes *me*.'

I pull on clean jeans and a faded red t-shirt and wander out to the kitchen barefoot, dragging my hair back into a ponytail. Jude is bent over the bench, shirtless, his weight on his elbows. Daisy is checking the wound on his back. Her head comes up when she hears me.

'Come and look at this,' she says.

'Settle down,' Jude says. He starts to straighten but Daisy puts a hand on his neck to keep him in place.

'Stay there and let your sister see what a mess you've made of yourself.'

'If memory serves me correctly I didn't do this to myself, Daisy.'

'But you could've had it stitched up before you threw yourself back in harm's way.'

He sighs at me as I round the bench.

'Give it up, Jude,' I say. 'You know you're not going to win—'

I falter. His back *is* a mess. The gash across his shoulders healed while it was still open and the wound looks like an angry mountain range bursting out of his tanned skin. I feel queasy. 'Bloody hell, Jude, have you seen this? Does it hurt?'

He shrugs. 'A few more shifts and it'll settle down.'

Rafa joins us, poking his head through a threadbare t-shirt. 'Shit, buddy, you'll need to go under the knife if you're still keen on scoring at the beach.' He winks at Daisy.

She glowers at him and her fingers drop from Jude's neck. 'I'm going home.'

'What about breakfast?' Jude asks, straightening.

She shakes her head, not looking at him. 'I'll find something at the Sanctuary.'

'The commissary's a smoking ruin.'

She ignores him, catching my eye as she reaches for her weapons on the bench. 'See you when you get there.' And then she's gone. I give Rafa a dirty look. I forgot how much he enjoys winding her up.

The kitchen smells of Thai food and stale beer. I open the window over the sink, careful not to bump the empty bottles lined up behind the tap. I half expect to catch a hint of blood or sulphur or ozone on the breeze, but all I get is sea air and eucalypt. I breathe out.

'Where's everyone else?'

Jude's mattress is stood up against the wall out of the way, a stack of pillows and folded blankets and sheets on the floorboards next to it.

'The guys left for the Sanctuary about half an hour ago. Maggie and Jason have gone to get breakfast.'

'Jason was here all night?' I take the stool next to my brother. He shrugs into a lightweight hoodie and pushes up the sleeves.

'Yeah. Ez and Zak stayed with the girls.'

Rafa stretches in front of the open kitchen window, his back to us. He locks his hands over his head and twists until his shoulder pops. I want to ask him how he feels about seeing his father today, but my stomach dips and Maggie and Jason appear in the doorway.

'You're up,' Maggie says. Her steps wobble and she's pale, but she's more comfortable with shifting now. She's had enough practice the past few days.

'Morning, Margaret,' Rafa says. 'Goldilocks.'

Jason puts two paper bags on the bench and starts pulling out bacon and egg rolls and boxes of hash browns. Salty, greasy goodness. My stomach rumbles and Maggie smiles.

'*Now* the world feels normal again.'

'Your mum okay?' I ask, reaching for a roll.

She nods. 'She's shaken up, like everyone else.'

'What did you tell her?'

Maggie screws up one eye like she expects to get into trouble. 'That I'd explain everything today when she gets home. Is that okay? She's with Simon and I don't think he's said anything yet, but he might if I don't tell her *something*. And I don't want to keep lying to her.'

I look to Jude.

'As long as you think she can handle it,' he says.

Maggie fingers the corner of the bag on the bench. 'Mum's been struggling since Dad died – we both have. I think knowing there's more to the world, that the Rephaim exist and are looking out for us . . . it'll help her.'

'It's not like the whole town won't be chasing answers,' I say.

Last night everyone on the esplanade got a terrifying glimpse of a world they never knew existed. Demons stalking the beach. Monsters lumbering through town. There's no trace of any of them this morning, angel or demon. And if everyone else's phones are as useless as ours, there won't be any other evidence either. Our battle might be out in the open now, but maybe the truth will get lost in the hysteria. Maybe.

Jude nods but I see his attention drift.

'What are you thinking?'

He taps his thumb on the edge of the kitchen bench, exhales. 'Gabriel was in that forest last year.'

Rafa stops chewing his hash brown. 'You recognised his voice?'

'No, but who else has the power to change our memories?'

I try to swallow. The egg and bread and bacon feel like pâpier-maché in my throat.

'You swore fealty to the Second Lieutenant of the

Garrison?' Rafa says. 'What's he going to want in return?'

'No idea.'

I finally get my food down. 'Would Dani know?' I ask Jason.

He shakes his head. 'She can only see what Orias sees, and I doubt he has access to anything involving the Garrison.' Jason wipes his fingers on the dishcloth and then rinses it.

'Orias can see any of us whenever he wants to?'

'All of the Fallen can. The difference with Orias is that he also sees things that haven't happened – so Dani does too, whether she wants to or not. And it's a lot less precise.'

'But she goes looking for us whenever she wants to.'

He nods. 'When she meditates, she sees what we're doing *in that moment*. The things she sees in the future – those visions that take her completely by surprise – they've been intentionally given to her by Orias, but they haven't always come through as clearly as he's intended.'

Jason and his father must have had quite the chat last night. 'What else did he tell you?'

He folds the dishcloth over the tap. 'The Fallen communicate telepathically.'

'Yeah, I wondered about that.' Given how they shifted from the resort roof last night without Semyaza giving an audible command.

'That's how Dani reached out to Rafa when he was at the farmhouse. She somehow managed to tap into that too.'

I think about everything Dani's seen and done since Jude and I came into her life a year ago. Knowing the risks and wanting to help anyway. She's twelve years old and the bravest of us all.

Jason leans back against the sink, rubs his eye with his thumb. Sighs as if defeated.

'Jase,' Maggie says quietly. 'She's going to be okay.'

He brushes his fingers down her arm, almost apologetic. 'I've been trying to protect my family for so long – *lying* about myself to protect the people I care about. I don't know how to stop worrying. And now I've got you to worry about too.'

Maggie catches his fingers in hers. 'Orias is as curious about Dani as she is about him, he's not going to let anyone hurt her. Plus she's got the entire Rephaite army looking out for her. And I've got all of you.'

Maggie's tired and I can't imagine the nightmares she must be having after the last twenty-four hours, but she trusts us to keep her safe. Trusts *me*.

'Always, Mags,' I say and she smiles at me, eyes shining.

Jude nods his agreement, but he's not really listening. He's already thinking about the Sanctuary, trying to second-guess what's going to happen when we get there. I stand up, needing to move. My shoulders and neck are already tight again.

'Let's get this over with. You going to get Dani now?'

Jason blows out his breath. 'Do I have a choice?'

'Nah, Goldilocks, you don't,' Rafa says. He screws up the empty paper bag and lobs it from behind his back. It hits the wall and lands in an empty beer carton by the fridge. 'None of us do.'

ONE BIG HAPPY FAMILY . . .

Rafa, Jude and I arrive in the piazza under a cloudless night sky. It's after midnight here, and cold enough to make my breath mist.

The Rephaim are clustered outside the infirmary, no longer separated into Outcast and Sanctuary: we're a single group now, united not only by a common enemy – momentarily driven back – but by an uncertain future.

Light spills from the cloister lamps and a fat waxing moon hangs over the eastern wing of the Sanctuary. My eyes are good enough to find Ez, Zak and Daisy; Jones, Seth and Micah; Taya and Malachi. The Five. Nobody is armed. The tang of cold smoke still hangs in the air, sweetened slightly by lavender and rosemary.

I remember this place now. Everything's familiar again: the fountain where we cooled off as kids on the way back from training. The timber bench by the infirmary door, scarred with my initials and Daisy's. The downpipe on the residential wing, dented under the eaves where Rafa tried to hurl my boot onto the roof and missed. How long ago was that? Twenty years? Thirty?

Daniel breaks away from the others. He makes a point of glancing at his watch but resists the urge to comment on our tardiness.

'Where are Jason and Dani?'

'They're here,' I say. 'Jason's taken Maggie and Maria upstairs.' It was a smarter option than leaving them alone in Pan Beach. Zarael might be dead and his horde banished beyond the veil but I'm not taking any chances.

'Is Gabriel here?'

'Not yet. Nathaniel's gathering the Fallen now.'

'Did they get any sleep?'

'It took a few hours to find enough bedding for everyone, but they should have had at least a few hours' rest.'

I feel a little guilty. The Rephaim who came back here didn't sit around drinking beer and eating Thai food last night. They had to accommodate the Fallen.

'Where did you put them?'

'Semyaza, Barakiel and Orias took rooms in Nathaniel's compound – without an invite, naturally – and the rest bedded down in the gym and the rec room.'

'Cosy,' Rafa says. 'How's that going to work long term?'

'It's not. We'll need to convert the entire east wing into

accommodation.' Daniel says 'we' as if the Five still have authority at the Sanctuary. I check Jude. He's even more pensive now we're here. Fingers drumming his thighs, eyes scanning the piazza and the rooftop.

Fealty.

My stomach twists, and it's not purely from nerves. Mya and Jess have materialised a few metres away, backlit by the cloister. They head straight for us.

'What are you doing here?' Daniel asks Jess.

She eyeballs him, very cop-like. 'My family needs to know what Gabriel says tonight. There's no way my mother was coming back here, so you've got me instead.'

'It would have been a courtesy to ask permission to enter the Sanctuary. I'm—'

'Daniel, yeah, I know who you are. I've had access to my family's photo library, remember?'

His eyes drop to her holster and the handgun tucked against her ribs. 'You brought a weapon?'

She touches the butt of the gun. 'Don't panic, I know how to use it.'

He gives her a condescending smile. He can't help himself. 'I'm well aware of what you are capable of. I saw you in action last night and I've done some research of my own.'

Jess cocks her head. 'And what did you learn?' She's not remotely intimidated by him, which kind of impresses me.

'That your family has a long history of sociopathic

behaviour, and' – he concedes a nod – 'that you are very good at your job.'

She blinks, thrown by the compliment.

Doors scrape over stone on the opposite side of the piazza and the Rephaim fall still. Semyaza leads the Fallen out onto the grass. Nathaniel comes out last. Careful, tentative, as if every movement hurts. His wounds have healed but his face is a map of scars.

The angels fall into formation in the pale moonlight. Feet planted, hands behind their backs like well-drilled soldiers. They're scruffy, but at least they've washed. And they've come unarmed too. A good start.

Without being told, the Rephaim mirror the Fallen's formation, each line staggered so that every Rephaite has a clear line of sight to the ranks of the angels. The Rephaim in the frontline make room for us. Mya positions herself so she's facing Hadrial. I stand opposite Semyaza. His flickering gaze locks on mine and I feel that strange sensation again under my ribcage.

There's movement in the cloister by the infirmary door. Jason and Dani have come downstairs. Jess is with them and I vaguely register that she and Jason are shaking hands. I guess Mya wasn't the only one in her family kept in the dark about him all these years.

Nobody else speaks. There are nearly four hundred of us, but the only sound is an owl in the trees beyond the wall and water splashing in the fountain. In any other circumstance, Nathaniel would have taken charge now. But he's wounded, defeated, and his silence has paralysed the Five. All of them – Daniel, Callie, Uri, Zeb and Magda – are as uncertain as the rest of us about what to do now.

Beside me, Rafa cracks a knuckle. It's been less than a minute and he's already out of patience. Somewhere high above us, a jet cuts through the night. I glance up, try to find it. Spot something else closer. I reach for Rafa without looking, squeeze his wrist.

'Poser,' Rafa mutters. Murmurs spread through the piazza as the winged figure circles closer. Gabriel lands on the roof and paces across the tiles, taking us in, accounting for all of us. He launches himself again without warning, and with three powerful backbeats lands in the space between the Fallen and us. Cold air rushes over me, laced with pine needles and ice.

The archangel isn't dressed like a tourist tonight. He's turned up as a warrior – but not like the archangels in the paintings scattered through the Sanctuary. There's no helmet, no gleaming armour. This archangel looks more like he's about to climb into a Black Hawk helicopter: lightweight combat trousers, snug t-shirt and a vest that looks heavy-duty enough to withstand a dozen demon blades. If he's feeling the cold, he doesn't show it. He tucks his wings behind him but leaves them visible, every feather in place. Two broadswords are strapped between them.

Gabriel hasn't come to play.

I picture him with a hundred archangels at his back. A thousand. More. My mouth turns dusty. I clasp my hands behind my back to stop my fingers trembling.

'Take a knee.'

As one, the Fallen drop to one knee. It's probably more a reflex action than obedience, but the synchronisation is breathtaking. Gabriel turns to us. 'You too.'

Oh.

I look to Jude. He stiffens but then nods, once. Rafa grunts. The three of us kneel and I hear movement as the rest of the Rephaim follow. The knees of my jeans are instantly damp on the dewy grass. I copy Semyaza, rest one arm on my supporting leg. The Fallen haven't bowed their heads, so neither do we. The leader of the Fallen gives me the smallest of nods.

'You are no longer Fallen, Rephaim or Outcast,' Gabriel says, walking between our two forces. 'You are Ankida: where heaven and earth meet. When the final war comes, I shall call you to my cohort. I shall be your commander.'

So much for free will. I try to swallow but my throat is a desert.

Gabriel moves down the line, turns and comes back to us. He stops in front of Jude. 'Until that day comes, my ambassador will be Judah, son of Semyaza, adopted son of Nathaniel, former Sanctuary soldier and former Outcast.'

I forget to breathe for a good ten seconds.

Jude stares up at him. 'What does that mean?'

'It means, Judah, that after this day, if it is my will or the will of heaven to command the Ankida, it shall be done through you and no other. There shall be no more visions or revelations. No more lack of understanding about what is required of each of you.'

Jude's eyes flick to me and back to the archangel. 'That's it? That's all you want from me – to pass on your messages?'

Gabriel towers over my brother. He seems even taller, more threatening tonight. 'You do not understand. You are my agent in this realm. You carry my authority. These warriors, these philosophers, these academics . . . they are yours to command.'

The weight of those last five words presses down on all of us.

Holy shit. Jude's in charge of the Fallen – and us.

'What if I don't want your authority?'

'You have sworn fealty to me. This is what I demand of you.'

And there it is: confirmation it was Gabriel who saved us in the forest in Idaho and hid us from each other. Messed with our memories.

'You, Judah, will dwell here with your father and his cohort. You will work beside Nathaniel to ensure that my earthbound army is battle ready.'

I wait for Jude to push back, to argue, but he drops his head and stares at the ground, unseeing. He's accepted this fate. My heart lurches into my throat. My brother is now tied to the Fallen, to the Sanctuary, until the end of time. Literally.

Gabriel looks out over the rest of the Rephaim and then his gaze settles on me. 'The rest of you did not ask to join our war, so I give you a choice: leave tonight and live your lives beyond these walls as you see fit, or stay and take your place with Judah, Nathaniel and your fathers.'

The night holds its breath. The Rephaim stay silent, perfectly still. I have no idea what anyone is thinking. Except Jude, I can read him easily. He won't look at me. Won't ask it of me—of any of us. He knows how much worse the next battle will be. A full-scale war against hell. Just the thought of it wrings me out and makes my palms sweat.

But that's his future now.

And there's no way I'd let him face it without me.

I stand up, shaky. Ignore Rafa and Semyaza, both staring at me.

'Can we negotiate our terms?'

Jude lifts his head but I ignore him too, focus only on Gabriel. The archangel considers me for a moment. 'Ask what you will.'

I swallow. Take a steadying breath. 'We can't be prisoners here. If you want us to care about this world, we have to live in it.'

'What is your term, Gabriella?'

'That we have the freedom to come and go as we always have – including Jude.'

'Is that all?'

My mind races. What else does Jude need? 'We want the freedom to track and kill demons in this realm.'

'For payment?'

'Maybe, but mostly because it's what we should have been doing all along. If you want us to go to war against hell, it's only fair you give us a chance to thin the ranks first.'

'And?'

I glance across at Dani, standing between Jess and Jason. Watching me. *Proud.* 'I want our human friends to be welcome here. That no harm will come to any of them, especially Dani.' Opposite me, Semyaza shifts his weight on his knee. 'And we're not our father's keepers,' I continue. 'None of us is taking responsibility for the choices the Fallen make from this point.'

Gabriel raises his eyebrows. 'Do you wish to see your family expanded?'

'I expect them to work out how to use a condom.'

'Enough,' Semyaza says, rising. 'I do not need my child explaining when and how I can use my—'

'My point exactly.' I glare at my father, will him to shut up and not derail my negotiations. He glowers at me, but doesn't push the point.

Gabriel folds his arms, flexes bare biceps. 'I shall take a moment to consider your demands.' He launches himself from the ground and flies to the roof. Jude is on his feet before Gabriel touches down.

'Gaby, you don't have to do this.'

'Of course I do.' The others are already gathering around us.

'But—'

'Don't.' I stop him. 'There's no discussion here, Jude. I'm staying.'

'Fuck, man,' Rafa says. 'Talk about being careful what you wish for.' It's only half smart-arse. Rafa's as off-kilter as I am.

Rephaim crowd around us, hushed, but Jude doesn't acknowledge any of them, not even Rafa. He's still searching my face. 'You could have a different life, Gaby.'

'I don't want a different life if you're not in it. I thought we'd already established that.' My voice breaks a little but I keep going. 'I'm staying because you're my brother. Because I love you. Because you're tied to this place now and I've got your back until we die, whenever or however that day comes.'

'What about Pan Beach?'

'It's not going anywhere. I can still visit.'

The Fallen are all on their feet now but they give us space. Even Semyaza stays where he is.

'We go where you go, buddy,' Rafa says. 'That's the way it's always been, whether you like it or not.'

Jude looks from me to Rafa and back again. Blinks a few times. Swallows. 'Okay.'

'Looks like we're coming home for good,' Zak says. I

scan the faces around him, faces I've known my whole life. They're all with us: Ez, Taya, Malachi, Micah, Mya, Jones and Seth. They don't want a war any more than I do, but, like me, they won't abandon Jude.

And Gabriel knows it.

'We can probably fix up your old room,' Daisy says. Her freckled face is lit up in the moonlight. 'You don't get an upgrade just because you're calling the shots.'

'So you're staying?' he asks.

'Of course I am. I live here, remember? But don't think you'll be ordering me around.'

Jude smiles, finally, and some of the tightness leaves his face. 'Wouldn't dream of it.'

Daniel works his way through the crowd to us. Callie, Uri, Zeb and Magda are with him: the Five, still a united front. 'What do you need from us?' Daniel asks.

I study him, look for traces of resentment and find none. But then Daniel was never going to question an edict given by an archangel – even one that involves Jude being his new boss. Challenging authority has never been Daniel's style.

'What are you offering?' Jude asks.

'To do what we've always done: keep this place running. Provide structure and routine. Balance the books, keep food in the commissary, manage the day-to-day business.' Daniel glances back at the rest of the Five. 'And keep you accountable.'

'I'd expect nothing less.'

Daniel offers his hand. Their eyes meet as they shake and there's something new and uncertain between them: the first stirrings of something beyond rivalry. Daniel nods in Semyaza's direction. 'You're going to need all the help you can get.'

Rephaim part to let Semyaza through. The rest of the Fallen stay in formation, waiting for an order. If Semyaza accepts Jude's authority, the Two Hundred will fall in behind him. The Captain of the Fallen plants his feet and folds his arms, matted hair hanging over his shoulders. He's a head taller than us and stands so close we have to look up at him.

'I will not kneel before you,' Semyaza says. 'Neither shall any of my cohort.'

A muscle twitches in Jude's jaw. 'What have you seen in me over the last hundred and thirty-nine years that makes you think I'd want you to?'

'Authority does strange things to men.'

'Are you worried I'm too much like my father? Prone to bad decisions?'

Bloody hell, does he have to goad Semyaza right now?

The fallen angel's eyes flare, and then I catch a twitch of a smile under his wiry beard. 'I think that we have many interesting days ahead of us, son.' Semyaza's gaze meets mine, still amused, and then he turns away.

'He's going to be a handful,' I say.

Jude gives a short laugh. 'The irony is killing me.'

There's movement among the Fallen, the angels breaking ranks and mingling with the Rephaim. Orias goes to Dani and Jason. Hadrial to Jess.

Mya stands back, watching. Reunions – warm and frosty – continue around us, interrupted only when Gabriel lands on the rim of the fountain. He keeps his wings out to steady himself.

'It is settled?' the archangel asks me.

I raise my eyebrows at Jude, who nods. 'Seems that way.'

'Then I accept your terms.' Gabriel's relaxed now too. Did he expect more resistance?

Jude stands before him, more sure of himself now. 'It was you in Idaho.' It's not a question and Gabriel doesn't answer. 'Thanks for stepping in.'

The archangel inclines his head.

'But why did you change our memories?'

Gabriel's irises slow to a steady flicker. 'Your attempt to open the portal was premature.' His eyes cut to Orias under the cloister. 'I had hoped to buy more time to allow things to unfold as I had intended.'

I touch the thick scar on the back of my neck, finally understanding. 'Jude and I could have lived at opposite ends of Australia for decades, by which time Dani's gift would have passed and who knows how long it would be until the next seer came along – or if Orias would be able to influence her visions the way he did Dani's.'

Rafa reaches for me, brushes his thumb across the

damaged skin beneath my hair. 'Why give them back their memories yesterday?'

'The horde was gathering,' Gabriel says, 'and even united, you were no match for Zarael. You needed to bolster your ranks with warriors experienced in battle. I wished to see if you would make that choice, and I wished to see what the Fallen would do if freed.'

'You could've let them out yourself.'

'What is existence without freedom to choose? It is always about choice, Rafael.'

Of course it is. And free will has worked out so well for all of us so far.

'Ankida.'

It takes me a second to realise he means us.

We gather around, no longer in formation and no longer separated into Rephaim and Fallen. I'm shoulder-to-shoulder with Jude and Rafa. I think about the past – real and fabricated – all the moments that make me who I am. What it means to have lived as a half-angel warrior and a human. The value of my friends, human and Rephaim.

It's all led to this. But how do we make *this* work?

'You have life, you have freedom and you have purpose,' Gabriel tells us. 'Do not squander them this time.'

And then the Second Lieutenant of the Angelic Garrison, second only in authority to the Archangel Michael, leaves us alone to figure it out.

EPILOGUE: FOUR WEEKS LATER

'Are you nervous?' Maggie asks.

I glance down at my dress and my stomach does a tiny flip. 'No,' I lie and she laughs.

'I love that you'll face down an army of demons, but a gorgeous frock still freaks you out.'

It's not the frock that's freaking me out. It's wearing it in front of everyone I know. It's the strapless champagne dress I tried on in Melbourne with the fitted bodice and layers of silk flaring out from the hip, bought with some of the money I made from the LA job. Mercenary gigs have their perks.

Daisy lets herself into my room. My new room at the Sanctuary – which also happens to be Rafa's. Her hair is pulled back into a loose bun except for a few strands styled to frame her face, vivid against her pale skin. Her sleek gown is almost a perfect match for her red hair.

'How's the bride?' she asks.

I glance towards the bathroom and Mya steps into the doorway, make-up brushes in hand. She gives Daisy a once-over, says nothing. There's no love lost between them, but they can be in the same room without sniping at each other. Mostly. 'She's ready.'

Ez appears, a shy smile tugging at her lips. Soft white silk gently hugs her curves, her caramel skin luminescent against it. It's one of Maggie's designs, the halter neckline tailored to show off Ez's shoulders. Her dark hair falls in soft waves, her make-up light and natural. It turns out Mya can do more than slap on kohl when she puts her mind to it.

'Wow,' Daisy says, breaking into a wide smile. 'Breathtaking.'

Ez dips her head and reaches for a long white silk scarf. She carefully drapes it around her shoulders and over her hair so it hides the hellion scar on her cheek and throat. 'Shall we?'

Maggie hands me a crimson shawl – hand-knitted, of course – and the five of us head for the chapterhouse under a grey afternoon sky. It's fresh outside but not freezing. The lamps along the cloisters are lit, casting a warm glow on the cobblestones. We move out into the open courtyard and Ez's breath catches. The path to the chapterhouse is lined with tall rose bushes in terracotta pots, strung with fairy lights. Even the marble angel looks festive, his wings and sword draped in garlands of white flowers.

Music and laughter carry from the chapterhouse. Everyone's inside, except for Hadrial. He's waiting at the main door, hair and beard trimmed. Wearing a tuxedo.

'How are things between you two?' Ez asks Mya as we get near.

'Ugh, he wants to talk about my feelings all the time,' she says. 'It's exhausting.'

'It's good that he cares, though, right?'

Hadrial raises a hand, as if Mya might have missed him standing there. She sighs. 'I'd better go keep him out of trouble.' She gives Ez a quick, awkward peck on the cheek and then breaks away from us to join her father.

We make our way around to the side of the ancient building to an antechamber. I knock once and let myself in. Zak is waiting in a black suit, crisp white shirt and mint tie. He gives a curt, nervous nod, more interested in Ez, a few steps behind me.

Rafa and Jude are fiddling with their ties in front of a full-length mirror, both dressed in black suits. Rafa turns around. He's freshly scrubbed and clean-shaven, and wearing that suit like it was made for him – which it was. I drop the shawl so he can see my dress.

He takes me in, so slowly I feel heat creep up my neck. And then he steps closer, brushes a thumb across my bare shoulder. 'Good choice,' he says quietly and kisses the scar on my collarbone. I'm wrapped in a heady cloud of sandalwood and fresh cotton.

'Get a room, you two,' Jude mumbles, still fussing with his tie.

'Give that here.' Daisy crosses the room and strips it from under his collar.

By the door, Ez and Zak are holding hands and smiling at each other. Tender. Intimate. They're going to walk down the aisle the same way they navigate life: side by side. Ez's father is inside, but she doesn't need anyone to give her away.

'How do you know how to tie a Windsor knot?' Jude asks Daisy. He seems all too aware of how close she's standing as she loops it back around his neck and goes to work.

'I don't, but I'm confident I can do a better job than you.' She chews on her lip as she concentrates. He focuses on her ear, keeps his hands by his sides.

Maggie catches my eye, glances at Daisy and Jude and raises her eyebrows. I shrug. Nobody knows what's going on between them. I'm not even sure they do.

The door on the far side cracks open and Jason appears. He ushers Dani through in front of him. She's wearing a peach dress, carrying two bunches of white roses. She approaches Ez, shy, and offers her the larger of the two. Jason holds out a hand to Maggie. 'There's room up the front,' he says to us, and they disappear into the chapterhouse together.

I squeeze Ez's arm. 'I'm so happy for you.'

I don't know how seriously Ez and Zak talked about marriage before, but after the carnage at Pan Beach and the upheaval at the Sanctuary, they decided we needed something to celebrate. She blinks rapidly and dabs at her eye with the side of her finger. 'Don't get me started,' she says and laughs, embarrassed. 'Go on, I'll see you in there.'

The chapterhouse is unrecognisable. Under Maggie's instruction, it's been decorated to resemble a giant Bedouin tent, all lanterns, couches and hanging fabric. The stone floor is covered with dozens of giant rugs, the marble columns draped with scarves. I've never seen so much warmth and colour in here. Orange-blossom candles scent the air. I love it like this, without the bloodstains and scars.

Micah sits on the dais, playing acoustic guitar. Brother Stephen waits beside him, gnarled fingers clasped over his robe. His arm is finally healing from his encounter with Zarael in the car park last month, and his pale blue eyes are sharp again, hopeful.

The crowd is gathered at one end of the chapterhouse, divided by a makeshift aisle of plush red carpet. Fallen and Rephaim blended together. Ankida. The newest members of our melting pot are here too: Jess and Maria – not quite relaxed, but not uneasy either – standing together in solidarity. The Butlers and their crew, feet planted and arms folded like this is a normal Saturday night at the Imperial. Mick's already got a beer.

Rafa, Jude, Daisy and I slip through the crowd and squeeze in between Jones and Malachi. Taya is across the aisle, head bent in conversation with Simon. They lean into each other, relaxed, familiar.

I look around for Semyaza, find him waiting for me to notice him. He glances at my dress and raises his eyebrows in what I think is meant to express surprise that I own clothes other than jeans and t-shirts.

Nathaniel stands off to one side, watchful. He's still keeping his distance. I haven't worked out how I feel about him, and neither has anyone else yet. It's another one of those things that need time. He spends most of his days with the Fallen now, obviously burdened, wearing his guilt and shame like a heavy wool coat. Tonight, at least, his mood is lighter. His eyes flick to the back of the room and he holds up a hand. It takes a few seconds but everyone falls quiet.

Micah begins to play 'Let It Be'.

We all turn – all four hundred of us – and watch Ez and Zak walk up the aisle arm in arm. Dani walks ahead, smiling at everyone as she passes. A lithe angel with skin more coffee than caramel catches Ez's eye as she passes and puts his hand over his heart. She smiles, and a tear slips down her cheek. The bride and groom ascend the steps to Brother Stephen, then turn and face each other.

Zak reaches for Ez's scarf. He gently pushes it back from her face and slides it from her shoulders.

'You're too beautiful to hide,' he says.

For a few seconds, my heart is too big for me.

Brother Stephen isn't a licensed celebrant and technically the marriage won't be legal, but none of that matters. Today is about Ez and Zak showing us a way forward: that we may not be able to escape the training room and the battlefield, but we can live our lives beyond them.

When Zak says his vows, Rafa's fingers find mine.

Later – after everyone's had their fill of chargrilled lamb and flatbread and pickled vegetables – Jones and Daisy clear space for a dance floor.

Micah and Jude have rigged an iPod dock to a huge set of rented speakers. Now they're arguing over whose playlist to use. Daniel looks like he's about to get involved, but then spots Jess speaking quietly with Nathaniel and joins them instead, grabbing a bottle of wine from an empty table on his way. Nathaniel hasn't fully recovered in any sense from the Pan Beach battle, but he turns up for training every day, helps Jude plan the day's drills. And Jess has been teaching Daniel to fire a police-issue handgun, although I'm not entirely sure it's the gun that intrigues him.

Rafa's by the bar, trying to get away from Barakiel. I can see from here that Rafa's trying to hold his temper with his father. At least they're not throwing punches. Yet.

'Your brother thinks I should let Rafa and Barakiel spar,' Semyaza says behind me, making me jump. He always does this: approaches without warning and then launches straight into conversation. No polite small talk for my father. He sits down uninvited, taking up a lot of space.

'Jude's right. You need to let them sort themselves out on the mats.'

'Rafael is no match for Barakiel.'

'Don't underestimate Rafa. And trust me, he's never going to respect his father until they've thrown down.'

Semyaza tilts his head a fraction. His beard is trimmed to his jawline, his matted hair shorter and tied back. 'Do you wish to "throw down" with me?'

'Of course.'

His eyebrows go up.

'I want to test my skills, improve. That's why Gabriel threw us all together, right? We're supposed to reconnect you lot to humanity and you're supposed to make us better fighters?'

'Is that why? I thought it was to amuse himself.'

I blink and then burst out laughing. 'Holy shit, Semyaza, was that sarcasm?'

His lips quirk and his eyes crease like Jude's. 'You children, you think you invented everything.'

An up-tempo folk song starts. Daisy and Jones are first onto the floor, circling each other, grinning as they move to the beat. By the second verse, the dance floor is packed with Rephaim, waiting for the song to morph into a dance tune. Semyaza tops up my wine, fills a glass of his own. I reach over and clink my glass against his. He raises his in response. The synthesiser kicks in and the Rephaim erupt, hands in the air, bouncing in time to the thumping rhythm. Release.

Two songs later and Rafa slips into the seat on my other side. Jude is with him.

I bump my knee against Rafa's leg. 'How's your old man?'

He sits back and rests his arm behind me on my chair. 'Acting like a tool.' He nods at Semyaza, who ignores him. Jude watches Daisy and Jones carve a space for themselves in the crowd, showing off.

I lean across Rafa. 'Go dance with her.'

Jude shakes his head. 'I can't move like Jones.'

'Yes, that's a well-established fact.' I push his shoulder. 'Go on.'

'She's still pissed off.'

'No, she's not.'

'Then what do you call the way she acts towards me?'

'Self-defence.'

His eyes cut back to her. She's laughing at Jones hamming it up with pop-n-lock moves. 'She's not forgiving me any time soon.'

I think of the way her eyes have found him all night, regardless of where he is in the chapterhouse. 'I seriously doubt that.' I touch his wrist, make him look at me. 'But if you go to her, you better know what you're doing.'

Jude knows I'm not talking about his footwork. 'I know what I want.' He drains his beer. 'And it's not dancing to shit music.'

He skirts the dancers. He and Micah have a quick conversation and then Jude waits until the song is almost over before he goes to Daisy. She sees him and makes room. He and Jones bump fists and Jones melts into the crowd, still busting moves.

The song ends. Another starts, slower, melancholic. Daisy shakes her head, almost smiles: Foo Fighters. Dave Grohl singing about tortured souls and broken things. Jude holds out his hand and she hesitates only a second. He draws her to him and rests his hands lightly on her hips, a quiet question. They move together, watching each other. Jude says something and Daisy leans in. He slips an arm around her, still speaking into her ear, draws her closer. His other hand caresses her neck, and then his lips drop from her ear to her throat. She closes her eyes and melts against him. Okay. I guess they're working it out.

The dance floor is crowded now with slow-moving couples. Maggie and Jason. Taya and Simon. Even Malachi and Mya – barely touching and more awkward than everyone else, but that won't do either of them any harm.

And Ez and Zak, happier than I've ever seen them.

I sit back and lean into Rafa, feeling fuzzy. It takes a

second to register the sensation. It's not just the buzz from the wine. I'm . . . content.

It's not easy, all of us being here at the Sanctuary. The Fallen are far from domesticated, and there are heated arguments more days than not. And we're all still living on top of each other while we wait for the east wing to be renovated and the commissary to be rebuilt. But we're trying. It's not a comfortable alliance, but it's holding for the moment. And at least once a week I find an excuse to see Maggie in Pan Beach. There's something about our bungalow, about the rainforest and the ocean. It always feels like going home. Even if the town is still lousy with reporters.

Rafa's fingers brush my shoulder and trail down my arm. He leans in until I feel his breath on my ear. 'Do you want to hit the floor?'

I pull back to look at him. '*You* want to dance?'

A grin. 'Generally, no, but this seems like the time to make an exception.'

His tie and jacket are long gone. The top button on his shirt is undone and his sleeves are rolled up to his elbows. If Semyaza wasn't sitting with us I'd kiss Rafa right now. Probably inappropriately.

But I can wait until we're alone in our room.

Rafa's grin widens as if he can read my thoughts. 'So, *Gaby*, you want to dance with me or not?'

I'm not a librarian any more, I'm a soldier, and the future

holds more violence. More bloodshed. But not tonight. Tonight, there's life to be lived.

'Sure,' I say, winding my fingers through his. 'Let's see what you've got.'

ACKNOWLEDGEMENTS

Five years ago, I was frustrated and disappointed over yet another writing rejection—the latest addition to a fat folder. To cheer myself up I started working on something for fun. That scene turned into the beginnings of *Shadows* and an outline for the four-book *Rephaim* series. Less than a year later, my agent Lyn Tranter pitched the series to Mandy Brett and Alison Arnold at Text Publishing. They liked it and I was offered a contract. After all those years of writing and rejection, the thing I had wanted for so long happened 'just like that'.

Since then, the series has been published in the United Kingdom, North America and Turkey. I've been a guest at writers' festivals and a writer-in-residence at high schools, participated in blog tours, met lots of wonderful readers online and at events, and read countless reviews of my work (good, bad and otherwise).

I've rubbed shoulders with many of my favourite writers and met others who have since joined that list. I've chatted and shared book recommendations with a great bunch of dedicated bloggers and reviewers who do what they do purely because they love to read. The young-adult writing community in Australia is quite possibly the most welcoming, supportive and friendly writing sector in the world today, and that's been one of the greatest discoveries of all.

I still have a day job. Few people tell you how tough it is to earn a living as a writer. I'm just grateful to be in print, and especially grateful for publishers like Text Publishing who are still willing to take risks. There are plenty of writers out there who are where I was five years ago, so I take nothing for granted.

This is the fourth and last book in the Rephaim series, and there are plenty of people I need to thank.

Text Publishing: my editor Mandy Brett, for caring about a story filled with angels and demons. I'm well aware of how lucky I am to be able to work with you. And the entire team at Text, especially those I've worked with the closest: Anne Beilby, Alice Cottrell, Steph Speight, Alaina Gougoulis and Shalini Kunahlan.

Orion/Indigo Books: my editor Jenny Glencross and senior publicity manager Nina Douglas.

Tundra Books/Random House Canada: Alison Morgan,

Editorial Director Tara Walker and Publicity Manager Pamela Osti, as well as Val Capuani. Special thanks to Publishing Coordinator Sylvia Chan, for always going above and beyond.

Alison Arnold, for being there from the start of this series and whose influence still guides my writing (and inspires me to try to write beautiful sentences).

Rebecca Cram (Place), for nearly three decades of friendship and encouragement – and providing helpful feedback on an early draft of *Burn*.

Michelle Reid, fellow YA book nerd, for providing outstanding attention to detail at draft stage and again in the home stretch. (Thanks too for the 'arse' conversation!)

Tony Minerds, my brother, who can spot a typo at fifty paces. This time around he got a chance to find them *before* we went to print. Thanks bro.

Vikki Wakefield, a gifted writer who I'm proud to call a friend, for feedback and candid conversations that help me feel like I almost know what I'm doing.

Marianne de Pierres – a multi-talented writer, friend and mentor – for invaluable advice and much appreciated support.

My family and friends, many of whom had never read anything even remotely resembling urban/contemporary fantasy before this series came along, for taking the time to read every book and make appropriate noises of enthusiasm. You guys rock.

My amazing friend and business partner, Heather Scott, for her friendship and unwavering belief in me.

Mum and Dad, for their overwhelming love and support in all aspects of my life.

Murray, for knowing me better than anyone else on the planet, and for still being beside me twenty years on.

And last, but most certainly not least, all of you – readers, bloggers, reviewers, booksellers and librarians – who have picked up the Rephaim series. There is no writing career without you guys. Thanks for being a part of this adventure.

I know the Rephaim series isn't going to change the world, but I've loved writing this story and these characters – and they've certainly brought an amazing new dimension to my world.

For that, I will always be grateful.